MW01047745

# PRAISE FOR THE DIANA HUNTER SERIES

"Awesome."

"On the edge of my seat..."

"Page turner."

"I cannot tell you the last time a group of characters
endeared me as quickly..."

"Diana Hunter is a strong, intelligent, and very likeable
heroine."

"Grabbed me from the first page, and I sat up until 4:30 in
the morning reading it."

"The story line is quick-paced and attention-holding. This
one deserves 5+ stars."

"This book will keep you turning the pages to find out the
who, what, why, and how."

"Couldn't put it down!"

"Left me wanting more."

"Peter and Diana have a great chemistry."

"I love the author's writing."

"A pleasure to read."

"Really captivating."

"Fast-paced, well-written, fun stories."

"I can't wait to read the next book in the series."

"I'm hooked."

"Kept me reading until the wee hours."

"Diana Hunter is becoming one of my favorite characters"

"Super read. Cracking heroine."

"One of the most enjoyable books I've read in a long time"

"A gem."

"Diana Hunter is knowledgeable, experienced, quick-witted, and even sexy."

"Can you write quicker, please?"

# THE DIANA HUNTER MYSTERIES

ALSO BY A. J. GOLDEN

*Exposed*

# THE DIANA HUNTER MYSTERIES

BOOKS 1-4

A. J. GOLDEN

GABRIELLA ZINNAS

The characters and events portrayed in this book are fictitious. Any
similarity to real persons, living or dead is coincidental and not intended by
the author.
Text copyright © 2018 A. J. Golden
All rights reserved.

No part of this book may be reproduced, stored in a retrieval system, or
transmitted in any form or by any means, electronic, mechanical,
photocopying, recording, or otherwise, without express written permission of
the publisher.

Published by Mesa Verde Publishing
P.O. Box 1002
San Carlos, CA 94070

ISBN-13: 978-1720427261

Edited by
Marjorie Kramer

*"If you truly want to escape this reality, all you have to do is open a book and your imagination."*
*Unknown*

To get two free books, updates about new releases, exclusive promotions, and other insider information, sign up for Alison's mailing list at:

https://www.alisongolden.com/diana

USA Today Bestselling Author

# A.J.GOLDEN

## GABRIELLA ZINNAS

# HUNTED

## A DIANA HUNTER MYSTERY

# HUNTED

BOOK ONE

The characters and events portrayed in this book are fictitious. Any similarity to real persons, living or dead is coincidental and not intended by the author.
Text copyright © 2015 A. J. Golden
All rights reserved.

No part of this book may be reproduced, stored in a retrieval system, or transmitted in any form or by any means, electronic, mechanical, photocopying, recording, or otherwise, without express written permission of the publisher.

Published by Mesa Verde Publishing
P.O. Box 1002
San Carlos, CA 94070

ISBN-13: 978-1515313915

Edited by
Marjorie Kramer

# NOTE FROM THE AUTHOR

*Hunted* is a prequel to the other books in the Diana Hunter series of mysteries. The events in this story take place a few years before *Snatched*, the next book in the series. It is set in Vancouver. Unlike the other books, *Hunted* is not a complete mystery. It relates the events that create the backdrop to the series and fills in some of Diana's personality and motivations.

The Diana Hunter mysteries can be read and enjoyed in any order. I've made sure not to include any spoilers for those of you who are new to the characters and any existing fans of Diana's adventures will still find plenty of fresh action and mystery as well as perhaps a few answers to questions you may have. All in all, there is something for everyone.

I had an absolute blast creating this book – I hope you have a blast reading it too.

# CHAPTER ONE

"D O YOU REALLY have to go?" Lydia Hunter asked her daughter as she helped pack her things into boxes. She was trying to hold back the tears but was failing miserably.

"You know I have to, Mom," Diana replied.

"But why?"

"Because I'd rather not waste time commuting to school. I'll have plenty of work to do without going back and forth."

"But we live in South Cambie, not the North Pole! It's not even a 15-minute drive."

Diana sighed. They'd had this argument repeatedly. "Mom, I've signed up for two undergrad programs. I'm going to be spending every waking moment studying. Are you really going to be happy knowing that I'm out driving around at midnight?"

Lydia sighed, her light blue eyes glossy with unshed tears. "I know you're right. I know we've talked about it a million times, and your father agrees that it's safer for you to be on campus, but you're only sixteen! You're my baby."

She was sniffling by this point, trying to look anywhere except at her logical and highly driven daughter.

"It'll be okay, Mom. You'll see. You can come see me all the time, and I promise I'll come home at least once every weekend."

Diana smiled and pulled her mother into a hug in a rare exhibition of affection. It wasn't that Diana had any problems expressing love per se. It was usually a matter of her mind working on some problem or other and her simply not realizing what other people needed from her.

Lydia sighed again. "Why did I have to have a genius for a child?"

"Genetically speaking—"

"I didn't ask for a fully-fledged scientific explanation," Lydia cut her daughter off with a chuckle.

Diana was more than intelligent. She was far above the norm. She was reading by the age of two and a half. By the age of five, she was doing math far above the level of even a first-grader. By the time she had started second grade, she was so far ahead of the other children that she had become a problem in school. When the school counselor called her, Lydia had been worried. In the end, it was to suggest Diana be put into a special program for gifted children. And what could she do but agree? Diana was bored, and she was letting everyone know it.

Had it been up to Diana, she'd have already started her undergraduate courses by now. Probably finished them too. But Lydia had been adamant. Her daughter wouldn't spend her entire life with her nose in books. She needed to have as much of a normal childhood as possible. So, they had come to a compromise. She wouldn't head out to university until she was at least 16. After that, it would be Diana's decision what she did and how quickly she did it.

That's why Lydia wasn't surprised when Diana had chosen two undergraduate programs, biotechnology and computer sciences. Lydia didn't understand it. The two programs couldn't be more dissimilar. But then again, it had been a very long while since she'd been able to understand her daughter when it came to her academics.

She'd known the day she had discovered she was pregnant that her daughter would be special. That she'd do amazing things with her life. Of course, every mother feels that way, but it turned out Lydia had been right. Her daughter was special. And now, here they were. Her daughter was leaving home. And it was much too early, if you asked Lydia. But she couldn't, in good conscience, hold Diana back.

"I'm going to miss you," Lydia whispered.

Diana grinned. "I'll miss you too, mom."

Lydia glanced around her daughter's bedroom. There were no posters of her favorite actors or bands on the walls. There were no flashy clothes they argued over littering the floor. There was no make-up. There was nothing that would indicate this was a 16-year-old girl's bedroom. In fact, it looked more like a professor's study, with books covering every possible surface. A computer sat on a desk facing the windows. Every other available surface was covered in papers and notes, most of which Lydia had little chance of comprehending.

At one point, Diana had been interested in electronics, but thankfully, that messy phase had passed. Now her room was no longer covered with circuit boards, wires, and a myriad of tools. It was actually quite neat, compared to those days.

Her bed was a simple box frame tucked into the corner of the room. Her sheets featured a red and black geometric design. The rest of the room was dedicated to shelves for her books and various other projects she sometimes tinkered with.

Diana's closet mainly consisted of jeans, t-shirts, and sneakers. Fashion wasn't her thing. She wanted to be comfortable, and she really had no interest in clothing. As long as it was functional, covered her up, and didn't get in her way, Diana was happy. She was a girl who liked the simple things in life except when it came to solving problems. Then it was a case of the more complex, the better.

Lydia glanced at her daughter, who was stuffing some books into another box. "You do know you won't have that much space in your room on campus, right?"

Diana looked up. "I'll find a place for them," she said knowingly.

"I'm sure you will," Lydia smiled.

Knowing her daughter, she'd probably invent some trans-dimensional bag that would allow her to store an entire library's worth of books in a space no bigger than a purse. Lydia rolled her eyes at her own thoughts. She'd been spending too much time watching science fiction shows with her daughter. Though Diana tended to shout at the screen about the poor science on which these shows were based, she still loved them. They were her guilty pleasure. But to anyone who asked, she vehemently maintained she only watched them for research purposes, namely to see what she shouldn't do if she ever decided to write a book or a screenplay. Lydia just smiled knowingly without making a single comment.

"Are you two ready?" Diana's father, John, yelled up the stairs.

"Nearly, Dad. One more box to go."

"Well, hurry up. You'd think you were moving to the other side of the world, not basically down the road."

Lydia smiled to herself. Her husband was trying to pretend everything was all right, but he was even more worried about their daughter's move than she was. He'd signed her up for every self-defense class he could find when Diana had hit puberty. As a homicide detective, he saw the worst side of Vancouver every day, and he wanted to make sure his daughter was safe.

Lydia, though, had put her foot down when he'd wanted to sign her up for a firearms course. Diana had been fourteen at the time, and Lydia had told her husband point-blank that their daughter would not be learning how to operate those instruments of death at such a young age.

She'd also calmly reminded him that there was no way he could prove Diana was in imminent danger and that police protection wouldn't suffice, which was pretty much the only way a civilian could carry a concealed weapon in Canada. Of course, he'd ignored the logic of her arguments and had pouted. Then he'd wheedled. Then he'd begged.

He'd brought home photos of crime scenes and said that even if she couldn't carry a gun, it would still be an extra skill in Diana's arsenal, and it couldn't hurt. He'd also launched into a long lecture about how learning to shoot would improve her hand-eye coordination, her mental discipline, and her self-confidence. Lydia had just rolled her eyes. She held her ground, reminding him that there were many other activities she could engage in that would have the same effects without guns being involved.

Thwarted in his attempt to arm Diana, now that she was moving out, Lydia was surprised her husband hadn't turned into a raving lunatic. He was too calm. Something was up, and she planned to find out what it was, but not right this minute. Though she was sorely tempted to go downstairs and uncover precisely what was going on, Lydia refused to waste the last few minutes she had with Diana before she left home.

Half an hour later, John carried the last box of books to the car, shutting the back door of the black Ford Explorer parked in the driveway.

"Are you sure you didn't forget anything? Like the kitchen sink?" John asked with a cocked eyebrow.

"Don't be mean, Dad," Diana admonished as she swatted him on the arm.

"Ow!" he complained good-naturedly.

"Really, Dad?" Diana shook her head.

John sighed and pulled Diana into a hug. "I'm going to miss you, Didi," he said into her hair.

"Stop calling me that!"

Lydia smiled at the scene unfolding before her. Despite the fact that Diana hated the pet name, she didn't budge from her father's embrace. The two of them had always been close. And that was one thing Lydia had always been extremely grateful for.

"I'll miss you too, Dad," Lydia heard her daughter's muffled whisper. It had an edge to it, as if tears were about to fall. John glanced up at her, and his eyes were also suspiciously moist.

A few moments later, Diana began to fidget. "For you to miss me, I have to actually go, you know," she said.

Her father chuckled, letting her go, albeit half-heartedly. "Now, do you remember—"

"Not the lecture again, Dad," Diana groaned. "I've heard it five times already, and that's just in the past two hours."

Her father glared at her. "You don't know what—"

"Yes, yes, I know. The world is full of horrible people who are all out to get me, and boys are the spawn of evil who just want to impregnate me due to their biological drive to procreate with anything that moves. They don't care about me or my feelings." Diana recited in a monotone voice. "That about right?"

John's eyes narrowed. "Precisely. And, remember, don't go out—"

"...after dark because all the stalkers, rapists, and serial killers hang out right outside my dorm room just waiting for me, Diana Hunter, to walk out so they can grab me and do terrible things to me."

"Exactly, and—"

"I think she's got the point, John," Lydia said with a chuckle.

John looked at his wife with indignation. "If you saw what I do every day, you'd wonder how I let her leave the house. Either of you," he added, looking at his wife with concern in his gaze.

Lydia shook her head, but a loving smile curled her lips. "Do remember, honey, that we do see everything you do every day because you make a point of showing us the pictures. Let us never forget that we live in the city of Vancouver, which, despite so many people around the world thinking it is a lovely place, is a pit of evil and the crime capital of the universe, apparently."

"But it is!"

"This is fun and all, but can we get going, please? Pretty please?"

The puppy dog look Diana was giving her father was her most powerful, effective weapon. That, and her tears. Diana hardly ever cried. But on the rare occasions that she did, it destroyed her father. He was capable of taking on an entire army of serial killers by himself with only a rusty spoon, just to put a smile on her face. When she gave him that pleading look, though, he turned from one of the biggest hard-ass detectives into a complete sap. Lydia sighed. Diana had him wrapped around her little finger.

"Okay," he said, "everyone in the car."

When Diana had hopped in the SUV and closed the door, Lydia saw her chance. "What did you do?" she asked her husband pointedly.

"Me? What are you talking about?" His far-too innocent look said more than words. He knew precisely what she meant.

"John," she said warningly.

He ran a frustrated hand through his hair. "I may or may not have gone down to the local precinct near her campus and had a word with the boys there. And they may or may not have promised to keep an eye out for her. And they also may or may not have had a word with the campus security to keep her safe unless they wanted to deal with half the Vancouver Police Department breathing down their necks."

"Only half?" Lydia chuckled.

"Yeah, the other half will be busy dealing with the lowlife who hurt her," John replied sheepishly.

"You're impossible. You know she'll kill you if she finds out."

"*If* she finds out."

"You do know that your daughter is incredibly perceptive, right?"

"Well, it's my prerogative as her father to be overprotective." He paused for a moment. "She's our baby, Lydia. And she's leaving home."

"Don't start. If you start, I'm going to start crying, and she'll really kill us for making her late."

He nodded, enveloping his wife in a hug. "She'll be alright."

"Yes, she will."

"Are we going to be leaving this century?" Diana interrupted them.

"We're going, we're going," John mumbled.

They got into the car, and within moments, they left behind the three-bedroom townhouse that had been Diana's home almost since she had been born.

# CHAPTER TWO

## THREE YEARS LATER...

THE BLARING ALARM on his phone roused John Hunter out of a very deep and pleasant sleep. With his eyes closed, he hunted for the offending device and put the alarm on snooze. He groaned as he turned over, throwing an arm over his wife and nuzzling deep under the covers.

"We have to get up," Lydia said in a groggy voice.

"Five more minutes," he murmured. "I was having such a nice dream."

"Were you?" She scooted a little further back, cuddling into his warmth.

"Mhmm. It involved you, me, Paris, and a very, very romantic evening, if you get my drift," he purred.

Lydia giggled. "Now that I could get on board with. Of course, it would be nicer if it were more than just a dream so I could actually join in," she said with a soft sigh.

"We need a vacation," he grumbled.

"Yes, we do."

"You know what? How about we just do it? I mean, we

both have plenty of vacation time we can take, and Paris isn't that far."

"It's only halfway around the world. And do you have any idea how expensive a trip like that would be?"

Lydia had always been the practical one, at least in terms of finances. And that's precisely why she was in charge of all their money. Had it been up to him, they wouldn't have managed to buy a cardboard box, let alone own a house, have savings, and still lead a very comfortable life. But sometimes Lydia was way too tight with the money, like now.

"Yes, it's expensive, but it probably wouldn't even put a dent in our savings because my wife is a genius and a shrewd negotiator who could, in all likelihood, get us a great deal." After almost nineteen years, he knew precisely which buttons to push.

"I know what you're doing," Lydia said as she turned over.

He looked into her eyes that were the color of the sky on a beautiful spring morning and sighed. "Baby, we need some time to get away. Just the two of us. I want to go with my wife to the most romantic city in the world. Is that so wrong?"

Her eyes lit up, and she smiled softly. Cupping his cheek, she said, "I'll look over the figures and see if we can do it."

He grinned. Coming from Lydia, that was even better than a yes. It meant she would look over the figures and make it work.

"Paris, here we come."

She shook her head and poked him in the ribs. "If you want to see Paris sometime this century, it's time to get up." John groaned in protest.

"Or we could stay in bed and be late for work, after which there will be a rapid descent into poverty as we lose our jobs and never find work again. That would mean no Paris," she continued.

John rolled his eyes but still threw the covers off himself. "Yes, I'm sure we'll both be fired for being a few minutes late and end up dumpster diving."

That was his Lydia. Though she was generally a very optimistic person, she could exaggerate on occasion. He rolled out of bed and stretched. He heard Lydia sigh and looked back at her curiously.

"What?" he asked.

"Nothing," she replied with a blush. He grinned.

He found it amazing, and not a little sexy, that even after all this time, she could still blush. She'd obviously been checking him out. He told himself, it was understandable. Even though he was almost fifty, he kept himself in good shape with regular trips to the gym and a very clean diet.

"Like what you see?" He waggled his eyebrows at her and Lydia laughed, throwing a pillow at him.

"You know I do, now stop fishing for compliments and get ready."

"Yes, ma'am," he replied with a salute. With a grin still on his face, he made his way to the bathroom.

Fifteen minutes later, he was downstairs in the kitchen, pouring coffee for both of them. Two sugars and milk for Lydia and black for him. He placed the cups on the island and switched the television on to listen to the morning news.

Opening the fridge, he took out eggs, Canadian bacon, bell peppers, onions, and mushrooms. It was his turn to get breakfast ready. He chopped the vegetables and glanced at the clock.

"Hun, your coffee's getting cold," he called out.

"Coming," she shouted back. A few minutes later, she walked up behind him and looked around him to see what he was making. "Omelet? What's the occasion?" They tended to stick to simpler meals in the morning that didn't involve cooking.

"Can't a man do something nice for his wife without it being a special occasion?" he asked.

She cocked an eyebrow but smiled. She kissed his cheek. "Thank you."

"You'd think I never do anything for you," he grumbled.

She laughed as she sat at the island. "No, I just like to keep you on your toes. Can't have you forgetting to keep doing stuff for me. You know, to show me how much you care," she replied with a wink. Taking a sip of her coffee, she closed her eyes and moaned in satisfaction.

"Good?" he asked.

She nodded with a pleased look on her face. "Perfect."

He turned back to the omelets he was making. "We're still on for tonight, right?"

It was their date night, and he'd made reservations at a fancy French restaurant. He'd actually been secretly working on the idea of a trip to Paris over the past few weeks, dropping hints here and there. It seemed to have worked quite well.

"Unless some emergency comes up, sure," Lydia replied.

"We'll leave around seven. Our reservations are for half-past so that should give us plenty of time to get to the restaurant."

"Sounds good. My shift ends at six, so I'll be able to get home and change, no problem." She paused for a moment.

"But what about you? You don't finish until six-thirty. Please tell me you aren't going like that."

"I was planning on getting changed. I just don't need three hours to do it."

"Aren't we hilarious this morning?"

He grinned at her. "Just saying it like it is."

"You're lucky you're so good-looking, or I'd have booted you out ages ago," she grumbled.

He dished out the omelet onto two plates and set hers down in front of her with a kiss to her cheek. "I knew you only wanted me for my good looks," he said with a wink.

"You got that right," she replied with a sparkle in her eye.

He grabbed hold of his chest. "You wound me so, my lady."

She just rolled her eyes. "You can be so melodramatic, sometimes."

"That's precisely why you love me."

"Keep telling yourself that," she said.

He paused for a moment to look at her. He covered the hand she rested on the table with his own. "I love you more than my own life," he said seriously.

She turned her hand over and gripped his. "I love you, too, my darling."

That afternoon, John sat at his desk, glaring at the computer screen in front of him as if that would help him find something that apparently wasn't there.

"Who the hell sealed this file?" he muttered to himself. He would speak to his superintendent to see if he could gain access. It was the only lead they had on the case he'd been working, however vague it might be, and he really needed to get into that file.

Just as he was about to get up, he saw movement in the corner of his eye. Looking up, he saw a uniformed officer approach him. "Detective," the man said hesitantly. When the cop said nothing further and simply stood there fidgeting, John decided he'd better prompt him or they'd be there all day. He knew he had a reputation for being tough, but this was ridiculous.

"What is it, Constable?" he asked.

The man swallowed hard. "Detective Gregson would like to see you in the waiting room, sir."

"The waiting room?"

"Yes, sir. He wants to talk to you privately." The waiting room was hardly what one would call private since it was mostly glass, but it was less public than the bullpen. That fact made John curious about what his longtime partner and friend, Liam Gregson, wanted to tell him. And why he hadn't come to get him himself.

John glanced up and nodded. "Thank you." He got up slowly and walked into the waiting room. He closed the door behind him and stopped to stare at his buddy. The man looked shell-shocked.

"Everything okay, Liam?" he asked. Something was up. He'd never seen Liam so shaken, and they'd been partners for more than five years.

"John, we need to talk," His tone was grave, which made John freeze. Liam was an easy-going guy who was always cracking jokes. Some thought his sense of humor morbid at times, but it was Liam's way of coping with the terrible things they dealt with day in and day out.

John looked at Liam. He really looked at him. The clenched jaw, the moisture in his eyes, the fidgeting, the stooped posture. It wasn't a demeanor that was unfamiliar to John. Liam got this way every time they had to deliver terrible news to a family. The only difference was that this time Liam looked even more devastated than usual.

"No," John whispered, suddenly catching on. "No, I don't want to hear it." He really didn't want to hear what Liam had to tell him. The younger man's body language was a clear indicator that whatever it was, he was not going to like it at all. Sending Liam to talk to him meant that whatever had happened, it affected him intimately, and it was serious.

"I'm sorry, John," Liam said, his voice strangled.

John began to pray. *Please, not my girls. Not my girls. Please, God, let them be all right. I'll do anything. Please...* "Diana?" John managed to choke out after a moment's hesitation.

Liam shook his head. "Is Lydia—", John's throat clenched, and he had to push the words out. "Is she okay?" he managed.

"I'm so sorry, John." John watched the lone tear that tracked down Liam's left cheek, his whole world reduced to that single droplet as it made its way lower and lower down the other man's face until it disappeared into nothingness. He couldn't process anything else. Not even what that tear meant. Certainly not what Liam's words meant.

His hands clenched into fists. The cheap plastic pen he'd been holding snapped in half. It sounded like a gunshot in the silence. He looked out into the bullpen and realized that everyone was completely silent. There were fifteen or so detectives and uniformed officers currently working out there. Normally, they were a curious and noisy bunch. Yet everyone was going about their business in complete silence, and they seemed to be doing their best not to even glance in the direction of the waiting room.

Everyone knew. They all knew. But no, there was nothing to know. "Lydia's fine," he muttered. "She's fine. We had coffee this morning. She kissed me good-bye. We're having dinner tonight at that fancy new place that just opened up on Alberni."

"John," Liam whispered as he grabbed his forearm. "I'm really sorry but..." his voice cracked. He cleared his throat. "Lydia's dead."

John's stomach heaved. His temperature ratcheted up until he felt as if he was burning from the inside. He stared at his hands, unwilling to look at Liam and the sadness he'd see in the other man's eyes. He took a deep breath to steady himself. He couldn't break down. Not here.

"What happened?" his voice was barely above a whisper.

Liam shook his head. "I'm not sure. The call came in a little while ago. They found her b—they found Lydia at the hospital, in the nurse's rec room."

"Maybe she's just sleeping."

He knew he was being ridiculous. It was a hospital. They'd know if someone was dead. But he couldn't believe it. He couldn't bring himself to acknowledge that he'd never again see the smiling face of the woman he had loved for almost two decades.

The pitying look Liam gave him made John want to roar at the other man. He wanted to rage at the world. He wanted to hit something. He wanted to... He wanted Lydia to be alive. He wanted to turn back the clock and tell her to take a day off. To tell her that she worked too hard and that she needed to rest.

"What happened? I need to know what happened,

Liam!" He hadn't even finished his sentence properly before he was surging to his feet, yanking open the door.

"John, they won't let you in!" Liam shouted after him. But John ignored his partner and stalked back to his desk. He grabbed his car keys and stormed out of the bullpen. He'd shout and scream and holler until they let him see her. His Lydia.

He heard running feet behind him. "Give me the keys," Liam said.

"I have to see her." He didn't break stride for a moment.

"I know. But give me the damned keys. I'll drive. You'll kill yourself."

John cut him a look. "Maybe I should."

"Don't be stupid! What about Diana?"

Diana didn't know. He'd have to tell her. Oh God, she was going to be devastated. He laughed humorlessly. He had no idea what he was going to say.

"We'll do it together," Liam promised. John hadn't realized he'd spoken aloud.

Shrugging, he threw Liam the keys and got into the passenger side of the SUV. He stared out the window, unseeing as the scenery flew past. He knew Liam would do the right thing. He could trust him with that. Just as he knew the younger man would help him break the news to Diana.

He wasn't even sure he could actually say his wife's name and that word in the same sentence. He couldn't say *dead*. He just couldn't even contemplate it. Not yet. But Liam would be there. And he had every right to be. He was practically family.

Since Liam had become his partner, Lydia had sort of adopted the younger man, making him an honorary member of their tight-knit group. He'd come over for Sunday lunch every week, and once Diana had left for university, Liam had spent more time at their home than he did his own apartment. Lydia always had a soft spot for the lonely, damaged ones. And the moment she'd spotted Liam, she'd known right away that he'd had a rough childhood. She'd seen right through his brash attitude, and Liam had been unable to keep his defenses up. No one could ever resist his Lydia. All she'd ever done was help people and make the world a more beautiful place.

Something wet hit the back of his hand, and he looked down in surprise. Raising a trembling hand to his face, he realized he was crying. No, damn it, no! Lydia couldn't be dead. Someone had made a mistake. They must have. Maybe it was someone else who just looked like Lydia. That was it. That had to be it.

A few minutes – and a lot of broken traffic laws – later, they pulled up in front of Mercy General Hospital. Lydia had worked there for almost fifteen years. She'd started a few years after giving birth to Diana, and with her quick intelligence and warm bedside manner, she had rapidly risen up the ranks to become head nurse. Everyone loved her. And now, she was gone? No! No, it wasn't his Lydia. It couldn't be.

He got out of the vehicle, his movements slow. He couldn't run. He wouldn't run. It would bring the truth that much closer, that much faster. No, it wasn't his Lydia. It would be some other poor nurse, and he would have to do his job. He would have to investigate what had happened to her. He squared his shoulders and walked into the hospital with Liam on his heels. He didn't stop to ask for directions. He didn't need them. As he rounded yet another corner in the maze of corridors that made up Mercy General, he stopped dead. Two uniformed police officers were holding back the curious. He walked toward them, determined. When they saw him, they froze.

"We can't let you in, sir," one of the men said respectfully.

He grit his teeth. "I need to work the crime scene."

They shook their heads. "I'm sorry, sir. We have strict orders not to let you in."

Just as he was about to snap at the two men, Liam intervened. "He needs to see her," he said, his tone low. The officers looked at Liam and nodded after a moment's hesitation. Raising the yellow tape, they let him through.

John looked at the doorway as if it was a portal into hell. And, in a way, it was. The moment he walked through it, he'd be living his own personal nightmare. He clenched his fists by his sides. He took a deep breath and took those final fatal steps that would bring him into the room.

He paused, looking around. It was a small room. The size of a closet. Two bunk beds took up most of the space, while a small table with two chairs and a refrigerator took up the rest of it. He took in everything. His eyes landed on the person lying on the bottom bunk furthest from the door.

He smiled gently. She looked so beautiful and serene, almost as if she were asleep. He even convinced himself of it for a few moments. She lay on her back, one arm curled under her head, while the other was by her side. Then he saw the hypodermic needle sticking out of her arm. He clenched his teeth.

"Come on," Liam said. "Let's get out of here. Let the crime scene unit do their job."

John shook his head. "No, I need to wake her up." He made toward her, but Liam grabbed him.

"No! You know you can't touch her!"

Liam practically had to drag him out of the room.

"Lydia!" he kept yelling. Liam dragged him down the corridor and out of sight of the other police officers, who were throwing him pitying looks. Pushing him against the wall, Liam got up in his face.

"John, Lydia is dead! Do you get it? She is dead. She's not asleep. She's not waking up. She's dead." By this point, Liam's tears were running down his face unchecked.

"No, no, no," John muttered, shaking his head in denial.

"Get it together! For Diana! You have an amazing daughter who has no idea her mother is dead. You need to pull yourself together for her, John."

John stared at Liam, his eyes glassy. He brought a fist up to his chest, rubbing the spot just above his heart, as if it would ease the pain. "My Lydia's dead?"

"I'm so goddamned sorry, John, but yes, she is."

John felt his knees give way. He crumpled to the floor and began to rock back and forth. "Lydia," he whispered through the tears.

# CHAPTER THREE

UNIVERSITY OF BRITISH COLUMBIA, VANCOUVER
CAMPUS

O
H MY GOD, did you see his face?" Teddy Van
Alst laughed as he threw himself down on
Diana's bed.

She rolled her eyes at his infantile practical joke, but she couldn't help a small chuckle. "Teddy, you are impossible. Why won't you leave Richard alone?" she asked as she joined him on the bed.

"Because he's a jerk," her best friend replied.

She and Teddy had met in Computer Science class, and though he was two years older than her, they'd become fast friends. They were geeks, the outcasts, the ones who were different. They'd bonded precisely over their different-ness. They'd pushed each other to be better, so they'd managed to get their degrees in two years, rather than the usual three. The fact that Diana had also gotten her biochemistry degree at the same time had resulted in Teddy declaring that she was a scary-smart dudette who would one day take over the world. She'd promised he could be her vice-whatever when she did.

He'd continued down the computer science path, while she'd gone to medical school. Even so, they were still best friends and saw each other every day. They would have shared the same room, if they could, but the university frowned on such things, even if Teddy wasn't interested in girls and never would be.

As it was, they met up for coffee every morning, spent their evenings studying together, and essentially spent every free moment in each other's company.

"Why is he a jerk?" she asked.

"Really? You really need to ask me that? After what I heard him say? He's lucky I didn't put him on a terrorist watch list and only froze his bank accounts." Among his myriad of hobbies, Teddy liked to "fiddle with" computers, as he put it.

"You're really making it sound a lot worse than it is."

He turned over and glared at her. "Diana Hunter, the idiot bet his friends that he'd get, and I quote, "the freaky smart girl into bed!" That is called being a massive jerk, okay? How could I let him get away with it?"

Diana rolled her eyes. "He wouldn't have gotten away with anything because that would imply that I am susceptible to his charms."

"What charms?" Teddy interrupted with a snort.

"Precisely. The day I fall into bed with Richard Morton is the day we get hit by an asteroid that obliterates the entire planet." When Teddy opened his mouth to say something, she held a finger up to silence him. "And even then, knowing I was about to die, I wouldn't sleep with him if he was the last man on earth."

Teddy chuckled then sobered. "He still deserved it," he mumbled.

Diana smiled and rolled over to give him a hug. She

kissed him on the cheek. "Thank you for always looking out for me," she said with a grin.

"Well, what am I here for? I'm your bodyguard. And that's official. Your dad said so."

Diana grinned. It was true. Her dad adored Teddy. The first time she'd brought him home for dinner, her father had scowled. Teddy didn't look like a geek at first glance. He'd been bullied as a child and again as a teen when the other kids figured out that he was gay. So, he started working out. A lot. He reasoned that if he were bigger than everyone else, they'd be too scared to bully him. And he'd been right. He'd left for summer vacation in ninth grade a scrawny kid. By the start of the next school year, he'd gained a lot of muscle mass, and by the middle of tenth grade, he was built like a tank. The bullies gave him a wide berth.

When she'd told her dad that Teddy was gay and would never be a threat to her virtue, he'd promptly declared Teddy her official bodyguard. And Teddy had been more than happy to oblige, claiming that her youth and naiveté in "matters of the heart" meant that she needed his protection. It was sweet. It really was. Except for when the two of them ganged up on any potential date she might have had. Between Teddy and her dad, it was a miracle she had any social life at all. Oh, wait, that's right, she didn't. Well, not much of one. Her IQ was already a huge impediment, since she found most boys her age boring as dirt and tended to avoid them. Anyone who seemed a little more interesting, from an intellectual point of view at least, was either way too old – as in they-could-be-her-dad-old – or felt the need to compete with her, which sucked.

"I'm going to die alone," she groaned.

Teddy looked at her in surprise. "Don't be stupid. Of course you're not going to die alone. We'll find you some hot, genius superstar who will worship the ground you walk on," he said with a grin.

Diana rolled her eyes. "You do know you are talking about someone who doesn't exist, right?"

"Just you wait. Everyone has a soul mate, and you will find yours," Teddy said knowingly.

She looked at him like he'd lost his mind. "Are you insane? I don't need a soul mate. I just want to have some fun." She huffed. "And maybe lose my virginity sometime before I'm a hundred years old," she muttered under her breath.

Teddy's eyes widened. "Oh, no! No! No! You will be a virgin until the day you die. Your father's orders. I really don't want to spend the rest of my life locked up in isolation somewhere."

Diana rolled her eyes. "He was kidding when he said that."

"It didn't sound funny when he growled at me while cleaning his gun."

She laughed. "Yeah, Dad can be a bit overprotective."

"A bit? I mean, okay, I get it. I'd be the same as him if I had a daughter like you."

"Like me?" she asked.

"Fishing for compliments are we? Come on Di, you're hot as sin, you can kick most guys' asses – I really gotta thank your dad for that one – and you have a sick sense of humor. If I were straight, I would have married you by now."

Diana giggled. "Teddy, you do amazing things for my ego. If you were straight, I would have married you too," she said with a wink.

"I've got a brilliant idea," he said, sitting up excitedly.

He repositioned himself cross-legged on her bed and looked at her expectantly. She moved into the same position.

"Go on, I'm listening, oh, Great One."

"Let's make a pact. If we haven't found our soul mates by the time we're thirty-five, we'll get married to each other."

Diana's eyes widened. "What kind of idea is that? Do you think people die at thirty-five?"

He rolled his eyes. "Don't be ridiculous. But I'd rather spend my life with you than alone."

"Thanks, that makes me feel really good," she said with a laugh.

"That's not what I—"

The sound of her phone ringing interrupted him. She rolled over to look at the caller ID. "Hi, Liam, what's up?" she said when she answered.

*"Diana, we need to talk to you."*

His grave tone didn't sit well with her. "Is Dad alright?"

*"Yeah, he's fine. He's here with me."*

"Well, then, spit it out. What is it? And why are you calling me and not Dad if he's there with you?" she asked suspiciously.

*"Diana, could you come outside, please? I'd rather we not do this over the phone. We're parked right outside your building."*

"I'll be right out." She hung up and stared at her phone for a moment.

"Everything okay?" Teddy asked.

Diana shook her head. "I don't know. I don't think so. Liam and my dad are here. They want to speak to me outside."

Teddy knew enough about her family to know that

something was very wrong if both Liam and her father had shown up.

"Do you want me to come with you?"

She looked up at him. "Please," she said.

Teddy slipped his hand into hers. She squeezed his hand hard. "Okay, let's find out what's going on," he said, trying to sound a lot more confident than he felt.

As they made their way outside, Diana could feel the icy fingers of fear squeezing around her heart. They were getting tighter with every step she took. When she finally saw her father and Liam, her heart plummeted. Her father looked like death warmed over, and Liam didn't look any better. She stopped in her tracks, pulling Teddy back.

"I don't want to go over there," she whispered at Teddy's questioning look. "They're going to tell me something I don't want to hear. I just know it."

Teddy nodded. "It doesn't look like they're here to give you good news." He tried to start walking, but Diana's feet were planted.

"Di, honey, we have to go over there. Standing here won't change anything, whatever it is."

"I know, but it will delay it."

"You're only putting off the inevitable. Come on, Di, whatever it is, I'll be here for you. Always." He gave her hand a gentle squeeze and tugged her forward. Her feet moved of their own volition.

"Dad?" she asked softly when she reached him. She saw the tears in his eyes, and the panic began to well up inside. Her palms were clammy, yet her hands felt frozen.

"Oh, baby," her father managed to get out.

"What's going on?" she demanded, her voice sounding just as panicky as she felt.

"Your mother—" her father's voice broke.

"Mom? What's happened to Mom? Dad, tell me what happened to Mom!" she was already screaming. She didn't care that everyone milling around the campus was staring at her. She didn't care that Teddy was trying to calm her. She wanted to know why her father looked as though her mother was dead.

"Baby, I'm so sorry. She was found a few hours ago at work..." he trailed off, unable to talk.

"No! No! No! You're lying!" she flew at her father, hitting his chest with her fists. "You're lying! Why are you lying to me?" she sobbed.

John looked down at his daughter. He had to be there for Diana. He was her father. He was supposed to be the strong one. He controlled his emotions as best he could, burying his pain deeply so he could focus on supporting her. Squaring his shoulders, he gathered her into his arms, holding her tightly. "I wish I was, Didi. I wish I was."

Diana broke down in her father's arms, her legs giving way. He held her up, holding her tight, realizing finally that he could no longer protect her from the world around her, from the pain, as he'd always tried to do. "Daddy," she sobbed into his chest.

"Shhhh," he soothed as he petted her hair. "It's okay, sweetie, Daddy's here." And in that moment, he made a promise. Whoever had done this to his wife, he would find him. He would find him, and he would destroy him.

## CHAPTER FOUR

"EXCUSE ME?" JOHN growled, his tone so menacing that Nico Stavros, the detective who'd been assigned Lydia Hunter's case, paled and took a step back.

"Lydia's death has been declared a suicide. I'm sorry," he whispered.

"My wife did not kill herself." John's jaw clenched. He could feel his temple begin to throb in earnest.

"I'm sorry, but that's what the evidence points to." Stavros was practically mumbling, looking for all the world as if he wished the ground would open up and swallow him.

"What evidence?" John snapped. He was moments away from throttling the small man standing in front of him.

Stavros' Adam's apple bobbed like crazy. "There was no evidence of a break in, no one's fingerprints but hers were found on the hypodermic, and her therapist said she was suffering from depression."

"And just based on that, you think my wife killed herself? How the hell have you closed so many cases if you take just five minutes to rule this a suicide? If you'd looked a bit deeper, you would have discovered my wife didn't even have a therapist!"

Faced with the towering fury that was John Hunter in that very moment, Stavros practically squeaked. "Some of the nurses said she saw one of the psychiatrists from the hospital every now and then. Something to do with dealing with all the death at the hospital," he said quickly.

"That doesn't mean she was seeing a therapist on a regular basis and it definitely doesn't mean she was depressed or that she killed herself."

"She left a note," Stavros said quickly.

"What?" John froze.

No, it wasn't possible. His wife could not have killed herself. He would have known something was wrong. But she had seemed just as happy as always. He'd have noticed. He would have.

Stavros nodded quickly. "She left a suicide note."

"Don't call it that!" John roared, causing the man in front of him to go white as a sheet.

"I'm sorry," he said quickly. "Let me get it for you." Moments later, he returned with the note.

John yanked the plastic bag containing the piece of paper from Stavros. "Has it been dusted for prints?"

Stavros opened his mouth but then stopped. "Well?" John demanded. He hadn't even looked at it yet.

"No one else's prints except Mrs. Hunter's were found on the note," Stavros said quickly.

John nodded and paused before finally working up the courage to look at the piece of paper he held in his hand.

*My dearest John,*

*I know this will come as a shock to both you and Diana, but I can't deal with life anymore. There are so many things you don't know about me, my dear, sweet*

*John. If you really knew me, knew about my past, you'd never look at me the same way again. I couldn't bear the thought of you knowing how weak I am, and that's why I never told you how much I was suffering. I couldn't. I wanted you to be happy, and if you'd have known how much I was hurting, I know you would have suffered right along with me.*

*It would have been just like that time when we went hiking and I fell and broke my leg. It wasn't your fault, and there was nothing you could do to take the pain away, but you suffered with me. Remember what I told you then? Well, I meant every single word and still do.*

*I just want you and Diana to know that I love you both dearly, and I'm sorry to hurt you like this. I'm just tired, John. Tired of fighting every day to put on a face that isn't mine. To act like someone I'm not. This is the best solution.*

*I don't want you and Diana grieving over me. You have to move on with your lives. It is best this way. Please believe that.*

*Your loving wife,*

*Lydia*

John's hand was shaking. There was no way this was happening. Lydia had been fine. She had been happy. They'd had coffee that morning. She'd laughed. They were planning a vacation to Paris, the most romantic city in the world. Lydia had not been suicidal, no matter what anyone said to him.

Then he glanced down at the piece of paper in his hand. His heart was screaming that Lydia would never do this, but the cop in him was shouting at him to accept the facts. He had physical evidence in his hands that Lydia had been deeply unhappy and that she'd managed to hide it from him so well that he hadn't noticed a thing until it was much too late. Tears were running down his cheeks. It took every ounce of strength he had not to fall to his knees.

Someone snatched the letter out of his hands. "You idiot!" Liam snarled at Stavros. "You choose the middle of the bullpen to tell him this? To show him this! You don't deserve to wear that badge." Stung, the detective slunk away.

Liam turned to John. "And you! What are you doing here? You should be at home with Diana. It hasn't even been two days!"

John looked up at him, his jaw clenched, "I needed to know what happened."

Liam nodded. "Come on, I'll take you home."

"How am I going to tell Diana?" John asked. His hand twitched.

Liam looked at him. "The only way you can tell Diana anything. Clearly and to the point."

John smiled sadly. "That's our Diana. No beating around the bush, or she'll take our heads off."

"Exactly. So, come on, let's go."

John had a sinking feeling that the news would change Diana irrevocably. But what could he do? He couldn't lie to his daughter. And even if he wanted to, Diana was a walking, talking lie detector. At least with him. She knew every single tell of his and would figure out he was being less than truthful within a second.

He stopped walking. "Get a copy of the letter, or she won't believe it."

Liam didn't wait for a second invitation. He turned and stalked back into the bullpen, shouting at Stavros. Within a few minutes, he'd returned, a manila envelope clutched in his hand.

Diana sat on the couch in the living room, her back ramrod straight. Dressed all in black, she was struggling to hold her emotions in check. She felt like breaking down and crying every second she spent in the house. Everywhere she looked, she saw something that reminded her of her mother, and it hurt. It hurt so badly.

Now, she was sitting here as Liam and her father loomed above her. Thankfully, Teddy was sitting next to her, holding her hand. He had been a steadying presence ever since she'd found out about her mother's death. And she had never been more grateful for his friendship than right then.

"What is it you want to tell me?" she asked, though she feared the answer. She thought back to the last time they'd given her news together; it had been the worst moment of her life.

Her father sighed, running a hand through his hair. "They've discovered what happened to your mother," he said softly.

Diana's eyes widened. "They found whoever did this to her already? Are they sure?" The sad look on her father's face stopped her. "What happened to Mom, Dad?"

He looked at her. "All evidence points to the fact that she took her own life."

Diana froze. "Excuse me?"

"Diana, it looks like your mother killed herself."

"No, that's not possible. Mom would never... No, you've got it wrong." Diana looked back and forth between Liam and her father. They really believed what they were telling her. That didn't mean it was true, though. It wouldn't be the first time they'd made a mistake.

But then Liam handed her an envelope. She took it with trembling hands. She tried to remove the piece of paper that was inside, but her hands were shaking so badly she couldn't grasp it. Teddy took the envelope from her gently and pulled the paper out, handing her the white sheet.

She took it and began to read, her hands clenching the paper tighter with every word. She looked up at her father. She had no doubt that this was real. She knew her mother's handwriting.

"She left us," she said with a sob. As he had many times over the past two days, her father sat down and pulled her into a hug, holding her tightly.

"I know it hurts, baby girl. But think how much pain she was in if this was the only way out she could see," he tried to soothe her.

"She never said anything. Why didn't she say anything? We could have helped her."

"I know, Didi. I know. I wish she'd said something. I wish…"

He pulled her onto his lap. She curled up against his chest as she had when she was a little girl. It felt so good to let her father comfort her like this. She'd tried to be stoic and strong, but losing her mother and now finding out she had abandoned them made her feel just like a little girl again. A little girl who wanted her mommy but would never see her again.

"You won't leave me, too, will you, Dad?" she asked, her voice small and terrified.

John was torn between grief at losing his wife and resentment at her for doing this to them. For taking the coward's way out. And to hear his smart, courageous nine-teen-year-old daughter revert to a little girl begging him not to leave her made him angry. So, so angry at Lydia for being so selfish.

He groaned, hugging Diana even more tightly. "Of course not, baby girl. I'll never leave you. Not if I have a choice."

Those words sounded familiar somehow. They felt important. A flicker of a memory stirred deep in his brain, but as he tried to concentrate on it, his daughter's quiet sobs distracted him.

"Shhh, it's okay, Didi. We'll be okay. I promise." He hoped it was a promise he'd be able to keep.

Diana lay on her bed, her head pillowed on Teddy's bicep. He was spooning her from behind, holding her tightly against him as if he could lend her some of his strength.

"How could she do this to me, Teddy? How could she do it to Dad? How could she do it to all of us who loved and cared for her?" she asked in a small voice.

Teddy sighed behind her. "I know it hurts. I know it's killing you that she did this, but Diana, she must have been in such a bad place to see this as the only solution."

Diana sighed. "It's not fair, Teddy. She could have said something. Why didn't she say anything? We could have helped her. All of us. We could have been there for her and helped her get over whatever it was."

"I know, Di. And you know we'd have all done anything we could to help Lydia. She knew that. The pain she must have been in.... Try not to be angry with her, Di. She did the only thing she thought she could."

"You know, I just realized. She'll never see me get

married. She'll never meet my children. My kids won't have a grandma because she was... so selfish," she uttered.

Diana knew she wasn't being fair, but part of her didn't care. Her mother had had so many people in her life who loved her, and she'd chosen to give them all up.

"Your dad will be there," Teddy reminded her.

Diana laughed though it was a cold, harsh sound. "Who knows? Maybe he'll decide to kill himself too. After all, he might not be able to take the pain of losing my mother," she said sarcastically.

"Diana!" Teddy snapped. When he used her full name, she knew Teddy meant business. "You have no right to belittle his pain. He's been doing the best he can, trying to be strong for you."

"I'm sorry," she said with a frustrated sigh. "I just wish I could understand what happened. I wish I could understand how and why my strong, happy mother suddenly turned into a depressive coward who chose to give up rather than fight."

"Don't, Di. Please, don't. You'll regret these words later."

Diana shook her head. "No, I won't. You know why? Because everyone has problems. You think being the brain box in every class is easy? Do you know you are the only true friend I've ever had? Do you know that I haven't even as much as danced with a boy because I scare them all off? I know it sounds pathetic, but you know as well as I do that growing up as an outsider isn't easy. We could have killed ourselves, couldn't we? We could have given up, just like her. Then other people would be hurting instead of us."

He sighed, nuzzling her hair. "It's not the same thing, and you know it."

She turned over to look into his eyes. "How isn't it the

same thing? We were in pain, but we chose to fight back rather than just roll over and die!"

"Di, you're not being fair. You have no idea what your mother was going through, and until you find out – if you ever find out – you have no right to judge. I'm sorry, but that's the truth."

Diana huffed out a breath. "Let's agree to disagree for now."

Teddy nodded. Diana had a strong stubborn streak. Arguing with her wasn't always the best option. Like now.

"Thanks for being here, Teddy," she whispered.

He smiled. "Where else would I be? You're my little sister, and I'll always be here for you, no matter what."

Diana closed her eyes and snuggled into Teddy's warmth. She was exhausted from the roller coaster of emotions she'd been riding ever since she'd heard of her mother's death. It was all too much for her to comprehend and for now, what she needed most was to rest. Luckily, blissful oblivion overtook her senses in moments as she fell asleep in Teddy's arms. Tomorrow was another day, and she was in no rush for it to arrive.

# CHAPTER FIVE

J OHN LOOKED AT Karen Elwin, the medical examiner, who was currently cringing under his murderous gaze.

"What?" He couldn't believe what he was hearing.

"I'm sorry, Detective Hunter. I have no idea what happened."

"Well, find out!" he exclaimed. "You can't just lose a body! And I'm pretty damn sure she didn't get up and walk out of here on her own."

"Let me call my assistant. He was in charge of the night shift. Maybe he knows more."

The woman looked terrified, but at that very moment, John couldn't bring himself to care. How could she just stand there and tell him his wife's body was missing but that she had no idea what happened?

The medical examiner scurried into her office to make the call. Or to call John's superintendent and report him for shouting at her. Well, let her. He doubted his super would say anything when he found out precisely why he'd lost his temper.

Two minutes later, she came back in wringing her hands.

"Did you find her?" he snapped impatiently when it seemed she wouldn't be saying anything of her own accord.

"It seems an order came down from the Deputy Chief Constable's office that your wife was to be cremated. Her body was shipped out this morning."

"That's it?" He was going to kill someone. "Who gives the Deputy Chief Constable's office the right to decide what will happen to my wife's body?"

Karen Elwin shook her head. "I'm sorry," she murmured. "The orders came down, and we had to follow them."

"When's the cremation scheduled for?" he asked, realizing that was probably the first thing he should have said after her revelation.

She looked at him and winced. "It was scheduled to start three hours ago."

John's eyes widened as he realized what she was saying. "You're kidding me, right? Are you telling me you turned my wife into ashes without consulting me? What is wrong with you people?" He was screaming, and he knew he was scaring the woman by the way she flinched, but he felt justified. Some moron had turned his Lydia to ashes without his permission.

"I'm sorry, Mr. Hunter," Karen Elwin whispered.

"I don't want an apology, I want my wife's body! I want to be able to give her a proper burial. I want my daughter to be able to say goodbye to her mother. I want to say..." his voice cracked and he swallowed back the tears that were threatening to fall.

He tilted his head back and took a deep breath. "An apology isn't enough. I want to know who signed that order. I want to know who is responsible for this."

The woman looked contrite. "I'm sorry, Mr. Hunter, you know I can't release that information to the family."

He glared at her. "I'm a homicide detective with VPD. This order was issued by mistake. My wife's death was ruled a suicide, which means that there is no ongoing investigation and that means you can damn well tell me who is responsible for cremating my wife's body without my permission!" His voice got louder and louder as he unleashed his venom on the woman.

She squared her shoulders. "Sir, I'm sorry, but I'm not authorized to release this information to anyone. If you wish to learn more, I suggest you take it up directly with the Deputy Chief Constable's office."

John was about to launch into another rage-filled speech, but seeing the mulish look on the woman's face, he realized he was wasting his time. He turned on his heel to leave before immediately turning back round again and placing his face just inches from the medical examiner's. "Mark my words, this is not over. Not by a long way. Someone, somewhere *will* pay for this!" He stormed out of her office, slamming the door as he did so.

He wanted to hit something he was so angry. How could something like this happen? How could he have lost her all over again? And then it hit him. How was he going to tell Diana? Dropping yet another bomb on her was not a good idea. It had been one thing after another. The last thing he wanted to do was put her under even more stress, but he didn't have much choice. He'd have to explain to her why she couldn't say good-bye to her mother. He'd have to tell Diana that they'd once more lost the woman they both loved so deeply.

John sat nursing a glass of scotch that evening. He was worried about Diana. She had taken the news of her mother's unexpected cremation rather well. Too well, in fact. He thought over all the events that had taken place over the past few days. Something wasn't right. He knew that if he had been Nico Stavros, he too, given the evidence, would have reached the conclusion that Lydia had killed herself. However, Stavros didn't know Lydia. He didn't know what a fighter she was or how much she'd overcome.

Lydia used to go out of her way to avoid hurting people. It just didn't fit that she would have killed herself and left them all behind to cry for her. He hoped. One minute his heart was screaming that she didn't kill herself. Then his brain intervened with cold hard logic, showing him the facts, the suicide note.

Sighing deeply, he mulled over the circumstances surrounding the cremation of Lydia's body. The action felt utterly invasive, leaving John feeling bereft and humiliated. He had had everything taken from him – his life, his wife, and even her dead body.

Yes, it looked on the surface like a simple clerical error. In fact, that's what they had said at the Deputy Chief Constable's office when he'd checked. The cremation order had been intended for a body that had remained unclaimed for the better part of a fortnight. John couldn't accuse them of lying, at least not without proof, but the explanation he had been given, that someone had accidentally written "Lydia Hunter" on the order instead of "Jane Doe #46," defied belief. It wasn't as if it were a simple spelling mistake or that there were two people with the same name lying in the same morgue. So, it was either a monumental error or something else was going on. Something extremely suspicious. It was as if someone wanted to cover up evidence...

"Dad?" he heard Diana's voice. He was tempted to share his thoughts with her, but then he gave himself a mental shake. His daughter had been through enough without him giving her false hope. After all, he had no evidence to support his thoughts. Just a few suspicions. Suspicions that would probably get him branded a nutcase if he took them to his superintendent.

"What are you doing up and about at this time?" he asked.

Diana walked into the gloomy living room and sat next to her father on the couch. "Couldn't sleep," she replied, staring into the cheerful fire that was a complete antithesis to her mood.

"Me neither," he replied.

"Why do you think she left us?" Diana asked after a moment's hesitation. She needed to understand why her mother had chosen to die. The more she thought about it, the harder it was to come up with an explanation and the harder it became to accept that her mother had preferred death over her daughter and husband.

"It had nothing to do with you, Didi," her father said softly. "It's not a case of preferring death to you."

"Then what is it? Was death really her only option? Was it really the only way to solve her problems?"

John sighed. "How do you think I feel, Didi?" he asked softly. "Think about it. She was the love of my life. I saw her every day, and I'd sworn to protect her. Yet I didn't notice anything. I couldn't see that she was so unhappy she'd rather end her life than keep on going. How do you think I feel knowing that I should have, could have noticed something, yet didn't? How do you think I feel knowing she obviously didn't trust me enough, wasn't confident enough in me, to let me help her."

He ran a hand through his hair. He exhaled slowly. "I'm sorry, Didi. I shouldn't take my frustrations out on you. You're dealing with enough as it is."

Diana shook her head. "No, Dad. I'm here for you. Just like you're here for me. After all, all we've really got is each other, no?"

"Well, there's Teddy and Liam, too," he reminded her with a small smile.

"Yeah," she replied. "You're right." She got to her feet. "I think I'm going to try to get some sleep."

"Good. Get some rest. I'll see you in the morning."

"Good night, Dad."

"Good night, Didi."

She smiled sadly and made her way up the stairs. She dropped down onto the bed, curling up into Teddy, who was snoring loudly enough to wake the dead. It was a comforting sound. One that kept her grounded.

Ever since she'd learned of her mother's suicide, she'd been battling against herself. Trying hard not to let herself withdraw from the world. It was so tempting. She knew she could simply withdraw into her studies, into her mind, and let science take over. She knew she could stop the pain like that. She'd done it before, when she was younger, when she hadn't been able to deal with all the bullying. She'd retreated from the world, barely exchanging two words with anyone.

Her mother had been so worried, she'd taken her to the doctor and then the psychologist, who'd figured her out pretty quickly. The shrink had explained to her mother that burying herself in her studies was Diana's coping mechanism and that she'd come out of it when she wanted to or when an external factor forced her. At the time, she'd been ten. Chocolate cake had worked pretty well.

Now? Now she was worried that if she allowed herself to slip into that place, she'd never come out of it. She'd be stuck in that emotional limbo for good, never connecting with anyone, not truly. Never loving. Staying remote from all those who loved her, and whom she loved back. While she pondered these things, she was slowly lulled to sleep by Teddy's snoring, her grief abating as she slipped out of consciousness, preventing her from seeing the irony of her thoughts as she snuggled into her friend.

# CHAPTER SIX

I T HAD BEEN a month since the death of his wife, and to say that John was worried about Diana was putting it mildly. She'd gone back to school soon after the funeral but had refused to return home even once since then. She also completely refused to talk about her mother. Whenever he tried to broach the subject in an attempt to help them both work through their feelings, Diana immediately shut down and changed the subject.

Had it happened only once, he would have ignored it and chalked it up to grief and needing time. But last night, he'd taken her to dinner. It must have been the tenth time he'd attempted talking to Diana about Lydia, only to be confronted with his daughter's implacable resolve not to discuss her mother at all. In the first two weeks, they'd talked quite a bit. He understood that Diana was angry with her mom. And he couldn't say he blamed her. But this avoidance she was engaging in wasn't healthy for anyone, least of all her.

He sighed, turning over and punching his pillow, trying to find a more comfortable position. Diana's distress weighed heavily on his mind, and he couldn't sleep. He figured he would have to seek some advice. He wasn't a psychologist so he didn't know what to do. He also knew, though, that not just any psychologist would do.

Slowly, he nodded off. His sleep was fitful. Restless. He kept reliving a portion of the same unpleasant dream, over and over and over again. And then, with a start, he jack-knifed into a sitting position. He wiped the sweat off his brow with the sheet, staring at the wall in front of him blankly. "Lydia *was* murdered," he whispered into the darkness. The despair in his heart began to change. It soon morphed into determination, creating a force field around him as it took shape and strength. Somebody had killed his wife. But why? As he sat there in the dark, he thought hard. He'd find out who had done this to his Lydia, and why. No matter what it took.

The following morning, John sat in his kitchen sipping coffee. It was so strange, so empty. Lydia had filled his life with love and laughter. And now? Now, everything was so quiet. So dead. Just like her.

In the previous days, his anger and resentment at her death had started to fade as guilt begun to assail him. Guilt that he hadn't tried harder, hadn't noticed her pain. But last night, thanks to a dream – a memory – all those destructive emotions had galvanized into a determination to catch her killer.

Now, he was absolutely certain Lydia hadn't chosen to take her own life, and no one could persuade him otherwise. His wife hadn't killed herself. She had been murdered. Yet it had been done so well that even seasoned detectives had declared it a suicide. The big problem that faced him was that once a death was ruled a suicide, it meant a crime hadn't been committed. There was no reason to call in the crime scene unit or any other police resources for that matter.

It would be difficult now to find strong evidence considering how many people used the room in which she'd been killed, but he might get lucky. The issue was, he'd need permission to comb through it. And that meant convincing his superintendent he wasn't going crazy. To support his theory, he needed evidence; hard evidence. Otherwise, his super would not only dismiss his suspicions as the ravings of a man stricken by grief, but he might very well suspend him.

He debated what he should do. Should he try investigating this on his own? At least until he found something concrete? Then he could present it to his senior officer in support of having the case reopened. He scratched his chin, then shook his head. He didn't have to do this by himself. He'd get Liam's help. The younger man might discount his suspicions at first, but his partner had cared for Lydia like she was his own mother. He was sure Liam would help even on the off-chance that he was right.

He picked up his phone and called his partner. "Liam, we need to talk. When can you come over?"

"Is something wrong?" he asked.

"No. At least, I don't think so. I don't know. Look, I just need you to come over as soon as you can. It's about Lydia."

"John," Liam said warningly. Apparently, his partner knew him better than he had thought. They had worked together every day for the past five years, and Liam had become an important part of his life outside the job too.

"Look, Liam, this is serious. I'm not imagining things nor am I hallucinating and talking to the dead. And no, I'm not having a nervous breakdown. I just need to talk to you as soon as possible."

Liam sighed and John could see him running this hand through his hair. It was a nervous gesture the younger detective engaged in whenever he wasn't certain he was making the right decision. "Fine. I'll be there in an hour," he said and the line went dead.

John sighed in satisfaction. It was a good thing they both had the day off. They had time to go over everything and come up with a plan. It would be much easier than having to do it at the precinct, with everyone listening in and thinking him crazy. He just hoped he'd be able to convince Liam.

Precisely an hour later, the doorbell rang. If there was one thing to be said about Liam, it was that the man was incredibly punctual unless something catastrophic had happened. In the five years since they'd worked together, Liam had only been late once. And that was because someone had put a bullet in him and left him to die. He got a pass on that one.

John opened the door and tried to smile. He knew it was strained. He knew his eyes didn't shine. But he was trying. That's all anyone could expect from him, right?

"Hey, Liam," he said as he stood back to let the younger man in.

"Everything alright?" Liam asked. As usual, he got straight to the point.

"Not right now, but it will be," John replied. He knew he was being cryptic, but the front doorway wasn't the best place for this discussion. "Coffee?" he asked.

Liam nodded. "Sure." John headed over to the kitchen with his partner right behind him. Liam slid into a chair at the kitchen island while John poured him a cup of coffee and handed it to him.

Picking up his own cup, John took a seat opposite his partner. Liam was watching him intently, but now that he was faced with actually having to say the words out loud, he was having trouble voicing his thoughts. This was his only chance to convince Liam he wasn't insane. If he couldn't do that, life would get much tougher, because he didn't stand a chance of convincing anyone else.

As he paused, Liam took a firm hold of the space between them. "Look, John, I know you're hurting. We all are. Lydia was an incredible woman. Those of us who had the privilege to have her in our lives were blessed, but she's gone." His voice had lowered to a whisper, as if it was almost a sacrilege to say the words out loud.

John glared at him. "Don't you think I know that?" he hissed. "Don't you think I don't feel it every moment of every day, especially when I'm here? Alone? Everywhere I look, something reminds me of her and the fact that I'll never see her again. So, yes, I damn well know she's gone."

Liam's eyebrows had climbed into his scalp. John thought for a moment. He had delivered his diatribe with a little more force than he had intended, but he was sick and tired of everyone tiptoeing around him as if he were a ticking time bomb likely to go off at the slightest provocation. Yes, he was angry. Yes, he had lost his wife. Yes, he was grieving. Yes, he was worried sick over his daughter. But he wasn't out of his mind.

"Okay," Liam said gently. "What did you want to talk about?"

John hesitated for a moment and then decided to say it point blank. It was the best way. "Lydia didn't kill herself."

He could see the pity in Liam's eyes and for the first time since they'd known each other, John really, truly, wanted to reach across the island, yank Liam over it, and demonstrate how he felt in a way the younger man would never forget. His nostrils flared and he took one, two, three, deep, calming, breaths. Attacking Liam wouldn't help his case. He'd give the other man even more ammunition to tear down his theory.

"Don't give me that look, Liam. I know what I'm talking about."

"I really believe that you think you do, John. But I also know just how hard it's been for you to accept that Lydia decided to take her own life and I think you're grasping at straws."

John glared at him. "Really, Liam? You haven't even heard what I have to say, and you're already judging."

Liam sighed. "I'm not judging you, but there's a reason we aren't allowed to investigate cases involving someone close to us, just like doctors aren't allowed to treat their own family members. You lose any form of objectivity and start seeing what you hope is there rather than what is *literally* there."

John rolled his eyes. "I taught you that, remember?"

One of Liam's childhood friend's had been the victim of a drunk driver, and Liam had wanted to be assigned the case. When their super had said no, Liam had flipped. He'd calmed down, though, when John explained precisely why it wasn't a good idea for Liam to be investigating the case. Not only would he find it difficult to be objective, but it would also hurt their chances in court. The defense could use Liam's connection to the victim to cast doubt over any evidence they presented. It had taken a few hours, but Liam had finally and grudgingly admitted that John was right.

"I know, John. So, maybe it's time you took your own advice."

"I'd love to do that. I'd love to sit back and watch as someone else does their best to catch the killer who murdered my wife. I mean, I'm sure that the detectives on the case are great at their job and all. Oh, but wait... No one is assigned to the case. You know why? Because it's been ruled a suicide!" John was shouting.

Liam opened his mouth but closed it without saying a word. John could see the wheels in the man's head turning. "Tell me what you have," he said finally.

John pulled out a copy of Lydia's suicide note from his back pocket. He unfolded the paper and pointed out a short passage he'd highlighted.

*It would have been just like that time when we went hiking and I fell and broke my leg. It wasn't your fault and there was nothing you could do to take the pain away, but you suffered with me. Remember what I told you then? Well, I meant every single word and still do.*

"This paragraph has been bothering me since I read it but I couldn't put my finger on why for the life of me," John said.

Liam nodded. "I remember that trip. You called me in such a panic that I thought the world was coming to an end. She'd fallen down into a small ravine and you were so sure she was going to die. I remember I had to calm you down because it sounded like you were about to throw yourself after her."

John laughed ruefully. "Yeah, my heart pretty much stopped for the few minutes it took me to reach her. She wasn't moving, and she wasn't answering me. Luckily, it was only a concussion and a broken leg, but I swear I thought I'd lost her."

"Yeah," Liam replied, "and you seemed pretty determined to follow her." He gave John a pointed look. The latter just snorted.

"I'm not suicidal," John muttered. "Not now. Because I know that this wasn't an accident and it wasn't a suicide."

"How?"

"As I said, I couldn't see the significance of this passage at first. I guess I'd blocked out most of that day because it took me until last night to remember. By the time I'd managed to get down to her in that ravine, she was regaining consciousness. And my reaction was probably a little over the top because as soon as she came round and took one look at my face, she tried to comfort me, even though it should have been the other way around."

Liam smiled. "I'm not surprised. That was Lydia. She was always looking out for everyone."

John nodded. "The thing is, I remember clearly what happened now. I was terrified that she had died, and I told her so. She smiled and shook her head. She swore to me at that moment that she'd never leave me if she *had a choice*."

There was silence for a moment as John paused to let those words sink in.

"And you think that she referred to the incident in her letter to give you a message?" Liam asked. Where moments before he'd been skeptical, now it was clear that he was beginning to wonder.

"Yes, I do. Otherwise, what was the point? As she lay there in that ravine, I said a million times that I wished I could take her pain away. I berated myself constantly for not looking after her better, but the only thing she said to me that would even be slightly relevant here was that she'd never leave me if she had a choice."

"Maybe you're on to something. So you think she was

being coerced into writing the letter and this was her way of telling you, is that it?"

John nodded. "And don't tell me that you don't think the fact her body was cremated by 'accident' isn't suspicious at all."

Liam shrugged. "At the time, I did think it was an honest mistake, but if we assume Lydia was murdered, then we have to consider the cremation being a mistake as bogus as well."

"I thought it was strange at the time, but I dropped it because there was nothing else to go on. She'd killed herself, so why would anyone purposely have her body cremated? But if she was murdered..."

"If she was murdered, the only reason to have her body cremated would be to hide evidence."

John nodded. "Exactly. What I want to know is how the killer managed to get that cremation order filled out."

"What do you mean?"

"The coroner's assistant had arranged to ship the body out and said the cremation order had come down from the Deputy Chief Constable's office. The story they gave me was that it was supposed to be issued for an unidentified and unclaimed body but that someone accidentally put down Lydia's name instead of "Jane Doe #46" on the order."

Liam's eyes widened. "Are you kidding me? How can you make a mistake like that? Why didn't you tell me this sooner?"

John shrugged but gave him a pointed look.

"Because I was being an ass and kept accusing you of being in denial," Liam said, answering his own question. "I'm sorry."

"It's okay. I guess I would have thought the same thing if I were you."

Liam gave him a grateful smile. "So, the order came from the Deputy Chief Constable's office? That's strange."

"Yeah, it is. And I'm telling you it's got me seeing conspiracies left, right, and center. I mean, my first instinct was to think that it must have been a genuine mistake because the alternative would mean that someone in that office, someone who is supposed to be on our side, is on the side of a killer. And that's a massive accusation. But now I can't help but think that it's a possibility."

Liam nodded. He was getting on board with the murder theory, John could tell.

"Whoever it was, they were obviously desperate or in a big rush because it was done so sloppily. They left a clear trail back to the Deputy Chief Constable's office," John continued.

"Hmm, that was a stupid move. Maybe something went wrong. Do you think the DCC is involved?"

"Not necessarily. The order could have been actioned by someone lower down the chain of command - a secretary or an assistant. All they'd have to do is change the name on the order and slip it into a stack of other documents that needed signing. Do you think the Deputy Chief Constable stops to read each and every piece of paper he signs?"

"So, we're basically looking for anyone who had access to the cremation order."

"Pretty much." And then John realized something. "We can't take this to the super, can we?"

Liam shook his head. "Even if he believed us about Lydia being murdered, without solid evidence, he'd shut us down the moment we mention the Deputy Chief Constable's office. And the only evidence we have so far points to a suicide and a clerical error. It's hardly substantial."

"I hate to say it, but that's pretty much the way things stand," John agreed.

"We're also too close to the case. You know he'd never let us investigate this ourselves, if he knew."

"I know. I have no choice, Liam. I'm going to have to do this on the side," John said.

"You won't have to do it by yourself, John. I loved Lydia too."

"I know, but I can't ask you to do this. We have no idea who or what is involved, and I won't ask you to risk your career over this."

Liam rolled his eyes. "You're not asking me to do anything. I've decided, and there's jack all you can do about it. So, instead of arguing and wasting time, why don't we get to work so we can put Lydia's killer behind bars."

John's nostrils flared. He'd been avoiding mentioning Lydia's name in an effort to distance himself from the case. He needed to be objective. But every time Liam mentioned her name, his objectivity flew out the window and was replaced with a desperate, raging need for vengeance. One thing was certain, no matter who killed Lydia, they would pay. He'd make sure of it.

# CHAPTER SEVEN

EDDY SAT ON the floor outside Diana's dorm room. With his back against the wall, he was trying hard not to fall asleep. It was already two in the morning, and he'd been waiting for her for four hours. Maybe he should have tried to find her. Maybe just sitting here hadn't been his smartest idea, but when he'd taken a more proactive approach a week ago and hunted her down at some frat party, she'd totally freaked out on him. Of course, it might have had something to do with the fact that she'd been blind drunk at the time and he'd tried to drag her home, against her will. Even so, maybe he should go track her down again.

He groaned. He'd give her another half an hour, then he'd go look for her. He'd sling her over his shoulder and bring her back to her room if he had to.

Diana was spiraling out of control, and he was worried about her. She'd started ditching class, her grades were slipping, and her professors were just as worried as he was. He knew that the only reason they hadn't come down harder on her was because of the death of her mother.

He grimaced and slammed his head against the wall behind him. He would not allow himself to shed any tears. Not here at any rate. He'd do it in the privacy of his own room, as he always did. Lydia had been a wonderful woman. She'd accepted him for who he was and had welcomed him, something his own mother hadn't been willing to do once she'd discovered he was gay.

Teddy hadn't been comfortable with the idea of revealing the truth about his sexuality to Diana's parents – mostly because of the reaction of his own family – but as it was, he needn't have worried. There were a few awkward moments, but ultimately he'd been welcomed into the bosom of her family. He grinned at the memory of the first time Diana had brought him home.

*"Di, please don't tell your parents I'm gay," he'd begged. "I don't want them... I don't want them to look at me with the same disgust and disappointment my own folks do."*

*Diana had rolled her eyes. "Teddy, my parents aren't like that. And, anyway, I think you'll really want to tell my dad."*

*"Why?" he asked suspiciously.*

*"Well, if he doesn't know you're not into girls, he'll assume you're either my boyfriend or are simply pretending to be my friend to get into my pants. That means you will get 'the talk'."*

*"The talk?"*

*"Yeah, the one where he describes in gruesome detail what he'll do to you if you hurt me and then promises they'll never find your body. I think that's the long and short of it. I've never actually heard him deliver the speech, but a few of my potential boyfriends did provide a few details as they were running out the door at full speed," she said with a wink.*

*"It's alright," Teddy replied. "It can't be that bad."*

Diana gave him a look that said he was delusional. "Why do you think I'm still a virgin and will probably remain one until I get married?"

"You just haven't found the right guy?" Teddy asked hopefully.

She snorted. "Keep telling yourself that if it makes you feel better."

Teddy nodded. "Doesn't matter. I'd still prefer you didn't tell them."

Diana leaned over and kissed his cheek. "Teddy, I'll do as you ask because you're my best friend and I love you. But that doesn't mean I agree with your approach. You should be proud of who you are."

Teddy snorted. "And what's that? A gay nerd who hides behind his appearance as a jock, or, as my father so eloquently describes me, a satanic curse on my family and an abomination."

Diana turned and slapped him on his arm. Hard. "Ow!"

"Stop talking like that about yourself. Your dad's a moron who doesn't deserve to have a son as awesome as you are. And my dad is nothing like that."

He was still adamant. He wanted to feel normal for once. He didn't want to be the freak. "Please, Di, for me. Don't tell them."

She nodded and cuddled up against him, putting an arm around his waist. "I do love you, you know," she whispered.

Teddy dropped a kiss on the top of her head. "I love you too, Di. More than you'll ever know." She'd saved him. He'd been so alone until she'd come along and brightened his world.

Of course, his resolve to keep quiet about his sexual orientation swiftly evaporated when he'd arrived. Lydia had hugged him tightly, kissed him on the cheek, and thanked him for being a good friend to her daughter, though Diana had assured him she knew nothing. But then came John Hunter. Teddy was tall and well-built thanks to his five weekly training sessions at the gym. John Hunter, however, was slightly taller and seemed even bigger than Teddy. His eyes narrowed threateningly as he looked Teddy over. That was the moment Teddy started to doubt his resolve.

Fifteen minutes later, John invited him into the den to look at his gun collection. Teddy had swallowed hard and followed the other man apprehensively. The moment the door closed, Diana's father turned and pointedly sized him up and down.

"Did Diana tell you what I do for a living?"

"Yes, sir," Teddy replied, proud that his voice was steady, despite the fact that he was decidedly uncomfortable.

"As a homicide detective, I catch murderers every day. I go after some of the worst scum in this city, from drug addicts killing each other for a fix to psychopaths who torture and murder others for fun."

Teddy tried to smile. "Thank you for keeping us safe, sir."

John snorted. "The point I'm trying to make is that if you hurt my little girl, they will never find your body," the older man growled. In that moment, along with the menacing look being thrown his way, Teddy decided that telling the truth would be preferable to spending Thanksgiving weekend being glared at with threatening intent.

"I'm gay, sir," Teddy said quickly, and then braced for impact. He was expecting a look of disgust. He was expecting a snort of derision. He was expecting to be told to get out of the house because he was "an abomination". He was expecting anything other than what happened.

"You're gay?" John Hunter asked, visibly taken aback.

"Yes, sir."

John quickly went on the offensive again. "How do I know you aren't lying?"

Teddy opened his mouth to say something, though he wasn't quite sure what it was going to be when the door opened and Diana's mother sailed in.

"John Hunter, are you terrorizing the poor boy?"

And Teddy watched in fascination as the towering man who had just a moment before looked ready and able to kill him, turned into a puppy in front of his wife. "Me? Of course not, darling. Teddy and I were just getting better acquainted."

Lydia glared. "Right. I believe you. Teddy, dearest, why don't you come with me? I just pulled out a batch of cookies from the oven."

Teddy looked at John and hesitated. "Oh, don't mind John. His bark's worse than his bite."

The glare John was giving him made Teddy doubt that very much. But thankfully, the decision had been taken out of his hands. Lydia grabbed him by the hand and pulled him after her.

Later that evening, after dinner, they'd sat down to watch a movie. Halfway through, Lydia and Diana had gotten up to make more popcorn.

"So, you're gay," John said, looking him up and down.

"Yes, sir," Teddy had replied defensively. He had been expecting the insults to begin. Instead, he got the shock of his life.

John Hunter had nodded in satisfaction and looked back at the television. "I believe this is going to be the beginning of a beautiful friendship," he'd said. Teddy's jaw had fallen open in shock.

"Sir?" he'd asked.

*"We'll talk tomorrow, son, but you and I are going to become great friends because you'll be looking after my little girl, right?"*

*Teddy nodded quickly. "I've been doing my best, and I always will. She's my best friend. She's closer to me than my sisters are."*

*"That's good. That's very good," John had said with a pleased smile.*

*Teddy had relaxed, and things only got better from then on. The following day, Lydia had marched into the kitchen and promptly given him a hug.*

*"Teddy, you'll always be welcome here. If you ever need anything, even if it's just someone to talk to, you call us, you hear?"*

*Teddy stood there in shock but nodded and thanked her. He'd looked at Diana questioningly. "Dad told her," she whispered. "Then she asked me why I hadn't said anything to her, and I might have told her a bit about your issues with your family."*

*Teddy groaned, feeling embarrassed. But it wasn't long before he relaxed into the Hunter family dynamic. They were so close and relaxed with each other that it was a completely new experience for him. And instead of making him feel like an outsider, Lydia went out of her way to make sure he felt like part of the family. It was the first Thanksgiving of his life that he had truly enjoyed.*

The sound of giggling brought him back to the present with a start. Diana was stumbling down the hall with a guy in tow. Teddy got to his feet and glared at the idiot holding on to Diana as they tried to walk. She was swaying and obviously drunk out of her mind.

"Teddy!" she exclaimed happily. "What are you doing here?"

"Waiting for you, obviously," he replied.

"Who's this guy?" the jackass had the audacity to ask.

"Oh, this is Teddy. Teddy, this is..." she trailed off, obviously either not knowing the guy's name or having forgotten it because of one too many shots.

"Ethan," the guy slurred. "Why's he here? Weren't we gonna have some fun?"

Diana paled. "Actually, I don't think that's a good idea," she said quickly. "Teddy and I have some things to talk about."

"What?" the guy snapped at her. He was probably going to say something else, but it never left his lips. Teddy's hand had snapped out and grabbed him.

"Watch your mouth," he said.

"Or what?" the guy wheezed. Teddy rolled his eyes.

"Or I'll rip your arms off and beat you with them," he growled.

The guy blanched. "Sorry," he croaked. Teddy nodded.

"If I hear that you've been running your mouth off to your friends about her or that you've insulted her in any way, I will find you, and I won't be as nice as I was tonight. Got it?"

"Yes, absolutely." Teddy let go of him and the guy began backing away. "I swear. Not a word. I'll forget I even met her."

"Good." The guy turned and ran.

Diana chose that moment to snort. "You've been hanging out with Dad too much."

"We have to talk," Teddy said seriously.

She pouted. "I don't want to. You have that look on your face that says I'm not going to like this talk, so how about we don't?"

"You don't have a choice in the matter."

Diana sighed and turned to unlock the door to her room. She poked her head in and almost swore out loud. Her roommate wasn't back so she couldn't use that excuse. She knew precisely what Teddy wanted to talk about, and she wasn't in the mood. She was still pretty tipsy, and she really didn't need a lecture on her conduct.

"Teddy," she whined, "have mercy. I really don't want to talk now."

He eyed her for a moment and glared at her. "Fine. But I'm spending the night here, and in the morning we'll go out for coffee and talk."

It wouldn't be the first time he'd spent the night in her dorm room. Her roommate didn't mind at all. But at the moment, Diana was the one who didn't like the idea of him spending the night.

"Why don't you go back to your place, and we'll just meet up for coffee in the morning."

Teddy snorted. "Why? So you can ditch me? No thanks. I'll spend the night."

Diana turned and stomped into her room. She whirled around quickly and tried to slam the door in Teddy's face, but she wasn't fast enough. He caught the door long before she could shut it. And since he was twice her size, she didn't stand a chance in the brute force department.

Defeated, she threw herself down on her bed. She felt the mattress next to her dip down as Teddy sat down next to her. "Aren't you going to change out of those clothes?"

"Uh-uh," she replied, her eyes drifting shut. "Too lazy."

She could practically feel the disapproval roll off Teddy. With a sigh, he got to his feet. She could hear him rifling through her things and moments later, he dropped her favorite pajamas on the bed next to her.

"Still too lazy," she mumbled.

"I'll help you. Now, come on."

Sure enough, Teddy did help her change into her pajamas, but before she could fall into bed, he stopped her.

"Wait a sec," he said. He walked into the bathroom and moments later came out with a glass of water. He handed her two pills and the glass of water. "Take these, or you'll feel terrible in the morning."

She nodded and quickly downed the pills. Teddy put the glass on the nightstand, and then tucked her in. He lay down beside her, and that was the last thing she remembered before falling into a very deep sleep.

The following day, Diana woke with a groan. "Come on, sleepy head, it's almost noon," she heard Teddy's much too cheerful voice. She opened one eye and shut it just as quickly.

She pulled a pillow over her head and tried her best to ignore Teddy. "Nope, you're not getting off that easy." She lost the grip on her pillow as Teddy pulled it away from her. Then he did the unthinkable. He pulled the covers off her and she was left to shiver on the bed.

"I hate you," she mumbled.

"I know, but you still need to get up."

"Don't wanna," she whined.

"Don't care. Now move!"

"Fine," Diana snapped, rolling over and out of bed. She padded to the bathroom with a glare thrown Teddy's way. Ten minutes later, she was feeling better, and she knew she had Teddy to thank for that. If he hadn't given her those aspirins last night, she'd be clutching her head in agony right about now.

"You're looking better," Teddy remarked.

"I feel better," she replied with a small smile. She hesitated for a moment. "Thank you."

Teddy nodded. "Come on, get dressed. We'll go get some coffee and talk."

"Do we really have to?" she asked as she began to discard her pajamas. Teddy, ever dutiful, picked up behind her. She had become a slob recently. Even she had to admit that.

"Yes, we do," he replied adamantly.

Sighing, she got dressed. "Fine. Let's go." She wasn't looking forward to the lecture she was about to receive, but everything came a distant second behind her priority to get some caffeine into her system.

Fifteen minutes later, they were walking into a small café just off campus, a place they usually went when they wanted to spend some quiet time together. Diana sat down as Teddy went to get their coffee.

A few minutes later, he was placing a long espresso with milk and two sugars in front of her. She leaned over and inhaled. It smelled wonderful. She wrapped her hands around the cup, letting the warmth seep into her skin. Bringing the cup up to her lips, she took a tentative sip and groaned in pleasure as the liquid ran down her throat.

"Ambrosia," she whispered. She glanced up at Teddy with a smile that faltered when she saw the exasperated and concerned look on his face.

"Diana, what are you doing?" Teddy asked.

She looked up at him in surprise. "I'm pretty sure it should be quite obvious. I'm drinking coffee," she replied, indicating the cup in her hand.

"Don't do that. Not with me. You can pretend with everyone else, but I know you too well for that."

Diana rolled her eyes. "What do you want from me, Teddy?"

"I want to know why you've suddenly turned into someone I don't know. I want to know why you seem so hell bent on destroying yourself."

"Just because I'm having some fun doesn't mean I'm trying to destroy myself," she replied with a huff.

"Really? This is the third time this week you've gotten drunk, and it's not even the weekend yet! And last night, you show up with some dude whose name you didn't even know."

"I did know his name. I'd just forgotten it. And anyway, everyone else is doing it so why can't I?"

"Because you aren't everyone else," Teddy snapped. "You are a highly intelligent, beautiful woman who I thought had more respect for herself than to act like a tart."

Diana froze. "What did you call me?"

Teddy glared at her. "Don't give me that. I didn't say you are a tart, just that you're acting like one. And you know I'm right." He frowned in frustration. "Do you have any idea what could happen to you at one of these parties? Don't you watch the news? Don't you know how many girls get attacked at these things? Especially girls who drink too much. Do you really want to end up like that?"

"So, you're trying to tell me that if I get into trouble, it's my fault."

"Are you insane? I never said that! I am saying that you'll be a lot safer if you don't put yourself in harm's way."

Diana sighed. "Look, Teddy, just drop it. I'm having a great time, and I don't need you raining on my parade."

"Are you serious? Diana, don't shut me out. Tell me what's going on. Your grades have slipped, and your professors are worried."

"You've been talking to my professors?" Diana snapped.

"Yes, I have. They know we're friends, and they're worried about you. So, what is going on?"

Diana snorted. "Like you don't know. My mother killed herself two months ago, remember? She didn't think I was important enough to stick around for, and I'm having a bit of a problem dealing with it."

"And you think that this is the best solution?"

Diana shrugged. "I don't really care. It makes me feel better, and that's all that matters."

He looked at her sadly. "Di, you can't keep doing this. It won't solve anything."

"I don't care. I just need to forget for a little while. Let me forget, Teddy, please."

Like her dad, he'd always been a total sucker for that puppy dog look. "Fine, but you aren't allowed to go out alone anymore. I'm going with you. At least that way I can protect you."

Diana nodded with a smile. "Okay."

Two months later, Teddy was lying on his bed, staring at the ceiling. He didn't know what to do about Diana anymore. She'd kept her word and hadn't gone out without him ever since they'd had their talk, but he knew it wasn't really helping. She was partying hard, and her grades hadn't picked up any. He needed to get her some help before the situation became irrevocable. He had to call her father. She'd hate him, of course, but he was more interested in making sure she got the help she needed. Hopefully, she'd forgive him. He'd call Mr. Hunter in the morning. He'd know what to do. He'd know how to help Diana.

Just as he was about to drift off to sleep, his phone rang. It was Diana. "Hey, Di, what's up?" He really hoped she didn't want to go out because he really wasn't up to it. She'd already dragged him to two parties that week, and he was exhausted.

"Teddy," he heard Diana whisper with a sob. He shot bolt upright, instantly on high alert.

"Di, what's wrong?"

"Teddy, please help me."

"Where are you? What's going on?"

"I'm locked in a bathroom. There are two guys trying to get in. Oh God, Teddy, what have I done? Please, you have to help me."

Teddy was already out the door and running down the hall. "Tell me where you are."

"At the Alpha Kappa Delta house," she whispered.

He growled into the phone. The party fraternity of UBC. They were known for throwing the biggest parties on campus and also for being utter and complete jerks. "Stay with me on the phone, I'm on my way there."

"Okay," she sniffled.

Before he could say anything else, though, he heard a crash and Diana screamed. "Teddy!" The line went dead.

Half an hour later, Teddy was rocking an uninjured but traumatized Diana in his arms. She was crying into his shirt, and he was shaking. He had brought her back to her dorm room, where she could feel safe.

"God, Di, you just took ten years off my life," he whispered into her hair.

"My hero," she said, her voice cracking.

He'd gotten to her before anything had happened and had made it extremely clear to her assailants that they had made some very poor decisions. In case the message hadn't been clear, he'd also given both of them a pummeling they wouldn't soon forget. When he'd left the frat house with Diana in his arms, the crowd had given him looks ranging from fear to respect. He knew that word would spread quickly that no one was to mess with Diana or Teddy would come after them. But there was no remorse, not from Teddy. It was the only way to deal with that crowd, in his opinion. The gossip would act as a deterrent to any other idiot who contemplated making such "poor decisions" in the future.

"It's okay, baby."

"I know. You've got me," she said as she burrowed deeper into him.

Things couldn't keep on going like this. They'd been lucky on this occasion. He'd made it in time. But what if it happened again, and he wasn't close enough? What if he couldn't find her? No. There would be no next time. Enough was enough. He was going to drive her straight to her dad's house. If anyone knew how to deal with Diana, it was Mr. Hunter.

He tried to lay her on the bed, but she whimpered, refusing to let go of him. So, he held her until she fell asleep. He then laid her down gently and packed a quick bag for her with some essentials. He sneaked out and brought his car round to the front of her dorm. Going back inside, he picked her up gently, doing his best not to wake her. Ten minutes later, he was driving toward her childhood home.

Despite it being two in the morning, John and Liam were

still hard at work, which was why it didn't take John long to answer the door when the bell rang. When he saw Teddy standing there with a black eye, holding his daughter in his arms, his heart stopped beating.

"What happened?"

John held the door wide and stood back to give Teddy room to carry Diana inside. He had already cataloged every inch of her. She seemed unharmed and apparently asleep.

"Can I take her upstairs, first?" Teddy whispered.

John nodded, though he grit his teeth. His heart was racing, and he felt as if the world was crashing down around him. This was all too much. What had happened to his daughter?

As Teddy climbed the stairs, Liam came out into the hall. "Everything alright?" he asked.

"I don't know," John replied.

A few minutes later, Teddy came down the stairs. Liam took one look at him and grunted. "You're gonna need ice for that."

They all went back into the kitchen, where Liam and John had been working on Lydia's case. John shut the door and then rounded on Teddy.

"What has happened to my daughter, Teddy?"

The younger man blanched but stood his ground. "She needs help, Mr. Hunter. I got to her before anything happened, but we were lucky this time."

"What are you talking about?"

Teddy proceeded to tell John about Diana's recent behavior. When he got to the part about the two who had tried to attack his daughter, John went to pick up his gun.

"John, you can't go around shooting frat boys," Liam said.

"Watch me," he snapped.

"You are a detective. A representative of the law. You do not go around shooting kids, no matter how much they deserve it."

"It's okay, Mr. Hunter, they won't do it again, I made sure of it," Teddy said.

John paused for a moment and looked at the boy standing in front of him. "Thank you, Teddy." His tone was grave because he knew if it hadn't been for Teddy, the unthinkable could have happened.

"There's no need to thank me, sir. She's like my sister. I only wish I could have done more."

John nodded. "Do you know who they are?"

Teddy shook his head. "No, sir. I don't really hang out with those guys. They're all grade A idiots. But don't you worry, I'll recognize them if I see them again."

"Good. I'll speak to the local precinct. They'll need to handle this because if these kids tried to do this to Diana, there's a good chance they've already done it to other girls."

"I think so too, sir."

"Why don't you go up and get some rest? Your room is where it's always been," John said with a small smile.

"Thank you, sir," Teddy replied.

"No, thank *you*, Teddy. Thank you for protecting my little girl."

Teddy nodded and left.

"You need to tell her, John."

John sighed. "I don't know. I really don't know. What if it makes things worse?"

"Can things get worse? The girl thinks her mother abandoned her. I'm pretty sure finding out that her mother didn't kill herself will make her feel better than she does right now," Liam retorted indignantly.

John sighed. His partner had a point. "I guess you're right. I'm going up to check on her."

He walked up the stairs slowly. Liam was right. He needed to tell Diana that Lydia had not committed suicide but been murdered instead. But things would get tricky when he did this. He knew that. He knew his daughter. She'd probably want to get involved. It would be dangerous, because even though they'd found out little so far, they had discovered enough to realize that there was a good chance someone powerful was involved. And though he wanted to protect her, he knew it would be much more perilous to let Diana keep believing her mother had killed herself. She'd end up imploding.

He quietly opened the door to her room and waited for his eyes to adjust to the darkness. She was sleeping on her side. She looked so innocent. His little girl. He walked in quietly and sat down on the edge of the bed, watching her sleep. A tear formed in the corner of his eye. If it hadn't been for Teddy, he could have lost her. He'd been so focused on the case that he hadn't taken the time to find out how his daughter was doing. And he'd nearly lost her too.

"My little girl," he whispered.

She fidgeted, and he froze. He didn't want to wake her up. She needed to sleep after her ordeal. However, he saw her eyes open slowly. She turned over and saw him. "Daddy?"

"Hi, baby," he whispered softly.

"Daddy!" she cried and launched herself into his arms.

"It's okay, darling. I've got you."

She sniffled into his chest and looked up at him. "Teddy?"

He nodded. "Teddy brought you home."

"He saved me, Dad."

"I know, honey. You go back to sleep. We have some things we need to talk about in the morning."

She nodded and lay back down. "I'm happy Teddy brought me home," she whispered as her eyes closed.

"So am I. You have no idea how much."

She smiled and within moments, she was asleep. He sighed. Tomorrow was going to be a difficult day.

# CHAPTER EIGHT

T HE FOLLOWING MORNING, Diana was
sitting at the kitchen island across from her father,
holding a cup of coffee. He looked relaxed but she
knew this was the calm before the storm. She was in for a
massive lecture that she knew she deserved. She'd been
reckless, and she'd landed herself in a lot of trouble. If it
hadn't been for Teddy... a shiver ran through her at the
thought of what could have happened.

"You'll be pressing charges." It wasn't a question. It was
a statement.

Diana nodded. "Yes." And she knew she would. Not for
herself as much as for any other girl who had been, or would
be, subject to unwanted attention from those guys. Yes, she
would be pressing charges.

"Good." He paused for a moment. "Diana, I need to tell
you something."

She looked up at him. "What is it, Dad?"

"It's about your mother."

Immediately, she shut down. She did not want to have a
conversation about the woman who had abandoned her and

her father. The woman who had taken the coward's way out. "I'm not interested," she said as she rose to her feet.

"Sit down," her father snapped. She froze. He'd never used that tone of voice with her. "I've had it with you acting like a spoiled child."

"Excuse me?"

"You heard me. I have something important to tell you about your mother, and I don't care whether you want to hear it or not. You will sit down, shut up, and listen."

"I don't want to talk about her," Diana stated adamantly.

"I said, I don't care. Sit down," her father snapped.

Diana sat, even though she wanted to be anywhere else but where she was. But she knew well enough that she'd pushed her father too far and she wouldn't be getting out of it.

"Fine," she snapped. "What do you want to tell me about Lydia?"

She practically spat her mother's name out. She couldn't bring herself to refer to that woman as her mother.

Obviously, by the way her father's face darkened, that had been a mistake. "You will never again refer to your mother like that or I swear, even if I've never laid a hand on you, I will take you over my knee and spank you."

Diana glared at her father. "I will refer to her anyway I like. She was supposed to be my mother, but she chose the easy way out. She was a coward, and she left me, so I can call her whatever I want."

"You are an ungrateful, spoiled little brat," her father growled. "Your mother loved you more than her own life, and this is how you repay her? By insulting her? How dare you? Did you ever stop to think, for even a moment, about her? Or are you so damned selfish that you've made this all about you? Let me tell you something, Diana, the world does not revolve around you, and only you, no matter how brilliant you are. And no matter what you think your mother did, you don't have the right to judge her or to treat her with anything less than complete dignity."

Diana's eyes had widened. Her father had never spoken to her like this. She'd always been daddy's little girl.

"She left us both, Dad. How can you forgive her?"

John glared at her. "First of all, your mother did *not* kill herself. Secondly, even if she had, I wouldn't be walking around with my head stuck up my own backside like you are doing. Instead, I'd have enough respect for her to realize the choice she made was the only one she felt she could make at the time. And I damn well wouldn't be pretending she didn't exist!"

Diana's mind had come to a screeching halt. "What did you say?" she asked, her voice trembling.

John sighed, a hand on his head clutching his hair. "Your mother didn't kill herself. She was murdered."

"No," Diana gasped. "You're lying," she said as she covered her ears with her hands, her eyes closing tightly. "I don't want to hear another word."

"I thought you'd be happy to know your mother didn't commit suicide."

Diana opened her eyes, tears shining in them. "I've been blaming her all this time. The things I've said and thought about her. If she didn't kill herself, I've been hating her all this time for nothing." She wrapped her arms around herself. "I'm a monster," she whispered.

John sighed and shook his head. He put his hands on her arms and forced her to look at him. "You aren't a monster, baby. You were just lost for a bit there."

Diana sniffled. "Dad, I cursed her very existence. I wished she hadn't been my mother."

He got up and circled the island. Hugging her from behind, he whispered, "Mom loved you very much. She'd understand."

She shook her head. "How could she? Even *I* don't understand." It was as if a spotlight had suddenly exploded into life, shining straight on all she'd said, thought and done over the past few months. And it wasn't a pretty picture. She'd been wallowing in self-pity without a thought for anyone or anything else, including her mother's memory. No matter what her father said, she was a monster.

"We all deal with pain in our own way," he said softly.

Diana nodded. Then it really hit her. "Mom didn't kill herself?"

"No, honey, she didn't. She was murdered, and it was made to look like a suicide."

A shiver ran through her. She hunched her shoulders and tears spilled down her cheeks. "Why would anyone want to kill Mom?"

"I don't know, baby, but I'm doing my best to find out."

"How long?" she asked.

"How long what?"

"How long have you known Mom didn't kill herself?"

"I suspected from the beginning, but I've been certain for the past three months."

"Three months?" Diana asked softly. And then she erupted. She wrenched herself out of her father's arms and turned on him. "You've known for three months, and you didn't say anything?" she shouted. "How could you? You knew how I felt. You knew I hated her because I thought she'd killed herself. And you let me keep on hating her when you knew she hadn't done it!"

"I didn't have any proof," he shouted back. "I didn't want to raise your hopes for nothing. What if I'm wrong? What if I'm so desperate to think that she didn't leave us of her own accord that I'm seeing stuff that isn't there? I couldn't do that to you."

Diana's anger fizzled out at the pain on her father's face. "But you're sure now?"

He nodded. "Pretty sure. Liam and I have been investigating the case in our spare time. It's not as if we can get it reopened," he grumbled.

"Why not?" Diana asked.

John sat back down and started explaining the situation to her about the Deputy Chief Constable's office and their involvement in what he and Liam believed to be a cover-up.

"We can't go into the precinct shouting conspiracy because we'll end up suspended, and we'll lose all access to some very valuable resources. So, we've been investigating on the sly, but it's been slow going. Doesn't help that there's nothing basically to investigate since there's no body, no crime scene, and we have no idea who would want her dead."

He choked on the tail-end of his sentence. Sometimes, he simply couldn't separate Lydia from the case, like now with his daughter sitting across from him, staring at him intently. He swallowed back the lump in his throat.

"I could help," Diana said softly.

John shook his head. "No, it's too dangerous. We have no idea who's involved and who we can trust. I don't want you poking around and getting into trouble."

"Come on, Dad. I can help. I promise not to go poking around anything, but maybe if you tell me what you have so far, I might find something you've missed."

John paused for a moment. "Okay, but only as long as

you promise me you won't go off on your own. Remember, I'm the one with the experience. And the gun."

Diana nodded quickly. This was more than she had been expecting. Her mind was already working furiously on certain changes she'd be making once she got back to school, but they weren't anything her father had to be made aware of just yet.

One hour later, everyone had gathered in the dining room. Diana had convinced her father that Teddy's hacking skills could prove useful. He had loved Lydia too, so he deserved to be in on the investigation she argued. Though reticent, her father had finally agreed.

"Okay, Liam, tell them what we know so far."

Liam began to explain how John had first become convinced that Lydia hadn't killed herself, thanks to the message she'd managed to get to him with her "suicide" note. He then explained about the cremation order from the Deputy Chief Constable's office.

"Now, we've been doing some investigating on the quiet, but as you can imagine, we can't go around asking questions at the Deputy Chief Constable's office. They'll kick us out so fast, we won't know what hit us."

"And if we do get found out, whoever is involved will know we're onto them, and they'll go to ground. We'll never find them."

"Do we know who was in charge of filling out orders that day?" Diana asked.

Her father shook his head. "There's no way for us to find out."

"Are they recorded digitally, or are they paper forms?" Teddy asked.

Liam shrugged. "I'm really not sure, but there's a good chance a digital record is kept. Since they've rolled out their new computer system, it's become pretty much mandatory to complete digital forms in all the precincts."

Teddy surged to his feet. "I'll be right back," he said as he rushed out of the room.

Moments later, he walked back into the dining room with his laptop. "You do know that hacking is a felony, right?" Liam asked the younger man.

Teddy looked up at him. "Who said anything about hacking?" he asked with an innocent look.

"Right," Liam replied, giving him a do-you-think-I'm-stupid look.

"Look, you guys have said yourselves you've been spinning your wheels for months. I can hack into the records and maybe find out who issued the order. It might give you a little more to go on. Or," he paused, "You could just keep doing what you've been doing."

John nodded. "He's right, Liam. Go for it, Teddy. Just make sure they can't trace it back to us."

"Please. This isn't my first rodeo."

John gave him a look, and Teddy sobered. "Nope, I've never, ever hacked into a government agency before. I've never hacked into anything. In fact, I don't hack. This will be my first time."

John nodded with a grunt. Diana had been quiet the whole time. She'd been thinking about everything she'd heard, wondering what they weren't seeing. And then it hit her.

"What about the therapist?" she asked.

Everyone was paying attention to what Teddy was doing but John turned to look at her curiously. "What do you mean?" he asked.

"Well, have you looked into the therapist? I mean he's

the one who said Mom was depressed and suicidal, when she obviously wasn't."

John's eyes widened. "You're right," he whispered. "Someone must have gotten to him, somehow. Liam, we need to find out who the therapist is and have a little chat with him."

Diana said, "Maybe just find out who he is? If you start talking to him, he might alert whoever's involved, and that's the last thing we need. Teddy can dig into his past, and maybe we can find something out that way. If we can't, then you can go talk to him."

John grinned. "My daughter is definitely a genius."

## CHAPTER NINE

I T HAD BEEN two months since Diana had discovered her mother had been murdered. In that time, they'd continued the investigation but come up with precious little. They had managed to find out who had signed the cremation order, but Ms. Jillian Stoltz had disappeared off the face of the planet. After a few discreet inquiries, they discovered she had received a large deposit into her bank account on the day the order was issued, which would most likely help toward addressing the serious gambling problem she had. But that was all they could find because the payment had traced back to a shell corporation in the Cayman Islands.

They'd also looked into the therapist. Robert Baldwin had been with the hospital for three years and, at first glance, he seemed to be aboveboard. Then they had found that he too had received a large payment. $50,000 had been deposited into his bank account on the day Lydia died. Unsurprisingly, it traced back to the same shell corporation. When her father and Liam had gone to question him, the man had been tight-lipped. A week later, Baldwin turned up dead. The official story was that he had committed suicide. Naturally John didn't believe it, and neither did Diana. And that was precisely why her father had sent her back to school with a warning to stay out of the case. He wasn't going to put her in danger.

She promised her father she'd keep away. At least for now. They didn't have any other leads for the moment, anyway. However, that didn't mean Teddy wasn't still digging around. He was determined to follow the very long and complicated trail of the shell corporation back to its source.

Diana had returned to school with new determination. She would make her mother proud, and she would help her father find out who killed Lydia and why. She signed up for a criminal psychology class and a forensic science class. She had been tempted to transfer completely from medical school, but she decided she wanted to finish what she'd started. It would mean a lot of work, but she knew she could do it.

It was on one of those really hectic days that she was approached by two men. She had been rushing to one of her classes, when they stopped her.

"Diana Hunter?" one of them asked. She sized them up. If she were to go by the movies, then these two would be the poster boys for government agents.

"Yes. Can I help you?" she asked.

"My name is Stewart Duvall," said the older man. He looked to be about the same age as her father, though nowhere near as fit. "This is Kieran Black." He indicated to the younger man next to him, who looked to be in his late twenties.

"Nice to meet you. I'm sorry, but I'm in a rush to get to class. How can I help?"

The older man fidgeted a little. "We're with CSIS, and we need to talk."

Diana's eyebrows climbed into her scalp. "The Canadian Security Intelligence Service?" When the older man nodded, Diana's heart froze. What if they had discovered Teddy's hacking? Or were working for whoever killed her mother? "Do you have IDs?" She wasn't taking any chances.

The two men nodded and pulled out their identity cards. Diana looked at each one closely.

"What can I do for CSIS, gentlemen?" she asked.

"That would be a conversation best held in private, Ms. Hunter. Is there anywhere we can go?"

Diana thought quickly. She didn't really feel comfortable taking two men she didn't know to her dorm room, especially if they worked for the government. Then she got an idea.

"We can go to the gardens," she said, referring to UBC's Botanical Garden and Centre for Plant Research. "There are benches there and it will be quiet at this time.

The older man nodded quickly. They followed her to the gardens where she chose a bench and took a seat. "Well?"

Duvall sat next to her. "Ms. Hunter, you have come to the attention of my superiors."

"I have?" she asked, her voice a little strangled.

"Yes, my superiors have tasked me with recruiting you to the agency."

Diana's jaw practically hit the ground. "You're offering me a job?" she squeaked. She had been terrified that they were about to arrest her and Teddy and they'd never be seen or heard from again.

"Yes," Duvall responded.

"Why?"

"All I can tell you is that my superiors feel you have certain skills and qualities that would make you an asset."

"And what would this job entail?"

Duvall hesitated. "I'm not at liberty to say. My superiors, though, will be more than happy to answer all your questions."

Diana hesitated for a moment and then made a quick decision. "Thanks. I'm flattered. I really am. But I'm not interested." She made to go.

"We understand that this is a big decision," the man cautioned. "Here's my card. Why don't you think about it for a bit longer and then give me a call?"

She took his card but shook her head. "I won't change my mind, but thank you for the offer. Now, if you'll excuse me, I have to get to class."

"Of course. It was nice to meet you Ms. Hunter. Oh, and it would be preferable if you kept this conversation just between us."

"Certainly. And it was nice to meet you, too. Goodbye." She turned and walked quickly to her class without looking back, her mind clamoring with thoughts about what the visit from the two men could possibly mean.

Diana was sitting on her bed, staring at the ceiling. They were on summer break. She and Teddy had moved back into her childhood home so they could help with the investigation. Her father hadn't been happy about it at first, but Diana warned him that if he didn't give in, she would go off on her own. Her father had caved immediately.

They still had squat. Nothing. Not even an idea of why someone might have wanted her mother dead. All they had was the name of a shell corporation, a dead therapist, and a clerk who had disappeared. It was madly frustrating, especially since their hands were tied fast. Had it been an official investigation, her father could have interrogated witnesses and suspects. As it was, however, they had no official status, no access to police databases, and no idea whom they could trust. They had to work stealthily and sometimes illegally so that no one found out. It was slow going.

Just then, the door to her bedroom burst open and Teddy ran in, his face flush with excitement. "I did it!"

"You did what?" Diana asked.

"I found a lead!" he said excitedly.

Diana jumped out of bed. "What are you talking about? Show me!"

She followed him back to his room where he showed her his laptop. "I've finally managed to find a connection to that damned shell corporation. It's only the address of a warehouse owned by a company that is very indirectly connected to the shell corporation but..."

"But it's a lot more than we had before. You're a genius, Teddy," Diana said as she kissed her friend on the cheek. "I've got to call Dad."

She ran back to her bedroom and grabbed her phone. "Dad, Teddy's got something," Diana said excitedly into the phone.

"We're on our way." This case had become an obsession for all of them, so Diana wasn't surprised her father would drop everything. Fifteen minutes later, John Hunter arrived with Liam in tow.

"Tell me," he said before he was even through the door.

Teddy quickly explained how he'd managed to locate the warehouse. "Great job, Teddy. You'd make a great cop," Liam said with a grin.

Teddy blushed at the praise. "I don't think I'm cut out for it, but thanks."

"Okay, let's go check this place out and see what we can find." John was anxious to leave.

Diana glanced outside. It was already dark. "Shouldn't you wait until tomorrow?" she asked.

"We'll be fine, Didi," her father soothed.

Diana wasn't so sure. "I'd rather you not take the risk. It's dark out, and that's not the best part of town."

"Don't worry, we'll be fine. I promise," John said with a smile and a hug for his daughter.

As she watched her father walk out of the house, she had a terrible feeling in the pit of her stomach. She ran after her father. "Dad, wait!" He turned around and she launched herself at him, hugging him tightly. "I love you, Dad," she said.

Her father hugged her back just as tightly. "I love you too, baby." And then he was gone.

Two hours later, Diana was pacing back and forth. "They've been gone too long, and they're not answering their phones. I'm telling you something has gone wrong."

"I'm sure they're fine. Maybe they don't have cell coverage in that area."

Diana sighed, rubbing her eyes with the heels of her hands. "You're right. I'm just being paranoid."

Another two hours later passed. Diana was still pacing. Teddy was trying to trace her father's cell phone with no luck.

"Damn it," he said as he slammed his fist against the table. "Their phones are off."

Diana went white. Her father would never turn his cell phone off. Especially not when he knew she was worried about him.

"Something's wrong," she whispered.

"What shall we do?" Teddy responded, fear etched on his face.

Diana looked up at him, determination shining in her eyes. "We follow them," she said.

"Are you crazy? They are seasoned police officers with guns. If they're in trouble, what do you think we can do? Shouldn't we call the cops?"

"And alert whoever is behind my mother's murder to the fact that we might be onto them? I'd rather not, thank you very much."

"Diana, we can't just go charging into a situation like this. We could get them killed!"

Diana glared at him. "So what do you expect me to do? Just sit around and do nothing? Well, that's not going to happen. Either come with me, or I'll go on my own."

"Like I'd let you go off on your own. Crazy woman," Teddy muttered under his breath.

Before Diana could give him a suitable retort, there was a knock at the door. Diana gasped. Her father wouldn't be knocking. She rushed to the door and wrenched it open. A uniformed officer stood in the doorway with another man.

"Ms. Diana Hunter?" the man asked. She nodded. "I'm Superintendent Steven Michaels. I work with your father." She remembered him vaguely. They'd met a few times when her father had taken her into the precinct as a kid.

Teddy moved up behind her and put his hand on her shoulder. "Is something wrong?" She asked the question, but she knew what the answer would be.

He sighed for a moment. "I regret to inform you that

while answering a 911 call, John Hunter and his partner Liam Gregson were ambushed. There was a shoot out. They were both killed. I'm so sorry."

"No," she whispered and closed her eyes, tilting her face upward. She crumpled to the ground, sobbing her heart out. This couldn't be happening. She couldn't have lost her father, too. And Liam. Oh God, no, no, no! She was rocking back and forth when she felt a pair of strong arms come around her.

"Teddy, they're gone. Everyone's gone," she cried into his chest.

"I'm so sorry, Didi," Teddy's voice broke. "I'm so, so sorry."

She'd lost everyone. Her mother. Her father. Even Liam, who had been like her younger, cool uncle. She'd lost them all.

Diana walked into her bedroom, throwing her purse on the bed. She had just come from her father's funeral. It had been a wonderful funeral. It had seemed like all of Vancouver Police Department had shown up to pay their respects. They'd handed her a flag. She'd almost laughed. They thought a flag would ease the pain? That it would make her feel better?

She could hear the voices downstairs and knew she had to go back down and entertain a slew of people who barely knew her father. The hypocrisy of it all made her skin crawl, especially since she was convinced that someone in the department had had something to do with her father's death.

The policeman at the door had been lying. Or been lied

to. John and Liam had gone to the warehouse to follow up the lead Teddy had uncovered, not because they'd been answering a 911 call. They weren't killed in the process of carrying out their police duties. As she stood there in the middle of her childhood bedroom, it seemed to Diana that there was a good chance that someone among all the people at the funeral today knew more than they were saying about her parents' deaths.

She sighed and squared her shoulders, getting ready to go back downstairs. That's when she noticed it. A manila envelope on her bed. It had her name printed on it. She picked it up and looked at it curiously. She opened it and dumped its contents on her bed. She froze. They were pictures. Dozens of pictures of her and Teddy over the past year. And there was a note. She picked it up gingerly as if it was a poisonous snake.

*Back off or he's next. Tell anyone about this and he dies.*

Diana's heart began to race. They were threatening to kill Teddy. She couldn't lose him too. He was all she had left. She had to protect him. But why were they threatening him? Why not just kill her as well, like they had her parents? Wouldn't that be a more logical route to assuring the outcome they obviously wanted?

Now her mind was racing as well as her heart. Something didn't add up, but she had no idea what. And she didn't have time to figure it out. Not immediately. Not without giving herself away. Not without putting Teddy in danger. No, first she had to make sure Teddy was safe. Then, she'd deal with whoever thought they could scare her into dropping the investigation into her parents' deaths.

She quickly picked up the pictures and the note, stuffed them back in the envelope, and put it in the bottom drawer of her dresser. That they had gone into her room creeped her out and demonstrated their audacity. These were people willing to stop at nothing and no one to get what they wanted. Her mind continued to whirl with thoughts. She didn't know whom she could trust, and she couldn't show the pictures and the note to Teddy. If she did, he'd never agree to back down and stay safe. No, this was for her to do alone.

She went back downstairs and pretended everything was just fine. She put on the brave face everyone expected of her, even though she wanted to curl up in a fetal position and shut out the world. She had made a decision and she had to carry it through.

That night, she sat Teddy down. "Teddy, I've decided to go to Europe," she said.

"What?" he squawked.

"I need to get away from all this. I need to forget for a little while. I feel as if I'm falling apart, and that if I don't get away, I'm going to explode."

Teddy nodded. "Fine, when are we leaving?"

Diana shook her head sadly. "Not us, Teddy. Just me."

"You've got to be kidding me. If you think I'm letting you go off on your own, you're insane."

"It's not your choice to make. I have to leave, and I'm going alone."

The sullen look on his face told her he was ready to start arguing. She cut him off before he could even begin. "Don't you get it, Teddy? Every time I look at you, I remember what I've lost. I can't do it anymore. I can't be your friend anymore. We need to part ways."

She knew she sounded unkind, and she was dying

inside with every word she said. But keeping him safe was more important than anything. He was all she had left. She'd rather he be out of harm's way but far from her, than end up like her father, her mother, and Liam.

"Diana, you can't do this. I loved them too, you know." Tears filled Diana's eyes at the broken look on his face. But she had to be strong. She was doing this to keep him alive.

"I know, Teddy, and I'm sorry, but I've lost my entire world, and I can't be reminded of it every day. I need some time. Please, you have to understand."

"But I can look after you, protect you. God knows, you need it."

Diana said nothing, her eyes pleading.

Teddy looked back at her for a moment, his eyes moist. He took a deep breath, "Okay, I'll give you some space because you've been through more than anyone should have to in a lifetime, but if you think I'm giving up on our friendship, you are sadly mistaken, girlfriend."

"Please, Teddy, just leave," she begged. "I need to be alone." If he didn't go now, she might not let him go at all and he'd end up like everyone else she cared about.

"Fine," he said. He stomped up to his room. Fifteen minutes later, he came back downstairs. He stopped in front of her and hugged her, though she held herself stiffly. "I don't know what you think you're doing, but I will never give up on you. I love you, Di. You hear me? I love you, and I always will. You'll always be my baby sister."

"Please, just go," she whispered. Jaw clenched, he nodded. Turning on his heel, he walked out of the house and out of her life, slamming the door behind him.

Diana crumpled to the ground and began to sob. She really was all alone now. She cried for what seemed like hours, but when she was done, she felt almost as if she had been reborn. Getting to her feet, she started wandering through the house, looking over the family photos from happier times. With every photo, her determination grew.

She was a Hunter. She was not some weakling they could intimidate into doing what they wanted. And now? Well, now they had no one they could threaten her with. She would find out who had killed her parents and why. She just had to come up with a plan. And then she remembered.

She rushed up to her room and dug through the bag she used in school. She breathed a sigh of relief when she found what she was looking for. It was a white card with a name and number printed on it.

She dialed the number. After a few rings, a man answered.

"This is Duvall."

"Mr. Duvall, this is Diana Hunter," she said.

"Hello, Ms. Hunter. I heard what happened. I'm very sorry for your loss." Diana wasn't surprised he knew about her father's death. It had been all over the news. And Duvall was CSIS, after all.

"Thank you."

"How can I help you?" he asked.

"Is that job offer still open?"

"Of course. Have you reconsidered?"

Diana hesitated for a moment but she'd made her decision. "Yes. I've reconsidered."

"That's very good to hear, Miss Hunter."

"So, what do I do now?" she asked.

"I will pick you up tomorrow at 8am and bring you in to meet my superiors."

"Thank you," she said.

"I will see you tomorrow, Miss Hunter."

"Good-bye," she said softly. She terminated the call.

*Hunted* is a prequel to the Diana Hunter series. Unlike the other books, *Hunted* is not a complete mystery. It relates the events that create the backdrop to the series. Read further books in the series to find out what happens.

USA Today Bestselling Author

# A. J. GOLDEN

## GABRIELLA ZINNAS

# SNATCHED

## A DIANA HUNTER MYSTERY

# SNATCHED

BOOK TWO

The characters and events portrayed in this book are fictitious. Any
similarity to real persons, living or dead is coincidental and not intended by
the author.
Text copyright © 2016 A. J. Golden
All rights reserved.

No part of this book may be reproduced, stored in a retrieval system, or
transmitted in any form or by any means, electronic, mechanical,
photocopying, recording, or otherwise, without express written permission of
the publisher.

Published by Mesa Verde Publishing
P.O. Box 1002
San Carlos, CA 94070

ISBN-13: 978-1517642907

Edited by
Marjorie Kramer

# CHAPTER ONE

DIANA HUNTER BENT over, taking deep breaths of the salty air. She'd pushed herself hard on her run today. She'd felt the need to after being stuck behind her desk almost around the clock for the past seven days.

Standing up, she began to stretch her muscles. That's when she saw him. A man sitting under a tree right outside her apartment. Usually, she wouldn't have taken any notice. He looked engrossed in the book he was reading, and it wasn't unusual for people to come out and sit by the ocean.

But there was a problem. First of all, it was seven in the morning. No matter how much you loved reading, being out at this time was odd. Yes, it was beautiful, but then Royal Bay Beach always was. The sun sparkled off the deep blue water, the grass was lush and green, and the pale sand looked as inviting as always. Diana had spent many an afternoon enjoying a good book curled up under a maple tree or admiring the flowers and shrubs that dotted the promenade running right alongside the beach. But not so early in the morning, when it was still pretty chilly.

She'd first noticed him when she'd started her run, almost an hour ago. And he hadn't moved an inch since then. Something was definitely wrong.

She walked over to him. "Sir? Are you feeling alright?"

No response. She tried again, a little louder this time. "Can I get you anything? Do you need a doctor?"

Again, nothing. Kneeling next to him, she took a closer look. Her breath caught in her throat. *This isn't good.*

He was pale. Much too pale. His chest didn't seem to be moving, either. She reached out a trembling hand and, using two fingers, tried to find a pulse in his neck. He was as cold as ice. There was not even a flutter of a heartbeat to be found.

This man was dead. And she was fairly certain that he hadn't died of natural causes. Especially considering that, other than having no pulse, the man looked to be in good health and was certainly in his prime.

The urge to shout was strong, but she kept it in. "Breathe, Diana, breathe. You've seen dead bodies before. Get a grip." The last thing she wanted was to turn a crime scene into a circus, which would make the job of the police impossible.

She looked up to see if anyone was around. The beach was deserted. She pulled out her phone and dialed 911.

"What is your emergency?" the operator said as soon as the call connected.

"I'd like to report a dead body." Diana cleared her throat. "Could you send an ambulance and the police?"

"Did you say a body, Ms. ...?" the operator inquired, her tone disbelieving.

"Diana Hunter. And since he isn't breathing and is as cold as ice, I'm pretty sure he's dead." Diana's voice had gone up a few octaves, so she took a deep breath, trying to regain control. "Please send someone."

"Of course," the woman was suddenly all business. "Tell me where you are, and I'll dispatch units to your location."

"I'm right on the promenade near Royal Bay Beach, close to Stanley Park."

"Stay there. The police will be there in five minutes."

"Thank you." Diana disconnected the call and looked down at the body again. Her brain started working overtime. What could have happened to him? Who was he? Who could have left him there? Why take the time to position him like that?

Part of her wanted to turn away and ignore the whole situation. She had been looking forward to spending a quiet weekend at home catching up on some chores. But questions kept nagging at her. With a sigh of defeat, she took a closer look at the body, making sure not to touch anything. She didn't want to contaminate evidence and make the police work harder.

Clearly, whoever had dumped the body had wanted to make sure people didn't notice it right away. And one thing was certain. He hadn't been there last night. She'd got in after midnight, and would have noticed someone sitting on the grass at that time. So the body must have been deposited between one and six this morning.

Diana took another quick look around her and leaned in to examine the body. There weren't any visible marks on him. She was tempted to stand up and move away, but her curiosity got the better of her. His shirt was unbuttoned part way down – a fact she hadn't noticed earlier – so she pinched the fabric with the tips of her nails, trying to touch as little as possible. She pulled the shirt out slightly and looked down, but before she could be sufficiently horrified in her reaction, she heard sirens. The cops would get rather touchy about someone getting too close to their crime scene, so she jumped up and as far away from the body as was feasible without looking like a crazy person.

An ambulance, a patrol unit, and an unmarked police car pulled up beside her. As the paramedics rushed to the body – she could have told them rushing wasn't necessary – she watched the policemen get out of their patrol vehicle. One of them looked young, and she tried to hide a small smile at the terrified look on his face. This was probably his first dead body. Just then she felt a light touch on her elbow. She nearly jumped out of her skin.

"Ms. Diana Hunter," the man asked. This had to be the man who'd pulled up in the other car.

"Yes."

"Ms. Hunter, I'm Detective Peter Hopkinson. Can you tell me what happened?"

She gave the man a quick once over and noted that he wasn't exactly what she had been expecting. She'd dealt with the police quite a bit in her career and found that detectives were usually middle-aged men with significant paunches and constantly irritated demeanors. Her experience had never involved a man who looked like he'd stepped off the cover of *GQ* magazine, sexy stubble included.

She cleared her throat. "Well, I found a dead body." Great going, Diana. That was deep. Really. Like he hadn't figured that out by himself.

"Yes, I think we've established that," he said gently. "Could you be a little more specific?"

For some reason, his quiet disposition annoyed her. She wasn't in shock, and she definitely didn't need to be coddled.

She drew her shoulders back and, in a much stronger voice, explained to him precisely what had happened.

"So, the body was here when you left on your run?" he asked, taking notes on his tablet. It was the first time she'd seen a detective with something other than a notepad.

"Yes, I told you he was. But, at the time, I didn't know he was dead. I thought he was reading a book, though it did strike me as odd. It was pretty chilly this morning, and no one comes out quite this early." Great, now she was babbling.

"And what made you stop to speak to him on your way back?"

Diana rolled her eyes and gritted her teeth. "As I said, he hadn't moved at all from his position, and I wanted to check he was alright."

"You noticed he hadn't moved?" For some reason, the detective seemed rather skeptical.

"Didn't I just say that?" Why was he asking her to tell him the same things over and over again? Didn't he believe her?

"It's unusual for people to be quite that observant." His strange look set her teeth on edge.

"You think I killed him?" Her tone clearly showed her shock.

"Of course not," the detective said gently. "I'm just covering all my bases."

Diana felt her temperature rise up another notch. She was seriously starting to dislike the detective. Logic said he needed to ask her all these questions, but it just felt like he was wasting her time. Not to mention, also insulting her. First, he treated her like a silly little woman, and now he was inferring that she might have been involved. Male cover model looks or not, she had the sudden and overwhelming urge to tell him to shove it. Or slap him.

"Finding a dead body drained of blood outside my building is certainly suspicious," she snapped. "And of course I'm involved. I'm such a criminal mastermind that I killed him, drained his blood into my bath tub, dragged him out here, let him sit around for a couple of hours, and then called the police on myself to deflect suspicion." She snapped her mouth closed in irritation.

"Is that what happened?"

Diana clenched her teeth. She took a deep breath and realized her imagination had taken off without her permission, creating a realistic scenario of what could have actually happened. Except for one thing. "And just how exactly would I get a dead body that weighs at least 180 pounds down from my apartment, on my own, without leaving a trail of blood, and without being seen?"

"I don't know. That's for you to tell me." He was watching her closely, his face betraying nothing.

"You're being serious? I can't believe this. I wish I'd never made the call. I should have simply walked on by."

"I'm sorry, Ms. Hunter, but all of this is a bit strange, especially considering how much you seem to know about the body." Great. She'd done it again. She'd put her foot in her mouth, and now she had to extricate it without letting on how close she'd got to the body. In her experience, offense was the best form of defense. So, she attacked.

"How much I know? What are you blathering about?"

The detective stiffened. "Well, I would be quite interested in how you know the body was drained of blood." His tone was much colder than it had been before.

Diana took a deep breath to calm herself before she went off again. Maybe insulting him hadn't been the best course of action. "I got up real close and personal with him to make sure he was dead, and his color suggested he'd suffered severe blood loss." She knew that all dead bodies had the same waxen pallor whether or not they had lost blood, but she had to say something.

The detective cocked an eyebrow. "Is that the only reason you assume he was drained of blood?"

"Why else would I think that?" She really hoped he was buying this. The last thing she needed was to be charged with obstruction or tampering with evidence or whatever else they charged people with for fiddling with dead bodies when they shouldn't.

"I don't know. Maybe because you killed him and are now trying to throw us off your trail?"

"You know, I was having such a nice morning."

"I can see how a dead body could ruin your morning."

Diana snorted. "It wasn't the dead body that did it," she replied with a pointed glare at him.

Now the detective was gritting his teeth. Good. He was an ass who thought she'd killed this guy and then called the cops.

"If there's anything else..." he trailed off stiffly.

She debated whether she should tell him what else she had noticed, but decided against it. If she said anything more, he'd probably arrest her.

"No, that's all I know."

"Very well. If you could come down to the station later on today so I can take your statement, I'd appreciate it."

"Didn't I just tell you what happened?" Diana knew it was proper procedure but the fact that he wanted to go through what she had seen a *third* time was extremely irritating. Maybe it had something to do with the condescending look on his face.

"As I'm sure you are well aware, it's just a formality. So, please, come to the station."

"No."

"No?" He stared at her as if she'd lost her mind. "What do you mean, no?"

"Just what it sounds like. You want my statement, you can come to my place and get it." And then she realized just how much like a proposition that sounded – especially when his eyes widened slightly – and a blush crept up her cheeks. "I meant that this is the first weekend I've had some free time, and I want to catch up on some chores at home. I need to get some vacuuming done. My fridge hasn't been restocked in ages, and everything is covered in dust." Great, now she was babbling like an idiot. Could this day get any worse? "So, if you want that statement, I'll type it out, and you can pick it up later," she finished in a rush.

The detective paused for a moment, looking at her carefully, "Yeah, sure. I'll come pick it up later on this afternoon." He was still giving her a weird look. What was it about this man and his very attractive face that made her fly off the handle so easily?

"Okay." She rattled her address and phone number off while he took note of them and then turned to walk away. She would absolutely not give in and tell him what he could do with the stupid placating look he had on his face.

"By the way, Ms. Hunter, what was it you said you did?" Hopkinson was looking at her as if he'd already judged her. Just because she wasn't exactly looking her best with her rather worn and faded T-shirt and her running shoes that had seen better days, that didn't mean he had the right to judge.

"I'm a magazine editor," she snapped.

He inclined his head, eyebrow cocked again. "That

explains it," she heard him mutter. Did all law enforcement officers come with a built-in disdain for magazine editors? It wouldn't be the first time she'd been insulted by a detective because of her job.

"Are you implying that my imagination has run away with me?"

He looked at her with a small trace of surprise. "I didn't say anything."

"You didn't need to. I know your type."

"Wouldn't that be the pot calling the kettle black?" he asked with a smirk.

She huffed in irritation because he had her. Deciding retreat was the better part of valor, she turned on her heel and marched toward her building. Of course, Diana being Diana, she couldn't help but throw a parting shot at him.

"Just to make your job easier, I'm pretty sure this was a body dump."

Before he had a chance to say another word, she'd marched off, leaving him with a bemused look on his face. That's when she realized she might have implicated herself even further. Why couldn't she have just kept her mouth shut? She didn't have any proof of it being a body dump. It might be the logical conclusion, especially after she'd seen the wicked cut the man sported from sternum to navel. But still.

**D**IANA WALKED INTO her apartment, shutting the door behind her and making sure to lock it. Her job as a reporter and then a magazine editor for a news and crime publication meant that she'd met and interviewed many people, including some pretty tough characters. She knew quite a lot about how the under-world worked, and it wasn't a pretty sight; abused mothers and children prostituting themselves to make money for food, pimps taking advantage, and various other hardened criminals out to make a buck, regardless of who they had to trample over. She'd met a few serial killers, too.

So, she always made sure to lock her door. It might not stop someone really determined, but it would give her a few extra minutes to get out of her apartment using the fire escape, if push came to shove.

But before she could take a step, a small cannonball of white fluff hurled itself at her, yipping and barking. She laughed as she got down on her knees, holding her arms open. Max got the message and bounded up to her, licking her face, his tail wagging energetically.

She hugged him until he started to squirm. She smiled down at the Maltese terrier who was her constant companion and the official love of her life. He always knew how to make her smile. He sat down, wagging his tail, his tongue hanging out of his mouth, looking up at her expectantly.

"Alright, alright. Come on. Let's get breakfast." She walked into her stylish, modern kitchen with its red and black lacquered cabinets, black granite countertops, and an island with her collection of copper pots and pans hanging above it. She opened the door to a cupboard and pulled out the dog food. Measuring out the right amount, she put Max's dog bowl down on the kitchen floor. Like a good boy, Max waited to be invited. "Eat, Max." In a flash, Max dived into the bowl. She giggled and rolled her eyes. Typical male. As soon as food was present, Max completely forgot she existed.

Now that he had been taken care of, she walked into her bedroom that featured the same modern lines and red and black color scheme as the rest of her apartment. A king size bed with a black curved headboard, chrome accents, and inbuilt lighting dominated most of the space. Two small glass and chrome tables stood either side of the bed, in lieu of more traditional nightstands. Floor to ceiling mirrors hid her walk-in wardrobe. The wall facing her bed had red and black lacquered shelving units that held her makeup, some of her favorite books and magazines, and a single photograph in an ornate silver frame.

Diana paused for a moment and trailed her fingers over the frame with a small sigh. The photograph was one of her most cherished possessions. It was a shot of her parents. Whenever she saw it, her heart shuddered. The way they looked at each other in the picture showed how much love they had shared. She ached to hear her mother's soothing voice and her father's deep and contagious laugh. She yearned to be held and told everything would be all right. She longed to be not so alone. Angrily she dashed away the single tear that rolled down her cheek.

Giving herself a mental shake and putting the past firmly where it belonged – in the past, for now – she began to take off her clothes. She dumped everything into the hamper and padded into the bathroom. Turning the shower spray on, she waited a moment for the room to steam up. She knew at that point, the water would be perfect.

She washed herself as she thought back to the dead body and the detective. Admittedly, the detective looked better than the dead body, but the latter wasn't snarky or a know-it-all. Insinuating that she was the killer, indeed. What a moron. Or he thought she was one. She sighed, pretty certain she was overreacting to the man.

It probably had something to do with the fact that he was too attractive for his own good. Or for her peace of mind. And she might have a wee chip on her shoulder when it came to detectives talking down to her.

She promised herself she'd be more careful when she next met him. She wanted in on this case, not only because it would make for a great article, but because she was curious why someone would leave a body on Royal Bay Beach right outside her home.

She turned the water off and stepped out of the shower. Drying herself with a fluffy white towel, she padded back into her bedroom and put on her I-want-to-kill-myself-I-have-chores-to-do outfit, which consisted of a pair of yoga pants, a sports bra, and a tank top. She pulled her long, light brown hair into a ponytail, flicking her bangs back. They had gotten too long and kept getting in her eyes. She needed a haircut and her highlights refreshed.

Diana grabbed a cup of coffee from the kitchen and sat at her desk, a frosted glass and chrome affair that faced the floor-to-ceiling windows overlooking the bay. She fired up her computer, bringing the three-monitor setup to life.

She was going to get that statement done before the know-it-all detective turned up on her doorstep. The less time she spent in his company, the better. She glanced outside, and that's when it hit her. Her balcony looked out over the crime scene. She grinned. This was a sign. She walked outside and looked down. The area was now devoid of life, with only a cordon of yellow plastic tape with *Crime Scene* printed on it indicating anything had happened. She'd definitely be down there soon to take a closer look. She knew it.

Of course, Max chose that precise moment to come barreling into the room. Apparently, he was in the mood to play. She got down on one knee and petted the bundle of energy that was her dog. "Not now, boy. Mommy has work to do." He looked up at her with such a sad face that her heart almost broke.

"This is emotional blackmail," she grumbled. But, unfortunately, she didn't have time to play with him. She really needed to get that statement done.

She went back to her computer with Max at her heels. Seeing he wasn't getting anywhere, he curled up beneath her chair, waiting patiently. Sort of. Except for the odd lick and nip at her heels that would make her jump now and then. She sighed and focused on the statement she had to write out.

Opening up her word processer, Diana began to type. She made sure to include as much as she could without actually stating she'd done the unthinkable and touched evidence before the police had arrived. She was so engrossed in what she was doing that she jumped when her doorbell sounded.

Of course, the moment the bell rang, Max was off like a shot. He skidded to a stop, almost crashing into the door, and he proceeded to bark as menacingly as he possibly could. He was a tiny Maltese terrier. Menacing was not an adjective one could use to describe him.

She sighed. She had better open the door before Max had an apoplectic fit. Anyway, it could only be Detective Hot-kinson. Jeez. Since when did she have a nickname for the guy? It was a pretty fitting one, though.

"Max, sit. Stay." Dutifully, Max sat. She took a deep breath and schooled her features into a mask of welcome. She had to be nice. She opened her door, a smile frozen on her face. Yes, he was still as good looking as earlier. Not her overactive imagination, then. Sigh. No man had the right to look that good.

"Hello, Detective," she said.

"Ms. Hunter," he replied, inclining his head.

"Come in, please." She stepped back from the door to make room for him and he swept past her with a gruff thanks. She closed the door behind him, taking a deep breath to steel herself for what was to come.

Unfortunately, Max chose that moment to make himself known. This was his home, and other males were not welcome. And since this was the first time a man had come onto his turf, Max was not pleased. So, the 6'2" detective came face-to-face with a growling fur ball that he could easily dispatch with a single, swift kick.

"Max, no." Apparently, Max wasn't interested in

listening to her. He wanted the male off his turf, and that was that.

Surprising her, Detective Hot-kinson sat on his haunches. "What have we here?" He reached out a hand, palm down and held it out without moving any closer to Max, who kept growling, baring his teeth. The detective just kept staring him down. After a few moments, Max stopped growling. He looked at the extended hand quizzically and sniffed it. A moment later, apparently deciding the detective wasn't the enemy, he yipped and pushed his head under the man's hand.

"Who's a good boy?" the detective murmured, petting her supposedly loyal dog.

"Traitor," she muttered under her breath. "Max, bed," she ordered. Max looked up at her as if she'd kicked him. "Now." With a disappointed whine, he turned and dragged himself into her bedroom.

"Nice dog."

"Thanks." Her tone said it all. She wasn't going to engage in small talk with the annoying Detective Hot-kinson.

"So, can I get your statement now?" His low rumble sent a shiver up her spine. No, this was not right. She could not, would not, be attracted to the condescending jerk of a detective. Unfortunately, now that the excitement had passed and there was nothing else to focus on except him, she found herself noticing more and more about him. Like his square jaw line and that brown stubble she found so fascinating. Or those smoldering blue eyes that were looking at her so intently.

She cleared her throat, blushing that she'd been caught staring like a schoolgirl. "Yes, of course." Why did her voice come out so breathy? Ridiculous. He was a fool. She had to keep repeating that to herself. "I have about a paragraph left. Do you want a cup of coffee while you wait?"

He was watching her closely, which made another shiver skate up her spine. She almost missed his nod of acceptance. She walked into the kitchen, closing a door that was cracked open as she passed it, and poured a cup of coffee. That's when she realized she hadn't asked if he wanted milk or sugar. For greater efficiency – and if she was honest, to give herself time to recover – she raised her voice. "Do you want milk and sugar?"

"I take it black, thanks." She jumped. Again. Somehow, he'd materialized next to her. Thank goodness the cup was on the counter or she would have spilled it all over herself.

"Here," she said, shoving the cup at him. He took it, and of course, just like in every cliché romance novel she'd never admit to reading, their fingers touched, and it was like touching a livewire. She felt the shock all the way down to her toes. "Uhm, I'll go finish that statement." She rushed out of the kitchen without a backward glance.

She sat at her computer and took a deep breath. "Focus, Diana," she muttered to herself. Squaring her shoulders, she forced her mind to address the task at hand. Whoever had been killed deserved justice, and she needed to do her part. She had to help if she could. Engrossed in what she was doing, she didn't hear him come back into the living room.

"You seem to have a perfect view of the crime scene from here. Did you see anything this morning that was out of the ordinary?"

She shook her head. "No, I'm not in the habit of hanging out my window at such a crazy hour." She grimaced. Okay, that had been a bit bitchy. "Sorry," she said with a sigh. "I think finding a dead body first thing in the morning has thrown me slightly." *It has absolutely nothing to do with you.*

He smiled softly. "It's okay. Don't worry about it."

She nodded, though that smile had, once again, thrown her for a loop. With some effort she refocused and printed off a copy of her statement. Grabbing a red pen, she started proofing it. Finding a passage that read awkwardly, she tapped the pen against her lips as she thought of how to rephrase it. Once she was done, she fixed the mistakes on the computer and printed off a final copy.

"So, I'm guessing I need to sign it."

He nodded. "That would be great."

She scribbled her name on the piece of paper, pulled out a manila envelope, and slid the paper inside it. She handed the envelope to him, making sure her fingers were in no way within touching distance.

"I have a few other questions for you," Detective Hopkinson said.

"Fire away." Getting up from her computer, she moved to the couch, then realized it was a mistake. He towered over her when she was standing. Now, she'd end up with a crick in her neck. He apparently noticed her discomfort because he took pity on her and sat in the armchair opposite.

"The victim's name was Leonardo Perez. Did you know him?"

"No, that name doesn't sound familiar at all. And I'm pretty sure I haven't seen him before. I think I would have noticed."

"And you have no idea how he ended up under that tree?"

She sighed, rubbing the bridge of her nose. "This again? I

already told you that I saw him like that this morning when I left for my run. I'm pretty sure he wasn't there last night. I got in late – past midnight – and there was nothing unusual out there. I would have noticed a guy trying to read under a tree in the middle of the night. But I've explained all this in my statement."

Detective Hopkinson nodded. "I'm just double-checking."

Diana accepted his reply. "Was he from around here?" she couldn't help but ask.

"I'm sorry, but I can't discuss an open case with a civilian." He looked apologetic. Sort of.

"Sure, I get it. No problem. Just wondering if I should bolt my doors and windows? Or hide from a psychotic killer?"

"You should always bolt your doors and windows. But no, there's no indication you have anything to worry about in terms of a psychotic killer."

They lapsed into an awkward silence, which he broke after a few moments. "You have a nice place. It's not what I expected."

She glanced around, trying to see her living room from his point of view. Like the rest of her apartment, it was minimalistic. A couch with red cushions and a black frame curved around one corner of the room facing the windows, with a matching armchair sitting across from it that separated her actual living room from her work area. An oval coffee table with a lacquered geometric stand and glass top sat right in front of the couch.

On the opposite wall from the couch was a frosted glass and chrome media center that matched her desk. The other side of the room was her workspace. Her desk was positioned right in front of the windows, while a black bookcase stood off to the right. On the left, she had two low cabinets with red and black lacquered doors.

She looked at him curiously. "What were you expecting?"

He looked slightly nonplussed. "I'm not sure. I guess I expected something a little more...girly." The last word came out on a choke, as if he'd realized half-way through that it might not have been the wisest thing to say.

Diana started to laugh. "Let me guess. You were expecting lots of pink, lace, and frills. Maybe even a doll collection?"

He grinned. "The doll collection was the first thing on my list."

"I don't know if I should be insulted."

"No, it's just that..." he trailed off. "I really didn't know what to expect but this was definitely not it."

"You didn't expect to like my taste in decorating, did you?" What Diana found remarkable was that he'd actually thought about what her place might be like. And he'd given it enough thought to formulate expectations.

"Honestly, no. Then again, considering how much of an idiot I was earlier, I certainly wasn't expecting coffee, either." Even more remarkable. The detective was apologizing? Okay, it was in a rather roundabout way, but it still qualified as something of an apology.

"Don't worry, I slipped cyanide into your coffee," she replied sweetly.

Detective Hopkinson actually paled and looked down quickly at his cup of coffee. "I'm joking," she said, rolling her eyes.

He grinned. "I think I've been doing this job for too long. I've become suspicious of everything and everyone."

She nodded. "I understand."

Again, silence descended. But it was slightly less awkward than before.

"Out of curiosity, why do you think he wasn't killed here?" he asked suddenly. "Why do you think it was a body dump?"

They were back to that were they? "Are you going to suggest I did the killing again?"

He chuckled. "I never thought you did. It was just funny to see you get so worked up."

"What?" Okay, she had almost screeched right there. Not good.

"You have to admit, it did look a bit suspicious."

"How do you figure that?"

"Well, it's not every day that someone finds a body and is quite so calm about it. Plus, you seemed to know so much about what was going on."

"Like?"

"You did say something about massive blood loss. How did you know that?"

Diana sighed. She was going to get into so much trouble. "I may or may not have looked down his shirt to see if I could get a better idea of what was going on."

"So, it was the gaping wound that gave it away?"

She nodded. "And that's also why I think he was killed somewhere else." He cocked his head, inviting her to continue.

"With a wound that big, he would have been bleeding. A lot. But there was no blood on the ground around him. So, where did it go? Last time I checked, there were no reports of vampires living in the Vancouver area. And even if a few are hanging around, they couldn't do that good a cleanup job."

She was babbling again. Vampires? Really? For some

reason, Detective Hot-kinson gave her foot-in-mouth disease. When she glanced at him, though, he was grinning. Maybe he liked her sense of humor.

"Good call," he nodded in approval. "Well, thank you for the coffee. And for only joking about the cyanide." He grinned. "I have to get back to the precinct."

She nodded with a small smile. "Thanks for coming around to pick up my statement."

"You're welcome," he responded graciously and she let him out. Closing the door behind him, she took a deep breath. Max came scampering out of the bedroom. She turned to look at him. "That was one interesting morning," she muttered.

Peter Hopkinson sat at his desk and pulled out Diana Hunter's statement. The woman was as opinionated as hell, so he was curious to read what she had written. When he was done, he was frowning. It read more like a forensics report than a statement. She'd included every damn thing, including the fact that the victim's clothes had seemed rather shabby. He was surprised she hadn't performed an autopsy on the body herself, right under that tree.

She'd been so irritating at first with her I'm-smarter-than-everyone attitude and those grey eyes and haughty looks. It was why he'd made her go through the story twice; three times if he counted the statement sitting on his desk. Just to cut her ego down to size.

She was a magazine editor, for crying out loud. What the heck did she know about crime scenes and dead bodies? And that was the problem because judging by her state-ment, she knew quite a lot.

When he'd gone to her apartment, he'd expected a repeat of the scene at the beach. In other words, he'd been on his guard and had expected her to skewer him. Surprisingly, other than one sarcastic remark, she'd been rather pleasant. She'd been really pleasant, in fact.

Of course, when she'd opened her door to let him in, he'd had to use every ounce of willpower to keep his eyes on her face. What was wrong with the woman, answering her door looking like that? Didn't she know there were a lot of bad people around? A gorgeous, single woman living alone attracted a lot of unwholesome attention from the types of people he came into contact with on a daily basis. She needed to be careful.

He looked at the statement once more. He had a feeling that he and Ms. Hunter would meet again. Her observations were very interesting. They were actually better than the forensics report he'd received. Since the tree hadn't been the scene of the crime, the forensics unit hadn't spent too much time on it. He shook his head. He'd have to go back. This case was weird enough without taking Ms. Hunter into account.

He groaned. That was going to be awkward. He reached for his phone and dialed the medical examiner. "Doctor Riddle, do you have anything for me?"

"Hello to you, too."

"Sorry, Doc."

The man huffed. "Actually, I do. And you can come down here to find out what it is."

Great. He really loved visiting the morgue. Not. "I'll be right down, Doc."

A few minutes and an elevator-ride later, he walked into the morgue. The smell of industrial disinfectant assaulted his nostrils. He hated visiting the morgue, a dislike that only intensified when he saw the body of their murder victim on one of the tables, the medical examiner leaning over it.

When the Doc called, the body was usually covered or sewn up or something. It was rare for the doctor to still be working on it, like he was now, his arms almost disappearing into the corpse as he pulled out the organs.

Peter prided himself on having a strong stomach. He'd been a member of the Canadian Special Forces. He'd been deployed overseas to more war zones than he could count. He'd seen death. He'd dealt out death. But seeing the Doc playing around with a man's guts? He struggled to stomach it.

"Doc?" he said, breathing in through his mouth. The body was giving off a unique perfume that was not wholly pleasant.

Doctor Riddle looked up. "Good, you're here."

"So what was it you wanted to tell me?"

"Come here, I need to show you something." When Peter hesitated, the Doc glanced up at him again. "I don't have all day, you know."

Peter took a deep breath and stepped forward. He clenched his teeth and looked down. "What am I looking at, Doc?"

"This man has no kidneys or liver."

"Excuse me?"

"His kidneys and liver have been removed. And that's not the worst part."

"Someone killed him, took his kidneys and liver, and there's something worse?" Peter didn't really know if he wanted to hear what else the doctor had to say.

The Doc nodded. "The cuts were precise. They were definitely made by someone with medical training, but the victim wasn't dead when his organs were removed. He was alive. In fact, I'm pretty sure he was conscious when they cut into him."

Peter felt bile rise up in his throat. "What makes you think that?"

The Doc closed the body up, pulling the edges of the initial wound together. "I can find no traces of anesthetic. And take a look at this incision. It starts off almost like a zigzag and then becomes straight and smooth."

Peter nodded, not trusting himself to say anything. Doctor Riddle continued. "Part of the incision is surgical, but part of it looks like it's been done by someone whose hands were shaking. The only logical explanation is that the patient was awake when he was first cut into and was struggling. Then he probably passed out or someone held him down..."

"Jesus."

"Uh-huh. Horrendous."

"But why would anyone take out his liver and kidneys?" Peter knew the answer, but he didn't want to say it out loud.

"You know why. Organ trafficking. It's the only explanation as to why this man was alive when his organs were removed. Obviously, they didn't need him after they took what they wanted, so they just let him bleed out."

"He didn't die from his liver and kidneys being removed?"

The Doc shook his head. "Without them, he might have lived for a few hours, maybe even a day, if he'd been patched up. But, they didn't bother. They just cut what they needed out of him and let him bleed to death. Utterly callous."

"So, he clearly didn't die under that tree."

"No. They would have needed equipment and a sterile environment to perform the procedure. They wouldn't have been able to risk contaminating the organs, or they would have become worthless. And the amount of blood this man lost would have saturated the area."

"Organ trafficking? Wow. I thought I'd seen it all, Doc. But this is beyond belief."

Doctor Riddle nodded. "It was a terrible way to go, that's for sure. No one deserves to die like this."

Peter agreed. He'd seen people getting blown apart by IEDs, people gunned down in the streets, murder victims with gunshot wounds – or in police vernacular, GSWs – and people who'd died from overdosing on whatever drug was popular that day, but this was an entirely new level of cruelty. To torture someone like that, remove his organs, and then throw the person away like they were trash was grotesque.

"Thanks, Doc." Peter turned to leave.

"Peter, you have to catch these people. This is the first one we've found but..." Doctor Riddle trailed off.

Peter nodded. "I know. There might be others and even if there aren't yet, there will be."

"I'd rather not see a body like this on my table again."

"I'll do everything I can to stop them, Doc." And he would.

The following morning, Diana stood on her balcony with a steaming cup of coffee in her hands. She took a sip every now and then as she looked out over the bay. Max was curled at her feet, snoring. Though it was too early in the morning for him to be up and about, he still liked being close to her.

She'd glance down every once in a while, the crime

scene acting like a magnet for her eyeballs. She couldn't seem to ignore it. She knew she shouldn't get involved. In fact, she should stay as far away as possible from this case. But there was something about it that drew her like a moth to a flame.

Diana hated mysteries. She couldn't just ignore them. It was impossible for her to simply leave questions unanswered. And in this case, she had so many questions.

Who was Leonardo Perez? Why had he been killed? Why had he been left outside her building? And what was with that cut from sternum to navel? It took gutting to a whole new level. Who would kill someone like that? It certainly didn't seem like a crime of passion, unless the killer was beyond disturbed.

Diana groaned. "I'm not going down there." But the yellow tape had been removed, and the tree beckoned to her. She shook her head. "No." Determined, she went back inside to get her breakfast, with Max hot on her heels.

She put out dog food for him and got her chocolate granola and yogurt. Before long, though, she found herself wandering back to the balcony, breakfast bowl in hand. She glanced back down at the tree while munching on a spoonful of cereal. It was still early enough that there were only a few people strolling on the beach. There was a woman sitting on a bench, but she seemed to be engrossed in a magazine. And she was at least a hundred feet away.

Maybe she could just take another quick look, Diana thought. She'd only be doing her civic duty. After all, the forensics team had seemed to be in a rush, and they hadn't come back, so maybe they missed something. It would be the right thing to do. She wouldn't technically be poking her nose in. She'd just be helping. She nodded to herself. Yes, it was definitely the right thing to do. She was halfway out the door before she even finished the thought.

She walked out of the elevator and smiled a greeting at Jimmy, the day doorman, before bumping into one of her neighbors.

"Good morning, Mrs. Latham."

"Good morning, Diana. Off for your run?" Mrs. Latham lived right across the hallway from Diana. She was a sweet old lady who didn't have any family around, which was why Diana made sure to check in on her from time to time.

"Not this morning, Mrs. Latham. Just a quick stroll." If she told the woman where she was going and why, she'd worry her needlessly. She was surprised the old lady hadn't heard about the body. Mrs. Latham's apartment was on the other side of the building from hers, so she wouldn't have seen the commotion, but news traveled fast. Especially that type of news.

Mrs. Latham leaned in conspiratorially. "Did you hear that they found a dead body right by that tree yesterday morning?" The apartment block's grapevine was working in its usual efficient manner, then. "They're saying he had a huge gash on his chest and that it probably has something to do with drugs." Apparently, the grapevine wasn't just efficient, it was almost an information superhighway.

"Yes, I did hear about it, though I really have no idea what happened to him." Diana was loathe to admit she'd been the one to find the body. She still wanted the chance to look over the crime scene before the area filled with people. If she told the old lady she'd found the dead man, it would be noon before she got away.

"I would have thought with you being a magazine editor, you'd know all about it." Mrs. Latham looked positively dejected.

Diana smiled. "Well, I promise to find out what I can and tell you all about it."

The woman's face lit up. "You're such a sweet girl. Thank you, Diana."

"I'm sorry, Mrs. Latham, but I really have to go."

The old lady nodded with a big smile on her face. "I'll be waiting for news," she said with a wink. Diana laughed and nodded.

Within moments, she was walking up to the tree. The beach was still relatively free of people, except for the woman on the bench, who was still reading. She seemed to be paying close attention to her magazine, though, so Diana focused her attention on the tree and the surrounding patch of grass and dirt.

With another look around to make sure she wasn't attracting too much attention, she sank to her knees. There was a small smudge of blood at the base of the tree. Could it be from the victim? But if she remembered right, that spot of blood would have been immediately behind the man. So, how did it get there? Maybe it was old? It didn't look old, though. As a matter of fact, it looked quite fresh.

She shrugged, trying to decide what to do about it. She could cut the piece of bark off the tree, put it in a plastic bag and take it to the police to be analyzed. But what if she contaminated it somehow? She didn't have latex gloves with her or sterile equipment. Maybe she should just call Detective Hopkinson and let him take it from here. Yes, that's what she'd do. She'd call the detective. But after she checked out the scene a little more. Who knows what else the forensics team had missed? She got down on all fours, just to make sure she didn't miss anything. Like more blood stains.

As she circled the tree, she saw sunlight glint off something. Crawling over to it, she spotted what looked like a small triangle of plastic. Ignoring her earlier thoughts, she impulsively picked it up. She saw it was actually a plastic card. A keycard. And most of it had been buried in the dirt. It was also green. No wonder no one had noticed it. She tried to handle it as little as possible and put it in her shirt pocket. Of course, she had no idea if the keycard was related to the case, but it was a coincidence finding it that close to the tree.

She continued to study the ground, looking for anything else that might have been buried or overlooked. As she moved forward, a pair of oxfords suddenly appeared in her field of vision. The shoes paced forward and stopped right in front of her. Diana swallowed down a lump. She knew exactly to whom those shoes belonged. So, she took a moment and then raised her head slowly, taking in Detective Hot-kinson from feet to chest. She thought he'd been tall when she was standing. From this position, he looked even more imposing. And, she decided when her gaze locked with steely blue eyes, he didn't look happy. "Busted," she whispered to herself.

"This is probably a waste of my breath, but what exactly do you think you are doing here, Ms. Hunter?"

CHAPTER THREE

D
IANA SMILED AT him sheepishly and
jumped to her feet. "Enjoying the scenery?"
Rather than a statement, it came out as more of a
question.

He cocked an eyebrow at her, taking in her dusty
appearance. "Enjoying the scenery?"

He said it as if he was testing the words. As if he
couldn't believe she'd actually said it. To her surprise,
instead of reading her the riot act, he burst out laughing. He
had a nice laugh. It was a deep rumble that pulled at the
corners of her own lips. Before she knew what was happening, she joined in his laughter.

"I guess I could have come up with a better excuse," she
said, trying to take a deep breath.

"I think even walking your turtle would have been
better," he replied, still chuckling.

"Well, I wasn't expecting you to show up, now was I?"
she admonished.

"Oh, excuse me. Please accept my apologies. Next time
I want to check over one of my own crime scenes, I'll make

sure to call you in advance and ask for permission." He was still smiling. So, he was joking. Not being an ass. Not yet, anyway.

"Apology accepted, and it's only polite to ask for permission," she winked and he grinned.

Suddenly, they both sobered, remembering why they were there in the first place. A man had died. In a gruesome, diabolical way. "Did you find anything?" he asked, his tone brisk and all business.

She nodded. "I think so. See here?" she lowered herself to her haunches, indicating the spot of blood on the tree. "I'm assuming this is blood."

He crouched to get a better look and nodded. "I think you're right."

"But it's a bit strange. I'm sure the forensics team has photos, but if I remember correctly, this is about where the body was positioned, right?"

He nodded. "So, how did the blood end up on the bark behind him?"

"Precisely. The only explanation is that either it was there before and is unrelated to this case, which would be heck of a coincidence. Or, maybe it isn't his."

Detective Hopkinson gave her a curious look. "Why assume it's not his? You have no idea how the body was handled when it was placed here. Maybe they dropped it and spattered the tree with blood."

"Then wouldn't there be more blood on the ground and over a larger area of the tree?" And since Diana always paid attention, she caught the slip. "And I was right. He wasn't killed here, was he?"

"I shouldn't have said that. I shouldn't be discussing an open case with a civvie." The detective glared at her accusingly.

"Hey, don't look at me like that. I didn't force you at gunpoint to tell me anything."

"Yeah, I put my foot in my mouth all by my lonesome," he replied ruefully.

"Well, now that the damage has been done, let's get back to it. So, he definitely wasn't killed here, which makes it even more likely that the blood on the tree is someone else's." Diana looked at him expectantly, waiting for him to agree with her.

He looked at her curiously for a moment. "Enlighten me."

She let out a frustrated growl. "Don't you see? If he was killed somewhere else, by the time they brought him here, he'd already bled out. Otherwise, if he had still been bleeding when he was dumped, we'd have seen more evidence of blood. At least a few directional drops as he was being carried. But there's nothing anywhere except for that spot on the bark." She indicated the area around them, which was completely pristine. Not a drop of blood in sight.

"Now," she continued without pausing, "I'm pretty sure whoever carried him here wouldn't have had their hands or other body parts covered in his blood as it would have drawn too much attention. So, it stands to reason that this is the blood of one of the people who put him here. Maybe they nicked themselves when they leaned him against the tree, or maybe they were involved in whatever was done to him and they got cut without realizing it. Doesn't matter. I'm pretty sure it's not his blood, and it could be an important clue."

Diana took a deep breath and looked at Detective Hopkinson. By the look on his face, she'd done it again. Why did she never stop to think how her theories sounded when she said them aloud? To her, it was simply a matter of logic. To other people? Well, most people had the same reaction as the detective. They couldn't understand how her mind worked, so they thought she was implicated in some way. But she never learned her lesson. She'd just keep rambling until everyone gave her the same suspicious look the detective was wearing now.

"You know what? Forget it," she snapped.

He looked at her in surprise. "Just forget it," she repeated. She got to her feet and started to stomp off. He called after her, but she ignored him. And then she remembered the keycard. Damn! She stopped for a moment and turned around. Leonardo Perez was more important than her pride. So, she stalked back.

"I also found this," she said, her tone curt. She pulled the card out of her pocket, making sure to only touch the edges. "It was buried in the dirt." She glanced at the card, curiosity getting the better of her. She raised her eyebrows in surprise. "And it looks like it's a keycard from a hotel that's about two blocks from here. I recognize the address."

"Do I really need to explain the concept of tampering with evidence and contaminating it?" Hopkinson barked. "What possessed you to even touch it? You should have called me right away." He pulled out a latex glove and used it to take the keycard from her. He dropped it into an evidence bag, which he sealed and put back in his coat pocket.

"No, you don't need to explain evidence tampering to me, but it was your forensics team that did a terrible job of covering the scene. I was just trying to help."

Hopkinson sighed, shaking his head. "Next time, just call me before you pick evidence up. Please." She nodded. "So, where did you find it?"

"Over there," she said, pointing to the spot on the

ground where she'd found the piece of plastic. "It was mostly buried under the dirt and grass, which is odd to say the least."

He nodded. "It would be too much of a coincidence for it not to be related."

Diana shrugged. She wasn't feeling all that forthcoming anymore.

"If you say so," she said.

The detective looked at her in surprise. "No more theories?"

"I think I'm all theory-ed out for now. I'll let you get on with your," she waved her hand around, encompassing the crime scene, "investigating."

"Why did that sound like an insult?"

Her eyes widened. He was too perceptive by far. "I'm sorry, I have no idea what you're talking about."

"Really?" he stared at her for a moment before his face relaxed. "Fine. Have it your way," he said mildly. Apparently, he was going to let it go. "Before you leave, though," he said, stopping her mid-turn, "did you happen to find anything else?"

She turned back to him, her temperature starting to rise. "If I had, I would have told you," she snapped.

"Really?" he said again. The way he drew that damned word out ratcheted her temperature up yet another few degrees.

"Really," she said.

"So, you're absolutely sure you haven't found anything else and you don't know anything more about this...situation."

Blood roared in her ears. Her jaw was clenched so tight she was pretty sure she'd have trouble opening her mouth. Her eyelid twitched. Her hands curled into fists by her sides. She took a deep breath. She. Would. Not. Explode. "Well?" That demanding tone and the suspicious look erased all her good intentions as if they had never existed.

"You pompous ass!" she shouted.

"What did you say?" He stared at her, his eyes wide, as if he couldn't believe the words that had left her mouth.

"You heard me. You are a pompous, ungrateful ass. All I've done is try to help you, and what do I get in return? I apparently end up at the top of your list of suspects. And hell, I wouldn't have cared. It's not as if it's the first time this has happened. But where I draw the line is having my integrity questioned." She was shouting. She knew she shouldn't be. But she had expected more from him.

"Stop shouting, you insane woman." He wasn't quite shouting himself, but he wasn't far off. "What do you expect from me? You seem to know so much about what's going on, yet you claim no involvement. You find things that apparently the forensics team missed, and your damned conclusions are as good as any detective that's been on the job for more than a decade. But you claim to be a magazine editor. So, what the heck am I supposed to believe?"

"Maybe that I have more than two neurons and know how to use them? For goodness sake! You're a detective! Use your brain! If I really were involved, why the hell would I give you all this information? Wouldn't it be logical for me to completely derail your investigation instead of helping you?"

"How do I know you're helping me? Maybe you're trying to slow me down while your accomplices clean up the real crime scene. Maybe by this time tomorrow, you'll be in the Cayman Islands, sunning yourself on the beach, enjoying the proceeds from your organ trafficking ring."

Diana's mouth fell open. "Organ trafficking?" She

paled. She didn't know what shocked her more. The fact that there was an organ trafficking ring active in Vancouver or that the detective thought her capable of something as heinous as being involved with one.

"Damn! I shouldn't have told you that." He ran a hand through his hair in frustration. Apparently, she wasn't the only one who got foot-in-mouth disease.

"You actually think I'm capable of doing something like that?"

He looked at her defiantly. She could see the indecision on his face. "I don't know," he admitted softly. "I've seen a lot of things. I'm not surprised by much anymore..." he trailed off.

Though the look on his face tugged at her heartstrings, she steeled herself. "Well, that's your problem, not mine." Her tone was glacial. She didn't have to put up with his crap. "You know what? Get on with your investigation. Pretend you never met me. I hope, for your sake, that you catch these people before we're knee-deep in bodies missing organs." She turned on her heel and marched away.

Diana didn't look back. She stalked over to her building. Only once she was safely in the elevator did she crumble. Tears fell. For some reason, she had expected him to be different. But he was just like everyone else. A judgmental bonehead.

She let herself into her apartment and slammed the door behind her so hard that Max woke up and started barking like crazy. When he realized it was only her, he quieted down and launched himself at her. She smiled softly and sat on the floor cuddling him.

"You love me, right Max? You'll always love me. And you'll never think me capable of killing someone to steal their organs, right?" Max whined and licked her face. Diana giggled. Then she sighed. Could she really let it all go? She shook her head at her own stupidity but the fact was that she couldn't. A man had died. If she could help in some small way to bring him justice, then she had to do it.

So, she got to her feet and walked out onto her balcony. She glanced down at the crime scene to see that the detective hadn't left yet. Apparently, he'd decided to do some more investigating. He searched the area for at least another fifteen minutes but didn't appear to find anything else. She watched him as he sat on his haunches in the area where she'd found the blood on the tree. He pulled a knife out of his back pocket along with an evidence bag and cut a piece of bark off. He bagged it. So, he was going to get it analyzed. Good call. He got to his feet and walked away. He never once looked up.

Before she turned to go back inside, Diana noticed the woman from earlier still sitting on the bench, reading her magazine. Diana really hoped she hadn't heard too much of their argument. She didn't want the neighbors to think she was crazy. She shrugged. It wasn't as if it mattered, anyway. She'd likely never see the woman again. She walked back into her apartment, forgetting all about her.

After a quick shower to get rid of the film of dust that had settled on her skin after her foray around "the tree", as she'd come to think of it, Diana grabbed another cup of coffee. She eyed the chocolate bar that she kept for emergencies but decided against it. This wasn't a chocolate situation. At least not yet.

She walked back into the living room and fired up her computer. It was time to do some work. But first... She opened up a file marked *DB_Royal_Bay*, ignoring the lengthy list of other files in the folder that all started with DB but featured different locations and dates. She read through the file, made a few more pertinent notes and closed it. She'd discovered that allowing information to percolate in her subconscious for a while helped her gain a better understanding of what was going on. It let her "see" connections that she may have otherwise overlooked.

Diana navigated to another folder and opened up an article she had been editing. It wasn't long before she was engrossed in her task. An hour later, she saved the changes she had made and stretched with a satisfied smile. Now, she could relax for a while and then turn her attention back to the body by the beach. She checked the time. Time for lunch.

As she was staring into her fridge trying to decide what to eat, her doorbell rang. She didn't have to wonder who it was for long. By the way Max started to yip and scratch at the door in excitement, it could only be one person. She was not in the mood for another argument. She could pretend she wasn't home.

Peter started banging on the door. "Diana, I know you're home. Open up!"

She was Diana now? And how did he know she was home? She decided to keep quiet. "Diana, I know you're in there." He kept banging on the door. Diana realized that she was going to have to talk to him or all her neighbors would find out she was involved in a murder case.

She walked over to the door. "Go away! I don't want to talk to you," she said.

"Please, open up," he said, more gently this time.

"I'd rather not, thank you very much."

"We need to talk." He hesitated for a moment. "I need your help."

Diana snorted. Though her curiosity was like a fire in her stomach, she wasn't ready to back down just yet. "You should have thought of that before insulting me."

"Look, this is ridiculous. Just let me in so we can talk." Diana was intent on getting him to grovel some more when he suddenly said the magic words. "I went to the hotel and found the scene of the crime."

## CHAPTER FOUR

DIANA YANKED THE door open so fast, Peter nearly fell into her apartment. She tried to hide her grin at the very ungraceful way he caught himself on her doorjamb. That should teach him not to lean against people's doors in future. She closed it behind him.

Max, ever the traitor, made a beeline for the detective. "Max, no. Bed!"

Peter shook his head. "It's okay," he said with a smile. He lowered himself and gave Max a good scratch. Her dog was in heaven. And that's when Diana realized she was starting to hate Peter Hopkinson. One moment, she was arguing with him, ready to kill him, or at the very least, rearrange his face. The next moment, he was so gentle and cute. Ugh! He was driving her nuts.

She leaned against the door, watching him. He made such an unusual picture. He was a big man. And she had a small dog. He could easily pick Max up with one hand. But he was being so sweet. She felt her heart soften.

"I was just going to grab some lunch." Her voice was not

supposed to come out like that. Husky. She cleared her throat. "Do you want something?"

He looked up at her warily. It struck her that he resembled a wild animal in that moment, his eyes assessing and calculating. Was she being serious with her offer of food? Or was she going to go supernova on him again? It was written all over his face.

She huffed in irritation. "I'm not going to poison you," she said, thinking back to her cyanide joke. "It's just an offer of food."

He smiled at her sheepishly. "Sorry, I'm just not sure where I stand with you."

She shrugged a shoulder. "At the moment, you don't stand anywhere. I'm just offering you some food. Now, do you want something or not?"

"Sure, that would be great," he replied with a cautious smile.

"Smoked salmon and cream cheese sandwiches with salad." She pulled shut a door that was slightly ajar and sailed into the kitchen.

"Sounds amazing."

He followed her and took a seat on one of the bar stools surrounding the island. "So, tell me how I can help you, Detective Hopkinson." She opened her fridge and pulled out the ingredients she needed.

"You know, I've never done this before, and I'm still not sure I'm doing the right thing talking to you now. I'm used to following the rules. I'm a military man. Following the rules is in my blood. But this case..." he paused for a moment and looked up at her. "I need a fresh perspective."

Diana nodded. "I'll do what I can," she said. She busied herself making the sandwiches, giving him the time and space he needed to get over the fact that he was going to break the rules. He was clearly uncomfortable with the idea, but he was affected by this case. It had disturbed him enough that he was willing to go against some very ingrained principles.

He watched her as she started chopping vegetables for the salad. "Those are some serious knife skills you've got there," he said. Diana looked up in surprise at the comment.

"I like to cook," she said by way of explanation.

He cocked an eyebrow in disbelief. She was still chopping away while staring straight at him. Most other people would have chopped off a finger by now. He let it slide, though, clearly more interested in solving his case than her ability to slice raw onion into transparent slivers while looking elsewhere. She breathed a small sigh of relief.

"So, you said you went to the hotel?" she prompted him.

"Yeah, and found our crime scene."

She raised her knife, pointing the tip at him. "Hang on a second. Before I get back on this merry-go-round, we need to get one thing straight. If you accuse me of being behind all this one more time, even if it's just with a suspicious look, I swear I'll show you precisely how deadly a frying pan can be when I hit you upside the head with it."

He let out a bark of laughter. "I promise, no funny looks or accusations. Though seeing you wield a frying pan might just be worth the risk."

She smiled and shook her head, going back to her task. "So, I'm assuming the crime scene was a hotel room?"

He nodded, his face serious again. "Exactly. The thing is that Doc Riddle – that's the M.E. – found that the guy's kidneys and liver had been removed and he'd been left to bleed out."

The knife paused for a fraction of a second. "Organ trafficking," she said with a nod. "I'm not surprised they took the kidneys."

"Why do you say that?"

"I did a story a few years ago about organ trafficking. I learned more than I ever wanted to know about how the black market for organs works. It's a very big and very lucrative trade. It's active all over the world. And kidneys tend to be moved most often because they are the cheapest and easiest to get."

"Killing someone is easy?" Peter sputtered.

Diana rolled her eyes. "Don't be ridiculous. They don't have to kill anyone. We all have two kidneys and can survive just fine with only one. And a healthy liver will regenerate once part of it is removed and transplanted. Live donors are used all the time, especially when a family member is a match. As I'm sure you know, if there's no live donor, you go on the transplant list and wait for a match. The third option, if you are rich, unscrupulous, and desperate, is to buy an organ on the black market."

"Go on."

"These rings often source organs from places like China and India where they can pay upwards of $500 for something like a kidney. They bring the candidates over here, perform the surgery, and then ship the patient back home, with no one the wiser. They then sell the organs for tens or hundreds of thousands of dollars."

"But if they can do it like that without attracting attention to themselves, why kill this guy? Wouldn't it draw down more heat than necessary on what they're doing? We may never have learned of them if it hadn't been for the body showing up practically on your doorstep."

"The only explanation I can come up with is that Mr.

Perez is unique in some way. He must have a very rare combination of blood and HLA typing."

"What's HLA typing?"

"It's a criteria used to match organ donors to recipients, along with blood type."

"So, what you're saying is that Perez was the only person to match the buyer. He must have refused to donate willingly so they took the organs by force and killed him?"

Diana nodded as she tipped the vegetables from the cutting board into the bowl. "Or they planned to kill him from the outset. Clearly, compassion for the victim wasn't their top priority. I'm sure you'll find that a crazy amount of money changed hands to get hold of those organs. As you said, this is a ridiculous risk for an organ trafficking ring. They've basically exposed themselves, so the money must have really been worth it."

Peter nodded, watching Diana as she dressed the salad and pulled out two plates and two forks. She set the plate of sandwiches and the bowl of salad in the middle of the table, just to his right, and took a seat on the bar stool next to him. "Dig in," she said, after placing a plate and fork in front of him.

"Thanks." He reached over and grabbed a sandwich. He took a bite out of it and munched thoughtfully. After he swallowed, he said, "There's something I don't get. Doc Riddle said that they didn't use anesthesia, that Perez was cut open while he was awake."

Diana's fork froze halfway to her mouth. "What?"

Peter nodded. "The Doc didn't find anything in Perez's blood work or lungs to indicate the presence of anesthetic and the shape of the cut led him to conclude Perez was awake and aware when the procedure started."

Diana took a bite out of her sandwich, analyzing what

she'd just heard. "There's something very bad going on here."

"I agree."

"What did you find in the hotel room?"

"It was almost completely spotless by the time I got there, but they forgot to check one thing." Diana rolled her eyes. Something so simple, yet so important.

"And so did the maid." Peter carried on. "I found a piece of blood-soaked gauze under the bed."

"Bingo! I'm guessing it was Perez's blood."

"I think so. I'm still waiting for the DNA results but, unlike what you see on TV, these things can take a few days."

"In a few days, these guys will have cleared out never to be heard of again," she said.

"Yeah, I know. And that's my problem. My hands are tied until I get the results from the lab. My superintendent doesn't want me going around asking questions until we're certain that the hotel really is the scene of the crime."

"So, he'd rather wait and risk these guys escaping?"

Peter nodded. "It's politics," he said with a shrug.

"What does politics have to do with a bunch of thugs stealing people's organs and killing them?"

"I have no idea. All I know is that the super told me to back off until I had proof that the hotel room was the scene of the crime."

"Very curious. I wonder..." Diana muttered to herself. "What was the name of the hotel again?"

"The Hazeldene Inn."

She stood but held up her hand when the detective went to follow her. "Stay here. Finish your lunch. I'll only be a moment."

Diana sat down at her computer and fired up her

browser. She ran a couple of searches online until she found what she was looking for. She printed off an article and took it back into the kitchen.

"Guess who has a controlling interest in the Hazeldene?"

Peter looked up at her and then at the piece of paper she'd slid in front of him. "Oh, great," he said with a groan.

"Yes, Mr. Barry D. Gutierrez." Gutierrez was one of the richest men in Vancouver. Though he had a number of legitimate businesses, he was suspected of having ties to every illegal activity in the city, from gun running and prostitution to drug distribution and human trafficking. Unfortunately, no one had ever been able to find any evidence to indict him. On the rare occasion a witness had stepped forward, they would end up disappearing soon after, usually turning up in a lake, face down, on the other side of the country. Unsurprisingly, no one stepped forward to speak against him anymore. It was like he was covered in a film of oil. Nothing ever stuck.

"No wonder the super told me to back off." Peter grunted.

"You think your superintendent is protecting him?"

Peter shook his head. "Donaldson? No way. He's been after Gutierrez for more years than I can count."

"Then why did he tie your hands like this?"

"I may, at some point, have had a run in with Gutierrez, and I may have overstepped the mark slightly, and Donaldson may have warned me that he'd have my badge if I ever went near Gutierrez again."

Diana hid the smile that curled her lips. Harassing Gutierrez definitely sounded like something Detective Hotkinson would do. "So, your superintendent is trying to protect you."

"Looks like," he said, drumming his fingers on the table in frustration. "But it's not doing my case any favors."

"You know, just because Gutierrez owns a stake in the hotel, it doesn't mean he's involved in this."

Peter cocked an eyebrow in disbelief. "Gutierrez would gut his own mother if he thought he could make a buck."

Diana lifted a hand to stay his tirade. "Listen for a sec. Gutierrez isn't stupid, as evidenced by the number of times he's gotten off and the fact that he isn't rotting in prison, right?" Peter just nodded with a grunt. "So then why would he get his people to perform a clearly illegal procedure and let the guy die in one of his hotels? He would have known it would lead us directly to him."

"You're right," he said with a sigh. "I was just hoping that he may have made a stupid mistake this time."

Diana shook her head. "I'm sorry, I can see you hate him, but I really don't think he's involved in this. He's not that stupid."

Peter nodded.

"What name was the room registered under?" Diana asked out of the blue. She needed more information if she was to come up with a working theory.

"Give me a moment." He pulled out his tablet to check. "Montclair."

The name set alarm bells ringing in Diana's head. It sounded so familiar but she just couldn't place it. "Maybe the name is connected somehow," she said.

He shook his head. "Unlikely. It's such a common name that it was probably the first thing they came up with."

She decided to ignore the alarm bells for the moment. The detective was right. It was a pretty common name. Then she had an epiphany.

"You know, in a situation like this, if I wanted to find out who was involved for a story I was writing, I would follow the money."

Peter glanced up with a wry look on his face. "I did think of that. But I have no idea where to start, remember? We don't know who the buyer is."

"But you have all the information you need already," she pointed out.

"What are you talking about?"

"Leonardo Perez. Get your M.E. to do a full work-up on him and work backward —"

"Find out who he would be a match for. That's a great idea! I can run the results against the national transplant waiting list —"

"The buyer will definitely be on it because most people don't resort to buying organs on the black market until the situation is pretty dire."

Peter jumped to his feet. "You, Ms. Hunter, are a genius," he said with a wide grin. "I have to go." He grabbed his sandwich and dashed out of the kitchen. He popped his head around the door. "Thank you."

Diana smiled and waved him off. "Find the buyer." He nodded and disappeared. She heard her front door slam and in the silence that followed, she found herself wondering more and more about the detective. Fifteen minutes later, she was sweeping the floor before she realized that she'd cleaned up after their lunch but couldn't remember a thing about doing so.

On the way to his car, Peter called Doc Riddle. "Doc, can I get a full work-up on Leonardo Perez?"

"What do you need it for?"

Peter didn't take offense at the Doc's curt tone. He was like that with everyone. He didn't have patience for small talk – most of the time – and that suited Peter just fine, especially today.

"I need to find out who he could be a possible organ match for," he explained.

"Ah, I see. Good idea. I'll get right on it. It will take a while though."

"How long?"

"You'll have the results first thing in the morning."

Peter sighed in disappointment. He had hoped to make further progress on this case today but there was little he could do about it except wait. At least he had a lead to work with now.

He ended the call with the Doc and got behind the wheel of his car. He fired up the engine. Pulling away from the curb, he got to thinking about the magazine editor. He'd been right to go to her. Her insight had been very useful. His limited experience with organ trafficking would have had him going around in circles. And then, once he'd discovered the Gutierrez connection, he knew he wouldn't have been able to let it go. He would have wasted more time barking up the wrong tree. This way, if Gutierrez was connected, he'd have concrete proof, and if the snake wasn't involved for once, he wouldn't be wasting any more time.

Diana Hunter was unusual. The way the woman's mind worked was uncommonly logical and smart. It was rare that he came across someone who could process information or make connections on the fly like she did. Especially a civilian. And that made him wonder. How did she know as much as she did and how had she honed her skills? And who the hell was she, really?

As his mind turned over, he became restless, and a

feeling of paranoia reared its ugly head. He was familiar with it. Hyper vigilance had become his constant companion ever since the murder of his brother, Matthew. Matthew had been found shot in the head – execution-style according to the detective on the case at the time – and the killer never found. The crime scene had been immaculate, with every trace wiped away. Even the bullet had been removed, so no ballistics match could be made. According to the police, it had been an intricately planned killing committed by someone who knew police procedure well. Since then, Peter had had a lot of trouble trusting people, especially those who seemed to know more than they should.

Yes, Diana's mind was fast. Too fast. What if he was kidding himself and she really was involved? What if she was engaged in some elaborate game? She knew too much to be an innocent bystander. And he'd had the feeling ever since he met her that she knew a lot more than she was saying. She was hiding something. And that feeling hadn't disappeared when they'd eaten lunch. In fact, if he thought about it, the feeling had become even more acute.

While she seemed to keep the doors in her apartment open, including the one to her bedroom, she shut one partic- ular door. She had tried to act like it was no big deal, but she got this slightly pinched look on her face when she'd real- ized it was open. And, every time he'd glanced at it, he'd seen her stiffen slightly. Maybe she was hiding a dead body in there, he thought with a rueful grin. No, if Diana Hunter was playing him, she wouldn't be hiding evidence in her apartment. But she was definitely hiding *something*.

He parked outside his precinct and walked in. He had to talk to his superintendent. He needed a second opinion on the whole situation. No one came up to talk to him as he walked through the bullpen. Most of his colleagues gave him a wide berth when he had what they called his intense face on. They knew that talking was pointless and avoiding him was in their best interests.

Superintendent Donaldson's door was open as usual, but Peter still knocked. He stuck his head in his superior's office. When the man looked up, he asked, "Can I have a word, sir?"

Donaldson nodded and waved him inside. Peter closed the door behind him and hesitated for a moment. Was he doing the right thing? He was going to be admitting he'd broken the rules.

"Out with it, boy," Donaldson barked. The man was in his early fifties and a great police officer. Only problem was he'd stuck his neck out for his team once too often and had angered the powers that be, which was why he'd never got the promotion to Chief everyone knew he deserved.

Peter sat down, drew a deep breath, and took the plunge. He told his superintendent everything about Diana Hunter and what had happened from the moment he'd met her to just now, when he'd left her not fifteen minutes earlier.

"I just can't help the feeling that she's hiding something," Peter confessed. "I mean, it almost felt like she was the detective and I was the civvie."

Donaldson scratched his chin. "We'll discuss the fact that you shared information with a civilian later," he said with a pointed glare. Great. And just when Peter thought he'd got away with it. "But what I want to know is whether you really think she's hiding something or you're just pissed that she's smarter than you are?"

Peter stared. "Sir, you know me! I just want to close the case. And fast. Maybe she can help —"

"But you say you suspect she's not being truthful," Donaldson probed further.

"I don't know what it is. Yeah, she seems to know a lot about the case, but I keep getting the feeling she is holding something back. I don't know, sir, maybe I'm just being paranoid."

Donaldson glared at him. "What have I always told you?"

"Listen to my gut until it's proven wrong," Peter replied automatically.

"Precisely. Dig into the woman. Find out if she is who she says she is."

Peter stood. "Thanks, sir." He left Donaldson's office and headed to his desk and, more importantly, his computer. It was time to find out who Diana Hunter really was.

Two hours later, after reading more articles she had edited or written than he would ever care to admit, Peter stared at his screen and contemplated his next move. There was a file on her in their database. Ms. Hunter *was* hiding something. Significant parts of her personnel file were classified. Every time he'd tried to access her data, he'd come up against the same wall. He thought for a moment. He picked up the phone and put a call through to his former military commanding officer. If anyone could get him into that file, he could.

Another hour and a lot of bitching later, he'd finally gotten his answer. At least, part of an answer. He knew why Ms. Hunter's file was classified, but his CO had said that he couldn't get him any more information. Now, he had to decide what he should do next.

Now that she had gotten involved in the case, Diana decided that taking another look at "the tree" couldn't hurt. Maybe she'd find something she had overlooked earlier. After all, she would have missed the keycard if she hadn't been crawling around on all fours.

Ever since she'd found that piece of plastic, she'd had the nagging suspicion someone had left it there on purpose. That someone had hidden the keycard. It was starting to seem more and more as if whoever had left it was trying to leave clues for the police to find. Clearly, Leonardo Perez couldn't have been the one to drop it there. Maybe it was someone who had been forced into this awful scheme and wanted out. And maybe she was getting ahead of herself. She needed to go down and have another look around.

She left her apartment, making sure to lock the door. She gave Max an apologetic look. "Sorry, boy, promise we'll go out a bit later." She couldn't take Max down to the crime scene because he'd contaminate everything with his need to mark every tree and piece of dirt in his vicinity.

She rode the elevator down, nodding to the doorman as she passed through the lobby, and strode out of her building moments later. She walked over to the crime scene and paced it back and forth. Getting back down on all fours, she crawled around. Her hand knocked against something hard. It was a Swiss Army knife, mostly hidden among the scrub. She extended her hand but froze, remembering Detective Hopkinson's admonition about contaminating evidence. She growled in annoyance. She was going to have to call him.

Just as she reached for her phone to do just that, she got a strange feeling she was being watched. She glanced around surreptitiously. And that's when she saw her. The woman she had seen this morning. She was still sitting on that bench. And she was still holding the magazine. No one spent more than six hours sitting on the exact same bench, reading the exact same magazine.

Diana palmed the knife quickly, deciding it was better to pick it up, evidence tampering and all, than it was to leave it there. She got to her feet and brushed herself off. Her instincts were screaming at her to get going while she could. And she planned on listening to those inner voices. As she took a step toward her building, the woman saw her and got up, heading in her direction.

In response, Diana turned and walked the opposite way. The Starbucks on the corner. People knew her there and the crowd would make it difficult for anything to go down without witnesses. But before she managed more than a dozen steps, the woman cut her off.

"So, did you find anything else, Ms. Hunter?"

# CHAPTER FIVE

U P CLOSE, DIANA realized the woman was much younger than she had at first thought. She couldn't have been older than twenty-five, but she had a look about her that said she had been through a lot in life and most of it unpleasant.

"I'm sorry, I don't understand what you mean." Diana was going to play it safe. Better act ignorant than give the game away.

The woman snorted. "I think you know perfectly well what I mean, Ms. Hunter. I'm referring to the dead body that was discovered here yesterday. Leonardo Perez."

"Why would you think I have anything to do with that?" Diana asked. She had started walking again, forcing the woman to follow her. She was getting to that Starbucks if it was the last thing she did.

"Come on, Ms. Hunter. It's okay. You can tell me the truth. My name is Sergeant Brodeur, and I'm working with Detective Hopkinson on this case."

"I see." Diana wasn't going to say anything else on the subject. Hopkinson would have never sent someone else to see her. He'd been so freaked out about breaking the rule of not talking to civilians she was pretty sure he'd never send anyone else to see her ever again. Plus, she'd seen the woman on the bench that morning. Had she been who she said she was, Hopkinson would have made the introductions. He had said nothing about any sergeant.

"Look, I'd like to go over some more details we've uncovered about the case. Would you mind having a cup of coffee with me?" the woman asked, nodding in the direction of Starbucks.

And that's when Diana's self-preservation instinct decided to exit stage right. Instead of politely refusing and high-tailing it out of there, Diana did the exact opposite. She agreed. This woman had to be connected to Leonardo Perez's murder. Otherwise, why would she be digging around for information about the case and seemingly impersonating a police officer while doing so? This would be a golden opportunity for her to discover more about what was going on. It could take days before Hopkinson found this woman again. She'd disappear into the woodwork and they might never find her.

They walked into the Starbucks together, and Diana waved at the baristas she'd known for a couple of years. They waved back. Jenny was one of those working behind the counter. She was taking orders today. Jenny had been her barista – if one could have a barista – ever since Diana had started coming to the coffee shop on a regular basis. She was a sweet girl and always went out of her way to make Diana's coffee special, even if it was just a more elaborate design in the milk foam of her drink. Diana always made sure to leave her a nice tip.

Sergeant Brodeur indicated an empty table in the

corner of the crowded coffee shop. "Have a seat. I'll get the coffee."

Diana nodded. She didn't even bother to tell the other woman what she wanted to drink. She had something else to do. She sat down and quickly slipped her phone out of her pocket. Since she rarely jumped to conclusions, she had to verify that she wasn't being paranoid. She took a quick picture of the woman as she stood at the counter and sent it to Hopkinson along with a message.

*Is this your Sergeant? Goes by Brodeur. Asking a lot of questions about Perez. At Starbucks around corner from my place.*

She quickly hit send and, a few taps and swipes later, had turned her phone into a recording device. Now, Sergeant Brodeur's every word would be caught on tape.

"Who were you talking to?" the so-called Sergeant asked, nodding at the phone. She set their coffees on the table and looked at her strangely. Diana did not like that look.

"No one. It was just an email from work about an article that needs to be published on Monday. They needed my input." Damn it, she was babbling. She always babbled when she was nervous. And she'd give herself away if she didn't calm down.

Brodeur gave her a critical look and nodded, relaxing. She took a seat opposite Diana.

"So, I'll ask you again. What else did you find at the crime scene?" Apparently, Brodeur wasn't one for small talk.

Diana gave a small shrug. "Actually, I didn't find anything except the body." She was praying the woman hadn't noticed her pick up the Swiss Army knife.

"Then why were you nosing around the crime scene again today? Twice." Brodeur was definitely suspicious.

"Because I was curious," Diana replied with a shrug. "I'm a magazine editor, and I used to be a reporter. It's in my nature to scrutinize things."

"Maybe this time your curiosity has done more harm than good," Brodeur said cryptically.

"Let me guess," Diana said with a sigh, "you're going to throw the old cliché about curiosity and cats at me, right?"

Brodeur stiffened. "If the shoe fits…" the woman snarled. Great, now she'd pissed off a woman who probably had a gun hidden in a shoulder holster under her jacket. Genius, Diana, genius.

"Well, my curiosity has gotten me in trouble before, so the shoe does fit," Diana tried to smile, but it felt as if her face was about to crack. At least her words seemed to mollify Brodeur, who smiled back. Only there was nothing comforting about that smile. It was like staring a shark in the face.

"So, tell me, how exactly did you find the body?" Brodeur asked.

Diana's first instinct was to query why she needed to ask her that. If she was a police officer and working with Hopkinson, then she should know. But she didn't want to give the game away. She didn't want to alert Brodeur to the fact that she already knew the woman wasn't who she claimed to be.

So, she shrugged. "He was leaning against a tree. I asked him if he needed help, and that's when I realized he was dead. I called the police, and that's pretty much it."

Brodeur cocked her head. "Ms. Hunter, I'm getting the distinct impression you're not telling me the whole story." She emphasized the word, "whole".

"I'm sorry if that's the impression I'm giving. But that's all there really is to it. I know finding a dead body should probably sound more exciting, but it's not. In fact, it's rather unpleasant." She scrunched her nose in what she hoped was a good imitation of disgust.

Brodeur shook her head. "You must really think I'm a fool, Ms. Hunter. I know Detective Hopkinson visited you twice at your home and that you were at the crime scene together this morning. And now I find you nosing around the same crime scene again. So, tell me, Ms. Hunter, if all you did was find the body, why are you still involved in this case?"

"I promise you, Sergeant Brodeur, I am not involved in this case. I'm just an unlucky bystander who happened upon a murder victim, that's all." Diana was starting to like this situation less and less. She needed to do something about the Swiss Army knife in her bag. She needed to make sure it got to Hopkinson.

"You'll have to excuse me for a moment, Sergeant, I have to head to the ladies' room." Diana got to her feet. Though she could see Brodeur was conflicted about letting her go, she didn't give the woman a chance to say anything. Diana wound her way through the tables and made it to her destination with a sigh of relief.

Locking herself in one of the stalls, she dug the Swiss Army knife out of her bag and wrapped it in toilet paper. At least that way, the only contamination would be from her. Thinking quickly, she scribbled a quick note with a pen she found at the bottom of her bag. Writing on toilet paper isn't easy, but she finally managed to get a few words down.

*FAO: Detective Peter Hopkinson c/o Vancouver Police Department*

She placed her valuable package on top of the toilet's

water tank. Pulling out her phone, she paused the recording and typed out a quick text to the detective.

*Found knife at scene. Left it in bathroom stall at Starbucks.*

She hit send. That's when she saw she'd already received a message from him.

*That woman is not Vancouver PD. Get out of there now! On my way.*

Diana grimaced. It was too late for that. Another message pinged. It was from Hopkinson.

*Give it to me yourself. Be there in 10.*

Just as she was about to type out another text, she heard the door to the toilets open. "Ms. Hunter, I think you've been in there long enough," Brodeur's silky yet threatening voice echoed around the room. Damn! She couldn't let the woman see inside the stall. She put her phone back in her pocket and pressed the flush. She slipped out of the stall, making sure not to open the door too wide, and closed it behind her quickly.

"Sorry," she said with an apologetic look on her face. "I had something that didn't agree with my stomach and... Well, you get the idea." Brodeur's face wrinkled up with distaste. It was exactly the effect Diana was going for. She headed over to the sink, put her purse down, and made a big spectacle of washing her hands. She was trying to stall, hoping to give Hopkinson more time.

Brodeur cleared her throat, and Diana glanced up, looking at the woman in the mirror. She was holding her jacket open, showing Diana her gun plain as day. "Let's drop the pretense, Diana. You know I'm not a cop, and I know you have more information on this case than you're letting on. So, you and I are going to take a quick trip." Diana tensed. They were about the same size. The woman hadn't drawn her gun yet. She had a chance. Her muscles tensed.

Before she could make a move, however, Brodeur issued a threat that made her freeze in her tracks. "If you try anything, I promise you I won't hesitate to put a bullet through the head of that pretty little barista out there. The only way to stop me doing that is to kill me or do as I say. And since you are no killer, Diana, and I'm the one with the gun, I suggest you go with option two."

Diana wanted to punch the woman in the face. But Brodeur was right, Diana wasn't a killer. She might be able to incapacitate the woman for a short while, but there was no guarantee Hopkinson would arrive in time to stop Brodeur from carrying out her threat. She would not put an innocent in harm's way.

Diana threw Brodeur a frigid look. "Option two it is. Lead the way."

"Oh no, Ms. Hunter. Please, after you. I insist." Diana clenched her jaw but did as she was told. She stepped out of the ladies room with Brodeur following closely behind. "Outside." Diana nodded. This was amazing. She was being kidnapped by a madwoman in the middle of the day, with people milling around, and a detective a few minutes away. But she followed Brodeur's instructions, unwilling to put Jenny at risk.

As they left the coffee shop, Diana saw a black SUV with tinted windows parked just to the right. The back door was open. "Get in the car," Brodeur growled at her. Just as the woman was about to push Diana in, a voice called out her name.

"Diana, you forgot your order!" It was Jenny. She was standing on the sidewalk holding up a bag and a cup of coffee.

Brodeur looked at Diana suspiciously. "I get a chocolate muffin and a latte every day," she lied. "Jenny must have thought I forgot my order. If I don't pick it up, she'll know something is wrong."

Brodeur glanced back at the barista. She wasn't convinced but finally relented. "Go, but remember, you say anything, and I will put a bullet between her baby blues."

Diana glared at the woman. "I hate you."

Brodeur actually laughed. "Good."

Turning around, she stalked over to Jenny. "Is everything alright?" the girl asked, looking at her worriedly.

Diana subtly shook her head. "Check the toilet stalls," she whispered. Jenny nodded. Diana grabbed the bag and coffee and turned. She couldn't risk saying anything else.

Once she got back to Brodeur's side, the woman plucked the latte out of her hands. "Can't have you wielding hot coffee, now can we? Someone might get burned." To be completely honest, Diana hadn't thought of that but, given time, she would have. Now she didn't even have the small comfort of being able to scald someone's lap. "Get in the car before I push you in."

Diana obliged and found herself seated behind a man dressed in a dark suit. The driver, unlike her guard, was short. She couldn't see much of his face, but she could see he wasn't built like a bull. He actually looked quite frail. But he had a gun pointed at her, and his smile was just as predatory as Brodeur's. Was there some crime school they all had to attend where they were taught to smile like that? Unlike Brodeur, though, this man didn't look like he'd ever visited a dentist in his life. A dental plan was not part of the employment package, it would seem.

Brodeur slipped into the front passenger seat. She

turned back to Diana, holding out her hand. "Phone!" she snapped.

"Excuse me?" Diana tried to play stupid.

Brodeur sighed. "Diana, give me your phone, or I'll ask Mr. Smith here to take it from you." She indicated the man sitting in front of Diana, who grinned widely. Diana swallowed back the bile that rose in her throat. She pulled out her phone and handed it to Brodeur. The woman turned around. "Drive."

The man nodded and put the car into gear. They tore away from the curb with such speed, she was thrown back against her seat. After a few minutes of driving, Diana began to worry. They hadn't blindfolded her. They were letting her see precisely where they were going. That could only mean one of two things. Either they weren't planning on using the location they were taking her to for very long, or, the more likely scenario, they planned to kill her.

Pulling up in front of Starbucks with a squeal of tires, Peter jumped out of his car as soon as he killed the engine. He tore into the café, oblivious to the curious stares he was getting. He looked around but couldn't see Diana.

One of the baristas hurried up to him. "Are you Detective Hopkinson?" she asked. He nodded. "I'm Jenny Masterson. I was just trying to find you," she said, showing him her phone.

"What's wrong?" he asked, though he dreaded her answer.

"Diana left this for you in one of the toilet stalls." She handed him an object wrapped in toilet paper. He assumed it was the knife but barely spared it a second glance.

"Where is she?" he asked.

The girl looked worried. "She was with this other woman, and I think she was kidnapped. It looked as if she was being forced into an SUV."

The blood drained from Peter's face. "Are you sure?"

"Yes. I tried to get her to tell me what was going on but she just told me to check the toilet stalls, which is where I found that." She pointed to the object in Peter's hands.

"I don't suppose you got a license plate?"

Jenny looked stricken. "Oh God, how stupid am I? I'm so sorry, I didn't think to look."

Peter shook his head. "You did great. Really. Can you tell me more about the car?"

Jenny nodded quickly. "I think it was a Chevy Suburban – a black or dark blue one. It looked black. And it seemed pretty new."

Peter's mind was galloping ahead. He needed to get an APB put out on that car and the woman who had taken Diana. What the hell had he done? She was going to end up dead and it would all be his fault.

"Can you tell me what the woman with Ms. Hunter looked like?"

"Well, she was about 5'9" or so. She had short black hair, brown eyes. She looked athletic, like she worked out."

Peter nodded. He took out his phone and scrolled to the photo Diana had sent. "Is this the woman?"

Jenny nodded. "Yeah, that's her."

"Stay there a moment. I need to talk to you some more."

Peter turned away. He pulled out his phone. This wasn't a call he was looking forward to making.

He scrolled to his superintendent's number and hit the dial button. "Sir? Look, I need the tech guys to trace Diana Hunter's phone pronto."

*"Well, why are you calling me?"* Donaldson asked suspiciously.

"I need you to make it a priority. Diana Hunter's been kidnapped and –"

*"Kidnapped?"*

Peter winced. "Yeah. Some woman forced her into an SUV. I've got a witness and a description of the vehicle. I've also got a photo of the woman who kidnapped her. It's not great—"

*"But it's better than nothing. Get back here now. I'll get the boys from tech to see if they can trace her cell, and we'll put out an APB on the woman and the vehicle."*

Peter sighed. "Thanks, sir."

*"Don't thank me yet. You better hope to hell we find the Hunter woman before something happens to her."* He didn't need to say anything else. Peter turned back to Jenny.

"I need you to start at the beginning. I you need to tell me everything you saw from the moment Diana arrived to the moment she left."

"Well, I saw Diana walk in, but she wasn't alone, which is pretty unusual. I mean, she's been coming here for years, but she's almost always by herself."

Peter nodded. "Then what happened?"

"Diana sat at a table and that woman came up and ordered two mochas. That was weird too."

"What do you mean?"

"Diana always orders the same thing. A skinny caramel macchiato with an extra shot of espresso, no cream. Except for her birthday. That's when she gets the full-fat version."

"Keep going. What else?" Peter was trying to be patient.

Jenny shrugged. "Diana's a regular. She comes in almost every weekday. She's always really nice and leaves a tip. We've become friends, sort of."

Peter nodded. "Go on," he encouraged the girl.

"Yeah, anyway, it was the order that got my alarm bells going. So, I kept watch. Diana seemed really uncomfortable while they talked. She headed to the bathroom, and after a few minutes, that woman followed her. Then they came back, and Diana looked really angry. But worried too.

"I didn't know what to do. I knew something was wrong. So, I grabbed the first completed order and a muffin and ran outside, shouting for Diana, saying she'd forgotten her usual order, which she hadn't because she never gets a muffin. But I just wanted to make sure she was okay."

"That was quick thinking. You did really well," he praised the girl, urging her on.

"Yeah, well, apparently I didn't do so well since she was still kidnapped."

"It's not your fault. You did much more than most people."

Jenny gave him a grateful smile. "Anyway, I called to Diana and after the other woman said something to her, she came over, and I asked if everything was okay. That's when she shook her head and told me to check the toilet stalls. She grabbed the coffee and the bag and went back to that woman, who pretty much pushed her into the SUV. Then they drove off like a bat out of hell. Will Diana be alright?" she asked after a moment's hesitation.

"I'm going to do everything in my power to make sure she gets back home safely." He meant every word, but he couldn't promise Jenny he would find Diana. It was a promise he might not be able to keep. "Thank you, Jenny. You've been a lot of help."

"Please, find her."

He nodded. "I'll do my best," he said. Turning on his heel, he left the café. He paused on the sidewalk for a moment, hoping against hope that there would be some surveillance cameras around. His heart sank when he didn't see any.

He quickly got in his car, his mind racing. How had he got in this position? His career was about to go down the proverbial toilet and that weighed heavily on him. But it was the thought of an innocent woman dying because of his stupidity that had him tied up in knots. He shouldn't have got Diana involved. He slammed a fist against the steering wheel. To say he had handled the whole situation badly was putting it mildly.

He tore away from the curb. All he could think of was Diana's smart mouth and how much trouble it could get her into. The people who had taken her were killers.

Ten minutes later he parked in front of the precinct and marched straight into his superintendent's office.

"We got anything, sir?"

The older man leveled a glare at him. "This is why we don't involve civilians in police business. They cannot protect themselves. They aren't trained for this kind of work. What were you thinking?"

Peter knew the super's assessment wasn't strictly accurate but he still cringed. He knew he'd messed up. All he could do now was fix things. "I don't know," he admitted. He really didn't know. She'd been so helpful, but it hadn't been her place to get involved and he should have stopped her.

"Obviously," Donaldson snapped. "I've got the boys in tech trying to track her phone. Nothing so far. Same with the APB."

"Damn it! Hunter hasn't got any family in town. In fact, she doesn't have any family at all. Who are they going to contact?" he muttered.

"You're hoping for a ransom call?" Donaldson looked at him with surprise in his eyes.

Peter drew his shoulders back and took a deep breath. He needed to think straight. "Yes, they'll call. If they just wanted her dead, they could have killed her in her apartment. They could have taken her into the alley behind Starbucks and shot her there. Instead, they kidnap her in front of witnesses. So, I'm assuming they want something."

Donaldson nodded. "Your logic is sound, I suppose."

"I'm going to need some surveillance equipment."

"What for?"

"I want to watch her apartment. In case someone shows up."

"Do you think they know of her involvement in the Perez case?"

Peter nodded and told his super about the message he'd received from Diana. "Impersonating a police officer? These people are smart. Get that surveillance equipment. I'll let you know the moment that tech has anything."

Peter nodded. "Thanks, sir." He turned and left. He had surveillance equipment to requisition and a Swiss Army knife to drop off with the forensics team for further testing. Maybe they'd find something useful on it. Something that would lead him to where Diana was being held.

"So, this Detective Hopkinson is your knight in shining armor, is he?" Brodeur's saccharin tone made Diana wince.

"I have no idea what you're talking about." The fact that the woman was going through Diana's phone felt like more of a violation than being kidnapped.

"Well, he was the first person you texted when you thought you were in trouble."

"Only because you claimed to be working with him," Diana retorted.

Brodeur snorted. "Not the smartest move I've ever made, I admit. So you are more involved in the case than you let on. Of course, I knew that."

Diana rolled her eyes. "Good for you. I'll give you a gold star later on, when I don't have a bulldog pointing a gun at me." She looked at the bulldog in question who was still aiming his gun in her direction while driving the car. "No offense."

The guy looked at her but only issued a confused "Huh?" Diana rolled her eyes. He had obviously not been hired for his intellectual capacity.

The driver laughed. "I like her."

Brodeur shot him a glare. "No one cares what you think."

The driver's face darkened. "Shut it, woman. Remember, we're both in on this. And if he finds out the plan, we're going to be in deep doodoo," he growled.

Brodeur said nothing further. *So, the woman isn't in charge. She has a boss. And whoever this "he" is, any mention of him silences her immediately.*

In the reflection of the front passenger window, Diana saw Brodeur pull out her phone. She fiddled with Diana's and then did something with her own. Moments later, she opened the window and threw Diana's phone out.

"Hey!" Diana exclaimed. They were out in the middle of nowhere, having left the city a while ago. She was never going to get her phone back.

"What?" Brodeur snapped.

"What did you do that for?"

"Not that it's any of your damned business, but I will not have the police tracking us."

"But that was my phone!"

"Do you ever shut up?" Brodeur was getting increasingly annoyed. Diana clenched her jaw. A swift retort came to her lips, but she kept quiet. The last thing she wanted was to goad the woman into shooting her.

"That's better. Now, maybe we can finish our drive in peace," she said with a glare thrown at Diana. "Unless, of course, you'd like Mr. Smith here to shut you up. Permanently."

Diana shook her head quickly but refrained from saying anything else. Brodeur nodded in satisfaction and settled back into her seat.

Watching as the scenery flew past them, Diana's heart sank deeper with every mile. The further they got from the city, the harder it would be to find her, especially now that her phone was gone.

An hour later, after they had passed through a small village, the SUV turned off the main road. After a few miles, they turned again onto a dirt track, which led to a farmhouse. Other than the house and what looked like a small barn, there was no sign of civilization for miles in any direction. And it was all flat. There was nowhere for her to hide, even if she did manage to escape. She thought of Leonardo Perez and swallowed hard. Hopkinson was her only chance.

Peter looked around Diana's living room, trying to find a good spot to hide the surveillance camera. He'd appreciated her minimalistic décor earlier. Now it just infuriated him because there was nowhere he could hide the camera that would give him a good view of the room, her computer, and the entryway.

Max whined, and Peter looked guiltily at the dog. The moment he'd walked into the apartment, Max had gone insane. The dog probably knew something was up with his mistress. He glared around the living room again, and then an idea came to him. The camera was small enough. He could put it on top of one of the monitors. The one that was angled slightly toward the door. Anyone would think it was part of the equipment.

After he finished setting up the camera, he glanced back at Max, who was staring at him with a pitiful look on his face. Peter got down on his haunches and held his hand out. Max came to him with a whine and nudged his hand. "She'll be alright, little guy." She had to be. "You'll see. We'll find her safe and sound," he said with much more confidence than he felt. He got to his feet with a sigh. He walked into the kitchen. He couldn't, in good conscience, leave without setting some food out for Max. It could be a while before Diana was back.

He rummaged through the cupboards until he found a bag of dog food. He filled Max's bowl up and put it down for him. Max came over and sniffed at his food, but he backed away without touching it. He turned and looked at the front door with another pitiful whine.

Peter clenched his jaw. He was tempted to take Max with him. If the kidnappers did decide to check out Diana's apartment, there was a good chance they would kill Max. Just as he was trying to decide what to do with the dog, his phone rang. It was Donaldson.

"Sir?" he asked as soon as he picked up.

"Hunter's phone has been found."

His heart skipped a beat. Finally, a lead! "I'm guessing she wasn't found along with it?"

"No. It was found at the roadside off Capilano Park Road in North Vancouver."

"Thanks, sir. I just finished setting up surveillance in her apartment. I'm heading back to the precinct now."

"Good," Donaldson replied and terminated the call without saying another word.

"We're getting close, boy," he said to Max. He looked into the dog's eyes and that's when he decided to take Max with him. His interference had already disturbed Diana's life enough. The last thing he wanted was for her dog to get hurt in the process. As he bent over to pick Max up, his phone pinged.

He quickly looked at it, hoping that Diana had found a way to contact him. He let out a sigh of disappointment when he saw the text wasn't from her. And then he froze as he read the message.

*If you want to see Diana Hunter alive again, deliver $5 million as unaccompanied luggage to Vancouver International Airport. Leave the baggage stub and a ticket to Mexico City at the VanAM Airways airline counter. Otherwise, Diana will be sold off as spare parts. You have until midnight. One minute late, and I start cutting her up.*

P ETER STARED AT his phone, then took a deep breath to calm himself down. In reality, this was good news. At least they had a way of finding the woman who had kidnapped Diana. A way of getting Diana back.

He looked down at Max. There was no need to take him after all. He was out the door in moments, slamming it shut and locking it behind him. On the way to his car, he made another call.

"Ryan, this is Hopkinson. I need you to trace a number for me. I just got a ransom demand for Diana Hunter. I need to know where it came from."

Ryan Scott was a genius with computers. He'd been a hacktivist once upon a time until Peter arrested him as part of a larger case. Back then, Ryan was facing a minimum of five years in prison, but Peter had seen something more in him. The kid had only been trying to do some good, even if his approach was misguided. So, he'd convinced Donaldson that Ryan would be an asset. The superintendent had agreed, albeit reluctantly. It had taken Peter reminding him that they'd never be able to afford someone with Ryan's level of technical skill that sealed the deal.

At first, Ryan was adamant that he'd rather go to jail than work for the system. That was until Peter took him on a tour of a high-security corrections facility. After a while, Ryan had realized that he was able to help more people working for the police than against them. He'd worked on the "inside" for over three years now and enjoyed it. Even if it did sometimes feel like he'd sold out.

If Peter knew one thing about Ryan, it was that if anyone could trace where that ransom message had come from, it was him. "Send me the text and the number, and I'll get right on it."

"Thanks, man."

"No worries." The line went dead. Peter quickly forwarded the message to Ryan, making sure the phone number was included.

He got into his car and fired up the engine. He debated whether to call his superintendent or just go down to the station. He was only fifteen minutes away, but every second mattered. It was already six in the evening.

So, he made the call.

*"What?"*

"I got a ransom message from the people who kidnapped Hunter. I've already sent Ryan the text and number."

*"What do they want?"*

Peter explained the contents of the message.

*"That's just great. Where are we supposed to get $5 million at this time?"*

"Sir, if it's unaccompanied luggage, she has no way of

knowing if there's any money in the bag. Not before she lets Diana go, anyway."

*"Are you willing to risk it? How do you know she doesn't have accomplices waiting to kill Diana if the money isn't there?"*

"Because I'm pretty sure her accomplices won't be in a helpful frame of mind considering she only asked for one ticket," Peter pointed out heatedly. It looked like whoever this woman was working with was about to be double-crossed.

*"Yeah, well, I'd rather be safe than sorry. Let me speak to the Deputy Chief Constable. We'll see what he says."*

"Okay, sir, I'm on my way in."

He put his phone back in his pocket and quickly made his way to the precinct. When he got back, Ryan was already waiting for him. By the look on his face, the news wasn't good.

"Sorry man. I traced the message to a burner phone."

"Crap! What about the GPS? Any luck?"

Ryan shook his head. "Whoever it is, they know what they're doing. The GPS wasn't operational."

"Damn it."

"Sorry I couldn't do more." Ryan gave him a pitying look.

"Hopkinson," Donaldson barked, "get in here." Peter rushed into his superintendent's office, hoping for better news.

"Ryan tracked the message to a burner—"

"I know," Donaldson interrupted him. "Burton's authorized me to buy a ticket to Mexico City. He's also letting us have $5 million."

"He is?" Peter was surprised to say the least. The Deputy Chief Constable wasn't known for his largesse.

"Don't get too excited. Remember that case a couple of years ago with the counterfeiters?" Peter nodded. "The cash is still in the evidence locker. Apparently, it's being kept for situations such as this."

Peter heaved a sigh of relief.

"I've got to warn you, though, Burton's mightily pissed. I tried to cover for you, but there's only so much I can do."

"Thanks, sir." He was grateful. Burton was a vindictive tool who had always disliked Peter for some reason. And that meant that even if Diana came out of this alright, he'd still have to be really careful for a while. At least until he dropped from Burton's radar. Right now, though, Burton was his savior and Peter took a moment to say a silent prayer of thanks for the Deputy Chief Constable's decision.

"We still need to find out where Hunter is being held. We can't run the risk of the kidnapper pulling a fast one."

Peter nodded. "I'll speak to the forensics team to see if they found anything."

"Fine. Go. Keep me in the loop."

"Yes, sir."

Rather than calling Tina, the crime scene unit's supervisor, he decided to run up to her lab. He knew she was always extremely busy as her team handled all the precinct's cases, but he needed her help and quickly.

He knocked on her open door and stepped inside. "Tina." She looked up from a microscope.

"Hi, Peter. I'm glad you dropped by. I was about to call you."

"Please tell me you have something," he knew he sounded desperate but that's exactly how he felt.

"Actually, I do." She swung around in her chair. "Let's start with the Swiss Army knife you brought in. Now, I don't have to tell you how I feel about evidence being contaminated, but luckily for us, Ms. Hunter's fingerprints were in the system, so we could eliminate them. Unfortunately, any other prints on the surface of the knife were compromised when she picked it up. However, as you know, when most people open a Swiss Army knife, they tend to grip the flat of the blade to pull it all the way open."

"You got a fingerprint, didn't you?" Peter breathed.

"Yup," she replied, popping the 'p'. "It's only a partial, but we got a match. It belongs to a Dean Browning. According to his employment records, he works as a registered nurse."

"A nurse? I guess that makes sense considering what we're dealing with."

Tina nodded. "What's even more interesting is that Browning is currently in the private employ of Jonathan Abbott, who seems to be extremely well off and on–"

"The national transplant waiting list, right?" Peter was getting excited. They finally had a connection. He finally had a real lead! "Tina, you are a lifesaver!"

"I'm not done." Peter's eyes widened. "We went over that hotel room with a fine-tooth comb, and while it was wiped pretty clean, we did find something interesting. We found traces of soil containing various pesticides that were banned more than a decade ago. The composition of the soil indicates it comes from West Vancouver, relatively close to Capilano River."

Peter's mind was going at a thousand miles a minute. Maybe Diana was being held around there. Or perhaps in one of Abbott's houses. "I have to go check what properties Abbott owns." He rushed out with a "Thanks, Tina," thrown over his shoulder and didn't stop running until he reached his desk.

Peter pulled up everything he could find on Jonathan

Abbott. Tina had understated the situation. Abbott was rich as sin. He owned a number of businesses, many of which provided services to the oil industry. Now in his mid-forties, he'd been very active his entire adult life, often in the public eye, attending charity events and various galas, always with some model or starlet on his arm. However, about two years ago, he became a recluse. It had never been confirmed, but rumors were that he'd contracted some tropical disease that had done a number on him. Judging by the fact that he'd been on the national transplant waiting list for the past eighteen months, whatever disease he'd developed must have seriously affected his liver and kidneys.

Peter's mind continued to work furiously. He analyzed every piece of evidence and information he had, connecting the dots. Those connections were telling him that Jonathan Abbott might be behind the whole thing. Maybe this wasn't an organ trafficking ring. Maybe this was all about one man.

Then he remembered the ransom demand. Clearly, the woman who had kidnapped Diana couldn't be working for Abbott anymore. He'd have cut her and her crew loose after getting what he wanted. She was looking for another payday. But would she be using one of Abbott's properties? Maybe a remote one, off the beaten track. It was a possibility, especially if that's where they had holed up while looking for the perfect candidate to get Abbott the organs he needed. He knew he was doing a lot of speculating, but, at this point, it wasn't as if he had much choice.

So, instead of looking at Abbott's entire list of properties, he pulled up details of farms in the area indicated by Tina's soil analysis. He was looking for one that linked to Abbott. Thankfully, there weren't that many around Capilano River as most of the area was protected regional parkland. Eight of the nine properties appeared to be owned by private individuals. One, though, was owned by a shell corporation, which had purchased the property a little over a decade ago. Could that be the one he was looking for? No matter. It was all he had.

He quickly printed off the information about the farm and Abbott, then went to see Superintendent Donaldson. After explaining the situation to him, Donaldson agreed.

"It is all a bit coincidental. I'd be more comfortable if we could dig deeper and see if this shell corporation is connected to Abbott in any way—"

"But, sir, we don't have time!"

"But it all lines up too well to be a complete shot in the dark, and we are running out of time," Donaldson continued as if Peter hadn't even opened his mouth. "I've got the Emergency Response Team on standby. They're waiting for you."

"I'll send Johnson and Tate with a few constables to apprehend the kidnapper at the airport. She's not going anywhere. But we need to make sure Hunter is safe first, so get going."

When Donaldson looked up, he grimaced. He was talking to an empty room.

Peter joined up with the ERT, which consisted of a dozen men and women armed to the teeth, wearing black uniforms and protective gear. They looked ready to fight a war. Which was a good thing. Peter really had no idea what was waiting for them in that farmhouse.

An hour later, they stopped some distance from the

farm. Considering the lay of the land, there was simply no way for them to approach without being seen. It was dark out, though, which made things a lot easier. The moon and stars provided the only light. They'd shut the headlights off as soon as they'd turned off the main road. They had to be cautious. The last thing they needed was for the kidnappers to put a bullet through Diana's head as they approached.

They all got out of the three SUVs they'd arrived in. "We're going to go in low and quiet," Michael Stockton, the team leader, said. "We don't know how trigger happy this lot are. They might kill the hostage if we startle them."

"Wouldn't they want her alive so they could use her as leverage?" one of the women asked.

Stockton nodded. "That would be the intelligent thing to do, but we don't really have any idea who we're dealing with, and I'd rather not take the risk. Hopkinson here will engage them first, so I want everyone out of sight, got it?"

"Yes, sir," everyone replied, their voices coming almost as one.

"Hopkinson, there's a megaphone in the first truck. You might need it." Peter nodded and ran over to get it. These people took being prepared to a whole new level. He wouldn't be surprised if they had a chopper tucked away somewhere close by.

"Okay, everyone, gear up, and let's head out."

Within moments, they were all crouching low to the ground and making their way toward the farmhouse. When Stockton felt they were close enough, he signaled everyone to stop. Hopkinson looked around and knew he wouldn't see anything or anyone. They'd all hit the ground, fading into the darkness.

Stockton spoke into his communications unit, his voice

sounding clearly in Hopkinson's ear thanks to the earpiece he wore just like the rest of the team.

"Hopkinson, you're up."

He rose to his feet. "This is the police. Come out with your hands on your head!"

There was no response. Then he caught a glimpse of someone pushing back the blinds to look out. He waited some more to see if the kidnappers would acknowledge him. Nothing.

"Apparently, they don't want to play nice," Stockton said. "Lynda. Johnny. Rob."

The three people he'd called began to move.

"Hopkinson, keep them busy."

Peter nodded. He took a deep breath. "We are armed. We know you have a hostage." He watched Lynda, Johnny, and Rob circle the building and start to creep closer to it. He searched his mind for what else to say that wouldn't alarm the kidnappers but keep them focused on him for as long as possible. "Your accomplice has abandoned you. She called in a $5 million ransom for the woman you're holding." He paused to let that sink in.

"She tried to pick up the money and a plane ticket at the airport. She was apprehended and is now under arrest," he lied.

There was more movement behind the blinds. Peter glanced over to Stockton, who nodded at him and then indicated the house. Peter looked but didn't see anything at first. Then the sound of glass breaking startled him. He saw smoke begin to billow out of the broken windows. They had thrown smoke grenades inside.

"Give it a minute or so," Michael said. Sure enough, four men stumbled out of the farmhouse, coughing and spluttering. "Gets them every time."

Peter didn't wait to share pleasantries. He grabbed a gas mask and rushed into the farmhouse. "Diana!" he shouted. Damn mask! It was muffling his voice.

He opened doors, one after another, practically throwing them against the walls in his panic. Each room he looked into got worse and worse. A thick layer of dust covered everything. Cobwebs hung from almost every available surface. The few bits of furniture still in the house were old and broken.

One room looked a little more lived in. There was a half-eaten hamburger on the table that had become dinner for a cat with missing clumps of fur. When he'd opened the door, the hideous thing had turned and hissed at him. The room was littered with fast food wrappers. They must have been here for a while. He backed out of the room and tried the next door. That's when he found her. The blood drained from his face.

Diana was unconscious. Her skin was pale and mottled with bruising around her wrists and ankles. There was a bruise forming on her cheek. Her hair stuck to her forehead. Her clothing had been removed. She wore a paper hospital gown and was strapped to a table. She was corpse-like.

Peter gasped which, through his mask, half-choked him. His guilt was becoming a living, breathing thing that was threatening to smother him. He rushed to her side and checked for signs of life. Thank God! A guttural sound escaped him when he saw the cut on her cheekbone and the skin around her left eye turning purple. But, he reminded himself, she was alive! He took his gas mask off and gently placed it over her face. Pulling out his phone, he called dispatch to send out the closest ambulance.

"The paramedics are on their way," the dispatcher

promised soothingly. He must have sounded really desperate.

Looking back at Diana, he grimaced. He undid the straps holding her down. He couldn't risk carrying her. He had no idea what they might have done, and he didn't want to injure her further. She looked so vulnerable. Nothing like the spitfire he had started getting used to. He wanted to go back outside and have a nice, up-close, and personal discussion with those goons. But he was already in enough trouble. Instead, he stood, silently waiting, standing vigil over Diana's inert body.

Eventually, after what seemed like an age, the ambulance arrived and the paramedics rushed in. He breathed a sigh of relief and stepped back to let them attend to Diana. It had been forty minutes since he made the call.

"Will she be alright?" he asked. One of the paramedics looked at him and nodded.

"As far as we can tell, she's been drugged and has some light contusions, but seems fine otherwise. She'll have further tests to make sure."

Another sigh of relief. His chest felt lighter, he could breathe again. She'd be alright. It was time to call Superintendent Donaldson and tell him the good news. Time to let the boss know they could take Brodeur down.

Diana came around slowly. She felt so groggy, she could barely lift her eyelids. When she did, the bright lights shot darts of agonizing pain through her head. She immediately closed her eyes again.

"You're awake. Good. That's an excellent sign. I'm Doctor Fraser, by the way."

Diana groaned. "Doctor, why do I feel like a rhinoceros sat on my head?" She tried opening her eyes again. More slowly this time. Now, the stabbing was a dull ache. She could live with that.

"You don't remember what happened? The kidnapping?"

"Oh," she said as the memories came flooding back. She'd discovered precisely how short a fuse "Mr. Smith" had had when she'd pushed him a little too far, hoping to get him off balance so she could make a run for it. She hadn't expected him to turn around and punch her. After that, she remembered little.

"It's alright," the doctor soothed. "You're safe now. The police rescued you. You're at Mount Sinai Hospital."

Diana groaned again. "What hurts?" the doctor asked worriedly.

"My head," she replied honestly. But to be completely truthful, she didn't like hospitals. In fact, she hated them because they reminded her of who and what she had lost. "When can I go home?"

"Well, you were really lucky. Other than a few bruises and a heavy dose of anesthetic that knocked you out cold, you seem to be fine. No concussion. But still, I'd like to keep you here another twenty-four hours for observation. Then you can go home. Is there anyone you'd like us to call?"

Diana shook her head. "No, thanks." She paused for a moment. "Actually, I think it was the punch to the face that knocked me out. I don't remember being injected with anything."

"They probably gave it to you after you were hit. To make sure you didn't give them any more trouble."

Diana nodded. It made sense. "How long have I been here?" she asked.

"You were brought in last night. A Detective Hopkinson asked us to notify him as soon as you were awake."

Diana nodded. "Thank you," she said softly. She closed her eyes when the doctor left. She'd rest a little more, and then she'd get out of there. She drifted off to sleep.

What felt like minutes later, but since it was now dark out, must have been hours, Diana awoke with a start. She opened her eyes and was pleased to find the pain was now almost non-existent. She got up slowly. That's when she noticed the flowers on the nightstand. She gingerly picked up the card with them.

*I'm sorry. Peter Hopkinson.*

She smiled gently. He must have come to see her while she was asleep. She glanced around. The walls were starting to press in on her. She needed out of the hospital, and she needed out now. She got dressed slowly, wincing every time the fabric rubbed against her chafed ankles and wrists. She was relieved to see her purse had been recovered, along with all its contents.

Grabbing the flowers and the card, she made her way out of the room. She walked out of the hospital, head held high, trying her best to hide the pain. She didn't need anyone stopping her when she was just moments from freedom.

She hailed a cab and gave him her address. Half an hour later, she was walking into her apartment to Max's happy yipping. She locked the door behind her and walked into the living room. After she had put the flowers down on the coffee table, she sank onto the couch and patted her leg. "Come on, boy." Max wasn't usually allowed on the couch, but if she bent over to pet him, she might just fall over. He jumped up happily, licking her face until she giggled. She hugged him. "I missed you, boy," she whispered into his fur.

She looked around and smiled. She felt terrible, but at the same time, she felt amazing. She was alive! She grinned. This was cause for celebration. She got to her feet slowly and made her way into the kitchen. She pulled out the dog food first. Her poor baby must be starving. But when she went to pick up his bowl, she found it half-full. Curious. She never left food out for Max. He had a regular feeding schedule, his food doled out in exact quantities to keep him from turning into a barrel on legs.

She picked up a bottle of red wine and opened it. She didn't have the patience to let it breathe, so she went ahead and poured herself a generous glass. She took a sip. That was good.

Next on the celebratory list? Chocolate! She pulled out the chocolate truffles she kept for special occasions and sighed with pleasure as she popped one into her mouth. Wine and chocolate. The best way to celebrate life.

Grabbing the bottle of wine, her glass, and the truffles, Diana slowly made her way back to the living room. She laid everything out on the table and sat down slowly. She put on some soft music and allowed herself to finally relax. She was home. She was alive. Life was good.

It couldn't have been more than ten minutes later that the doorbell started ringing. Diana groaned. She didn't want to get up. She didn't have the strength.

"Hang on," she shouted, then regretted it as a surge of pain ripped through her skull.

Before she could stand, Diana heard the lock rattle. The door opened.

As she expected, Peter Hopkinson walked through the door. "Hey, Detective," she said softly.

"I think we've gotten to the point where we can use our first names, wouldn't you say?" he said as he walked into the living room. He looked rather disheveled and more than a little contrite. For once, Max didn't move a muscle when he saw the detective. He remained curled around Diana.

"I guess you rescuing me from the clutches of death gives you the right to call me Diana," she said with a small smile.

"Yeah, and you nearly dying to help me solve my case definitely gives you the right to call me Peter. Jackass, too," he grimaced as he studied her, "but I think we should stick to Peter."

Diana laughed softly. "Wine?" she asked.

He shook his head. "I'm driving. I just came to check on you. I heard you disappeared from the hospital, and I wanted to make sure you were okay. Should you be drinking? After what you've been through, I don't think it's a good idea."

"I doubt a glass of wine or two will kill me."

"I still don't think it's a good idea."

"Noted. Now, will you please sit down? You'll give me another headache. How did you get in, by the way?" She nodded toward the front door of her apartment. "I locked it."

"I'm a police officer. I know a few tricks of the trade," Peter replied.

"Huh," Diana's response was muted. She thought back to Max's half-full bowl and looked at him curiously.

Peter sat down but he still looked like death warmed over. "I'm really sorry," he whispered then.

She looked at him. "It's not your fault. If anyone is to blame, it's that Brodeur woman."

"Georgina Dillon."

"Excuse me?"

"That's her real name. Georgina Dillon. "Jo-Jo" as she's commonly known. She's got a rap sheet as long as your arm. Jonathan Abbott hired her and her goons to help him get some replacement organs."

Diana gasped. "Jonathan Abbott, the oil tycoon?"

"Why am I'm not surprised you know who he is," Peter said with a smile. "It turns out he got some tropical disease two years ago. It damaged his kidneys and liver to the point where they couldn't do anything more for him. He's been living hooked up to machines ever since. He was on the transplant list but—"

"His typing made it difficult to find a match," she filled in.

"Precisely. And, apparently, when you have so much money and are knocking on death's door, your conscience takes a flying leap off the first cliff it can find."

"So, he decided to take matters into his own hands?"

"Pretty much. He hired Dillon and the others to procure Leonardo Perez for him."

"But who did the surgery?"

"A doctor who'd lost his license for engaging in unsafe practices. It seems that Abbott should be thanking his lucky stars he's alive. Then again, since he'll be going to prison for quite some time, I'm not sure that he will."

"I don't think he deserves to be alive," Diana said softly. "Having money doesn't entitle you to take someone else's life so you can live."

Peter nodded. "Dean Browning, Abbott's nurse, was the one who left the keycard, the blood, and the Swiss Army knife. He said he'd been paid a lot of money to participate in Perez's operation, but he had thought it was only to remove a kidney and part of the liver. He hadn't expected them to remove the organs without anesthetic or kill the man. He tried to leave us as many clues as he could."

"But why did they do it without anesthetic? It seems unnecessarily sadistic."

"No idea. They obviously had the stuff because they used it on you. Maybe they simply forgot it in their haste when they went to perform the operation at the hotel. They couldn't afford to delay, so just went ahead," Peter shrugged his shoulders.

"Ugh," Diana scrunched up her face and shivered.

"So, are you going to tell me what happened?" Peter asked.

Diana sighed. She quickly explained what occurred from the moment she left her apartment building to the moment she'd been punched, from which point she could remember nothing.

"He punched you?" The low and controlled tone made Diana look at him quickly. His jaw tightened, a vein pulsed on his forehead, and his fists clenched.

"Hey, I'm fine," she said softly.

He shook his head. "Sorry. I just hate it when men beat up women."

Diana chuckled. "It was my own fault. I should have contained him but he took me by surprise. I did attempt to kick him in the balls."

"You only attempted?"

"He was a lot faster than I gave him credit for," she replied with a shrug.

"I'm pretty sure you could have castrated him verbally," he said with a grin.

She laughed. "Thank you for the vote of confidence."

He smiled. "Well, I have to get going. I have a mountain of paperwork to get through." He stood.

"Thank you for coming to check on me," she said.

Peter turned to look at her, his face pinched. "No. You shouldn't be thanking me. I shouldn't have gotten you involved."

"It wouldn't have made any difference. You underestimate how determined I can be. I hate mysteries. I would have found a way to insert myself in this one, trust me."

"It doesn't matter. I shouldn't have let it happen. But thank you for your help. Without you, cracking this case would have been a lot harder."

"My pleasure, but I'm quite certain you would have managed without me."

He shrugged. "Thanks anyway."

She nodded. "Next time, though, try not to accuse me of being the perpetrator, okay?"

"Next time? Who said anything about a next time? You are not coming within a mile of anything this dangerous again. I won't allow it."

At that, Diana burst out laughing. "You won't allow it?"

"Look, I know you test out with a genius-level IQ and hold degrees in criminal psychology and forensic science. I also know that you have consulted for the Canadian Security Intelligence Service, and you could probably go over my head and get assigned to my cases, but I refuse to put you in danger like that again."

"If you know all that about me, then you know that it's not really your call, right?"

"I don't care. You will not be working on any other cases with the Vancouver Police Department if I have anything to say about it." With that, he turned and stalked out of her apartment. She watched him go and then gently squeezed her dog.

"We'll see about that, won't we Max?" She grinned.

The whole kidnapping experience had been horrifying, but she'd enjoyed the rest of it. She would have to make a few phone calls. She took another sip of her wine.

"After all, Max, we need to keep the good Detective Hot-kinson on his toes. Can't have him getting complacent, can we?" Diana popped another truffle into her mouth. And smiled.

USA *Today* Bestselling Author

# A. J. GOLDEN

## GABRIELLA ZINNAS

# STOLEN

# A DIANA HUNTER MYSTERY

# STOLEN

BOOK THREE

The characters and events portrayed in this book are fictitious. Any
similarity to real persons, living or dead is coincidental and not intended by
the author.
Text copyright © 2016 A. J. Golden
All rights reserved.

No part of this book may be reproduced, stored in a retrieval system, or
transmitted in any form or by any means, electronic, mechanical,
photocopying, recording, or otherwise, without express written permission of
the publisher.

Published by Mesa Verde Publishing
P.O. Box 1002
San Carlos, CA 94070

ISBN-13: 978-1530979288

Edited by
Marjorie Kramer

THE STREET IN front of the elegant building that housed the Four Seasons Hotel was packed. A throng of people crowded around the red carpet leading to the entrance. Camera flashes exploded almost every second. Dozens of limousines were queuing up, waiting to let their occupants out. As the long, black vehicles rolled to a stop, a team of valets swooped in to open the doors for Vancouver's élite, all dressed up in their glittering, shimmering finery. Rich businessmen, politicians, TV and film personalities exited the cars and, collecting themselves as they took their first strides toward the entrance, prepared to enjoy an evening of dancing and dining to support the British Columbia Children's Hospital.

Charlene Evans surveyed the scene with approval. She had been instrumental in organizing the evening and was pleased to see it turning out so well. She watched as men in tuxedos accompanied women in beautiful dresses adorned with sparkling jewelry as they walked the red carpet. They paused to have their pictures taken and then walked into the hotel, crossed the marble floor of the lobby, and into the winter wonderland that the ballroom had been transformed into.

White silk drapes hung from the ceiling. White tables and free-standing bars lit from within with blue lighting dotted the discothèque area, while the dining room featured large, round tables with snowy white tablecloths. Even the chairs had been draped in white fabric to add to the wintery feel of the room.

Music was playing in the background, and there was a stage set up for a band that would play later. As people walked in, they were met by staff with trays laden with glasses of champagne and hors d'oeuvres.

"I have to give it to you, Charlene. Everything looks amazing," said Neil Johnson, the chairperson of the BC Children's Hospital Foundation.

She smiled. "Thanks. I'm glad all that hard work paid off. Now, let's hope it pays off a little more literally in donations."

"I'm sure it will. Who can say no to helping sick kids?"

Charlene laughed. "Well, even if they could, they won't because they all want the good publicity that comes from donating to a cause like ours."

"I'd accuse you of being cynical if you weren't completely correct," he said with a laugh. "Now, let's get out there and rustle up some money for the hospital."

Charlene nodded and they went their separate ways.

A few hours later, after the four-course dinner had ended, the band started to play and several of the attendees made their way to the dance floor. Charlene picked up her glass and took a sip of champagne. She leaned in to her neighbor, who was trying to tell her something. Suddenly, she felt groggy. It was almost imperceptible and at first, she didn't realize anything was wrong. But something wasn't quite right. She could feel it. She put her hand up to her throat and froze. Her diamond necklace was gone...the diamond necklace she had been lent by a prominent jeweler and committed to wear in return for a hefty donation to the hospital.

Her heart began to pound. Exclamations of surprise sounded throughout the ballroom. It was like an echo that, instead of getting fainter, built up momentum as one person after another cried out in astonishment and indignation. The music petered out. Charlene looked around, her palms sweaty, her breathing picking up speed.

"My jewelry! It's all gone!" exclaimed one woman.

"My cash, too!" said a man. The same sentiment was repeated by one guest after another after another.

"We've been robbed!"

"But how? When?" cried a woman.

Charlene couldn't believe it. They *had* been robbed. But the woman was right. How? When?

"Someone call the police!" shouted a man with the face of an angry pit bull. He was so red, Charlene was afraid he would pass out.

When the operator answered her 911 call, she explained that all the attendees at the Annual Crystal Ball had been robbed. How many robbers? She had no clue. Had it been a stick up? No, there had been no gunmen. Pickpockets? Maybe. She just didn't know.

"I have three hundred guests missing all the jewelry, money, and other valuables they came into this ballroom with three hours ago. I don't know how it happened, when it happened, or who did it. Please send someone." She was trembling, and her voice had gone up several octaves. She had never felt so violated in her entire life. It wasn't just that she had been robbed. It was that someone had got their hands on everyone's valuables *without anyone noticing a thing*.

# CHAPTER ONE

D IANA HUNTER RUBBED her eyes with the heels of her hands and let out a satisfied groan. She had just spent five hours trying to polish an article into something that readers of the news and crime magazine she worked for would enjoy reading. She rarely spent so long on such a short piece, but there was something about this one that had kept her going. Initially it had been a diamond in the rough, so to speak, but now it was a beautiful, shiny gem.

She stretched her arms out behind her, working out the kinks in her shoulders. Max, her Maltese terrier, came bounding into the room and put the brakes on just a little too late as he crashed right into one of the chrome legs of her glass desk.

"Poor baby," she cooed as she leaned over to pet him. Max, of course, was pretending that nothing untoward had happened. If one thing was true about her adorable dog, it was that his ego was so big, it walked into the room five minutes before he did. Crashing accidentally was something he simply didn't do. Not our Max. At least, not according to the look he was sporting that said he had done it on purpose and that it was all part of some grand doggy plan.

Diana got up from her seat. Max clearly wanted some attention, and it was high time she gave him some. Maybe a nice walk would be a good idea. Both of them could use some fresh air.

As she headed toward her bedroom to change, her phone started to ring. She glared at the offending object she knew was about to ruin her plans but picked it up anyway. She cocked an eyebrow when she saw the caller ID. Bill Donaldson, Superintendent of Investigative Services, Vancouver Police Department.

"Hello, Superintendent. How can I help you?"

Thoughts rushed through her mind. Had Hopkinson finally relented? Had he gotten over his refusal to work with her all of a sudden? Did he know anything about the call his superintendent was making?

After getting entangled in Hopkinson's last case, determined to see some more action, Diana had made a few calls, pulled several strings, and called in a number of favors. The result was a position acting as a special consultant to the Vancouver Police Department. They could call on her to support their investigations whenever they felt her skills were needed.

But there, she had hit an immutable solid object. The Chief Constable had been more than happy to avail himself of her services, but no one in the Vancouver Police Department would work with her. Detective Peter Hopkinson included.

It had been totally frustrating. Diana's experience involved working with the Canadian Security and Intelligence Service, but most of the staff of VPD were not allowed to know that. All they knew was some simple-minded magazine editor was trying to get all up in their business. She sighed. The file on her was classified and had to stay that way, but it still rankled.

Hopkinson was a different story. He just didn't want her on the job. She didn't know why exactly, but he had been the first to lead the charge against her, and he had an ally in Bill Donaldson. The head of Vancouver Police Department may have been happy to have her, but his superintendent was not. Nor his detective.

"I just want to make one thing clear. I did not want to make this call, but—"

"Let me guess," she interrupted him. "You got a call from those above."

"Your powers of deduction are astounding." His view of the situation was clear. She couldn't blame him. She knew she had to prove herself; her role in their previous interaction hadn't covered her with glory. That didn't mean she was going to take the superintendent's snark lying down, however.

"Superintendent," she said, emphasizing his rank, "I would have thought that a man in your position would want to use all the resources at his disposal to keep the good people of Vancouver safe. I would have also thought that you'd value the opinion of the Chief Constable, a man you obviously greatly respect, and that you'd take the time to discover precisely why he believes I might be of use to you." She stopped there. She was being officious. She wanted to get into VPD. Antagonizing the Superintendent of Investigative Services was not the way to do it.

She heard a deep sigh. "I'm sorry," he muttered. "You're right. I shouldn't make assumptions.

"How can I help?" she asked without rancor.

Another deep breath. "I really don't know. Just come in. We can talk about the case and go from there."

"Very well, Superintendent. I can be there in forty-five minutes."

"I'll leave word at the front desk. Someone will bring you up to Major Crimes."

"Thank you."

A grunt was her only reply after which the line went dead. She looked down at Max, who whimpered, put his chin on the floor, and looked up at her with his most appealing eyes. He realized his walk was shot for now.

"Here we go again, Max," she said with a small smile. When she had first started out with CSIS at the age of twenty, she had faced the same resistance as she was experiencing with VPD. Many of the veteran, mostly male, agents had also been reticent to work with her, even after she had completed her training with flying colors. She had been thought too young and vulnerable. She had proved her value then, and she would do it again. The difference was now, ten years down the line, she had a lot more experience and confidence under her belt.

She missed the work. Missed putting bad guys away. She also wanted access to VPD resources. Progress on her own investigation had slowed since she had stopped working for CSIS. And there was something about a certain detective she had worked with previously that drew her like a moth to a flame. She wanted to show him what she could do. In their previous case, working on a murder inquiry related to organ trafficking, they had butted heads constantly, but there was something about him...

She went into her bedroom and opened up her wardrobe. A pinstripe pantsuit with a light blue buttoned shirt would do well enough. She dressed quickly, pulled her hair back into a neat chignon, tamed her bangs with some hairspray and applied a little makeup. Not enough to be noticeable, but enough to give her a polished look. She slipped on a pair of flat boots; high heels would have conveyed entirely the wrong message. She had also learned that, at 5'9", compounding her height with heels worked against her when trying to build bridges with shorter, flat-footed policemen. She glanced in the mirror and nodded in satisfaction. She looked professional, confident, and ready to take on the world.

Grabbing the keys to her Prius, she headed out. Along with recycling and buying locally, driving an environmentally friendly vehicle made her feel like a slightly smug, self righteous, though thoroughly good citizen. It was also helpful when she wanted to blend in with the crowd.

Five minutes later, she pulled out of her parking space and immediately hit traffic. It was a relatively short drive from Royal Bay Beach to VPD Headquarters, but today traffic on Beach Avenue was at a standstill. She groaned and drummed her fingers on the steering wheel, shifting anxiously in her seat. She wanted to make a good impression with Donaldson and arriving late was not going to do it.

Eventually, she turned into the parking lot of VPD headquarters. She had precisely three minutes to spare, so she broke into a run. She would not be late. Reaching the building, she paused to catch her breath and smooth herself down, then pulled open the doors to the place her own father had once worked. She steeled herself. This was not the time to be sentimental. It was show time.

She walked up to the front desk and smiled at the two constables manning it. "Hello, I'm Diana Hunter, and I'm here to see Superintendent Bill Donaldson. He's expecting me."

"Yes, of course, Ms. Hunter," said one of the constables cheerfully. She savored his friendly attitude because she knew it wouldn't be long before she would be eyed with suspicion and disdain. The constable turned to a woman who looked to be in her early twenties and whose uniform showed the rank of constable 4th class. If Diana remembered her insignias, that meant she was just one step above a lowly cadet. Diana smiled at the police officer with sympathy. "Stevens, take Ms. Hunter up to Superintendent Donaldson's office."

"Yes, sir," the woman replied as she stepped forward. "If you'll follow me, Ms. Hunter."

Diana made to walk after her, but the male constable stopped her. "You'll need this, Miss," he said as he handed her a visitor's pass.

"Thank you," she said radiating another smile. After putting her bag through the x-ray machine and herself through a metal detector, Diana followed Constable Stevens onto the elevator. The officer stood ramrod straight and was silent, which suited Diana just fine. The last thing she wanted was to make small talk. She needed to think. Why had the superintendent been driven to seek her assistance?

A minute later she was being led through a long corridor. There were offices and conference rooms of various sizes to the left and right, some of which were empty while others were bustling with activity. Most of the "walls" were actually glass, and though they did have blinds, they conferred little privacy. It was like being in a fishbowl.

A pang of emotion sliced through her. It had been over ten years since the death of her father. Ten years since he had wandered these very same corridors. She glanced around, looking for anyone older, anyone who might have known him. Maybe she would have the opportunity to speak to them. See if they had worked with her father. Even find more about what happened the night he had not come home.

Stevens stopped in front of a door that seemed to lead to the only office that didn't have glass walls. She knocked on the door. A gruff voice barked, "Come in."

"Superintendent, sir, Ms. Diana Hunter is here to see you," the female constable said.

"Well, bring her in," he snapped.

"Yes, sir," the constable stammered and moved out of the way to let Diana walk into the superintendent's office.

"Ms. Hunter," he greeted her with a curt nod.

"Superintendent Donaldson," she replied.

He looked up to see the constable still hovering. "That's all, Constable."

The woman quickly left the room, closing the door behind her as quietly as she could.

"Please, sit," the superintendent said. He was trying very hard to be polite.

"So, what can I do for you, Superintendent?" Diana got straight to the point. Wasting his time would not be appreciated.

He eyed her as if he was looking at some strange creature that had invaded his planet and was about to wreak havoc on his well-ordered existence.

"Damned if I know," he said with a shrug. "The Chief Constable seems to think you are the answer to all our prayers. I have no idea why. But, if the Chief Constable wants you, who am I to say no? He's the boss."

"You never know, I might be useful to you," she said, with a smile.

"Last time you tried to be useful, I had to put my reputation on the line to save your hide. I'm not in the habit of working with hot-headed women. I like my blood pressure where it is, thank you very much."

"So I'm not your favorite person then, Superintendent?"

"You are not. And I have a problem with you being forced down my throat, especially when I have no idea why."

"I'm not in a position to reveal my background, but I will be an asset to your team. I can show you, if you give me the opportunity to do so." Most of the work Diana had done for CSIS was classified far above the level that Superintendent Donaldson had access to. Even the Chief Constable was unlikely to know much at all.

She had been trying to coax the superintendent along, but her words had had the opposite effect, judging by the way his frown deepened.

"And that's precisely what I don't like. I have no idea of your background or experience. And no one will tell me. They want me to make use of you on my team, but that requires me to understand and trust you. We totally rely on each other here, often in life or death situations. How can I risk the lives of my people just because the Chief Constable is suddenly infatuated with you?"

Diana took a deep breath. She was trying hard not to take this all personally. Logically, Donaldson had a point. He didn't know her from Eve, so why should he trust her? In his position, she would have been just as reticent and wouldn't have relied on one man's word, no matter how much she respected him.

She changed gears. She likened it to flipping a switch in her head. One moment she could look at someone like a regular person, and the next she could observe and analyze the minutest of details, making deductions that were uncanny and eerily accurate.

"Superintendent, you've been Head of Investigative Services for ten years. Many might believe it was high time you made Deputy Chief Constable, especially with your track record. It would be natural to think so. People may assume that the reason you're not is because you've upset the powers that be. However, what most don't realize is that you haven't risen that far, not because you've been passed over for promotion, but because you've refused it every time. You'd feel too far removed from the action, lose touch with your people, nothing more than a paper pusher."

Donaldson probably thought he was being stoic and playing an excellent poker face, but his expression gave everything away. At least to her. "Right now, you're thinking that I could have researched what I just said online. After all, you can find everything online. Almost. And while it's true that I did research you, there is no way I could possibly have found out that your wife recently left you," Diana paused momentarily for effect.

"She's given up trying, hasn't she? Your kids are grown —you have two of them, by the way, and yes, I did find that out online—and she'd hoped that once they moved out, you'd be around more. But you are the job. You love the thrill of the chase. You find it easier to deal with criminals and people like you, those who love the adrenaline rush, than you do your own family. I bet you turned down a promotion recently too, and that was the straw that broke the camel's back."

She paused once again, for just a heartbeat. "Oh, and in your spare time you enjoy ocean fishing, gardening, and spending time at the animal shelter with the dogs," she finished crisply.

Diana took a deep breath and was about to launch into another monologue when he put his hands up. "Alright, I get it." He was trying to hide his shock but wasn't doing a good job of it. "How did you know all that about me?" he asked.

Diana sighed. "I'm very good at observing details and analyzing them. For example, I know your wife left you recently because your shirt is slightly crumpled. You are a stickler for rules, so the only reason you'd show up to work looking less than your best is because you haven't yet figured out how to handle all those mundane tasks your wife did for you.

"I can tell you like ocean fishing because of the calluses on your hands, as well as the tiny puncture marks on your palms, which are probably from handling bait. The photo of you with that impressive salmon on the shelf over there is a dead giveaway, too. I knew about the gardening because of the slight smell of fertilizer in here—you most likely picked some up on your shoe while cutting the flowers in that basket on your desk—which is rather incongruous, by the way. And you have a few strands of what appears to be animal hair on your suit. Considering the different colors, lengths, and textures, it either means you have a lot of dogs, which is unlikely given your work schedule, or you go down to the shelter to spend time with the animals there."

"That's good. But how did you know I'd turned down the promotions and why I did it? No one has ever figured that out before, not even my wife."

"The promotions were easy to deduce. First of all, you have more commendations than anyone can shake a stick at. Secondly, your track record is extremely impressive. These two facts would be more than enough to get you promoted. Now, some might argue that you have been passed over because your tell-it-like-it-is attitude rubbed certain people the wrong way and because you'll go to any length to protect your officers, even if that means a faceoff with a higher authority. However, were that the case, you wouldn't have been promoted to superintendent in the first place, and you certainly wouldn't still be in the same job. Ergo, it stands to reason that you were offered a series of promotions but turned them down."

"Hmm, not bad, Ms. Hunter. Not bad."

"Not bad?" Diana asked, letting a little cockiness bleed into her tone. She was good at what she did, and she knew it. He would discover it soon enough.

"You haven't told me how you worked out why I didn't accept the offers."

"That's simple. You like to be close to the action, which is why your people respect you like they do. Someone with your history and motivation would never accept a role that was far away from the sharp end. You like to be involved, a fact that became clear when you called me directly, and moving to the top of the building wouldn't afford you that opportunity. Your micro expressions are also a dead give-away. You wince slightly every time I mention the role of DCC, and you glance at the stack of paperwork on your desk that has been sitting there for so long that it's gathered a fine layer of dust. You wouldn't want to become Deputy Chief Constable because you already think you waste too much time on paperwork and other bureaucratic tasks."

Donaldson eyed her and then nodded with a satisfied look on his face. The sudden change of demeanor took Diana momentarily by surprise. "And you've just played me," she said with a grimace, "and I fell for it. Nicely done, Superintendent."

"What do you mean?" he asked curiously.

"You know more about me than you let on. You do know how I can help you and what my skills are, but for some reason, you played on my insecurities to get me to demonstrate precisely what I can do." Her gaze bore into his, and his wide-eyed, innocent expression was a dead give-away. "I won't be making that mistake again."

"Why would you think I'd do something like that?"

"Probably because you aren't at liberty to share any details about me with your team, and the easiest and fastest way to convince whoever will be working with me of what I can do is by showing them." She looked around Donaldson's office quickly. "I'm assuming you've rigged a camera and a mic in here somewhere. Probably in those flowers," she said nodding at the basket of colorful blooms that sat on his desk, "I thought they didn't fit."

Donaldson grinned. "You are quite impressive. You got me in less than ten minutes. No one has ever done that before." He paused. "You two can come in now."

She didn't think a second had passed before the door opened and two men almost fell over themselves to get inside Donaldson's office. Both were tall and well-built. What was it with VPD? Was being highly attractive a prerequisite to getting the job? Even Donaldson was a good-looking man, despite being a good twenty years older than the two who had just poured through the door. And then there had been her father. He had been a fine man, too.

"Satisfied?" Donaldson asked the two men.

"Very," said the dark-haired one.

"If she can shoot too, I'm going to marry her," his red-headed partner declared with a grin.

"I'm certain that Ms. Hunter can handle a weapon reasonably well," Donaldson said with a wink at her. Diana raised an eyebrow. The superintendent's presence had completely changed. Clearly, the Chief Constable had been a lot more forthcoming than he should have been.

"Please, call me Diana," she said. "And the Superintendent is correct. I can handle a weapon."

"I hear wedding bells in our future, Diana."

She rolled her eyes.

"You sure about that, Nik? You do realize the lady is probably a crack shot and could and probably would shoot you with searing accuracy when you inevitably messed up, right?" The dark-haired detective turned to her and smiled. "Excuse my oaf of a partner who apparently has no manners. I'm Detective Scott Rutledge, and this is my partner, Detective Nik Ericson."

She smiled. "Pleased to meet you."

Rutledge was about to shake her hand when Ericson shouldered his way in front of his partner and grabbed her hand in a strong grip. "The pleasure is all mine," he purred.

"You'll have to excuse my idiot partner. His IQ drops into single digits when faced with a beautiful and highly intelligent woman," Rutledge added.

Diana shook her head. They were as bad as each other. Ericson was more the playboy type, while Rutledge had a smooth charm that probably knocked most women off their feet. She wouldn't bite. She had to work with these guys, which meant laying down the law. And she also knew exactly what they were doing. They were trying to knock her off balance. It was a routine that probably worked well for them, especially when trying to get information. And she had a strong suspicion it was also a defense mechanism. So, she would play the game, for now anyway.

Before she could formulate an appropriate response, Donaldson intervened. "If you two have quite finished, I'd like to get some work done. Not that we're in any sort of hurry," he ended sarcastically.

The two men instantly transformed. Gone was the flippant attitude. It was replaced with a laser-like focus, like a cat closing in on its prey. Every muscle stilled, their gazes sharpened, and an air of danger surrounded the two men. The charming, laid-back attitude had been an act, too.

"We've set everything up in Conference Room 3."

"Lead the way," Donaldson said as he got to his feet."

CHAPTER TWO

THEY HAD MOVED to a conference room with a large, white, oval table, cream-colored chairs, and a touch screen mounted on one wall. There were a few files strewn on the table and a map of Vancouver on the screen with three red dots. Diana was finally going to find out why Donaldson had called her in.

"Ericson and Rutledge are part of the Robbery, Assault, and Arson Unit. They specialize in high-profile theft cases," Donaldson began. "Recently, we've had two major robberies that are unlike anything we've ever seen before. We have no leads, and the DCC," he paused to smirk at her, "and Chief Constable are coming down on us hard to find the perps and put them behind bars."

"Which is why you called me in."

"Exactly." He turned to look at the two detectives, who had been quiet so far.

Rutledge grabbed a file. "This is the first robbery. It happened exactly one month ago at the Four Seasons during the Annual Crystal Ball."

"What did they take?" Diana asked, as she reached for

the file. She had read about the heist in the local paper, but there had been scant details.

"Everything," Ericson replied.

Diana paused, "What do you mean, everything?"

"Everyone attending the Ball was robbed of all their jewelry, money, and other valuables." It was Rutledge who answered.

"And that's not the worst of it," grumbled Ericson.

"We'll get to that in a moment," Donaldson said. "What's interesting is how they're pulling it off."

When Donaldson didn't continue and the two detectives were just as silent, Diana prodded them. "So, how *did* they pull it off?"

"That's the thing. We have absolutely no idea," Rutledge answered, his palms up and fingers wide in obvious frustration.

"What do you mean?"

"All we know for sure is that everyone at the ball entered the building with their jewelry and valuables, then realized halfway through the party that it was all missing. It's as if someone waved a wand and everything worth anything disappeared."

Diana looked up from the thin file she was looking at to stare in surprise at Ericson. "Pickpockets?" she asked.

"That's what we thought at first, but we figured it couldn't be. There was no way for them to steal everything from hundreds of people in one place. Not without *someone* noticing their valuables were missing while it was happening. They'd have to steal everything from everyone all at once. It would have required a huge crew and been obvious," Rutledge said.

The file Diana was holding was mainly made up of photos of the missing items. There was also a list of attendees and staff. "No interview notes from witnesses?" she asked.

Ericson handed her a tablet. On the screen, there was a list of files, each labeled with a name. She opened one and saw that there were very few notes. She looked up at the detectives. "There isn't much here."

"That's the thing. There were no witnesses. No one saw anything. They all said the same thing. They suddenly discovered all their valuables were missing, yet they had no idea what had happened. One moment, they had everything, the next, it was all gone."

Diana looked through the other files, skimming through them quickly. Although there were slight variations, everyone had pretty much said the same thing, just as Ericson had explained.

"And that right there is the problem. How can we find these guys when we don't have a clue how they actually pulled the job off? We're not even sure where to start. We've gone through the regular stuff of interviewing everyone, checking out the staff, and so on. But no one knows anything. No one saw anything. It's almost as if it didn't happen. But obviously it did." Rutledge sounded as frustrated as Donaldson looked, which was very.

But Diana wasn't listening. This obviously hadn't been a run-of-the-mill robbery. The pickpocket theory was out. If the gala had been attacked by armed men of a number necessary to control a crowd of that size, they would have as many witnesses as they did victims. So, how did they do it?

"That's not all." Diana looked up at Donaldson. "That was the first one. They've pulled off another since then. The second one was at the Police Ball two days ago. We've kept the extent of it out of the press, but we won't be able to for much longer."

"You're kidding," she breathed.

Donaldson shook his head. "I'm dead serious. This crew have made the entire VPD look like a bunch of amateurs."

"And that's why the Chief Constable is having a fit, I'm assuming," Diana murmured.

"That, and the fact that Vancouver's elite are now afraid to leave their homes and are roaring for action. It must be charity ball season because there's another one being held in three days. We've got to find these guys before then. The last thing we need is another large-scale robbery going down."

"And the M.O. has been the same in both cases?"

The three men nodded.

"What about security footage?"

"The systems were disabled from the moment the gala started. We have nothing."

Diana kept skimming through the victim statements. Something caught her eye. She cycled back through all the notes and picked out fifteen files, leaving them open in the background. "Do you have the statements from the other event?"

"You got something?" Donaldson asked.

Diana shrugged. "I'm not sure yet. I need to see the other statements." She passed the tablet to Ericson who pulled up another set of files for her. It took her about two minutes to skim them.

"You read fast," Rutledge noted.

Diana ignored him. "Who took these victim statements?" she asked, indicating the files open on the tablet. Rutledge took a look.

"It seems they were all taken by Constable Roger Dunway. Why?"

"He made a note in all these files that the victims seemed slightly intoxicated."

"It was a charity event with lots of alcohol. Comes with the territory," Donaldson pointed out.

"True, but can I have a word with the constable? If possible," she added with a smile.

Donaldson looked at Rutledge, who pulled out his phone and dialed a number. "Shoesmith, can you send Dunway up to Conference Room 3? The Superintendent wants a word." He paused for a moment. "No, nothing's wrong. We just have a few questions for him." He turned to Donaldson and Diana. "He'll be right up."

"Thank you," Diana said.

"So, you want to tell us what you're thinking?" Ericson asked impatiently.

Diana sighed. "Not yet. I have a suspicion, but I'd like a little more information so I know whether I'm heading in the right direction or not."

Ericson huffed in obvious frustration. "You know," Diana said, in an effort to distract them while they waited for the constable, "some of these pieces are quite original. They should be easy to identify. Wouldn't that make them hard to sell?"

"Yeah, but they also made off with a lot of money and other easily saleable items. They'll probably sit on the larger ones until the heat dies down," Ericson retorted.

"Yet, they are the most valuable pieces of the lot. These three diamond necklaces are worth more than everything else put together," Diana countered.

"Quite possibly," Ericson replied.

"They're taking a lot of risk. Why go to such a public place? Why chance it? They could simply rob these people when they're at home. They'd get more loot with less attention and heat coming down on them."

"Maybe they're adrenaline junkies," Rutledge suggested.

"I don't think so," Donaldson said. "If it was the adrenaline rush they were after, they'd be more brazen about it. More open. They wouldn't go to the trouble of doing it so secretively."

"The rush could come from the very fact that they've managed to outwit VPD—no offense intended—but I agree with the Superintendent. I don't think this is a case of adrenaline seeking. There's something else going on, but I'm not sure what. First, let's figure out how they did it, then we can look at why and catch who while we're at it." Diana looked at the three men, in turn.

Constable Dunway walked in. "You wanted to see me, sir?" he asked Donaldson.

"Yes. Ms. Hunter here is a special consultant to VPD, and she has a few questions for you about those gala robberies."

The constable turned to her. "Yes, ma'am," he said respectfully. He was radiating tension.

"In almost ninety-five percent of the statements you took, you made a note that the victims in question seemed intoxicated."

"Yes, ma'am," Dunway tensed and a look of anxiety crossed his features. "Is there a problem?" he asked after a moment's hesitation, his eyes flicking to his Superintendent.

"No, of course not, Constable," Diana replied with a ready smile. The man relaxed instantly. "I would just like a few more details. What made you think they were intoxicated?"

"Well, ma'am, some of them had trouble with their coordination, some were slurring their words, and one of them even threw up on my shoes," he said, with disgust.

"I'm sorry to hear that, Constable."

"It's alright, ma'am. It wouldn't be the first time."

"Did any of them appear to have heightened color?" she asked.

"Ma'am?"

"Were any of them red in the face, Constable?" Donaldson asked impatiently.

"Yes, sir. As a matter of fact, they all seemed to be slightly redder in the cheeks than you'd expect."

"Thank you, Constable. You've been extremely helpful."

The man smiled shyly, "Glad I could help, ma'am."

Donaldson rolled his eyes when the man kept standing there, staring at Diana. "You're dismissed, Constable," he said, abruptly.

The constable blushed and saluted before he made his way out of the room. "So, can you share your little theory with us now?" Donaldson asked.

"I wish we could run a tox screen on a few of the victims to confirm my suspicions, but it's far too late for that."

"What suspicions?" Donaldson snapped.

"Devil's Breath," Diana said.

"Devil's what?" Ericson asked.

"Devil's Breath is the colloquial name for scopolamine."

Donaldson's eyes widened. "You think they were all dosed with scopolamine?"

"It's a distinct possibility. All the signs are there."

"Excuse me," Rutledge said, interrupting them, "but could you fill us in on what *scopolamine* is?"

Diana looked at them in surprise. She would have

expected them to know. But, maybe not. The few cases she had heard of in which scopolamine had been used involved rape. The use of it in a robbery, especially robbery on a massive scale, probably made this case a first in Vancouver.

"Scopolamine, or Devil's Breath as it is commonly known, is a drug that induces short-term amnesia. It also makes people highly suggestible. They'll do whatever they're told and won't remember anything. It's used extensively in Colombia in sexual assaults and thefts. People are drugged and assaulted or have their belongings stolen. Sometimes both. They don't put up any resistance. Later they have no idea what happened."

"So, you think our crew drugged everyone at these galas, got them to hand over their valuables and just walked out the door?" Rutledge was incredulous.

Diana shrugged. "It's the only thing that makes sense. No one seems to remember precisely how or when their valuables disappeared. And, thanks to Constable Dunway's diligence, we know that the victims appeared intoxicated, were nauseous, and had heightened color. These are all known side effects of being dosed with a higher than recommended amount of the drug."

"Have you considered that maybe people were acting drunk because they *were* drunk? They were at a party, after all," Ericson pointed out.

"True, but that's a large number of people to be inebriated. Most of these people are pillars of society with reputations to match. They wait to get drunk away from the prying eyes of the media. These aren't your regular Z-list celebrities. No, I'm quite certain that alcohol wasn't the culprit for the behavior the constable witnessed. And don't forget the memory loss. I'm convinced that's why no one knows when they were robbed. It's not because they didn't see anything, but rather because they can't remember what they saw. That wouldn't be the result of alcohol."

"It could be. Memory loss while drunk isn't unusual," Rutledge said.

"Sounds like experience talking," Diana said.

"I had some pretty wild times in college," he replied with a shrug. "And I can guarantee you that I'm still drawing a blank on some of those nights."

"I can believe it. But after you slept off the effects, you realized there was a lapse in your memory, correct?"

"Right. Okay, I see your point. People didn't actually report a memory loss. For them, it's almost as if time skipped forward."

"Exactly. Even if we were to assume it was alcohol, could almost two hundred people get so drunk that they all had blackouts at the same time? Or was it a deliberate attempt at ensuring that no one would remember what happened, certainly not that they'd handed over all their valuables without a single protest?"

"Okay, but if what you're saying is true, then how did they manage to drug everyone at the same time and with the right dosage? I'm assuming you'd need a specific amount for the drug to work as intended, right?"

"Right, Detective Ericson, which means that we are going to have to talk to some of the victims again to figure out the delivery system. While Devil's Breath can be put into drinks or food, it can also be blown into someone's face in powdered form. It acts in minutes. The problem with that approach in this case is that someone would have noticed. And no one did. We'll have to talk to at least some of the galas' attendees again to see if we can learn more."

"Diana's correct. You need to go out and re-interview some of the guests with this information in mind. If this theory is correct, then we've got an even bigger problem on our hands than a few jewels missing from a few top cops." Donaldson had started pacing the room.

"If scopolamine was used, they needed a large quantity of it to pull off something this big. I doubt they got it from a reputable source."

"Can you get it from a reputable source? Rutledge asked. "Isn't it illegal?"

"Scopolamine is a prescription drug used to treat common conditions like motion sickness and depression among others. But it has to be carefully managed or else the results are what we are suspecting here—suggestibility and memory loss."

"We're not hearing reports of it from other divisions — yet. But if scopolamine has hit the streets or will in the near future, we will end up with some major challenges landing on our desks," Donaldson said, now agitatedly walking back and forth as he thought through the ramifications. "It could send the city into crisis."

"Let's not put the cart before the horse. Let's first confirm it is scopolamine and then go from there," Diana was purposefully calm. The temperature in the room was starting to heat up. She didn't want to cause a huge uproar before they had clear proof that her theory was correct.

Donaldson turned to the two detectives, "I want you two to call in some of the guests from the Police Ball. It was the most recent hit by this crew, so people's memories will be freshest. Stick to some of the more low-profile guests. The last thing I need is more chaos and having DCC Burton breathing down my neck."

"Yes, sir," both men said as they stood. Diana rose to her feet as well.

"Do you need anything else?" Donaldson said, turning to Diana.

"I'd like to speak to the crime scene unit as soon as that can be arranged."

Donaldson nodded. "But they didn't find anything," Ericson intervened.

"Now that we know scopolamine may have been used, they could run some tests on whatever they collected to see if it's present."

"I doubt they collected any dishware or food and drink. No one suspected a mass drugging," Rutledge said.

"I don't think they drugged the food or drinks. They would have needed everyone to ingest it at the same time to avoid the alarm being raised."

"So what are you thinking?"

"I'm thinking they may have found a way to aerosolize it," Diana said thoughtfully.

Donaldson gaped at her. "Are you joking? If someone's found a way to distribute that drug through the air, it would be a disaster!"

"I know, but it's the only viable explanation I can come up with. At least for now."

"Rutledge," Donaldson barked, "take Diana down to Tina, then you can get on the phone and get those people in here for interviewing. We need to find out what's really going on."

"Yes, sir. Right, Diana, let's go."

Diana didn't take offense at Donaldson's brusque tone. She was as worried as he was. If scopolamine had hit the streets of Vancouver and was being aerosolized, there was no telling what someone could do with it. In the hands of a person with a desire to exert power and spread terror, it was the perfect, most devastating weapon.

As she followed Rutledge through the building, something nagged at her. Why go to all this trouble to steal? If they could come up with and execute a complex plan such as these gala jewelry heists, they could probably pull off some even bigger scores.

Suddenly, she was pulled out of her thoughts when someone grabbed her roughly by the arm.

"Hey, what's wrong with you?" Rutledge barked, stepping in threateningly. "Let her go!"

Diana looked up into the ice blue eyes of one very irritated but still highly attractive homicide detective. Peter Hopkinson was not happy to see her.

# CHAPTER THREE

"WHAT THE HELL are you doing here?" When he had first spotted her, Peter thought he was hallucinating. There was absolutely no way Diana Hunter, magazine editor and pain-in-his-ass extraordinaire, was wandering around the Major Crimes floor of the Vancouver Police Department. There was no way she was wandering around *his* floor, accompanied by Rutledge of all people. It couldn't be true. But it was.

When the Super had first broached the idea of Diana working with them, Peter made it clear that he would not work with her again, no matter who she called or what cases she had gotten herself working on. The one time he had been foolish enough to involve her in a case, she had been kidnapped. He had found her strapped to a table about to become the next victim. That was all he needed to know about working with Ms. Diana Hunter.

Within VPD, there had been arguments about her experience. CSIS skills were valuable. Peter hadn't been able to uncover information on precisely what she had done for the service, but he thought it likely that she had been nothing more than an analyst; someone who sat behind a desk and provided support and intelligence to field agents. That was it. There was no way she had been out in the field. So, her CSIS experience meant diddly squat. It was one thing to sit at a desk in the safety of the CSIS building and direct others. It was something entirely different to be out in the field, in the line of fire, where one mistake could cost someone their life. He would not make the same mistake again.

Peter had obviously taken Diana by surprise because she didn't say anything for a moment. She stared at him wide-eyed. And then he saw the precise moment when the situation caught up with her. Her eyes narrowed, and he swore that her lips curled back, baring her teeth, much like her dog, Max, had done when they first met.

"Get your hand off of me," she said slowly, emphasizing each word as if he were an idiot. Clearly, the woman was still a menace.

"I asked you a question," he growled. "What are you doing here?"

"That's none of your business," she snapped. "Now, you either get your hand off me, or I will shove it—"

"Now, now, children, let's play nice," Rutledge intervened again.

Peter glared at him. No one got between him and Diana. No one. "Back off," he warned Rutledge.

"Dude, chill," the other detective replied. "The Super asked her to come in and help us out."

"Us?" Peter snapped. Diana was standing as still as a statue. He could almost see the wheels turning in her head. She was working out a strategy to defeat him once and for all, no doubt. Good. Let her try. He would drag her out of there if he had to.

And then Rutledge's words began to sink in. The superintendent had called her? What the hell? The last time he spoke to Donaldson about her, the man was adamant that no civvie would ever be allowed to roam the halls of Investigative Services, and especially not the Major Crimes Division. Donaldson was as against the idea of Diana working with them as he was.

"Yeah, man, she's here to help Ericson and me on that robbery case."

"Why?" Peter demanded. Couldn't the two morons do their jobs? Why did they have to involve a civilian? The last thing he wanted was to get a call that Diana had been hurt, or worse, because of these two bozos.

"Look, it doesn't matter why. Just let her go. This is the 21st century, man. You're acting like a Neanderthal, for God's sake." Rutledge was getting irritated.

Diana turned to Rutledge and actually smiled at him. *She smiled at Rutledge.* "It's okay, Scott, I'm sure Detective Hopkinson was just about to apologize," she said. She turned to glare at him. So, it was *Scott,* was it? Not Detective Rutledge, but Scott. Why that irritated him even more, he didn't know. And it made every last shred of common sense disappear.

"No, I wasn't. You still haven't told me why you're here," he snarled.

She rolled her eyes and yanked her arm out of his grip. "You obviously have some sort of mental deficiency. I'm pretty sure Scott was quite clear on why I'm here. So, now if you'd be kind enough to move out of my way, I'll be getting on with what I need to be getting on with. And if you have any more questions, I suggest you go ask your superintendent."

"I made it clear that I wouldn't work with you," he

persisted. He knew he sounded stupid, but he still couldn't understand why Donaldson would do a one-eighty like this.

"Well, good for you. Seems not everyone agrees with your assessment of my skills," she said sweetly. She side-stepped and walked around him. "Oh, and in case you haven't noticed, I'm not working with you." She threw the words at him over her shoulder. "Come on, Scott, we've got work to do."

Rutledge followed her like a puppy. The fact that the younger detective turned around after a few steps, giving him a triumphant grin only made Peter angrier. Instead of following them, as every cell in his body was screaming at him to do, he turned and marched straight into Donaldson's office.

"Sir, can I have a word?" he asked, trying to contain his anger. What he really wanted to do was storm into the older man's office and ask him if he had gone off the deep end.

Donaldson glanced up from what he was studying to look at him. "What is it, Hopkinson?"

"I thought we'd agreed that involving Diana Hunter in any other cases was a bad idea."

The superintendent looked at him deadpan. "You do remember that she got herself assigned as a consultant to this department, don't you?"

"Yes, sir, but just because she has connections doesn't mean that she won't do more harm than good." Peter knew he was grasping at straws. But he was frantic. He took responsibility for involving her in the case they worked together, and if he had not gone to her for advice, this would not be happening. He had to stop her.

"Hopkinson, I'm only going to say this once, so you had better listen closely. Diana Hunter is here to stay. I've read into her background, and I believe that she will make a contribution to this division." He quickly raised a hand when Peter opened his mouth to argue. "All I'm at liberty to say is that she can handle herself in any situation. Now, this conversation is over. I suggest you find something better to do. Don't you have any open cases?"

Donaldson knew full well that Peter did not. He had just wrapped up his last case the day before, and no one had been murdered in the meantime. Detective Peter Hopkinson was free as a bird.

"No, sir, I don't. Seeing as I have nothing on, maybe you could use an extra pair of eyes on those gala robberies?" If he could not get her out of there, then he would keep an eye on her himself.

Donaldson eyed him critically. "Are you sure you can work with her?" he asked.

"Of course, sir. Why wouldn't I?" He tried to look innocent.

"The two of you weren't exactly quiet out there. I was expecting her to tear your throat out at any moment."

"I'll behave, I promise," Peter said, doing his best to appear contrite. He was going to kill her. He really was. Now his boss was deciding whether to put *him* on a case based on how well *he* could work with *her*.

"You better. Let me make this abundantly clear. This missing jewels case is a huge problem for us. I need her more than I need you at this particular juncture, so if you antagonize her in any way, or if I hear you got in her face at any point, you'll be directing traffic for the next month. You hear me?"

"Yes, sir!"

Donaldson eyed him warningly. "Fine. Go find Ericson and get him to brief you. You need to cool down. You know, just in case you can't control your temper around her." The raised eyebrow and the challenging look Donaldson gave him made Peter take a deep breath. A tempest of competing emotions was running through his body. He should have dealt with Diana differently. Maybe like a civil human being. But she just brought out the worst in him! He clenched his jaw, bit down his anger, and walked out of Donaldson's office to get briefed.

Diana was trailing behind Scott, paying little attention to where she was going. She was too angry with Hopkinson. "Ignorant fool. Who does he think he is? '*I made it clear I wouldn't work with you,*'" she muttered under her breath, parroting his earlier words. "Last I checked, he didn't own VPD. Does he think he's the only detective in Vancouver? And who gave him any rights over me? The man is *such* a pin head."

She didn't realize Scott had stopped walking. She crashed right into his back.

"Sorry about that," he apologized sheepishly. "Maybe we should exchange insurances?"

"Hmm?" Diana asked blankly.

"Well, we were involved in a crash." he said with a smile.

Diana smiled back, catching on. "I guess we were. I'm sorry, but I don't have my insurance handy."

"Oh well, then we'll have to exchange contact details to sort this out at a later date."

"You wouldn't happen to be trying to get my phone number for nefarious purposes, would you, sir?"

"Me?" he asked wide-eyed and all innocent looking.

"Of course not. I just want to make sure I haven't done you any grievous bodily harm."

Diana laughed. She patted his arm. "Don't worry. No bodily harm whatsoever."

They continued on their way. After a moment of silence, he spoke up again. "You know, Peter can come off as pretty gruff, and his social skills are lacking at times, but he's a good guy."

Diana thought it sweet how he was trying to defend his colleague. But she wasn't in the mood to hear someone defend the boorish oaf quite yet. "I'm sure he's a great guy. Still doesn't give him the right to order me around."

"I'm sure he believes he's got a good reason. He's always been the protective sort."

"I don't need protection. And I'm not some wilting wall-flower who will faint at the first sign of danger. Maybe if he opened his eyes and climbed down from his pedestal, he'd see that."

Scott smirked at her. "You like him, don't you?" Though couched as a question, it sounded more like a statement. And that ticked Diana off.

"Oh, I really like him," she said with a sneer. "I like him so much that I'd love to put my hands around his neck and squeeze—hard."

Scott's eyes widened, and he started to laugh. "Oh, this is going to be fun."

"What are you talking about?" she snapped. She knew she was acting nasty but that was Hopkinson's fault. He managed to push all her buttons.

Scott kept grinning. "Oh, absolutely nothing," he said innocently, the grin never leaving his face.

"You better be," she said.

"Swear. I didn't mean anything by it."

Diana knew Scott meant precisely the opposite, but no matter her personal feelings toward Hopkinson, they had a job to do. And time was running out. They had to catch this crew before the next charity ball took place in three days.

"Whatever," she said, shaking her head. "Let's get on with it. We can't afford to waste time." Diana cringed at her tone. She had been much too brusque, and Scott clearly thought so too judging by the tension that appeared around his jaw and eyes.

"I'm sorry," she apologized. "Hopkinson has a way of bringing out the worst in me. I have never, in my life, considered lobotomizing someone with a frying pan. Yet he inspires me to do so." She stopped talking when she realized she was revealing a little too much. She wanted to stomp her foot down like a kid and blame it all on Hopkinson. She really did. Because it was his fault.

Scott took it in his stride. He smiled gently at her. "It's okay. I'm sure everyone in this division has wanted to brain Hopkinson at some point or other. Must be his winning personality."

Scott made her laugh. She didn't laugh all that much anymore. "Shall we?" she said, making to continue down the corridor.

"We shall, my lady," Scott bowed with a flourish. Diana shook her head at his antics but couldn't help her grin.

A few minutes later, Scott led her into a large laboratory, where a woman in a white lab coat was studying something under a microscope.

"Here we are," Scott said. Tina looked up and smiled at the detective.

"What brings you to my humble corner of VPD, Detective Rutledge?"

Scott grinned. "I'd like you to meet Ms. Diana Hunter.

She's assisting us with those gala robberies. Diana, this is Tina Chu, the head of our crime scene investigation unit."

Diana smiled and shook the woman's hand. "So, *you're* Diana Hunter. The one who got kidnapped?"

Diana rolled her eyes. "I'm never going to live that down, am I?" she asked ruefully.

Tina giggled. "Peter Hopkinson told me the whole story. I don't think I could have done what you did. You were very brave."

Diana blushed, though she felt rather foolish. Had her old colleagues from CSIS heard about her little mishap, they wouldn't have let her forget it. She should have never let herself get into that position. Still, it was nice to hear some words of praise after having to deal with Hopkinson's hissy fit.

"Thank you. The reason I'm here, though, is rather urgent."

"Shoot," Tina said, all business.

Rutledge excused himself. "I'll leave you two ladies to it, if you don't mind. I have a lot of phone calls to make."

"So, what can I do for you, Diana?" Tina asked.

"Well, I think we might have a big problem. I think this crew of thieves is using an aerosolized form of scopolamine to carry out the gala robberies."

Tina eyebrows shot up.

"Aerosolized scopolamine?" The scientist was obviously intrigued by the idea. "Why do you think they're using that?"

Diana quickly explained her theory. Tina nodded thoughtfully. "You could be right. It makes sense. But why do you think they aerosolized it?"

"It's the only way they could ensure everyone would be exposed at the same time."

"R-i-g-h-t. If it's in the air, everyone would breathe it in. The time between the first and last person being affected would be a matter of seconds, especially if it was distributed from different points around the room."

"Exactly. We need to prove it, though. We need to check out the crime scene to confirm the presence of the drug before we go any further.

"If they did aerosolize it, then it must have landed on every surface in those ballrooms," Tina said thoughtfully.

"Precisely. But it's been two days since the last robbery, and I'm sure everything's been cleaned by now."

"But most places don't wash down the walls," she pointed out.

Diana grinned. "Good point! You are a genius. And maybe we should check the air conditioning, too. I'm thinking they got it into the room through the vents."

"Right," Tina said, looking extremely pleased. "I like how you think, Diana Hunter."

Diana laughed. "Thank you, Tina Chu. I like how you think, too."

"Okay, let's get going. We don't have much time to waste. The longer we wait, the more the trace evidence will deteriorate. Can you get Rutledge or Ericson to call the Fairmont and tell them we'll need access to the rooms where the event was held?"

"Of course."

"As soon as we get the green light, I'll gather my team together and we can head out."

"Great," Diana replied with a grin. "See you soon." She started to retrace her steps out of the lab, then came to a stop. She realized she had not asked Scott where she could find him and Nik. She had not even thought to get either of their cell numbers. It was all Hopkinson's fault, again.

Another rookie mistake. Her brain seemed to stop working properly whenever he was around. She groaned in frustration as she pushed the door out of the lab into the hallway beyond.

Speak of the devil. Really? Why now? Why her? Didn't he have a case to work on or something? Was leaning against the wall waiting for her the only entry in his job description? And why couldn't she look away? Admittedly, the whole broody, coiled-predator-ready-to-strike pose looked good on him, but still.

"Hey," said the bane of her existence, softly.

"What do you want?" she replied, entirely too snappily.

He held his hands up in supplication. "Look, I know we got off on the wrong foot and I'm sorry. I overreacted. I shouldn't have been so..."

"Disrespectful? Rude? Crude? Ignorant? Uncouth?"

"Okay, I get the picture," he interrupted her with a wince. "And I'm sorry. Truce?"

Diana glared at him. She was tempted to continue the hostilities, but she knew it would be mean-spirited and pointless. She did like him, which was precisely why he was able to push all her buttons. "Fine," she said with a massive sigh.

"Don't sound so happy about it, will you?" he said with a rueful smile.

Diana laughed. "Alright, alright, truce."

Hopkinson breathed a sigh of relief. "That's good. Because Donaldson's assigned me to work on this case with you, Rutledge, and Ericson."

Diana's eyes widened, then promptly narrowed. "What? So this is another scheme of yours. Donaldson told you to play nice if you wanted in and—"

"He did say that, but it isn't the reason I'm apologizing, and it's definitely not a scheme. I did overreact."

Diana looked at him. Now, like Rutledge, Peter also had lines of tension marring the side of his mouth and his eyes. Did she always have this effect on men? Something was going on. "And what?" she prodded him.

He sighed and ran his hand through his hair in frustration. "I still can't get the sight of you strapped to that table out of my head. You could have died, and it would have been all my fault," he said quickly, putting his hands in his pockets and looking down at the floor.

Damn this man. He always seemed to know what to say. "Peter," she said as he looked up quickly, almost hopefully, "*if* that had happened, it wouldn't have been your fault. I chose to get involved. You couldn't have stopped me if you tried."

"But I should have shielded you better. The moment I came to see you and asked for help with the case, I should have known something like that could happen, and I should have taken better care." He left off, *"Of you."*

"Peter, it was an unfortunate turn of events no one could have predicted. If anyone is to blame, it's me. I should have been much more careful. My guard was down. I've been through much worse, so I should have been better prepared."

"You've been through *worse*? Do you think that makes me feel better? Whatever you say, you were my responsibility. When I saw your face all banged up, I wanted to kill that brute."

"Don't worry, I wanted to kill him too when he smacked me," she said with a small snicker.

Peter didn't so much as crack a smile. Diana sighed. "Let's make a deal. You stop obsessing over the past and something that can't be changed, and I'll let you have my back, okay?"

"You'll *let* me have your back? How does that work exactly?"

"Well, I'll let you stick close to me, of course. That way, you can make sure the boogie man doesn't get me."

"And what if I'm not around? Who'll have your back, then? Rutledge and Ericson?"

"I think I'll be able to handle myself. This time, I'm not going in blind, and I'll be ready."

Peter sighed. "Look, just promise me that if I'm not with you, you'll be careful. No rushing into situations without backup and definitely no taking on strong, ugly men who might tie you up and hold you hostage, okay?"

"I promise," she said seriously. "I will not do any of those things. I will allow you to be my knight in shining armor and do your manly duty. Got it."

"Diana, come *on*," Peter was exasperated.

"Okay, okay, I promise, I promise! I will do as you ask and take all the necessary precautions. I won't do anything stupid."

"Good."

"Now that we've got that out of the way, I'm assuming you've been briefed on the situation."

Peter's countenance changed immediately. He was once again the experienced detective. "Yeah, and it sounds bad."

"If they did use aerosolized scopolamine, it could get a whole lot worse. I just hope I'm wrong."

"I have the feeling you are right on the money."

"I need to find Scott and Nik. Tina and I need to check out the crime scenes again but we need to speak to the venues to allow us back in."

"Scott and Nik is it?" Peter bristled.

She looked at him curiously. "Yeah. So?"

"If I remember right, it took you a whole lot longer to call me by my first name."

Diana turned and smirked at him. "You were so much harder to train," she replied, shrugging one shoulder.

"Excuse me?"

"Definitely much more pigheaded than your two colleagues," she said with another small shrug and a twinkle in her eye.

"Considering those guys, I don't know whether I should take that as a compliment or an insult," Peter seemed completely baffled, then he gave her a big smile. Diana gave herself a mental shake. She was much too tempted to stare at him. The fact was that when Hopkinson smiled, which was rarely, he went from handsome to devastating. So, she did the only thing she could to avoid embarrassing herself. She got down to business.

"So, shall we go find the boys? We really need to get those tests done." Her manner was brusque, but it didn't seem to bother Hopkinson.

"Let's go."

## CHAPTER FOUR

"THERE WAS ABSOLUTELY no need for you to come, too," Diana said as she got out of Hopkinson's car. She slammed the door, probably a little too forcefully. Peter was being irritating. Again.

They were just down the road from the Fairmont Hotel where the Police Ball had been held two days prior. From her vantage point, she could see the entire building. It was breathtaking. It was a majestic pile with architecture that mimicked a French chateau. It even came with gargoyles for that extra touch of authenticity.

"I told you I wouldn't leave you alone," Hopkinson muttered as he got out of the car. She tore her gaze away from the building to glare at him.

"I'm in the middle of the city, at the Fairmont Hotel, no less, with two of your colleagues, so I'm not alone."

"And what's Tina going to do if someone tries to kidnap you again?" he demanded.

"Now you're being ridiculous," she scoffed.

"Maybe, but I'm sure you could do with an extra pair of hands, and this way, I'll have peace of mind."

Diana rolled her eyes and decided to drop the subject. The fact was that his badge would come in useful when questioning people and he was a good detective. She was just annoyed that he had taken it upon himself to shadow her this closely, whether she wanted him to or not.

"Fine. Whatever. Let's go. I'm sure Tina's already arrived."

Peter shrugged, locked his car, and they were on their way. A few minutes later, they walked into the lobby of the hotel, and sure enough, Tina was there waiting for them. She had her lab assistant, Ruth Jennings, with her. Ruth was quite young, probably just out of college, but seemed confident and competent.

"I've spoken to the manager," Tina said. "He's gone to get the keys to the ballroom. He locked it up as soon as we called to avoid further contamination of any evidence that might still be in there."

"Excellent," Diana replied.

"Oh, here he comes." Diana turned to see a portly man with greying hair headed their way.

"This is Detective Peter Hopkinson and Diana Hunter, a special consultant with VPD," Tina introduced them.

They shook hands. "Robert Drummond, manager of the Fairmont Hotel. Pleased to meet you."

"Mr. Drummond," Hopkinson replied, rather tersely. Diana bristled. Did he really have to alienate everyone with his *winning personality*? They needed this man's help and the last thing they should be doing was antagonizing him.

"It's a pleasure, Mr. Drummond," Diana said.

The man, who had stiffened at Hopkinson's greeting, relaxed and smiled warmly at her. "Come, I'll take you to the Pacific Ballroom. We've cleaned it up, of course, but they've not yet started setting up for the Firefighters Ball on Thursday. "

"Thank you, Mr. Drummond. That's very kind of you," Diana said before Hopkinson could utter another word.

She glared at Hopkinson who looked at her blankly. *What?* He mouthed at her behind the manager's back. She rolled her eyes again and shook her head.

She turned her attention back to the manager, who was still speaking. "Nothing like this has ever happened at the Fairmont Hotel," he was saying. "It's simply not right. Our hotel hosts some of the most important people in the world and now our guests don't feel safe."

"Have you held any events here since the Ball?" Diana asked.

Drummond looked over his shoulder at her and shook his head. "No, ma'am. The ballroom's been free for the past two days."

Diana looked at Hopkinson. "Hopefully that will help," she said.

They reached the large doors that led into the ballroom, and Drummond bent over to unlock them. He threw the doors open wide and waved them in. They wandered into the room.

"Will you be needing anything else?" Drummond asked. He was fidgeting and kept looking over his shoulder. Obviously, he had other things to deal with.

"Actually, yes. We'd like the blueprints of the hotel," Hopkinson said.

"I'll have to get them from the office." Drummond sounded put out.

"We'll wait for you right here," Hopkinson said.

Drummond turned on his heel and left the room, closing the doors behind him.

"Blueprints?" Diana asked.

"Just a hunch. Blueprints are always useful. Besides it gives Mr. Drummond something to do."

Diana turned to Tina. "Okay, let's get to work."

"Ruth, let's start with the walls," Tina said to her assistant. They spent the next half hour taking samples from every surface available, even those that had likely been cleaned. Like all good scientists, Tina was thorough.

"We need to check the air vents, too," Diana said.

"Why the air vents?" Hopkinson asked.

"Well, if they did aerosolize the scopolamine, it would be the easiest place to hide the canisters or whatever they used as a dispersal system."

"Couldn't they have hidden them in these potted plants?" Hopkinson asked, indicating the shrubs in question. "That way, they could just grab them on their way out, without leaving any evidence."

Diana looked at the plants critically. They were quite bushy. Hiding something like a small canister wouldn't have been hard. No one would have considered looking there for something suspicious. Certainly not a canister. She glanced up at the vents.

"I guess they could have," she said slowly. "But if they used the air vents, it would ensure a more even dispersal. I suggest we test the plants *and* the vents. Better safe than sorry."

"If they used the vents, they could attach the scopolamine straight to the big A/C units up on the roof, couldn't they?" Ruth asked.

Diana considered this, but it was Tina who answered. "It's unlikely," she said. "Most of these buildings have multiple A/C units, but they service a large portion of the building. Using those on the roof would mean that people in other areas of the hotel would have been affected too."

"But are we sure no one outside the ballroom was drugged?" Hopkinson asked. "After all, they wouldn't know, would they? Scopolamine wipes their memory of whatever took place. And if the thieves were simply targeting the ballroom, the people in the other areas these vents reach wouldn't have noticed anything. None of their belongings were stolen."

"It's possible but risky. Using the air conditioning system would have been the easiest way for them to pull this off. They could hook up a canister to the A/C before the party. Then they could come back later, or even the following day, to recover the evidence."

Diana glanced at a vent. "Dispersing it throughout the hotel seems overkill and unnecessary. My bet is they restricted the release to just this room."

She pulled a chair over to the wall and got up. She still couldn't reach. Damn it. She was going to need a screwdriver, too.

She turned to jump off the chair and found Hopkinson standing behind her. He was holding up a screwdriver, a smug grin on his face. "Need help?" he asked.

She glared at him. "Yes, please," she said with a saccharine smile. She hopped off the chair and waved him up. "Be my guest."

Hopkinson snorted and climbed up. He unscrewed the faceplate and jerked it off with a loud grating sound. "I'm guessing no one does this too often," he said. He peered into the vent. "It's too dark to see anything."

"Need some help?" Diana held up the flashlight she grabbed from Tina's kit earlier. She was wearing the same smug grin that he sported only moments ago.

Hopkinson gave her a long, hard stare. "Thanks," he said, not taking his eyes off hers as he handed her the face-plate and took the flashlight. "So, what am I looking for?" he asked.

"I'm not sure. Anything that shouldn't be in an air vent. Possibly scopolamine residue. Let me get you a swab." She leaned the faceplate against the wall and went over to Tina's kit. "Tina, I need a tester."

"Top row, on the left," the woman replied.

Diana found the special test tubes that came with a swab inserted in the lid. She grabbed a few and walked over to Hopkinson. "Here you go," she said holding one up for him.

"Other than a dead rat—I think that's what that is anyway, it looks kind of furry—there's nothing in here," he said as he reached down to hand back the flashlight in exchange for the test kit. He ripped the plastic open, removed the tube and unscrewed the cap, then proceeded to run the cotton end of the swab over the floor of the vent. When he was done, Peter put the swab back in the test tube and screwed the lid on tightly, handing it back to Diana when he'd done so.

"Faceplate, please."

Diana picked up the faceplate and handed it to him. After screwing it back on, Hopkinson jumped off the chair. He eyed the rest of the tubes in her hand. "What are those for?"

"We're going to do all the vents."

"Are you kidding me?" he asked. "There must be ten of them in here."

Diana shook her head. "Twelve. I counted."

"But why do all of them?"

"It's unlikely they would have used every single vent.

There are just too many of them. But we don't want to risk swabbing only the ones they didn't use. It would give us a false negative."

Hopkinson nodded. "Makes sense, I suppose."

They spent the next ninety minutes removing face-plates and swabbing the inside of the remaining vents. Once they were done, Diana looked around. "Maybe we should check out the theory that they used outside A/C units, just in case."

Peter was hot and sweating with the effort it had taken to swab all twelve vents. He wiped his dusty face. "Good idea. I could do with some fresh air. It would help if we had those blueprints, too. I'm going to find that hotel manager and see where he disappeared to." He left the ballroom, the set of his shoulders determined.

"Well, we're done," Tina said as she walked back toward her kit. "We'll take all this to the lab and get to work."

"How long do you think it will take?" Diana asked. Tina checked her watch.

"Well, it's already pretty late, so it will have to wait until tomorrow morning. But I should have at least some results by early afternoon," she replied.

Diana glanced at her own watch, and her eyes widened. "Nine, already!" Time had flown. It had been around two when she arrived at the station, and since then, things had moved fast. Her track of time had slipped away from her. She needed to get home. Max was probably going crazy. But she still had a few more things to check.

"Why don't you two head on out? Hopkinson and I can wrap up here."

Tina looked at her. "You sure?" she asked.

"No worries," Diana said with a smile.

"Okay," Tina smiled warmly back at her. "Thanks."

"One thing. Could you leave me a few more of those testers?"

Tina pulled out ten test kits and handed them to her. "What do you need them for?" she asked.

"We're going to look into the possibility that they used the external A/C units to disperse the scopolamine."

"Uh-huh. You can swab those areas too."

"Yup."

"Well, good luck with that. Here, you'll need this," Tina said as she handed her the screwdriver Hopkinson had been using earlier.

Diana looked at Tina carefully. She was pretty certain Hopkinson had not put it back. Tina snorted. "If I didn't look after my equipment, I'd have nothing left."

Diana laughed. "I promise to take very good care of it."

"I'll hold you to that. Okay, we'll get going. See you tomorrow."

Diana waved. "See you."

Just then, Hopkinson walked back in. He was holding some papers in his hand. His trip had been successful, but he looked thunderous. "I knew I didn't like the look of that guy. He "forgot" to get the blueprints. And suddenly he was much too busy to find them. I had to explain the perils of impeding an investigation."

Diana sighed. "You didn't threaten him, did you?"

Hopkinson glared at her. "You do know I've been doing this job for quite a while, don't you?"

"Of course. Doesn't mean you're the nicest person to deal with."

"No, I didn't threaten him," Hopkinson declared. He turned to Tina, who was giving them an odd smile. "Are you leaving us?"

"Diana said you two could finish up here. We'll get on

with these first thing in the morning, and you should have some answers by tomorrow afternoon."

"Thanks, Tina," Hopkinson replied. Ruth waved to both of them.

Diana and Peter looked at each other. "Let's take a look at these blueprints. Try to figure out how the A/C system works." Peter walked over to one of the tables and spread the large plans out. There were a lot. The Fairmont was a big building.

Diana bent over to study them. She groaned. "I can't make a lick of sense out of these," she said in exasperation.

"So, you aren't perfect, after all."

She looked up at him quickly but smiled when she saw the humorous twinkle in his eye. "Looks like I'm not. And here I was thinking I was the embodiment of perfection. It's such a shame to discover I'm just a regular old human."

"It's a good thing that my brother," Peter's gaze darkened for a moment, "was in construction." He finished the sentence on a whisper.

Diana watched him. She wondered what was wrong.

"Your brother?" she asked.

Peter's eyes refused to meet hers, but she could see they were shuttered. "I learned a lot from him," he said abruptly. He bent over the plans, indicating loud and clear that the topic was closed.

Diana opened her mouth but shut it just as quickly. She decided to drop the subject. For once.

"So, can you understand anything?" she asked, pointing to the blueprints.

"Enough. And as far as I can tell, the A/C system runs through the entire building. See?" Peter traced the plans with his finger. "They would have had to gas the whole building. Someone would have noticed, and it would have been a massive waste of the drug. I think we can write off the idea that they loaded the whole place. "

Diana looked up at the vents in the room, "But if they didn't use the A/C units outside..." she trailed off. "Can you show me the venting system for this room?" she asked.

"This is it," he said, focusing in on one of the plans.

She bent over to take a closer look. "These are the inlet vents, right?" Peter nodded. "Then, if it were me, I would have put the canisters at these junctures. Here and here," she said, chewing on her lip. "They could release the drug and rely on the air forced through the vents to carry it into the room.

"Why not place the canister right at the lip of the air vents, to make sure the scopolamine was dispersed more directly?"

"Because I'd be worried about a maintenance crew finding them."

"Yeah, but as far as I can tell, they don't do a lot of maintenance on the air vents."

"They had no way of knowing that. And there's a good chance they brought in the canisters a few days before, to avoid any suspicion. The risk of someone finding them under those circumstances would have been high. Plus, they knew the cops would sweep the room right after the theft, and by hiding the canisters just out of sight, it would increase the odds of them being missed."

"Well, theories are great, but I guess we're just going to have to check, aren't we?"

"Pretty much."

Peter looked up. "Hate to break it to you, but there's no way I'm going to fit in one of those vents."

Diana eyed him and then up at the faceplate. "Great," she said with a sigh. He was right. His shoulders were too wide. He would get stuck. It would be her who would have the dubious pleasure of crawling around. In the air vents. Which had rats. The joy.

"Want a hand?" Peter looked much too pleased with himself.

"I'm so glad you're happy," she grumbled.

"Hey, no need to get touchy. Just offering to help," he replied, raising his hands. The twinkle in his eye and the valiant effort he was putting into not grinning belied his words. He was enjoying this.

"You're such a gentleman," she muttered. Diana was tempted to strangle him, but they had a job to do. She could restrict his airway later. She looked around the room and studied the vents. She wasn't short, but she was nowhere near Peter's height. Standing on a chair wouldn't get her into the vent. She would need a leg up. Or... There! There was her solution. A sturdy-looking cabinet stood against one of the walls.

She shrugged out of her jacket. Looking down at her shirt, she sighed. It was going to need a good dry cleaning after she was finished here. She unbuttoned her cuffs and rolled up the sleeves. "Come help me," she ordered.

"Yes, ma'am!" Peter said with a salute.

She glared at him again. "You do know you aren't funny, don't you?"

"Moi?" he asked, giving her an innocent look. "Actually, I think I'm hilarious." There was a small look of triumph in the smile he was now giving her.

"The size of your ego is unbelievable," she said as she walked over to the sideboard. She glanced at him. "So, you going to give me a hand, or are you just going to stand there?"

He shrugged, the smug smile still firmly planted on his lips. He walked over. "Do you mind?"

She moved out of the way. Taking her place, Peter pushed the cabinet until it lined up with the vent. "Happy?"

To be honest, she was impressed. That cabinet was damn big, and he had just pushed it across the carpet as if it weighed nothing.

"Here," she said, handing him the screwdriver. She climbed up onto the cabinet in what she hoped was a graceful move.

Getting to her feet at the top, she saw the air vent was now about the same level as her shoulders. It was going to be a tight fit, even for her. She held her hand out without a word and curled her fingers around the screwdriver Peter silently handed her. She quickly undid the screws on the faceplate and pulled it off. Thankfully, it came away easily. She handed the faceplate and the screwdriver down to Peter and looked into the air vent dubiously. It was dark. Black, almost.

"Don't suppose you still have that flashlight?"

"Of course I do," he replied, handing it to her. Her stomach tightened, and she swallowed. She didn't mind tight spaces. Hell, she didn't mind the dark. But the thought of what might be living in these vents gave her the creeps. She had gone up against terrorists, hardened criminals, and a whole slew of very scary people without a qualm. But rats? That's where she drew the line. She hated the disgusting, disease-carrying creatures. If one bit her, who knew what she would end up with?

She glanced back at Peter, who was watching her expectantly. She swallowed.

His gaze softened for a moment. "You okay?" he asked.

"Look, if you have a problem with tight spaces or anything, we can get someone else out here tomorrow to check the vents."

She shook her head. "I'll be fine," she replied. "I'm just not that fond of rats."

"You and me both."

She took a deep breath. She switched the flashlight on and checked the vent. It looked empty. She put the flashlight between her teeth and grabbed onto the edge of the vent, slowly hoisting herself inside, her top half resting on the vent floor. Grabbing onto the walls, she pulled herself inside. She got up into a crawling position. Her back hit the top of the vent. There was only an inch or so of clearance on either side. It was a tight fit.

She took another deep breath and coughed. How could an air vent have such a musty, stale smell? And so much damned dust.

"You okay in there?" Peter sounded a little worried.

"Yeah, I'm fine," she replied, slightly breathlessly. She was fine. There didn't seem to be any rats. No tell-tale scampering. Trying to breathe as little as possible, she inched her way forward. The juncture was only a few feet ahead of her.

Suddenly, she heard a scratching noise. She froze. Not rats. Please, anything but rats. She banged against the side with her flashlight making the vent clang and vibrate. The scratching noise stopped. She bit her fear down and moved forward. The faster she checked the juncture out, the faster she could get out of there. She hustled herself up that vent as fast as her hands and knees and the restrictive space would allow her.

When she got to the end of it, Diana's heart dropped.

The vent running perpendicular to the one she was in was empty.

"There's nothing here," she yelled, the frustration clear in her voice.

"Come on out then."

"I want to check the other vents," she replied.

"You sure?"

"Yes, I'm sure," she said with a small sigh. She turned to the left and began to inch her way forward as she started to investigate the maze of tunnels that ran above the ballroom.

After what felt like hours but which couldn't have been more than ten minutes, she hit the jackpot.

"Found something!" she shouted, excitement permeating her tone.

"Don't touch it," Peter immediately said. She heard some movement and then the faceplate of the vent closest to her came off. "I've got an evidence bag here," he said.

"Throw it over to me."

Peter threw it but the bag didn't make it too far. "Damn it," he said. He reached in but couldn't get to the bag. Diana sighed. She awkwardly made her way over the top of the oblong, shiny metal object lying in the vent—clearly a canister, like she had predicted—and grabbed the bag. She backed up, trying her best not to brush against the canister and wipe away any evidence that might still be on it. She picked it up using the evidence bag and worked her way back to Peter.

"Here," she said, handing it to him. He grabbed hold of it and disappeared from view. She sighed. She couldn't come out head first and there wasn't enough room for her to turn around. So, she backed up and turned around at the juncture. God, she felt ridiculous. She inched herself back down the way she had just come and started to climb out, feet, and butt, first. When she was about halfway, she felt a strong pair of hands grab her waist.

"I've got you," she heard Peter say. Her heartbeat picked up the pace a little, and she swallowed.

Peter helped her down, and she breathed a sigh of relief when her feet hit solid ground. He let go of her. "You okay?" he asked.

"I am now. Glad we found something," she said, indicating the canister.

She brushed herself off while Peter put the faceplate back on the vent. She looked like she had just come out of a coalmine. Her shirt was ruined. Next time she went to a crime scene, she was going to bring along a ratty T-shirt.

Peter looked at the canister quizzically. "It's pretty small, isn't it?"

Diana walked over to him and took a closer look. It was small. No bigger than her forearm.

"Tina will have to test the potency of the gas. I know scopolamine is pretty strong stuff, but I'm not sure this small canister would have been enough to cover this entire room," she replied.

"Then there's a good chance there was more than one canister. Better distribution of the gas through the room. Or as a backup, in case one didn't work," Peter said thoughtfully. "It's what I would have done."

"You're right. There could have been more. And that means someone removed them."

"So, leaving this one was a mistake."

"Or maybe someone interrupted them. They probably came back sometime after the gala to take them, after VPD had given the room the all clear."

"They could have removed the canisters any time in the last forty-eight hours."

"Well, at least we've determined the delivery system. Now, we just need to figure out who did it. Maybe we'll get lucky and find some prints on the canister." Diana looked at it again. "Look at this," she said pointing to something.

Peter took a closer look and his eyes widened. "That's a receiver," he said. "They're activating these things by remote." He had seen enough remote-activated explosive devices to know what he was looking at.

"That's smart. They don't leave anything to chance, do they? They probably waited to make sure everything was in full swing and then set them off."

"These guys are shrewd," Peter hesitated for a moment. "Look, why don't you go home?" he said. "There's nothing left to do here. I'll get the canister to Tina in the morning. And I'll return the plans to Drummond," he continued with a grimace.

Diana smiled. "Don't like him much, do you?"

"Not even a little bit."

"He was alright," she said. "In fact, I thought he was rather sweet."

"Sweet?" Peter cocked an eyebrow. "Maybe to you."

She snorted. "And you couldn't possibly believe that it was a reaction to you behaving like an ass, could you?"

"I was not an ass. I just got straight to the point."

"Peter, you practically snarled at the man until he ran out of here with his tail between his legs. People tend not to take kindly to that sort of treatment."

"Look who's talking—the queen of politeness."

"Compared to you, I'm a social butterfly," Diana muttered. It was true that she had no patience for fools and small talk was definitely not her strong suit, but she was also smart enough to know when being polite and kind would get her more of what she wanted or needed. "Guess you've never heard of catching more flies with honey than vinegar."

"Why would I want to catch flies? I'd rather swat them."

Diana groaned. "You can be so irritating, sometimes."

"Only sometimes?" he asked with a cheeky grin.

"You have your moments," she replied, "though they are very few and very far between."

"Aren't you funny? You know what? Why don't you talk to Drummond if you like him so much?"

"Uhm, no thanks. I've got a dog to get home to. I'm sure you can deal with this all by your little lonesome."

"Well, thank you for the vote of confidence, ma'am," Peter said with a half-smile.

"My pleasure. Any time."

Diana chuckled. "Call me tomorrow when you have news, and I'll come in."

"Sure thing. And thanks for getting your hands dirty —literally."

Diana smiled. It must have been painful for him to get those words out, especially after the scene he had made that afternoon. "No problem."

She picked up her bag and walked toward the door. She paused for a moment, her hand on the door knob.

"Everything okay?" he asked.

She turned to him. "You know, I'd ask Drummond if they've had any maintenance done recently on the air vents in this room."

"You think they came in as a maintenance crew?"

"It would be the easiest way. It wouldn't be hard to gain access."

"Okay, good thinking. I'll check with Drummond."

"Great. Speak tomorrow."

"Bye, Diana. Have a good night. What's left of it," he said.

"Thanks. You too."

Diana walked out, closing the door quietly behind her. She took a deep breath and then realized she had made a mistake. Her car was still at VPD. She turned to go back in and ask Peter for a ride but changed her mind. After the rollercoaster events of the day, she didn't want to risk the fragile calm on which it had ended. She would grab a cab.

After Diana left, Peter found himself staring dumbly at the door. However much he hated to admit it, Diana was good. She was a valuable asset. She had come up with more in a few hours than VPD had in a few weeks, ever since the first robbery.

He still wasn't sure that having her on board was the best idea, but he reminded himself that the super was convinced she could look after herself. And maybe she could. Maybe she had been more than just an analyst at CSIS. But one thing was certain: if she got in trouble this time, he would make sure she never left VPD HQ again. She would be consulting from the safety of a desk in the bullpen. He would make sure of it.

He brought himself back to the present. It was late, and he still had to talk to Drummond. He picked up the blueprints and the canister, checked to make sure they hadn't left anything behind, and left the room.

Ms. Diana Hunter had done enough for one night.

It only took Diana half an hour to get home. It was after eleven o'clock, and traffic had been relatively light. She let herself into her apartment and was greeted by a very excited Max, who was barking and yipping and bouncing. She put her bag down on the side table in the hall and got down on her knees.

"Hey baby," she purred to Max who promptly threw himself at her. She caught him and gave him a well-deserved hug. "You're such a good boy."

He began to struggle. She let go of him, and he went around her. He stopped in front of the door and looked at her expectantly.

Diana grinned. "Yes, it's time for a walk. Give me five minutes to change." She swore Max nodded at her. He was a very smart dog. Too smart sometimes. She got to her feet and made her way into her bedroom.

She quickly changed out of her suit and into a pair of jeans and a light sweater. She slipped on her sneakers and walked back out. Max was still in front of the door, waiting as patiently as he could. He began wagging his tail as soon as he saw her, and when she approached the hall to grab her jacket, he got to his feet. When she picked up his leash, he started to jump excitedly.

Diana chuckled. "So, you want to go walkies, do you?" she asked. Max yipped even more excitedly.

She hooked on his leash and opened the door. He shot out as if to make sure she wouldn't change her mind. She followed him and locked the door behind her.

Diana really enjoyed walking Max. It was their time. And it was relaxing, especially considering how hectic her life was becoming.

"Ready?" Max wagged his tail even harder, if that were possible. She took the elevator down to the lobby and then walked out into the night air. It was the end of November, and the air was crisp.

She took a deep breath, enjoying the sensation of the cold air working its way through her lungs. It was invigorating, especially after all the dust of earlier. She took the usual route that she and Max followed, and for half an hour, Max got the exercise he needed while she went over all the details of the case in her head.

She knew Peter was hoping they would find a fingerprint or other evidence on the canister, but she really doubted it. This crew had proven themselves to not only be professional, but also creative.

"I wonder," she murmured. She pulled out her phone and typed a quick text to Peter.

*We should get someone to check the air vents at the other venues. Maybe we'll find more evidence.*

She pressed "Send" and put her phone away. She immediately shook her head. Her first instinct had been to text him. Peter. She hadn't even considered contacting the guys from the Robbery unit.

"Forget it," she murmured to herself. She had other issues to deal with. She would think about this attachment she seemed to be forming to Detective Peter Hopkinson some other time. Like when they didn't have a really serious case and a tight deadline in which to solve it.

"Come on, Max," she said. He had obviously found something extremely interesting in a bush because he had been in there for the past three minutes. "What is with you and bushes?" Diana grumbled. She gave a short tug on the leash. Sure enough, he started backing out of the bush.

Diana giggled. She must have looked just like Max when she had been backing out of that air vent. The only difference was that she had been wearing pants. Oh, and she hadn't been sniffing anything. She had also had a strong pair of arms to fall back into.

Her phone vibrated. She took it out and saw that she had a message from Peter.

*Will send someone out first thing in the morning.*

Diana nodded in satisfaction.

*Thanks. Have a good night.*

*You too.*

She put her phone away and began the trek homeward. Ten minutes later she was in her apartment. She quickly changed into a pair of sweatpants and her favorite T-shirt. before going into the kitchen and eyeing the fridge. She didn't feel up to cooking anything, but she had to eat. Her favorite ice cream was in the freezer—mint chocolate chip—but she couldn't live off ice cream, however much she would like to. Sighing, Diana opened the fridge.

"Okay, something simple and quick." She pulled out everything she needed for grilled ham and cheese sandwiches. Her phone vibrated again.

*Forgot to tell you that you were right. Drummond confirmed they had a maintenance crew come in just before the party. He also said one of them came back on Monday, claiming he'd forgotten some tool.*

It felt so good to be right. Again.

*So, now we know how they got the canisters in.*

*Yup. We might be lucky. Drummond gave me security footage. I'll check it in the morning.*

*Great. Hopefully, we'll get a glimpse of our crew.*

*Hopefully. These guys are pros. I'm sure they managed to avoid the cameras. But we'll see. Anyway, have a good night.*

Diana grinned to herself. Even if they didn't have footage of the men, they still had a starting point. Now, she needed to find out where someone could get their hands on so much scopolamine. And she knew just the person to ask.

She took her sandwich out from under the grill and poured a glass of red wine. She would call Donnie after she finished eating. It was late, but she wasn't worried about disturbing him. Donnie's day was just getting started.

Donnie Cavanagh had been a good source for her on multiple stories. He was part of a local Irish gang that was involved in a long laundry list of illegal activities. Except for drug trafficking. The gang was adamantly against drugs and their turf was a no-sell zone. If anyone dared sell them in the 4LC area, retaliation would be swift. And permanent.

It was an interesting dichotomy. The gang was made up of professional thugs, yet the family that ran the gang absolutely refused to get involved in drugs. It was surprising and probably cost them a lot of money, but even so, with the Irish, it wasn't perceived as a sign of weakness. Most of the other gangs steered clear of them because they were so ruthless. At the same time, 4LC looked after their community and they didn't demand protection money as so many of the other gangs did. Ruthless, but with a heart, if you could believe it, that was 4LC.

Donnie was a senior member of the family. In fact, he was the middle son of Finn Cavanagh, the patriarch and head of the gang. The elder Cavanagh almost had a fit when Donnie first introduced Diana. He thought she was a cop looking to take them down. But eventually, she won his trust, and he had warmed to her, particularly after she helped them with a small problem Finn's daughter had had at a prominent nightclub in town. After that, Cavanagh had become more than happy to have Donnie give Diana as much information as she wanted on rival gangs who dealt in the drug trade. Their intel had been invaluable.

She wasn't sure why Finn Cavanagh was so against drugs, but there were rumors that his sister had died of an overdose. The two siblings had been close. So, when Finn took over the reins of the family business, he abandoned drug dealing and made it clear that no one else was to even think of selling drugs in his area. Now that Diana was looking for a very dangerous drug, she was sure Donnie and his dad would be happy to help.

She put her now-empty plate on the table and picked up her phone. She scrolled through her contact list and dialed Donnie's number.

He answered immediately. "Diana, chica! Where you been?"

Diana rolled her eyes. Donnie went through phases. Apparently, he was in a Latin American one right now.

"Donnie, how many times have I told you that your Irish accent is hot? Why do you keep insisting on trying to be something you're not?"

"Aw, come on, chica, don't be mean. I fit in better when I talk like this."

Diana didn't have the heart to tell him he was butchering the accent to the point that it was painful.

"I need your help," she said.

Donnie became serious. "What do you need?"

"First, in the interest of full disclosure, I'm working with the cops."

"What?" Donnie practically screeched.

"Relax, Donnie. This has nothing to do with you, unless your dad's changed gears and has gone into the drug trade."

"Never!" she heard another voice shout. She was on speakerphone. Brilliant! Another elementary mistake, Diana. You need to raise your game, girl.

"Hi, Finn."

"Hello, Diana. It's good to hear your voice. So, what's this about you working with the cops and drugs?"

"There have been some robberies in town, Finn, large ones, and I think someone is using scopolamine to pull them off."

"Devil's Breath? That's some dangerous stuff. Wouldn't touch it with a bargepole," Cavanagh grumbled.

"The problem is that someone's managed to turn it into a gas. And they would have needed a large quantity to pull off jobs of this size. Have you heard anything?"

"No, can't say that I have. But I don't like people using that stuff in my city. Shall I put some feelers out and give you a call?"

"Thanks, Finn. I'd really appreciate it."

"No worries, Diana. I'll do it. You should come in for a drink. We haven't seen you in a long time. We've redecorated the bar," Cavanagh said.

"I will. As soon as I wrap up this case, I promise I'll come in."

"Good. Look forward to seeing you. I'll have Donnie call you as soon as we have something."

"Thanks, Finn."

"No problem. Bye, Diana." The line went dead.

Diana sat in the dark fervently hoping that Finn could come up with some information for her. While the robberies needed to be stopped, what everyone was not saying yet was that finding the source of the scopolamine was even more critical. The last thing they needed was Vancouver turning into Bogota.

## CHAPTER FIVE

T HE FOLLOWING MORNING, Diana's alarm went off. With a groan, she reached out, searching for her phone blindly. Why in the world had she ever chosen such a shrill alarm? Eventually, she found it. She opened one eye and glanced at the time on the screen. Seven AM. She switched the alarm off and turned over. Just another five minutes, she promised herself as she snuggled under the covers.

What felt like moments later, she opened her eyes and stretched. She felt much better. She picked up her phone and glanced at the time. Her good mood evaporated. The five minutes she had promised herself had turned into two hours!

She jumped out of bed and ran into the bathroom. She had promised to go into the office today for a few hours and then get herself down to VPD. And there was Cavanagh to follow up with, too. Great! Obviously, there was no time for her usual run, but she still had to walk Max.

She rushed out of the bathroom and threw on a pair of white-washed jeans, a black shirt, and a blazer. She put on her boots and whistled for Max. He was still asleep. The late night must have gotten to him as well.

She went into the kitchen, made some coffee, and poured it into a travel mug. She measured out Max's food and put down some fresh water for him. With her coffee and Max's leash in hand, she picked up her keys. Sure enough, when he heard them jangle, Max came running out at breakneck speed.

"Good boy," she murmured. "You'll have to be quick today because Mommy was really, really late getting up." She snapped on his leash and took him outside.

For once, Max's schedule coincided with hers. He took care of business quickly and was quite desperate to get back home. He, too, seemed half asleep.

Half an hour later, Diana walked into the HQ of the magazine she worked for, *Crime & Punishment*. Someone had thought that would make a cool title. It wouldn't have been her first pick.

"Morning, Ana," she greeted the woman who manned the reception desk but who also took the role of office manager. It was a relatively small magazine with only fifteen permanent staff, many of whom worked from home. The office itself was small and quiet. Just how she liked it.

"Morning, Diana." Ana had already jumped out of her seat and was tailing her boss. That could mean only one thing.

"I'm guessing I have a lot to deal with today, right, Ana?"

"Yes, you do." Ana started to rattle off Diana's list of todos for the day. She had four hours, max. She would never be able to get through everything in that timeframe.

"Can anything be postponed until tomorrow?" she asked. "I don't have time to get all that done."

Ana looked down at her tablet thoughtfully. "Well, I can't exactly postpone anything, but I can make sure your meetings are short and to the point."

Diana nodded gratefully. "That would be wonderful, thanks."

Diana walked into her personal office and set down her coffee on the desk. She pulled out her laptop. After connecting it to the docking station, she switched it on. Time to deal with the queue of people and requests waiting for her. "Okay, let's get started," she said to Ana who was hovering at her door.

"Great," Ana said and rushed off.

Three hours and what seemed like a bajillion meetings later, Diana leaned back in her chair and rubbed the bridge of her nose. She could feel a headache coming on. Sometimes, people wanted to meet for the most mundane and trivial of reasons.

"No, you can't print the story before it's gone through fact-checking."

"Thanks, but we don't do puff pieces."

"Yes, you can use a stock photo for this article."

"No, a lost poodle doesn't make a good story for this magazine. Not unless it is a very valuable poodle and is one of many stolen by an international poodle rustling syndicate."

And so on and so forth. At least she finished most of her meetings. Ana, true to her word, had instructed everyone on proper meeting etiquette. They had fifteen minutes, and if they didn't get to the point quickly, they didn't get the answers they needed.

Diana stood and stretched. She hadn't moved in three hours. She rolled her shoulders and glanced at her coffee mug. Caffeine sounded like a very good idea. She grabbed her mug and made to leave her office, but the instrumental version of Pharrell Williams' *Happy* started playing loudly, stopping her in her tracks. It was her phone. Maybe it was Peter with some news.

She rushed to pick up the phone and saw an unknown number. With a shrug, she answered. "Diana Hunter."

"Hello, Diana, it's Finn." Diana froze. She wouldn't have needed the introduction. His pronounced Irish burr was more than enough to let her know who was on the other end of the line.

"Hello, Finn. What can I do for you?" she asked. She didn't want to presume that he had information for her. Assumptions and presumptions were rarely a good thing when dealing with men like Finn Cavanagh.

"You should be asking what I can do for you," he drawled, his tone light.

Diana's breath stopped in her throat. He had something for her. "Very well, then. What can you do for me?"

"I have some information for you. Have you had lunch? Why don't you come down to O'Malley's? We can talk and eat at the same time."

Diana glanced out of her office at Ana, then at her watch.

"I can be there in fifteen minutes."

"Great. See you soon." The line went dead.

Diana grabbed her things as quickly as she could. "Ana, I need you to reschedule everything else for the week. I'll be busy." They had just published this quarter's edition of the magazine, and she knew that most of her meetings could wait. "If something urgent comes up, I'll be on my cell."

Ana looked like she wanted to say something but seemed to change her mind at the last moment. "Okay, Diana. I'll call if anything comes up."

Diana had been lucky. Traffic was reasonable, and she made it to her lunch appointment just in time. You didn't want to keep Finn Cavanagh waiting. She walked into O'Malley's Pub. It was decorated with lots of mahogany that made it seem dark but also lent a cozy atmosphere. She would have loved to visit O'Malley's more frequently, but she didn't want to get too close to Cavanagh and his people.

"Diana, it's so good to see you," Finn greeted her enthusiastically. He was a tall man, and despite being in his late fifties, he was fit and trim. His ginger hair was streaked with gray, just like his beard, and was clipped close and impeccably styled. If you had no idea who he was, you would swear Finn Cavanagh was a very successful businessman. In a way, he was, but he didn't deal in any business Diana would want to get involved in.

"It's good to see you too, Finn," Diana answered. She allowed herself to be pulled into a bear hug.

"Come, sit," he said, indicating a booth with a very comfy looking bench. She sank into the cushions and smiled at him.

"Thanks for doing this for me, Finn," she said.

"Diana, you know I owe you. What you did for me that time can never be repaid," he said.

"It was nothing, really," she protested.

Finn shook his head. "That's our Diana. Never taking

the credit she's due. Another reason I like you so much," he said with a wink before his expression darkened. "But let's be honest, if it hadn't been for you, our Maggie wouldn't be here with us, now."

Maggie was Finn's daughter. She was a sweet but painfully shy girl. And because of her father's overprotectiveness and business activities, she had few friends. Donnie had introduced them early on in their acquaintance, and Diana had felt for the girl. The incident Finn was referring to had occurred when Diana was still working for CSIS. She had been undercover at Viper, one of Vancouver's most prominent clubs, when she had seen Maggie. The girl had been seventeen at the time and had no business being there.

Instead of blowing her cover, Diana spent the evening with one eye on her mark and another on Maggie. When she saw the girl swaying and a guy trying to lead her out of the club, she abandoned her mark and followed. As the man pushed Maggie into a van, Diana stumbled up to him, pretending to be drunk. She asked him for a light. When he refused, Diana became insistent, and he reached out to push her. Moments later, following a few moves honed during CSIS training with the help of a former Navy SEAL unarmed combat specialist, Diana zip tied the predator to a fence post. It had all been very quick.

Later, after she called Donnie to pick Maggie up and alerted VPD, she found out Maggie's attacker was wanted for a series of rapes and at least one murder. When Finn found out what happened, he grounded his daughter "until you retire, or I die." He then called Diana and asked her to pay him a visit. He had grabbed her up in a one of his signature bear hugs and told her that he would always be in her debt and whatever she needed, whenever she needed it, she was to call him.

"How is Maggie?" Diana asked with a gentle smile.

Finn's face fell. "In college."

Diana laughed. "It's killing you, isn't it?"

"She's my little girl. Among all those boys. Do you know the things they get up to? If you had any idea how many of them I've had to set straight," he said with a growl.

Diana lifted a hand quickly. "I don't want to know. It's best for both of us that way."

"So, what will you have?" Finn asked when one of the waitresses sauntered over.

"I'll have the chicken and mushroom pie and a very, very big mug of coffee," Diana replied. "Thank you," she said to the waitress, who smiled back at her shyly.

"Why don't you ever try anything else?" Finn asked.

Diana rolled her eyes. They had this conversation every time. "Because you make the best chicken and mushroom pie in the city."

"We make a lot of other good stuff."

Diana glared at him but with a twinkle in her eyes. "I like chicken and mushrooms."

"Fine, fine," he said, raising his hands, though he was grinning.

"So, you said you had some information for me."

"I do. I sent the boys out to do some recon, and I'm not liking what I'm hearing."

"Why's that?"

Finn sighed. "You were right. Someone has started bringing in scopolamine in large quantities. He's been advertising, and some of the gangs seem pretty interested." Finn didn't consider his outfit to be a gang. He thought of it as "an organization." Gangs were comprised of young idiots who thought waving a gun around and shooting people in the middle of the street was the way to do business. His organization had more finesse, in his own mind, at least.

To Diana, violence was violence, regardless of form, but the fact was that Finn preferred to avoid killing people if at all possible, and his aversion to drugs and murder made him one of the less repellent crime bosses she had dealt with. It was still a dance with the devil and an uneasy one from Diana's point of view, but necessary in the bigger picture.

Diana frowned. "This is not good."

"No, it's not. I don't like the idea of those little idiots getting their hands on a drug like this. It's dangerous enough stuff as it is, but putting it in the hands of goons? It's a disaster waiting to happen. The only good thing is that the source isn't actually selling it yet."

"Do you know who's bringing it in?"

Finn shook his head. "I don't have a name, but I do know that he's from an influential family in the city. They have old money."

"Great," Diana said with a groan. "Why do rich people do this? Don't they have enough money?"

Finn shrugged. "There is speculation that he was cut off from the family or something like that, but no one really knows who he is. He goes through middlemen and refuses to show his face."

"Smart."

"Yes, but not smart enough if he thinks he's going to get away with bringing that crap into Vancouver."

"Finn," Diana said warningly. "Let me deal with this."

Finn opened his mouth, then closed it. After a moment, he nodded. He handed her a piece of paper with a name on it. Andrew Krantz. "He's supposed to be one of the middlemen."

"Thanks, Finn."

Their lunch arrived, and Diana started eating with gusto. After a moment, she paused. "You said something about advertising. What's that about?"

Finn glanced across at her. "Well, I have to give him credit for this one because it's pretty impressive. Those gala robberies?"

There was a pause. "You're kidding!" Diana's jaw dropped when she realized what he was saying. "So, you're telling me that the robberies were just a way to show what scopolamine is capable of?"

"Pretty much. According to my sources, everyone's queuing up to get some of his product after the stunt at the Police Ball, but he's still refusing to sell."

"He's driving the price up," Diana muttered. "And this guy's the only source?"

"Looks like it."

"Well, that's something," she said.

"How's the pie?" Finn asked, changing gears suddenly.

Diana glanced down at her bowl. She was almost finished. "Amazing, as usual," she replied with a smile.

Finn paused for a moment. "Diana, I know you're working with VPD on this, but if you need any help or you get into trouble, you call me, okay?"

Diana was touched. The only problem was that if she did call Finn for help, heads would roll. Literally. "Thanks, Finn. I really appreciate it. I will."

"Promise," Finn pushed.

"I promise," Diana said. "And I'm sorry to eat and run, but I have to get to VPD. The faster we find this guy, the faster we can stop this stuff from spreading."

"It's fine."

Diana stood and grabbed her bag. "Thanks Finn."

"Don't be a stranger."

"I won't. Give Maggie my love, and tell Donnie I said hi."

"Sure thing."

Diana turned on her heel and left. Donaldson would be apoplectic when he heard they had been played. And it was about to get much, much worse.

# CHAPTER SIX

"WHAT?" DONALDSON EXCLAIMED. "They used us as guinea pigs? As an ad campaign?"

"That's the word on the street," Diana said with a nod. As she had predicted, the superintendent hadn't taken the news well. She, Donaldson, Hopkinson, Rutledge, and Ericson were sitting around the table in the same conference room that they had used yesterday.

"Are you sure your intel is good?" Peter asked.

Diana bristled but then took a deep breath. It was a normal question to ask. He wasn't questioning her integrity. "Yes, I trust my source, absolutely."

"And who is your source?" Scott asked.

She was tempted to keep her mouth shut, but if she didn't tell them, they would keep pestering her or discredit the information. They didn't know her well enough yet.

"Finn Cavanagh," she replied.

Donaldson's eyebrows climbed into his scalp. "*The* Finn Cavanagh? The head of the Irish mob?"

"The very same," Diana replied.

"Finn Cavanagh gives *you* information?" Nik asked, looking rather impressed.

"Yes, he does."

"Voluntarily?"

"No, I hold a gun to his head," she replied, sarcastically.

"Does he know you're working with us?" Scott asked.

"Yes, of course. Why?" she answered.

Peter felt like his brain was about to burst.

*Why? Because Finn Cavanagh is a notorious criminal, that's why.*

"Because he's a bad guy and doesn't like cops," Peter said, gritting his teeth in an attempt to keep his temper in check.

Diana knew Finn Cavanagh! Just when he thought he had gotten a handle on her, she turned around and pulled a stunt like this. *What was going on?*

"We go way back," she said with a shrug. "Let's just say that I did him a favor once and he helps me whenever he can."

Peter didn't like the sound of that. At all.

"When did you speak to him?" Donaldson asked.

"I just had lunch with him," Diana was nonchalant. Now, Peter felt his blood pressure skyrocket. Here he was, trying to keep an eye on her, and she was having lunch with mob bosses. *Why me? Really, why me?*

"You had lunch with Finn Cavanagh?" Scott, also, looked much too impressed by Diana. In two days Diana had found out more than they had in a month, but Peter didn't get why Scott and Nik were making stupid cow eyes at her. Didn't they know how ridiculous they looked?

"Yes, I had lunch with Finn. O'Malley's serves a mean chicken and mushroom pie."

"So, what else did he tell you?" Donaldson asked.

"He gave me a name. Andrew Krantz. He's a middle-man. Finn also told me that the mastermind behind all this is from an influential local family, but he doesn't know which one."

Donaldson nodded. "Tina confirmed your theory about the scopolamine, by the way, but there were no prints or other evidence."

"Well, at least we've got a name to start with now," Scott said.

"And I want you two to get right on that. Bring Krantz in. Diana, I want you to be there for the interview," Donaldson directed.

"Of course. What about the maintenance crew?"

"I went through all the security footage," Peter muttered, "and though the crew was caught on camera, their faces never show up. They knew what they were doing."

"Remember, the gala is tomorrow night, and the Chief will go nuts if this one's hit too. He's already promised everyone that it'll be secure," Donaldson added.

"Are we sure they're gonna hit the gala, though?" Nik asked. "I mean if the whole point was to advertise the effectiveness of scopolamine for less than legal endeavors, maybe they aren't planning on hitting this gala. They've already achieved their objective. Twice."

"Less than legal endeavors? Really? You sound like some Shakespeare reject," Scott grumbled. Nik elbowed him. Peter rolled his eyes. The two could be good detectives, but they were acting more like frat boys in Diana's presence.

"He does have a point," Donaldson said. He turned to Diana. "Is there any way we can confirm?"

"I can call Finn. They might have made their intentions for the gala known in certain circles."

*So, it's Finn is it?* Peter found this extremely irritating. He had only encountered Cavanagh once during the course of an investigation that he had run. The man had had an air of danger about him that had Peter agitated from the outset. Cavanagh had been extremely polite and cooperative, but Peter had snarled questions across the table at him. Diana, on the other hand, talked to him over *chicken and mushroom pie.*

"Please, call him as soon as you can," Donaldson said.

"I'll call him now, if you like." Diana took out her phone and dialed. "Finn?" she asked. She paused for a moment and then chuckled. "No, I don't need you to do that." Peter watched her closely. "Do you think you can find out if they have plans to hit tomorrow night's gala?" She paused again. "That would be great." Another pause, "Okay, I'll wait for your call. And yes, I will. Soon. Thanks, Finn. Bye."

She turned to the men. "He'll see what he can find out and call me tonight. But we have to keep in mind that these will be rumors, at best," Diana reported back to the four men in the room.

Donaldson nodded. "Better than nothing."

"Did the interviews with the victims turn up anything new?" Diana asked.

Scott shook his head. "Unfortunately, no. They had no idea what happened. There's nothing more they can tell us."

Diana sighed. "Then, I guess all we can do for now is to track down this Mr. Krantz and see what he has to say."

"We'll get right on it," Scott said quickly.

"Good. Go. All of you. The faster we get an arrest, the faster we get this drug off the streets."

"Yes, sir," the men muttered as they got to their feet.

"I'm going to speak to Tina. I want to take a closer look at the scopolamine they're using. Call me when you find Krantz," Diana said.

"Yes, ma'am," Scott and Nik said simultaneously. Diana looked up at them and smiled.

"Yes, ma'am," Peter parroted, albeit a little more sarcastically. Of course, she didn't smile at him. No, Peter got glared at. The daggers were a bonus.

Diana took the elevator down one floor and made her way along the corridors to Tina's lab. The door was open, but she still knocked. The scientist was bent over a microscope, looking at something intently.

Tina jumped. "Oh, hi Diana," she said enthusiastically.

"Sorry, didn't mean to startle you."

"It's okay. It always happens. I get very involved in my work," she laughed. "Anyway, I'm glad you're here. You actually understand what I go on about. You have no idea how rare that is," she said with a chuckle.

Diana laughed. "Trust me, I do. So, I was wondering if you have anything on the scopolamine. I'm curious about how they managed to aerosolize it."

"It is interesting. The first thing I noticed was that the canister isn't a regular canister. It's actually a custom made aerosol can."

Diana's eyes widened. "Are you kidding me? They made an oversized deodorant dispenser?"

Tina laughed. "Precisely. It uses the same principles, with liquefied gas as a propellant. They made a concentrated scopolamine solution using alcohol, put it in the canister, and then sealed it."

Diana responded, "Then all they have to do is activate the pumping mechanism remotely and the liquefied gas is forced out, dispersing the scopolamine solution as a very fine mist."

"Precisely. What I found interesting is that they added another compound. At first, I thought I'd made a mistake, but I triple-tested it. Air freshener. Why do you think they'd add that?"

Diana had to give it to the mastermind behind this operation. The guy was good. He obviously thought of everything. "I'm guessing the air freshener was designed to mask any strange odor the scopolamine might have given off. Since it's a mist, someone might have noticed something, but with the addition of the air freshener, no one would think anything of it."

"Oooh, that's a good idea." Tina's eyes sparkled. Like Diana, she was obviously fascinated with the mechanics and the thought process that had gone into creating the delivery mechanism for the drug.

Diana continued, "You know, to create something like this aerosol can, they'd need special equipment. Maybe we can track them through their purchases. Do you think you can get me a list of the items necessary for something like this?"

"Give me ten minutes, and I'll email it to you."

"What about the scopolamine itself?" Diana asked.

"As far as I can tell, it's pretty pure. It hasn't been cut with anything, which means there's a good chance that it's being obtained straight from the source."

"Maybe a pharmaceutical company?"

Tina shook her head. "No, this is much more potent than the grade of product used in pharmaceuticals."

"So, he's importing it directly, then?" Diana posited.

"I think so. But here's the catch. If they're not careful with the dosage, they could end up with people going around for a few *days* without realizing what they're doing."

"So, how do they determine the right dosage?" Diana was curious.

"The only way I can see is through trial and error. Maybe he tried it on his own people first. It's not like they'd know," said Tina.

"Hmm, nasty. If you could send me that list of equipment, I'll get on with some research. Maybe we can find an address. Thanks, Tina."

"No problem. I really hope you catch this guy soon. I hate the thought of a drug like this being freely available. I checked out some stories online as well as a documentary about what goes on in Colombia. It's terrifying." The scientist looked worried and with good reason. Countless atrocities had been committed with the aid of this particular drug. Vancouver and beyond would become very scary if it found its way into the wrong hands.

Diana left Tina and went back to the conference room where she had left her things. She pulled out her laptop and turned it on. She planned to do some research and then make some calls.

Before her laptop loaded completely, Peter walked in. He stood there, eyeing her with a very strange look on his face.

"What?" she snapped.

"You asked Finn Cavanagh for help?"

"Yes," she said, looking at him expectantly. "So?"

"Then you went to lunch with him?"

"I thought we already established that I did. Is there a point in there somewhere?"

Peter's jaw was twitching. His gaze had narrowed dangerously. So dangerously that she was surprised he could see anything. His nostrils flared. Wait for it. The explosion will start in ... 3...2...

"Are you insane?" he whisper-shouted at her. She had called that one, though she'd expected him to be a little more expressive. Louder.

"Why are you whispering?" she asked, completely ignoring his absurd question.

"Because Donaldson told me that—" he groaned. "Forget why I'm whispering. Just answer the question."

Diana sighed. "No, I am not insane. In fact, I'm in complete and total possession of all my faculties." She was talking to him like he was an idiot again. Diana glanced back at her computer screen. "Unlike some people I could name," she muttered under her breath.

"Do you enjoy putting yourself in danger?"

Diana looked up at him quickly. "What *are* you talking about now?"

"Finn Cavanagh," Peter ground out.

"Having chicken and mushroom pie is dangerous?" She knew what he meant, but she was feeling obstinate. And he was being a jerk. Again.

"No, but the company you keep seems to be," he snapped.

Diana opened her email. "Mmmhmmm," she paying little attention to him. Tina had sent the email she promised. Good.

She opened it and had a look over the list of equipment. Time to find out who sold this stuff in Vancouver. "Are you even listening to me?" Peter barked.

"No," she replied honestly. She heard Peter sputter next to her.

"You are the most infuriating woman I've ever met in my entire life."

"That's good," she replied. She was sure that if she looked up, he would be quite red in the face. But she didn't dare or she would ruin the charade.

"Good, she says," he muttered. "What are you doing, anyway?"

At that, she glanced up at him. "Working on the case, of course. You know, like you should be doing," she said sweetly.

He glared at her. "And what are you working on?"

"You're interested, are you?"

"Of course."

"Tina gave me a list of equipment these guys would have needed to make those canisters. They are oversized aerosol cans. As soon as I get some peace and *quiet*, I'm going to see who sells this type of equipment and contact them to see if they've made any recent sales of this specific combination."

"I see. Good idea," Peter said, tightly.

"You think?"

"I guess."

"Well, would you be so kind as to leave me alone so I can get on with it?"

Peter didn't move.

"Want some help?" he said, eventually.

"Aren't you busy with Krantz?" Diana asked.

He shook his head. "Rutledge and Ericson have gone to bring him in."

Diana shrugged. With his help, she would get through

the list much faster. "Okay, I'll email you half the list and we'll go from there."

"Okay, cool." He paused for a moment. "About Cavanagh, I want you to stay away from him. He's bad news."

Diana glared at him. "What makes you think you have the right to tell me what to do? I've known Finn for a lot longer than I've known you, and I've managed just fine, thank you very much."

He opened his mouth to say something more. Diana held up her index finger. "Don't," she warned before he could say anything. "Get used to the idea that you have absolutely no authority over me or my life. Otherwise, we'll have a problem."

Peter clearly wanted to say something more but swallowed his words. "Fine. I was just trying to look out for you," he grumbled.

"And I appreciate it, but I was doing well enough on my own before I met you. I'm pretty sure I'll be fine from now on, too."

He stared at her. "I'll go get started on that list."

"Good," she said, and he turned and left.

Diana rubbed her eyes with the heels of her hands. What was it with this guy? One moment he was all charming and courteous and the next, he was acting like a buffoon. Did he really think she couldn't handle herself?

*You did get your butt kidnapped and almost had your organs removed.* It was true. She had been kidnapped, but she had been out of the field for a while. Her radar for danger had been rusty. And now? Now she was on full alert. Her training would kick in. She wouldn't be caught out like that again.

She growled in irritation. Peter didn't know a lot about

her, and she had bungled things on their previous case, but that didn't mean he had the right to treat her like a child. She would make sure he got that fact through his thick skull, even if she had to beat it into him with a hammer.

But for now, she had work to do, and she couldn't keep focusing on Peter. They had a case to solve.

# CHAPTER SEVEN

TWO HOURS LATER, Diana had almost finished with her half of the list. Finding suppliers for the various canister parts hadn't been difficult. It was the sheer number of them that was the problem. She scanned the list again. She decided to start with the more sophisticated parts the thieves needed. Fewer companies supplied those. She would speak to Donaldson, too. An official communication from VPD to these companies would make her life a lot easier when it came to talking to them.

Someone cleared their throat. Diana looked up quickly and smiled. "Hi, Diana." It was Nik Ericson. "We brought Krantz in, and the boss would like you there when we interrogate him."

Diana jumped to her feet. "You found him? That's great!" She shut her laptop down and rushed to follow Nik through the maze of the VPD building.

"Yeah. He wasn't at home or at his place of work, but we put out an APB on his car, and a patrol spotted him near the industrial area."

"I wonder what he was doing there. Heading to wherever they've set up their lab, you think?"

Nik came to a halt outside a door to the interrogation area. "I have no idea, but he was pretty far away from his work and home."

Diana nodded. "Let's find out what Mr. Krantz has to say for himself, shall we?"

Nik opened the door for her. She walked into a dark corridor that was separated from the interrogation room by a one-way mirror. Donaldson and Peter were already there, watching.

"Diana," Donaldson said by way of greeting.

"Superintendent." She ignored Peter and glanced into the next room, studying Krantz. The guy looked like an upscale lawyer. "He probably paid more for his suit than I make in a month," she said.

"Yeah, it seems Mr. Krantz here is a partner in a law firm." Peter looked at the file. "Thomas, LeFavre & Blackman. Their client roster is made up of some of the richest people in the city."

"Interesting," Diana said under her breath. "I wonder why someone with such a cushy job would risk it all by getting involved in a scheme like this."

"Greed," Nik said, his tone matter-of-fact. "I know his type. They never have enough. It's always more, more, more. He probably figured he could make a ton of cash and then disappear. And if he got caught... Well, look at him. He's so calm and relaxed. Most likely figures he can get himself out of this mess easily. He's done it a thousand times for his clients, I'll bet."

Diana kept studying Krantz. "Maybe," she said softly.

"You don't sound convinced," Donaldson said.

"I'm not," she replied. "Do we know anything else about Andrew Krantz?"

"You mean beside the fact that he's pretending to be an upstanding citizen while actually being a scumbag?" Nik asked.

Diana levelled him with a glare. "Yes, besides that," she snapped. Nik darted a surprised look at her. She took a deep breath. "I've learned never to take anything at face value. There's always more to the story. And Mr. Krantz isn't quite as calm as you think. In fact, he looks decidedly uncomfortable to me."

"Probably because he didn't think he'd get caught," Nik said.

"According to the file we compiled on him, which is pretty thin, mind you," Peter said, "Mr. Krantz is forty-two. He's married and has a sixteen-year-old daughter. He made partner about two years ago and earns an obscene amount of money for the privilege. He has no priors, so on paper at least, he looks like a model citizen. That's about it."

Diana turned to look at Krantz again. Something was bugging her. He wasn't as relaxed as Nik thought him to be. His shoulders were stiff, there was tension around his eyes, and a bead of sweat was running down his temple. He kept throwing uneasy glances at the door, and every now and then he would take his hands off the table and hide them beneath it. She couldn't see them, but his motions indicated that he was fidgeting.

Most would assume he was guilty with the signs of nervousness he was exhibiting, but there was more to it than that. This was a man used to extreme levels of stress. He was a lawyer, after all. One that had made partner relatively young, considering the firm he works for.

It didn't make sense for him to throw away all his hard work on a deal like this. Scopolamine would fetch a pretty good price on the market, but he would be constantly looking over his shoulder. He was taking a huge risk. Something else was going on, she was sure of it. But she had to make certain.

"I don't think money is the issue," she said.

"What do you mean?" Peter asked, looking at her curiously.

"As far as we know, he's the middleman, right? That means he'll be getting chump change, at least when compared to how much he earns from his day job. The bulk of the profits will go to who's in charge. So, why would he put everything on the line for maybe ten—twenty thousand dollars, if he's lucky?"

"If he's getting that much every week, he might think it's worth it," Nik pointed out.

Diana cocked her head. "I don't think so. First of all, he has no way of knowing how much product they'll be able to move. This isn't like a retail store where you can draw up a projected cash flow based on previous sales. There are many more variables involved. Plus, if he was in it just for the money, he'd be much calmer than he is."

"He looks pretty calm to me," Nik said.

Diana glanced at him and sighed. "Trust me on this—calm, he is not."

At that moment, Scott opened the door. "Coming?" he said to his partner.

"Wait," Donaldson said. "Take Diana with you instead."

"Diana?" Scott asked.

"Yes, Diana. She'll be able to get a better read on him if she's in the room with you."

Diana walked toward the door. "Don't worry, Scott," she said, "I've taken part in an interrogation or two before. I can handle myself."

Scott opened his mouth but then nodded. "Come on, then. Let's see what this guy knows."

"Just a sec." She turned to Peter. "Is there a picture of his daughter in that file?"

Peter opened the file and looked through it quickly. "Yup, here it is," he said, holding out a photograph.

"Give me the whole file, please." Without a word, Peter gave it to her, and she followed Scott out into the hall.

Scott opened the door to the interrogation room, allowing her to walk in first, and then closed it behind them with a little more force than was necessary. Krantz jumped. Scott walked over to the table and sat down. Diana opted to remain standing. She opened the file as though scanning it, but she kept her eyes firmly on Krantz.

Peter watched Diana curiously through the one-way. Her remark about taking part in an interrogation or two before had struck him. Once again he wondered. What *had* she done for CSIS?

In the interview room, Scott was introducing himself.

"Hello, Mr. Krantz, I'm Detective Scott Rutledge. I'll be asking you a few questions. I'd appreciate it if you could save us both some time and be completely honest. The more cooperative you are, the less trouble you'll be in."

"Why am I here?" Krantz asked, his voice wavering slightly. His head was turned, and his eyes kept flying to the left trying to catch glimpses of Diana who was standing slightly out of his line of sight. Krantz fidgeted again.

"It has come to our attention that you might be involved with some less than reputable people who are responsible not only for a number of robberies that have taken place over the last month, but also for bringing an illegal drug into the country," Scott pressed.

Krantz blanched and fidgeted again, trying to see what Diana was doing.

"I have no idea what you're talking about," Krantz said quickly.

On the other side of the wall, Peter, Nik, and Donaldson were all watching carefully.

"Why is she just standing there? Why doesn't she sit down?" Nik asked.

Peter smiled. "She's making him extremely uncomfortable. He can't see her properly, and it's making it hard for him to focus. It means there's a better chance that he'll let something slip."

Nik bobbed his head, looking impressed.

Diana huffed. Krantz glanced back at her. "Mr. Krantz," Scott continued, "I strongly recommend you stop wasting our time. We know for a fact that you are involved. What happens from here on out depends on how cooperative you are. You help us find who's responsible, and we'll let the prosecutor know how instrumental you were in helping us. However, if you keep quiet, I can guarantee you will be spending a very long time behind bars."

"Look, I have no idea what you're talking about," Krantz repeated, turning slightly to look at Diana. She smiled at him encouragingly. "I swear. I wouldn't get involved with people like that," he said, straight to her. She nodded, the smile still firmly planted on her face.

"Why's she smiling at him?" Nik asked. Peter kept quiet. "Sir?" Nik prodded.

Donaldson looked at him. "She's establishing a connection with him. Making him feel as if she's on his side."

"Why?"

"Wait and see," Donaldson said, his tone irritated.

Back in the interview room, Rutledge was doing a good

job of appearing bored and frustrated. He sighed and shook his head and said, "Fine. What were you doing in the industrial area?" he asked suddenly.

Krantz swiveled back to him. "I was going to meet with a client."

"Really?" Scott asked. "That's strange. Your secretary told us you had taken a few vacation days and wouldn't be back at work until next week."

Krantz shrugged. "It was an unexpected emergency."

"And why would someone need the services of a lawyer for 'an unexpected emergency?'"

"I can't reveal that information. Client confidentiality."

"Mr. Krantz, you do realize that you could get into a lot of trouble if you don't tell us the truth?"

Suddenly, Krantz bristled. "Look, I'm a lawyer. I know my rights. I don't have to answer any of your questions."

"It would be in your best interest if you did," Scott said.

Krantz snorted in disbelief. "I've already said all I'm going to say. Now, if you aren't arresting me, I'll be on my way." He started to rise from his seat.

"Your daughter is beautiful, Mr. Krantz," Diana said suddenly, surprising him. He stared at her and sank back down into his chair. She circled around the table, taking the seat next to Scott.

"She is," Krantz choked out.

Diana cocked her head. "This is your daughter, right?" she said as she pushed the picture of a teenage girl toward him. He glanced down and nodded.

"Yes, that's Amanda," he said, grimly.

"You'd do anything to protect her, wouldn't you, Mr. Krantz?" Diana reached out and placed a gentle hand on his.

He looked at her and nodded vigorously. "Anything," he said hoarsely.

"That's what we want too, Mr. Krantz. We want to protect all the girls like Amanda in Vancouver who will become easy prey once this drug hits the streets. Rape, kidnapping, slavery. Those are all things that will happen to who knows how many sweet girls just like Amanda. Is that what you want?"

Krantz looked horrified. "N-no, of course not," he stammered. He had not withdrawn his hand.

"Then help us, Mr. Krantz," Diana urged him.

He looked up at her, his eyes a little too bright. "I can't," he said quietly. "I wish I could, but I can't."

Diana tilted her head slightly. Peter was expecting her to explode. He thought he had enough experience with her temper to know that she was probably going to go off like a rocket at Krantz. And then she surprised him.

"Have they taken Amanda, Mr. Krantz?" she asked softly.

He shook his head slowly, though he didn't say a word. "Have they threatened her?"

His eyes widened, and his breathing became erratic. "N-no," he stammered again. "Why would you think that?"

"If I promise you that your daughter and your wife will be safe, will you help us?"

He looked into her eyes and hesitated for a moment. He shook his head. "You can't promise me that. No one can," he said, his shoulders slumped.

"Mr. Krantz, we can pick up your wife and daughter right now and bring them here. We'll keep them at VPD until we put whoever is behind this operation in jail. It's not the most comfortable setting, but they will be safe here."

A glimmer of hope became apparent on Krantz' face.

Then he shook his head. "No, he's got connections every-where. I'm sorry, but no. I can't risk it."

"Great," Nik muttered, back in the observation room. "That worked really well," he said sarcastically. The intense silence in the room was broken.

"Shut it, Ericson," Donaldson snapped. The detective looked nonplussed. Peter returned his attention to the inter-view. He knew Diana wasn't done yet.

Diana said nothing for a moment and then yanked her hand away from Krantz'. He looked down in surprise and back up at her with a lost look on his face.

"Mr. Krantz, you've put me in a position I really didn't want to find myself in." Her whole demeanor had changed. She was cold and curt.

"W-what do you mean?" Krantz stammered.

"You have one of two choices, and please understand they are your only choices. First, you tell us everything— and I mean everything—you know, and we'll protect your wife and daughter. We'll also make sure word gets out that your boss has been very cooperative and is helping us catch the rest of the people involved, including his suppliers. That will ensure that his business partners won't want anything to do with him or his mess-up here in Vancouver." She paused, letting it all sink in.

"He'd never do that and they know it," Krantz said.

Diana smiled, but there was no warmth behind it this time. "Mr. Krantz, you'd be surprised at what people are willing to do once they find out what it's really like to be in prison. And even if he doesn't cooperate, no one needs to know that. The rumor mill is just as effective as the truth."

"And my second option?" he asked.

"Your second option is simply to walk out of here."

"You'll let me go? Just like that?"

"Yes," Diana replied. He looked relieved. For a moment. "Of course, the second you walk out of this building, I will make sure everyone knows precisely how helpful you were to VPD. By morning, every newspaper and TV news show will be running the story of how Andrew Krantz is helping the police find the people responsible for the gala robberies."

Krantz paled. "But my daughter..."

Diana looked at him and gave the slightest of shrugs.

"Holy hell," Nik breathed.

"You wouldn't. You wouldn't put my family in danger," Krantz said, shaking his head. "You're a cop. You don't do things like that."

"First off, I'm not a cop. I'm a consultant," she said. "Make of that what you will. Secondly, do you really think I wouldn't put one family at risk to save hundreds, maybe thousands of people? You think I wouldn't do anything and everything to keep this drug off the streets? We're facing a major threat here, Mr. Krantz. One that could affect many, many lives for years into the future."

Krantz was white as a sheet. His hands were shaking. "You can't," he said, his voice hoarse. "He said he'd take Amanda and hand her over to the Columbians. She's only sixteen!" he wailed. "You can't do this!"

"Try me, Mr. Krantz," Diana sat back in her chair and regarded him icily.

Krantz ran his fingers gently over the photograph of his daughter.

Diana leaned forward, placing her hand on his once more. "Mr. Krantz, look at me." Her tone was gentle again, like it had been in the beginning of the interview. When their eyes met, his were full of tears.

"She's my daughter," he whispered. "I can't let anything

happen to her. Even if I go to prison for the rest of my life."

"I know you'd do anything for her," Diana said, "so if you really want to keep her safe, then work with us. If that drug hits the streets, no one will be safe for a very long time, including Amanda. Help me stop these people, Andrew."

"And you'll protect my daughter? Like you said?"

"Yes."

He took a deep breath, squared his shoulders and looked her in the eye. "I'll tell you everything I know."

"Thank you," Diana said with a soft smile.

"Damn, she's good," Nik whispered. "Tough but good." Peter nodded in agreement. She was good. He blew his cheeks out. Analyst? He didn't think so. He would never have imagined she could be quite so ruthless.

"Tell me where Amanda is now, Andrew," Diana said.

"She's in school," he replied. "St. Mary's."

"Someone will go pick her up right now. She'll stay here at VPD until we can organize a safe house for her. You will join her as soon as we're done here."

"Thank you," Krantz whispered.

"You heard the lady, Ericson. Get a move on," Donaldson barked.

"Yes, sir!" Nik scurried out of the room.

Peter looked askance at Donaldson. "What exactly did she do for CSIS?" he asked. It had become clear that his boss knew a lot more about Diana Hunter than he let on.

Donaldson shrugged. "Need to know basis, son. Need to know."

Seriously? Ex-Special Operations Forces and he was being fed this line of bullshit?

Peter turned his attention back to the interrogation room. He would unravel the mystery of Diana Hunter, in time. Now though, he had to focus on the case.

# CHAPTER EIGHT

Diana took a deep breath and smiled at Krantz again, trying to put the man at ease. She had done a number on him. She would have taken a slower, softer approach if they had had more time, but Krantz had vital information she needed as quickly as possible. It wasn't her proudest moment, but it had worked. She had found his weakness and exploited it as she had been trained to do.

"So, Mr. Krantz, who is behind the gala robberies?" she asked.

"I don't know," he said. At Diana's disbelieving look, he continued quickly. "I received an email a few months ago with surveillance pictures of Amanda. It explained in detail what would happen to her if I didn't do everything I was told."

"Go on," she encouraged him.

He took a deep breath. "So, I did. I never had contact with anyone except a courier."

"And what were you told to do?" Scott asked, startling Diana slightly. She had almost forgotten he was in the room.

"I set up a company and purchased a property," he replied.

Diana gazed over Krantz' head, then back at him again, digesting the information. "And who are the shareholders of this company? Surely you must have been given names, documents."

"Yes, I was given some documents, but the company was set up as a branch of an offshore. The major shareholder is another company based in the British Virgin Islands. I didn't dare look any deeper."

"We'll need the name of the company and any documents you have. Also, the address of the property you purchased," Scott said.

"I have everything in my briefcase."

"Good," Diana said. "Thank you for your cooperation, Andrew. I promise you won't regret it. Now, if you'll excuse me, I'll leave you with Detective Rutledge. Remember, the more information you can give us, the faster we can find the men who threatened your daughter."

Krantz blinked as Diana got to her feet. "Thank you."

"You don't need to thank me," she said softly, laying a hand on his shoulder. She smiled again and left the interrogation room, closing the door gently behind her.

As soon as she was clear of the room, she leaned against a wall and closed her eyes. She drew in a shaky breath and rubbed her temples. She could feel a headache coming on. This was the part of the job she always hated. She had no compunction when it came to taking down criminals and terrorists. Even permanently, if necessary. But threatening a man's family? Putting them in danger for the greater good? It made her feel no better than the criminals she was trying to catch.

She heard a noise and opened her eyes to see Peter

coming out of the room next door. He leaned next to her. "You okay?" he asked gently.

She took a deep breath and nodded. "Fine."

"You sure?"

She shrugged. "It had to be done."

"You did the right thing. We can keep the girl safe, now. Who knows what would have happened to her? You probably saved her life, you know."

Diana glanced at Peter. He was perceptive. "I don't regret it," she said. "Doesn't mean I like doing it," she finished on a whisper.

"We do what we need to. There's nothing wrong with that. It's not as if you were going to follow through on your threat." He hesitated.

Diana glared at him. "Is someone picking up Amanda and her mother?" she asked suddenly.

"Donaldson sent Ericson the moment Krantz agreed to your terms."

"That's good." Diana said, still trying to convince herself that she had done the right thing.

"You did well," Peter said. "Stop beating yourself up over it. You made the right call."

"Thanks," she replied with a shaky smile.

"Once Rutledge is done with Krantz, I'll get Ryan— our tech guy—onto finding out who's behind this company.

"I think we need to check out that property, too."

"That's next on the list. But why don't you head on home and get some rest? It's been a long day, and Rutledge, Ericson, and I can handle it."

Diana shook her head. "No, I want to see this through to the end. I'll come with you."

He sighed. "You can be so stubborn," he groused.

She smiled up at him. "That's why you like me so much."

Peter snorted. "Keep dreaming, lady," he drawled. "You're nothing but a huge pain in my rear end."

Diana chuckled. "Well, at least I keep you on your toes."

Peter groaned. "Woman, I've lost years off my life since I met you."

She smiled. "Aw, come on, I'm not that bad."

"Not that bad? You're impossible! But you're starting to grow on me."

She chucked him on the arm.

"Now, in all seriousness," Peter continued, "this property Krantz mentioned could be nothing. Are you sure you don't want to go home? I promise to call you if we find anything so you can come check it out for yourself."

"It's a tempting offer. But I don't think we have time to waste. Whoever is doing this won't be advertising forever. He'll want to sell the product soon, and the longer we wait, the less chance we'll have of stopping him."

"Diana, we are detectives, and we do know how to catch criminals all by ourselves," Peter replied with a smirk. "We were doing it for a long time before you came along."

"Then why did Donaldson call me in?" Diana countered.

Just then, the door opened and Donaldson stepped into the hallway. "Because we needed all the help we could get on this one. That doesn't mean, though, that you need to run around, chasing every possible lead yourself." Donaldson paused and turned to Peter. "But Krantz just mentioned that the property he bought was an abandoned warehouse in the industrial area of the city. Given that it's probably the site of their operations, and since we're on a tight schedule, I think Diana should go with you."

Peter didn't look exactly ecstatic about this idea, but said. "Yes, sir. We'll head out right away."

"Good," the superintendent said with a nod. "I want regular updates. We have twenty-four hours. The DCC will have my head on a plate if we don't sort this before the Firefighters' Ball."

"Will do, sir. We'll go as soon as Rutledge is done with Krantz and we've given his info to Ryan to dig into further. Maybe he can hack into who's behind all these companies."

"Let me know what you come up with. And stake out the hotel. We don't want any maintenance crews depositing canisters in vents right under our noses." Donaldson paused and then looked at Diana. "Good job in there," he said.

"Thank you, Superintendent," Diana replied. "Now, if you gentlemen will excuse me, I need a cup of coffee. A strong cup of coffee."

"The break room is just down the hall, third door on the left," Peter offered helpfully.

"Thanks."

"I'd be careful, though. This place is full of excellent detectives and officers, but not one of them can make a decent cup of coffee." Donaldson added with a full body shiver. "I'm telling you that stuff's toxic."

Diana laughed. "I'll take my chances, thank you."

"I'll come get you as soon as we're ready to leave," Peter said.

Diana found the break room. There was a steaming pot of what looked like fresh coffee on the counter. She sniffed tentatively. It smelled like coffee. Maybe it wasn't as bad as Donaldson had intimated.

But when she grabbed a cup and started pouring, she began to wonder. It was dark. Really dark. Not like sludge, but still. She added some sugar, a dash of cream and took a tentative sip.

"Not bad," she murmured. It was strong. Strong enough to wake the dead. Diana had a resistance to stimulants. It meant she could take really strong coffee before feeling even a slight effect. She could down a six-pack of energizers and sleep like a baby. This was good coffee in her book.

She took a seat at the table, holding her cup in both hands, and thought back over the day's events. She had had to do something she was uncomfortable with in service of a bigger goal. Her CSIS persona was reasserting itself. The persona that was capable of doing much more than threatening someone.

Peter poked his head in. "We're ready to go," he said. Diana didn't move.

"Peter, what do you think will happen if we don't catch these guys?"

He raised his eyebrows and pursed his lips. He slowly sat down across the table from her and let out a big sigh.

"I imagine it will be hell. If this drug gets out, there will be lives ruined. The city will become a war zone. People will be afraid to leave their homes. Everyone will be a potential victim. The randomness of that would be terrorizing. We would be under siege."

Diana thought for a moment. "Hmm. With it being dispersed in the air, it would become a form of biological warfare. They could gas entire buildings, subway trains, banks, even government offices. The criminal possibilities are endless."

Peter continued her thought. "Ransoms could be extorted, evidence could disappear, locations of witnesses in protective custody discovered, juries tampered with and on. It will be a nightmare. But we'll nail this guy. I'm positive. It won't come to that."

"The length of the trail to the drug's source worries me. Whoever is setting up the operation is sophisticated."

"We are more so."

"But Peter, the robberies are extremely effective and audacious. The street criminals hankering to buy the drug will pay a higher price for it *and* the delivery mechanism. And we only have twenty-four hours to go. We still have no idea who is behind this campaign."

"Yeah, but with luck and some good detective work, this warehouse that Krantz bought for his paymaster will bring some results. Otherwise, we'll be spending a lot of time digging up who bought the different types of equipment needed to manufacture those canisters. That delivery mechanism is key to taking down this whole operation. Come on, less of this zombie apocalypse doomsday scenario, let's go. These guys aren't going to catch themselves."

Diana jumped to her feet and downed the rest of her coffee.

"Just a sec," she said as she quickly washed her cup. "I need to get my bag from the conference room."

"We'll be waiting for you at the elevator."

Diana made a beeline for the conference room where she'd left her laptop and bag. She gathered up all her things. She would head straight home after this, so she would follow Peter in her car.

She rushed to the elevator, where Scott and Peter were waiting for her. "Nik not back yet?" she asked.

Scott shook his head. "Stuck in traffic. But he has

Amanda, so everything's okay," he said with a smile. The elevator dinged, and the doors opened. They stepped back to allow people off the elevator and got on. There was only the three of them.

Peter hit the button for the second parking level. "I'm on level one," she said. At Peter's quizzical glance, she explained. "I'll be heading straight home after this, and I'd rather avoid another detour, so I'll follow you in my car."

Peter pressed the button for Parking Level 1. "I can come with you, if you want. Show you where to go," Scott offered.

Diana opened her mouth, but before she could say a word, Peter interfered. "I'm sure she can manage driving just fine on her own," he snapped.

"Yeah, but it's no fun being alone," Scott grinned. "Anyway, this way I can protect her."

Diana was about to tell him she didn't need protection when Peter intervened. Again. "From what? Traffic? What are you going to do? Shoot anyone in your path?"

Scott rolled his eyes. "What crawled up your ass and died?" he grumbled.

"Excuse me?"

Diana decided enough was enough. While this display of testosterone was certainly entertaining, it was becoming tedious. And Peter was being irritating again. Did he really think she couldn't make a decision for herself?

"While I can handle driving on my own and certainly don't need any protection, I wouldn't mind the company at all, so you're welcome to join me, Scott."

The man grinned triumphantly at Peter who turned to glower at her. Tough. She liked Scott.

Thankfully, both men kept quiet for a few moments. "Diana?" Scott said.

"Yes?"

"How did you know that Krantz' daughter had been threatened?"

She turned to look at him. "I didn't," she replied with a shrug.

"You didn't?"

She shook her head. "No, I made an educated guess based on the information we had on him. He was clearly a man who values his status, and since he's pretty much squeaky clean, they had to have swayed him somehow. Money definitely wasn't the reason because he would have been cockier. His entire body language screamed "terrified" but not of us. So, the logical assumption was that someone in his family had been threatened. His tone softened, and he got this faraway look in his eyes when he spoke of his daughter, so I surmised she was the target."

"But what if you had been wrong?" Peter asked.

She shrugged. "I wasn't. He clearly showed me that his daughter was very important to him—"

"But isn't that the case with any father?" Scott asked, interrupting her.

Diana snorted. "You'd be surprised at how ruthless some fathers can be or at least appear to be, even if they are bluffing or otherwise caught in a double bind. Anyway, once I knew for a fact that Amanda was important to him, I decided to use her. Even if she hadn't been threatened, I would still have used the strong relationship he had with her to our advantage.

"How?" Peter asked.

"It doesn't matter. We got what we needed, and Amanda will be okay." Her tone was curt and didn't invite further conversation on the topic.

A few moments later, the elevator doors opened. She

stepped out and headed toward her car, Scott following closely behind her.

"You drive a Prius?" Scott asked, looking surprised.

"Yes. What of it?"

"I'm just surprised, that's all. I expected you'd drive something bigger. Like a tank," he said with a grin.

Diana laughed. "I don't feel the need to compensate for anything," she said sweetly.

Scott went beet red. "Hey, not everyone drives big cars to compensate for inadequacies," he huffed.

She chuckled. "You drive a truck, don't you?"

"At least I don't drive an egg," he mumbled.

She rolled her eyes. "I'll have you know that I like the design of my Prius. And I'm helping the environment while I'm at it, so don't insult my car."

"But it does look like an egg. Get two of them and you can make an omelet. "

"You know, you could always walk," Diana said sweetly, as she opened the back door and put her bag and laptop inside.

"No, no, this is cool," Scott said as he quickly opened the door and got in.

"Worried I was going to follow through?" she asked as she settled into the driver's seat.

Scott glanced at her. "I decided not to tempt fate. I've seen what you can do."

"Good choice," she replied with a wink and started the engine.

## CHAPTER NINE

ALF AN HOUR later, they pulled up in front of a fence surrounding the warehouse Krantz had mentioned, a fair distance from the building. They turned off their headlights. Darkness had fallen and there were no street lamps to illuminate them. Peter got out of his car and walked over to Diana's. She opened her window.

"I think we'd best leave the cars here. The last thing we want is to alert them," Peter said.

"What's your plan?"

"We don't have a warrant," Peter was leaning casually on the roof of Diana's car and speaking down to her through the window, "so let's scout around and get a look inside through the windows. That way, if we see anything untoward, we'll have probable cause for a warrant and can come back tomorrow."

"If they haven't cleared out by then," Diana said.

"We'll have to take that chance," Peter replied.

"Wouldn't it be better if we just came back when we had a warrant?" Scott asked.

"We won't reach a judge before tomorrow morning, and we can hardly get him or her," Peter added with a quick look at Diana, "to sign off on a warrant based on hearsay."

"Your life is really complicated, isn't it?" Diana said.

Peter shrugged. "It's the way things are. Now, are we going to hang around here talking or get on with it?"

Diana and Scott got out of the car. "Okay, let's scout around. Look for cameras, just in case they have surveillance, and... try to look less..." she waved her hand in the air, encompassing them both.

"Less what?" Scott asked, suddenly looking affronted.

"Less like cops," she said with a grimace. "If he's got surveillance, we want to avoid tipping him off as much as possible. I'm hoping that we find something outside—" she broke off and looked back at the warehouse, an idea forming.

She looked down at herself. She took off her blazer and undid a few buttons until her cleavage was clearly visible.

"What are you doing?" Peter said. She looked up. Scott had his eyes trained on her chest.

"Scott!" Diana snapped her fingers at eye level and grinned when he apologized, stammering. She leaned into the car and got out her phone. She turned off all its alarms. "Now, wait here."

"Huh?" Peter asked. Before he could work out what she was up to, Diana was off like a shot toward the warehouse. He watched her, powerless to follow. The impotence he felt in the face of this woman's recklessness made him furious.

Diana came to a stop just before the warehouse door that was most worn and faded. She strolled casually up to it and leaned in. She could clearly hear the noise of activity inside the building. She banged on the door and waited, shivering in the cold. No one came. She waited for a few moments and tried again.

After what seemed like an eternity, she heard someone coming. The door flew open. "Who the hell are you, and what do you want?" Standing in front of her stood a very large, thickset man. He was a few years older than her. He was rasping. Diana looked down and saw an inhaler inside the man's large, meaty palm. A sheen of oily sweat formed a shiny mask over his features.

Diana donned her best helpless, "damsel in distress" look. "I'm so sorry to bother you but my car broke down, and my phone died, and I can't call for help, and I'm stuck out here, and I have no idea where I am," she babbled quickly, injecting fear into her voice. "Could you help me, please?"

The guy seemed to soften slightly when he studied her, his gaze stopping and faltering on her cleavage, just as she had intended. "Look, miss, there's nothing I can do to help you. We're not a car repair shop."

Diana's entire body shivered, and she brought her arms up to hug herself for added effect. "Please, at least let me make a phone call. I can get my sister to pick me up and come back for my car tomorrow. It's so dark out, and I'm afraid." Her lip quivered, and she looked at him beseechingly. "Please," she whispered again, her voice wavering.

He looked her over once more, leaned his head out of the doorway, and looked around. Seeing nothing, he sighed. "Fine, come in. You can use my phone and wait here until your sister arrives." He ducked his head so that it was close to hers, "But no poking around anywhere, got it?"

She nodded quickly and gave him a beaming smile.

"Thank you so much! You literally saved my life!" It was incredible what a little cleavage and a woman in difficulty could accomplish.

She walked into a dark hallway and followed him up a set of stairs into another dark corridor. He opened a door, and she squinted as the bright lights dazzled her. They were on a suspended walkway that crossed over a large space below. It was a space full of gleaming, sophisticated machinery. Workers wearing masks attended to the equipment in silence. Carefully, trailing the guy slightly, Diana pulled her phone out of her waistband and held it low, aiming so she could shoot some video of the activity beneath her. She needed enough to get that warrant. The guy ahead of her kept on walking.

Looking around nonchalantly as she walked, she saw something that almost made her freeze. Off toward the back of the large open space, there were at least twenty industrial-sized pallets with canisters stacked four feet high. Doing a quick calculation in her head, she figured there were between five and six hundred canisters on each pallet. That was a lot of scopolamine. There was no doubt in her mind that that's exactly what they were doing here: aerosolizing scopolamine.

A few moments later, Diana's knight in shining armor led her into a large, windowless office. "Use that phone. You can wait for your sister here," he said, pointing to a landline.

He looked at her suspiciously, but she smiled at him. She grabbed his hand gently, walking into his personal space. Extreme gratitude was printed on her features. "Thank you so much," she said softly. "You are a true gentleman. Not many of those around."

As expected, the guy flushed. "It's nothing," he said quickly. "Glad I could help."

"My name's Diana," she said with a flirty smile.

"I'm Ricky," he replied with a small, toothy grin.

She walked over to the phone and picked it up, dialing Peter's number. *"Hopkinson,"* he barked into the phone.

"Rose?" she said.

A moment's hesitation. *"Diana?"*

"Oh, hi Jim. Yeah, look, I got into a spot of trouble and my car broke down. Could you come get me, please?" she asked.

*"Diana Hunter, I am going to kill you."*

"Where am I? Well, actually I have no idea," she said with a grimace. She gave Ricky a pleading look.

He rattled off an address, and she relayed it to Peter, who was silent on the other end. Then,

*"If you aren't out of that place in fifteen minutes, I'm coming to get you,"* he said sharply.

"Okay, Jim, fifteen minutes it is. Thanks a lot." She put the phone down. She had got some time before Peter came barging in, waving his gun around, and shouting. That would screw the case up completely.

She turned to Ricky. "My brother-in-law is coming. He said he'd be here in fifteen minutes. I really don't know how to thank you," she gushed.

The guy grunted "Stay here. I'll be back before then to show you outside."

"Thank you again, Ricky. I really appreciate it."

He blushed again, turned on his heel and left, closing and *locking* the door behind him. Ricky was something of a contradiction. She shook her head. He wasn't very bright either. He had locked the door so she couldn't go poking around, but he had locked her in the office. There was a lovely, shiny laptop sitting on the desk top just asking to be rifled.

Diana waited for a few moments to make sure Ricky was gone and then took a seat. She spent the next ten minutes going through the computer, trying to find anything that could help. Nothing looked particularly useful but she pulled a thumb drive out of her pocket and backed up the entire list of files for later. Some CSIS habits never died.

She turned to the email client. Most of the emails were sent to a single address. She memorized it. Another CSIS habit.

Suddenly, she heard voices. She quickly closed all the files and shut the laptop, taking a seat on the couch. She heard Ricky's voice and that of another male.

"What the hell is wrong with you, Ricky?"

"She seemed really nice, Carl. And she was in trouble. I couldn't just turn her away," Ricky whined.

The other man groaned. "Get rid of her. I don't care, how. Shoot her if you have to. Just get her out of here."

"Yes, Carl. Sure thing. I'll get rid of her now."

The doorknob rattled and Diana sat up straighter. "Hi," she smiled shyly at Ricky.

"You have to leave," he replied.

Diana jumped to her feet. "It's okay, Ricky. You've been an angel. I don't want to cause you any trouble."

Diana followed the big man onto the walkway and quickly looked around. She couldn't see anyone except the workers below. "Carl" had disappeared. Damn it! She wasn't going to get the visual she wanted. As she and Ricky made their way back to the outside door, Diana tripped, and as she righted herself, surreptitiously took a couple more photos, hiding her phone as best she could. She crossed her fingers hoping she would have enough evidence for a warrant.

They reached the exit, and Ricky, no doubt rattled by

his conversation with Carl, quickly dismissed her. She left at a brisk pace. She turned the corner and saw Peter. He was staring at her. Hard.

Peter's heart was racing. He couldn't remember the last time he had been so scared. Actually, he could. It was the last time Diana had gone off without telling anyone. That time, he had found her unconscious and strapped to a table, waiting for her organs to be removed.

When Diana had raced away, he had wanted to go off after her but Scott had grabbed his arm and swiftly body-checked him against the fence.

"Leave her. She knows what she's doing."

"You know that, do you? She's unarmed."

"Chasing after her will put her in more danger."

Peter took a deep breath and shrugged himself out of Scott's grip.

"She can take care of herself," Scott repeated, while Peter paced back and forth, glancing at the warehouse every few seconds. He had been calculating how to get in. It wouldn't be hard. The place didn't seem especially secure. It looked abandoned.

Peter had checked his watch every thirty seconds, waiting for her to come out. And then she called. Her car had broken down? She needed a lift? He'd show her a lift. Running off half-cocked, without a plan. When he had said he would come in after her, he wasn't kidding. He was fully prepared to storm the place, no matter how many thugs were in there.

Then, out of nowhere, she came around the corner, cool as you like, and the world had righted itself. His fear dissipated, but left behind was unadulterated fury. Especially when he saw the big grin on her face.

"I'm pretty sure we have enough for a warrant now," she said, waggling her phone.

"You got pictures?" Scott asked excitedly.

"Nope. Even better. I got footage," she said gleefully.

Scott grabbed her and hugged her. Peter grit his teeth. Diana laughed. "You are amazing," Scott exclaimed.

Peter kept silent. If he opened his mouth, nothing pretty would come out.

"The guy who's running this operation was there. His name is Carl." Diana grinned. "Nothing to say, Peter?"

Peter glared. "Just send me the footage so I can get a warrant."

"Let's get out of here," Scott said."

"I'll come back to the precinct with you. We need to figure out who this Carl is." Diana was giddy. Adrenaline was pulsing through her veins.

Peter snorted. "Fine. Do what you want. You always seem to." He got in his car and slammed the door. If he stayed any longer, he would have turned into a raging beast. He was so angry with her.

"Don't worry, Diana. You did great. He's just being a jerk," Peter heard Scott tell her. Really? *He* was the jerk? Why? Because he was worried about her? Because he didn't want her putting herself in danger? Because his heart had nearly stopped when he realized what she was up to? Yeah, then he was a damn jerk alright.

The knot of tension that had formed in his gut over the past twenty minutes started to ease. He shook his head and fired up the engine. He would have a serious discussion with her as soon as they got back to the precinct. But he needed to cool down, first. He wanted to avoid another shouting match.

When he and Diana were together, it was like a match and kindling with a big dose of accelerant thrown in. And he was sure this time would be no different. But he would lay down the law with her, and she *would* listen to him. Or he would lock her up.

Diana threw herself down on her couch with a groan. It had been a long day. A really long day. She glanced at her watch. It was past midnight. She groaned again. Poor Max. He was sitting quietly, watching her. She felt like dead weight, but she had to get up and take him out. He was being so very patient.

She willed herself to her feet. When that didn't work, she decided she needed to engage her muscles and actually move. Once she was standing, she grabbed Max's leash, her keys, and was out the door in moments. The faster she got out of there, the faster she could get back.

Although the day had been tiring, it had been worth it. Thanks to the information Krantz had given them, what she'd found out at the warehouse, and Ryan's magical fingers, they had finally managed to put a name to the guy who was behind the robberies and the scopolamine gas. Carl Granger. As Finn had said, he was a poor little rich boy. His father had cut him off because he was too wild.

Carl Granger didn't have a rap sheet, but if his dad hadn't been one of the richest people in the city—in the country—he would have had one as long as her arm. From drug possession to violent behavior, Granger had done it all.

But none of the charges ever stuck, thanks, no doubt, to daddy's money.

Eventually though, Granger senior had had enough. She surmised that when Carl Granger realized that he did not have a cent to his name, he used his connections with the seedier element of Vancouver and beyond to put this scopolamine operation together.

Diana had to give him some credit. It was the first time anyone had considered running a promotional campaign for a drug. And what a campaign! Not only had Granger proven the drug and the delivery system were highly effective, but he had driven the price ever higher and created a revenue stream from the proceeds of the robberies in order to continue funding his operation. It was very clever.

Donaldson had been especially pleased with their results so far. When he had heard about Diana's little act at the warehouse, Donaldson had congratulated her and promptly put a call through to a judge to get a warrant.

But they still had a problem. They didn't have sufficient evidence to take the case to trial. They needed proof of a direct connection between Granger and the scopolamine. The Chief Prosecutor would never take the case to trial if they didn't have a stronger, more direct link. At the moment, all they had was a vague connection to a company in the British Virgin Islands and a voice Diana had heard. That wouldn't be enough.

Peter, of course, had brooded all night, giving her dirty glares every now and again. She knew he was angry with her for running off, but there was no way to placate him. No matter how often she told him she could handle herself, he wouldn't believe her.

While they were in the midst of this awkward standoff, Finn had called with interesting news.

"Diana, I've nailed two invitations to the Firefighters Ball. I wondered if you would do me the pleasure of accompanying me."

"Awesome! How'd you manage that, Finn?"

"Ah, you know, connections. But let me tell you the real news. There is no robbery planned, this time. Something completely different is in the works."

"Oh?"

"There's going to be an auction for the Devil's Breath. They're using the Firefighters Ball as cover for the great and the good and the decidedly criminal of Vancouver to bid for the drug. Bidding's going to be done via a mobile app. Unique access passwords will be distributed at the ball."

Diana had laughed when she heard this. It was an ingenious strategy. Anywhere else, Granger would have stuck out like a sore thumb. But at a charity event? He was in his element. And no one would think it odd that he was there, which was how he intended to maintain his anonymity.

Nik had suggested they just go and arrest him, but Donaldson reminded him they didn't have enough evidence. And that's when Diana got an idea.

"I can get him to talk," she'd said.

Donaldson cocked an eyebrow. "How?"

"I'll attend the Ball. I'll wear a wire and get him talking."

Donaldson considered this for a moment.

"Get him to incriminate himself? You sure you can do that?"

"I think so. We have no other options. It's worth a shot, isn't it?"

"It might be dangerous."

"We can look for evidence that places Granger at the warehouse, but that would be construed as circumstantial.

His lawyers could easily invent a story that would render it worthless. Getting him to admit his involvement in this scheme is the most effective way to resolve the case. It's a crowded event. I'll be fine."

Donaldson still hesitated.

"Sir, I think it's too risky." Peter was pouring cold water on her idea. Donaldson looked at him. "What if they do use scopolamine in the room again? Diana would come under his spell," Peter added.

"Granger's hardly likely to use it if he's there himself," Diana retorted.

"Did we ever see any sign of a crew installing canisters in the vents?" Donaldson asked.

"No, sir, nothing. The stakeout drew a blank," Scott replied.

"So it doesn't look likely that there will be an attack as before."

Peter tried again. "Sir, we're looking at a crowded room of innocents mixing with some of the shadiest people this city has to offer who are intent on criminal activity. All hell could break loose if we provoke Granger." Diana opened her mouth to argue, but Peter ploughed on. "I say we pursue the evidence angle at the warehouse and pick everyone up afterward."

They all stood in silence as Donaldson turned the idea in his mind.

"Okay, I think we should do it. Get Diana kitted up with a wire."

There was a big sigh from Peter. "You must wear an earpiece so we can talk to you." Would he ever give up? He was like a dog with a bone. Max had nothing on him.

Diana shook her head, "Too obvious. I'd be rumbled within minutes."

"You do know this is clearly no idiot. What makes you think he'll tell you anything?" Peter snapped.

She glanced at him. "Because men simply can't help showing off to a woman."

Peter snorted. "I'll go with you."

"No, I'll go with Finn. Showing up on his arm will make me credible to Granger. Everyone knows who Finn is, and Granger will think I'm part of his world."

"I don't like it," Peter grumbled. "If we're not there, how can we protect you?"

"I don't—"

"Yeah, yeah, I know. You're Wonder Woman."

Donaldson intervened. "She won't be alone. The three of you will be going in as wait staff. We'll speak to the Fairmont in the morning. Let's reconvene tomorrow."

When Max had finished, Diana went back up to her apartment, locking the door behind her. She had to get to bed. She had a busy day ahead of her tomorrow. There was shopping to do. She needed to find the perfect dress. Something elegant but sensual. Something that would draw Granger's eye and make him very, very talkative.

# CHAPTER TEN

DIANA EYED HERSELF critically in the mirror, pleased with her appearance. She had indeed found the perfect dress. It was a black, mermaid-style, evening gown with a short, sweeping train and a split up the side that verged on indecent. One side of the dress seemed transparent but was in fact lined with flesh-toned satin. The other side was covered in black sequins. A swirling appliqué snaked its way up the strapless dress stopping at the neckline. It was beautiful, and it fit her to a tee. Sensual, intriguing, dangerous.

She had teamed the dress with a pair of black stilettos with gold metal heels, a black and gold clutch bag, and long, gold earrings. Her hair had been transformed into a complicated up-do that had involved a lot of pulling, braiding, knotting, pinning, and poking of her hair and scalp. She classified it as cruel and unusual torture. Dark, smoky, dramatic eyes, sheer lip gloss and a little gold shimmer over her shoulders and chest completed her look.

Diana pursed her lips in satisfaction. She was going to do this. She walked out of her bedroom and stopped for a moment next to the guest room. She placed her hand on the doorknob and opened it. She glanced quickly over all the photos, newspaper clippings, and sticky notes that littered the walls. She walked over to one and smoothed her fingers across it.

"For luck," she whispered. "Don't worry, Dad. I haven't forgotten you. I will find out what happened. This is just the first step. Wish me luck." She smiled gently and walked over to the safe hidden behind a whiteboard. She punched in the code and took out her handgun and a magazine.

She loaded the gun and put it into her purse. If Peter discovered that she was carrying, he would have a fit. She giggled. She could just imagine his face. In truth, it was unlikely he would find out. She was taking it with her as a precaution. She didn't expect to need it. She highly doubted Granger would do anything stupid in such a crowded place.

She left the room and closed the door behind her. She walked over to the mirror in the hallway and picked up the pin-sized microphone she had been given. She affixed it to the inside of her dress. The microphone would transmit everything to earpieces that Peter, Nik, and Scott would be wearing, as well as to Ryan's laptop. Ryan would be sitting in the lobby of the Fairmont, recording everything.

Diana glanced at the time. She had better get going, or she would be late. Finn offered to pick her up from home, but she had declined, preferring to keep her personal address private. Of course, Finn could find out where she lived if he wanted, but she knew he would respect her wishes. She had suggested they meet outside O'Malley's.

Opting to call a cab to take her, Diana ordered a car and waited. Her phone beeped with a message about five minutes later, indicating it was waiting for her outside.

"Bye, Max," she said with a finger wave at her dog, who

was looking up at her so forlornly that she felt guilty. "You've become an expert at emotional blackmail, haven't you?" she asked. She bent over and gave him a quick scratch on his head, loathe to leave him looking quite so dejected. "Okay, now mommy really has to go."

She grabbed her shawl and swept out of her apartment, locking the door behind her. Shortly afterward, she was watching the Vancouver scenery pass her by from the comfort of her cab. She felt very alone.

Twenty minutes later, the cab pulled up in front of O'Malley's. Finn was already outside, waiting for her. There was a town car with a driver right outside the pub.

When he saw the cab arrive, Finn hurried over.

"I've got this," he said to Diana. He paid the cabbie while Diana got out.

"Thanks, Finn," she said with a smile when he straightened up.

Finn's eyes widened when he got a good look at her. "Good evening, my dear. You're looking a vision," he said softly. "More beautiful than any sprite or fairy."

Diana laughed. "Not a leprechaun, then. You are such a charmer, Finn Cavanagh."

He grinned but then sighed. "If only I were twenty years younger, I'd show you precisely how charming I can be," he said wiggling his eyebrows.

Diana gaped at him. "You are positively naughty, Mr. Cavanagh."

"That's me, alright. So, shall we go paint the town and get rid of some scum from this earth?"

Peter kept glancing at the entrance while trying to pretend

he was serving people and attempting to be unobtrusive. He still thought this was a crazy idea—cops undercover mingling among the criminal fraternity. Gave a new meaning to the phrase "hidden in plain sight." He recognized a few faces, but thankfully, they didn't seem to recognize him.

"Where is she?" he groused.

"Get a grip, man," he heard Nik say through his earpiece. "She'll be here. You know she will."

"That's what worries me." Peter did not like this plan. There would undoubtedly be trouble. Diana was a trouble magnet.

Two women in evening dress walked up to him and waited expectantly. After a pause, during which he wondered what they were staring at, he started into action. Recovering his poise, he quickly poured champagne into their glasses. Detective Peter Hopkinson was, most definitely, not in his natural habitat playing waiter to the well-heeled.

"Holy hell," Scott's whispered words drew his attention.

"What is it? We got trouble already?"

"Dude, if that's trouble, I want to be in trouble for the rest of my life," Nik replied.

"What the hell are you two talking about?"

"She's here, you moron," Scott said.

Peter looked toward the entrance quickly. When he spotted Diana, his brain simply stopped processing. He was used to seeing her in casual clothes. Even a suit. He had never seen her all decked out, certainly not like this. She was undoubtedly a beautiful woman, he'd clocked that the first time he met her, but he hadn't expected her to be this stunning. She was ethereal, graceful. She floated into the room, her skin shimmering in the soft lighting. Her hair was up, but tendrils framed her face, giving her a softness that made him want to pick her up and put her somewhere safe for the rest of time. And that dress? It made her the ultimate temptation. The way it climbed her body, like a vine that didn't want to let go of the treasure it had discovered...

That was it. He had to find a way to stick by her all night. There was no way he was leaving her on her own with Granger. He spared Finn a glance and clenched his jaw. The man was positively preening. Peter acknowledged that he would be puffing his chest out too if he had Diana on his arm. Half the room, the female half, was looking at Diana enviously while the other half was wondering what Finn could possibly have done to deserve such a woman.

"Check it out, guys. Hopkinson's mooning over Diana." Peter had been staring. He chose to ignore Ericson.

"Can it, Nik. We're here to do a job. Focus," Scott admonished his partner. "You too, Hopkinson. Granger's noticed her."

Peter managed to tear his gaze away from Diana to look over at Granger. Sure enough, he was watching Diana avidly.

"Anyone who isn't blind has noticed her," Nik added.

Peter rolled his eyes. As if he hadn't figured that out for himself. He watched as Finn leaned over to ask Diana if she wanted a drink. He walked off, leaving her alone, returning moments later holding two martinis. Finn handed Diana one and then held his elbow out. She snaked her arm into the crook of his, and they proceeded into the room. As they mingled, Granger watched Diana's every move. Getting him to take the bait was the first step, but Peter was rattled. He didn't want the slime ball anywhere near her.

At that moment, the music started. Peter watched

Granger make his way over to where Diana and Finn were standing.

"I'm sorry to intrude," he heard Granger say in his earpiece.

"No intrusion at all, son," Finn said. "What can I do for you?"

"I'm Carl Granger, and I was hoping for an introduction to your daughter," he said.

"She's not my daughter. She's a friend of the family," Finn replied gruffly.

"Oh, I'm sorry. I didn't mean any disrespect," Granger backpedaled quickly, but he didn't move.

Finn huffed, appearing to be put out. "Diana, darling, this is Mr. Carl Granger," he said.

Diana turned her hundred-watt smile onto Granger, who seemed to melt before her. "Diana Hunter, Mr. Granger. It's a pleasure to meet you." She practically purred. Peter squeezed the stem of the glass he was holding, nearly breaking it in half. He flat out ignored the couple standing next to him who were waiting none too patiently for him to serve them their drinks.

"The pleasure is all mine, Diana, I assure you. I was wondering if the most beautiful woman in the room would agree to dance with me."

Diana laughed. "Mr. Granger, you flatter me."

"It's not flattery when it's the truth. And please, call me Carl."

"Very well, Carl. I'd love to dance." She put her hand in Granger's and allowed him lead her onto the floor.

There was something incredibly repellant about Carl

Granger. He had the polished look one would expect of someone who had grown up in the lap of luxury. However, at the same time, he had an overly smooth manner about him. He was attentive, but in a cloying sort of way. He was too slick. When he put his hand on the small of her back, she fought hard to hold back a shiver, afraid to reveal her distaste.

"So, where have you been hiding all my life, Diana?" Granger asked, grinning at her. He thought he was charming, too. What a terrible combination.

"I'm not the type of person who hides, Carl," she replied.

"That's good to know. Do you live in our fair city?"

"Yes, I do."

"Then how come I've never seen you at one of these events before?"

Diana shrugged. "I travel a lot. The family business, you understand."

"I see," Granger hesitated for a moment. "Family business? Which family?"

"The Cavanaghs, of course," she replied.

"So, you're related to Finn?"

"Not exactly."

"You work for him, then?"

"Our relationship is a little more complicated than that. My parents died when I was very young and Finn stepped in. He looked after me. And now, yes, I work for him."

"That's interesting," Granger said, a speculative gleam in his eye. "What exactly do you do for him?"

"A bit of this, a bit of that," she said with a shrug. "I'm in charge of business development."

"You are, are you? So if I wanted to do business with Finn Cavanagh, you're the person to speak to?" he queried.

"Depends what kind of business."

"Just a bit of this and a bit of that."

The music switched to something with a faster beat. "Join me for a drink."

Diana smiled at him. "Of course." He took her hand and put it over his arm. They walked toward the bar. He ordered a glass of champagne for her. She cringed inwardly. She really hated men who presumed.

They walked over to a quiet corner. She sipped on her champagne as she studied him. "So, what do you do, Carl?"

He shrugged. "You could say I'm an entrepreneur. I'm in the middle of setting up a new business."

"That's interesting. What kind—" She noticed a man approaching them and froze. It was Ricky. Damn! He was dressed to the nines, but she still recognized him without any problem. She gave him a quick once-over. He had a weapon under his blazer.

Ricky glanced at her and nodded a greeting. He turned to whisper something to Granger, then looked back at her. "Aren't you the gal who broke down outside the warehouse?

Diana smiled. "Small world," she said. "It's good to see you, Ricky." The man didn't blush this time.

"Boss, this is the chick from the warehouse the other day. The one who needed help."

Granger swiveled to look at her. "Is she, now?" he asked suspiciously.

"Yup. Told you she was real pretty."

"Indeed you did. If you'd excuse us, Ricky." Granger's entire demeanor had changed. Gone was the charming if oily rogue, and in his place, a psychopath stared back at her.

"So you've been inside my warehouse, have you? What were you doing there?"

"My car broke down," she said with a shrug.

He snorted. "You expect me to believe that? Please. Yesterday you break down in front of my warehouse, and today you show up on Finn Cavanagh's arm? You'd better start talking now, lady, and I better like what I hear."

"Very well, Carl. You caught me. I was doing a little recon for Finn."

"Oh, yes?"

Diana sighed, looking put out. "Word was you had a lot of product to move, but Finn never does business with people he doesn't know. So, he sent me to check you out."

He looked at her suspiciously. "And why should I believe you?"

"You don't have to, of course. But do remember that I'm in charge of business development, which means Finn really values my counsel when it comes to choosing new business partners."

"But why are you even here? Everyone knows Cavanagh doesn't deal in drugs."

"I'm working on him. I think he's missing a major market opportunity."

Granger hesitated for a moment and then seemed to come to a decision. His demeanor changed again. The charmer was back. Finn was one of the most respected people in the criminal underworld. If he made a purchase, everyone would follow suit. Granger would be set for life. Diana was dangling the tastiest carrot in front of him—a way in with Finn.

"And what did you think of our little operation when Ricky so kindly took you on a tour?"

Diana shrugged. "I'm not sure what to think. You do have an interesting set up, but I'm not sure you can manu-facture the quantities we're interested in." Granger's eyes widened.

"That's just the test lab," he said quickly. "We're bringing in more equipment, and I'll be able to manufacture in far greater quantities in the future. However much you need, I can supply."

"I'm not convinced, Carl. Granted, I applaud your ingenuity. I mean, scopolamine complete with an ingenious delivery system certainly makes your product much more valuable, but if you can't cover the demand, what's the point in getting involved?"

"It is brilliant, isn't it? I came up with the idea of aerosolizing the scopolamine myself."

"Really?" she said, her eyes widening. "I'm very impressed." She stopped for a moment. "If you can guarantee delivery of at least a thousand canisters a week, for starters, we might be able to do business together."

Granger stiffened for a moment, but then he nodded. "I can definitely guarantee those figures." He paused, eyeing her a little more shrewdly than she would like. "If you don't mind me asking, why do you need so much?"

"I do mind you asking," she snapped. Then she softened. "But since you've been such a gracious host, I will tell you that we have partners all over the world who are interested in your product."

"You do, do you?" Granger sounded unconvinced. "Well, you don't need to worry your pretty little head, because when I make a promise, I always keep my word." There was a threatening undertone to his words. Had she given the game away?

"I'm glad to hear that," she said.

"So, when do you want the first delivery?" he asked casually.

"We're looking to start shipping out next week," she

replied, just as casually. He was studying her a little too intently. And he was leaning toward her.

He grinned wolfishly. His eyes hardened. "How about we go to the bar to order ourselves a celebratory drink?" It wasn't a request.

"We already have our drinks, Carl."

"I mean something *more* celebratory."

"I have champagne. How much more celebratory can you get than that?" She was stalling. "I'm sorry, but I have to get back to Finn."

"I'm certain Finn won't mind you having a little celebration with his newest business partner," he said with a hard smile.

Diana was caught in a bind. If she refused, Granger would become more suspicious than he already was. She considered calling in the guys, but he hadn't implicated himself enough yet. Granger was not as stupid nor as oblivious as everyone thought him to be.

"A drink it is," she said with a smile. She knew it was strained.

When he grabbed her elbow in a punishing grip, she knew he had caught on to her. "Who are you really?" he whispered in her ear as he guided her toward the back of the room. This was not the way to the bar.

"I have no idea what you're talking about. I told you exactly who I am. Where are we going?

Granger put his face close to hers and glared. "I'm no fool. You know Finn. You've been snooping around my warehouse. You are up to something. I'm going to find out what."

Diana stiffened. She readied herself to pull free from Granger. "Don't even think about it, lady" he hissed in her ear.

"One wrong move and I will gas this entire room with scopolamine. Then, do you know what I'm going to do?" Diana didn't reply. "I'll kill everyone, including your beloved Finn." He showed her the small dead man's switch he was holding in his palm. "You try anything, my thumb comes off this button and everyone here will become my puppet. Then, they will *die*."

She looked up at him in horror. "You wouldn't," she breathed, deciding to drop the charade. "You'd breathe it in too," she pointed out.

He shrugged. "That would be foolish of me. And I am nobody's fool, Ms. Hunter. You think I don't come prepared? Now, you and I are going to have a little talk, and you're going to tell me precisely who you are and what you're up to."

Diana knew Peter and the other guys could hear everything, but if they made a move, they risked a massacre. She prayed they wouldn't intervene. She had to deal with Granger alone.

"Fine," she snapped. "Let's go, then." She picked up speed, surprising Granger.

"Eager little thing, aren't you?" Granger asked, giving her a suspicious look.

She glared at him. "If Finn sees you manhandling me like this, he will hurt you. And I really like this dress. Blood stains are so difficult to get out of delicate fabrics."

He raised an eyebrow but didn't comment further. He moved faster. He was now dragging her behind him. They went through a door in the back of the room that was well hidden in a small alcove.

They ended up in a maintenance corridor. None of the elegance of the Fairmont here. Just concrete, metal pipes, and cables. No one followed them. Diana was purposefully silent. It was just her and Granger.

He pulled her down the corridor, bypassing a number of doors. He took her down a flight of stairs, turned left and then right. Finally, they came to a small, metal door that was so out of the way, she doubted it was ever used. Her suspicions were confirmed when the door opened with a loud whine and the sound of metal scraping on metal.

He pushed her into the room, and she stumbled, almost losing her footing. She looked around. The room was lit by a single bulb hanging down from the ceiling. Around her were old, metal, filing cabinets. This must have once been the Fairmont's archive, during the days when everything was done on paper. No wonder it was never used now.

She squared her shoulders and faced Granger. Her heart squeezed tight. This was not going to be pleasant, judging by the look of pure sadistic glee on Granger's face. He was still clasping the dead man's switch.

"You know," he said as he closed the door behind him and locked it, "I was hoping to have a little fun tonight, but you have surpassed my expectations tenfold," he said with a small sigh. She glanced at the switch he was holding.

He snickered. "Don't even think about it. I can do you some serious damage with one hand just fine. And with the other, I can do a whole lot more. But you're going to keep still like a good little girl. You don't want to be responsible for Finn's death, do you? Or those of all the other lovely people up there."

Diana snorted. "And how are you going to kill them from down here? Mind control?"

He shrugged. "The canisters are a special blend this time. In half of them, the scopolamine is laced with air freshener."

"And in the other half?"

"Cyanide." Granger put his hand in his pocket. "This

one," he said, indicating the dead man's switch in his hand, "is for starters. And this one," he pulled another switch, wrapped with tape, from his pocket, "is for dessert."

Diana felt a chill go down the back of her neck. What was going on? "You'd kill all your potential clients?"

He waved his left hand, the one holding the switch. "I can find more, easily enough. They're all scum anyway."

She cocked an eyebrow. "And what does that make you? A saint?" she asked sarcastically.

"Not a saint but a savior. I'm going to bring order to crime in this city," he said confidently. "All those mobsters in that room up there call it "organized crime," but not the way I like it. I'm going to do a little "restructuring.""

Dots connected in Diana's mind. "That was your plan all along, wasn't it? You were never going to sell the scopolamine. You got everyone here tonight to drug them and get them to turn their businesses over to you, didn't you?"

"Very good, Ms. Hunter. Yes, that was the plan. I'm going to take over this city, and no one will be left to oppose me, because everyone who's anyone in this city's criminal underworld is here tonight. And they'll all give me anything I want thanks to the scopolamine. Then they'll all die."

"How did you get the scopolamine inside the building? This place has been staked out for days."

"The cops were too clever by half. We went low tech, this time, precisely because they were expecting something sophisticated. The canisters were hidden around the room just before the party started." He was right. They had been expecting something much more imaginative.

"You are insane," Diana whispered.

"Maybe. But it's good to be me," he said with a cocky grin. "Now, your turn Ms. Hunter. Who are you, and what are you doing here?"

"I told you who I am and what I want."

"Please, Ms. Hunter. We both know you aren't inter-ested in buying from me. So, what are you really after? Were you and Finn planning to take over *my* business?" He paused for a moment, looking her up and down. He shook his head. "No, you don't strike me as the type to get involved in the drug trade. Maybe you're working with the cops," he spat out.

"Don't be ridiculous," she said, appearing to be insulted.

He walked toward Diana menacingly. She backed up until she hit something hard. Damn it!

He was way too close to her now. She could smell the excitement rolling off him, and it turned her stomach. He pulled out a knife, which he put down right next to her. Then he pulled out a gun, which he had stashed at his back, placing it next to the knife. Diana swallowed hard. He knew she was powerless. She wouldn't risk all those people's lives. There were at least two hundred partygoers up there who were completely innocent.

"Now, Ms. Hunter, are you going to tell me the truth or will you make me a very happy man and force me to have some fun with you?"

Diana raised her chin in challenge. "Bring it on," she snapped.

"Bring it on? Jesus Christ," Peter growled. His heart had sunk into his boots when he realized Diana's cover had been blown. And then, instead of slowing Granger down to give him a chance to get to her, she took off! Again! What was she playing at?

He continued down corridor after corridor, frantically

checking doors that led off hallways and alcoves that formed dead ends. See? Diana should have worn an earpiece. Didn't he say as much?

*Where the hell are you, woman?*

He was listening intently to Diana's conversation with Granger through his earpiece, trying to pick up clues that would help him find her.

"Rutledge, Ericson, did you hear that? Get everyone out. He's planted cyanide."

Both men acknowledged him. "Do it fast. No panic. Got it?"

He picked up his speed. She was somewhere. He just had to find out where.

"How will your plan work, Granger? Even if you do take ownership of organized crime in this city, how will you get the syndicates to do your bidding once their bosses are dead? They are notoriously loyal and will gang together against you. Did you think of that? You'd soon be toast. "

"Hah! But I have the scopolamine, remember? You have no idea the power that gives me." He walked up to her menacingly and ran a finger along her bare collarbone. "Anyone, *anyone,* will do my bidding. The consequences of not doing so are too devastating. Everyone will be eating out of my ha—"

Without warning the door was forced open and crashed loudly against the wall, startling the room's occupants.

"What the hell?" Granger snarled.

"Police!" Peter barked, leveling his gun at Granger's head. "Let her go!" The momentum of the force he had used to break the door open had propelled him into the room but his lightening fast reflexes and physical strength enabled him to recover his sure-footedness immediately. He stood panting, and glaring at Granger. He didn't move.

Granger also didn't move. He grinned.

"Peter, don't! He's got a dead man's switch," Diana warned. "Stand down."

Peter watched Granger drag Diana in front of him and secure her with his left arm, switch in hand, while picking up a gun with his right. He was still aiming his gun at Granger's head.

"Now, I have no intention of letting Ms. Hunter here go, so I suggest you back off unless you want her brains splattered across your starched white shirt and the deaths of three hundred or so people on your conscience."

"Stand down, Peter," Diana pleaded.

Peter hesitated. There was no way he could get a clear shot at Granger, nor could he get to the switch in time. He couldn't risk Granger carrying out his threat against Diana. Out of options, he lowered his gun and backed away as Granger advanced on him, Diana between the two men.

Peter continued to back away as Granger and Diana slowly retraced their steps to the ballroom. Maintaining a distance of a few feet, Peter's eyes never left the two as he willed Granger to make a false move. It had seemed a long, frantic search to find Diana in that small room full of files. Now the slow crawl back to the ballroom felt interminable. No one said a word.

Peter's back barged open the door to the ballroom. Diana and Granger followed him. Immediately, they saw that the room had been cleared except for Rutledge and Erikson who instantly raised their guns.

"Hold your fire!" Peter raised his hand, his back to his fellow detectives, his eyes never straying from Granger's.

"Everyone back off, or I will kill her," Granger snarled. "Ricky!" he hollered. Shouts were heard from outside the room, and a few seconds later, Ricky and three other men burst back into the room, brandishing weapons. "Drop your guns," Granger demanded of the policemen. When no one moved, he pushed the barrel of the gun harder against Diana's jaw.

"Fine, fine," Peter said, dropping his.

Granger snorted. "You think I'm an idiot? Take out the magazine and eject the bullet in the chamber." He looked around wildly. "All of you. Now!"

They did as Granger ordered.

Peter glanced at Diana. She kept looking at him, then lowering her eyes. Her fingertips were in her clutch bag.

"What are you going to do now, Granger?" Peter asked, "It's not like you can get out of here. The place is crawling with cops. You might kill us, but they'll never let you get away."

Granger laughed. "I'm holding three cops, make that four cops," he said as he tightened his grip on Diana, "hostage. I think I'll get out of here just fine."

"You're delusional if you think that," Peter said. He glanced at Diana who nodded very subtly. In her hand was a gun. He nodded back. She had a plan and this time, he would go with it.

Diana took a deep breath. She had one shot at this. She had to get that switch out of Granger's hand and make sure the button was not released in the process. She had to move fast. She had flipped the safety off her gun, without Granger realizing. She looked up at Peter. She was ready.

Peter stared back at her with stark fear in his eyes, but he nodded. She smiled gently. He didn't always have to play the hero, a fact he was about to find out.

Diana covered Granger's hand—the one holding the dead man's switch—placing her thumb on top of his.

"What—"

She threw her head back into his face as hard as she could. The scream that accompanied the sound of cracking cartilage as she broke his nose let her know she'd hit her target. She quickly brought down her heel on Granger's foot, giving it a twist for good measure. He hollered again, his grip on the dead man's switch loosening.

In the background, Diana was aware of a commotion. Peter pulled out the second gun that he had stashed under his jacket earlier and aimed it at Ricky. She heard shots. Nik and Scott dashed to retrieve their weapons.

Diana slipped the switch out of Granger's hand and replaced his thumb with her own in one smooth move, making sure not to release the pressure on the button. She turned around quickly and kicked Granger in the groin. He promptly went down on his knees. She brought her gun up, pointing it at his head.

"Tell your men to put down their weapons or I will put a hole in your head," she said. There was no question she meant it.

Granger whimpered but said nothing. "Do it," she snapped.

"You won't shoot me," he hissed. "It's probably not even loaded."

With the tiniest flick of her wrist, Diana moved the gun slightly to his left and fired into the floor, the bullet missing Granger by a hairsbreadth. He flinched. She brought the gun back to point directly at his head.

"Put your guns down," he whimpered. It was all over.

With Nik and Scott dealing with Granger's henchmen, Diana kept her hand on the dead man's switch as Peter came over. He dangled a pair of handcuffs in front of her.

"Would you like to do the honors?" he asked.

Diana grinned at him. "I'd love to, but I've got my hands full." She lifted her hand and showed him her thumb was still over the dead man's switch.

She watched Peter as he slapped the handcuffs on Granger and read him his rights. She noticed he tightened them a little too much, just to be safe.

"Where are the canisters, Granger," she demanded.

"You find them, " Granger replied petulantly.

Diana ground her metal heel into his ankle. "Where?"

"In the plants," he gasped.

"Get him out of here," Diana said as Scott came over. He grabbed Granger and roughly pulled him to standing.

Diana lifted her chin and looked Granger in the eyes. "Next time, know who you're messing with, okay?"

The ballroom was empty except for Diana and Peter. The bomb squad had deactivated the switches, and the room had been cleared of canisters. Nik and Scott had gone back to VPD to handle paperwork, after congratulating her for doing an amazing job and being "a kickass woman in an amazing dress."

"You're my every fantasy rolled into one. Please marry me," Nik had pleaded with her.

Diana laughed. "Nik, one of these days, some woman is going to say yes, and you are going to be in a lot of trouble." He had just grinned and walked away, waving at her.

She had spoken to Finn, who had waited outside for her throughout the whole ordeal. First, he wanted to make sure she was alright. Then, he spent the next five minutes berating Granger and his plan, providing gruesome details of what he would like to do to him for trying to hurt her.

After thanking him for his help and promising she would come have lunch with him again real soon, Finn left. He offered her a ride, but she was not quite ready to go home yet. She was on an adrenaline high. She returned to the ballroom to see if Peter needed any help.

"Those were some interesting moves you showed Granger," Peter said, when she took a seat beside him.

"It's been a while, but it's like riding a bike when your life is on the line."

"You did a great job taking him down. Especially in that dress. And those heels."

Diana laughed.

"The uniforms had to beat off all the firefighters who wanted your number, you know," Peter said with a grin.

Diana glared at him. "They drove them all off? What if I wanted to meet them? You do know that firefighters are on every woman's 'most wanted' list."

Peter rolled his eyes. "Very funny," he said. "But, seriously, I had no idea how well you would manage a situation like that."

"And now?" Diana asked.

He grimaced. "To be honest, I'm still going to worry all the time, but I'll try to be less of an ass. How's that?"

Diana chuckled. "It's better than nothing. And—" she paused for a moment, while Peter looked at her expectantly. "Well, I just want to thank you."

"For what?" he asked, looking honestly perplexed.

"For coming to my rescue," she said with a soft smile. "Again."

Peter shrugged, looking slightly embarrassed. "I didn't do all that much."

"It was more than enough."

"It was no big deal," he insisted.

"It was for me. So, thank you."

Peter just nodded, looking awkward.

"How did you find me, anyhow? It was like a rabbit warren down there."

"I can read blueprints, remember? And I've a good memory. You never know when something like that will come in handy. Like when you're searching for problem women who don't know when to leave well enough alone."

"Problem women?" They looked at each other for a long moment.

Peter changed the subject. "We got the warrant about an hour ago and raided Granger's warehouse. All the scopolamine has been taken in as evidence. There's no chance it will end up on the street. With Granger behind bars, it looks like the threat of biological warfare on the streets of Vancouver won't materialize anytime soon."

"That's a relief. Maybe you can do a deal with him to find out who was doing the supplying and how he was getting the scopolamine into the country."

"I'll suggest it to the prosecutor. It'll be his decision in the end."

Diana sighed and stretched. "You know what I could really use right now?" she asked.

"After what you did tonight, name your heart's desire, and it shall be yours."

"A slice of really rich, really dark, chocolate cake," she replied dreamily.

Peter laughed. "Well, I know this little place that's open all night and serves the most incredibly moist chocolate cake you've ever tasted in your life."

Diana jumped to her feet. "Well, what are we waiting for?" she barked.

"Okay, okay," he said as he got to his feet. "Wouldn't want to deprive the woman of the hour of her chocolate."

"You better not. I get mean if I don't get my chocolate. And I've still got my gun, you know." Diana smiled up at Peter. "Shall we?"

"Yes, ma'am,"

This time it was Peter who held out his arm as Diana slipped her hand through the inside of his elbow. As they traversed the hotel lobby, him in his black suit, bowtie hanging loose at his collar, Diana in her evening gown, her earlier complicated hair confection now slightly messy in a way Peter considered very sexy, they looked for all they were worth like a couple who had attended one heck of a good party. Peter caught sight of himself in a large ornate mirror in the hotel lobby. Was he preening? He didn't think so. Perhaps he was. Just a little. Okay, quite a lot.

Diana simply looked straight ahead, smiling. "Let's go, soldier."

USA Today Bestselling Author

# A. J. GOLDEN

## GABRIELLA ZINNAS

# CHOPPED

## A DIANA HUNTER MYSTERY

# CHOPPED

BOOK FOUR

The characters and events portrayed in this book are fictitious. Any
similarity to real persons, living or dead is coincidental and not intended by
the author.
Text copyright © 2017 A. J. Golden
All rights reserved.

No part of this book may be reproduced, stored in a retrieval system, or
transmitted in any form or by any means, electronic, mechanical,
photocopying, recording, or otherwise, without express written permission of
the publisher.

Published by Mesa Verde Publishing
P.O. Box 1002
San Carlos, CA 94070

ISBN-13: 978-1541154834

Edited by
Marjorie Kramer

# CHAPTER ONE

DIANA FORCED HER eyes open. She glanced outside. It was still dark. The bright green numbers on her alarm clock said four o'clock. AM. Why was she awake? She had had only two hours sleep.

She concentrated for a moment. No strange noises were coming from her apartment. No one had broken in. She sighed. Whatever had awakened her, she didn't rightly care. She turned over, burrowed deeper into her covers, and sighed. It was time to get back to sleep. A moment later, peppy, upbeat tones sprinkled their way loudly across the silence of her bedroom. Diana's eyes snapped open. Again.

She turned over with a grunt and glared at her cellphone. She considered her options. Throw it across the room and smash it to pieces? Or answer and explain a few facts of life to whomever was calling at this ridiculous hour?

Choosing option two on the basis that it would be less expensive in the long run, she picked up her phone and looked at the caller ID. Hopkinson. "What?" she barked.

"Aren't you cheerful?" Peter's sunny voice rang in her ear.

"Do you know what time it is?" She was in no mood for Peter's quips. Her soft pillows called out, tempting her to rest her head in that lovely softness and let the warm cocoon of sleep take her back to Neverland. And Peter bloody Pan here just had to ruin it.

"Yup. Four o'clock. Were you still asleep?" he asked.

"No, I was wide awake. Like everyone is at four in the morning. I was lying here thinking about how I'm going to torture you the next time I see you," she replied.

"And that's precisely why we get on so well," he said.

"Why? Because I threaten to do you grievous bodily harm all the time?"

"That, and the fact that you're such a sweet, caring person."

"Peter, if you just called to irritate me, you're doing a damn good job of it," she growled into the phone.

"Unfortunately, murders don't have the decency of occurring on a nine-to-five schedule," he said gravely, the light and teasing tone gone in a flash.

Diana's eyes flew open, and she was instantly alert. "You've got a new one?" she asked. They had been working together for seven months, but it had been more than two weeks since their last case. Diana was itching for some action. She had reached her limit with egotistical writers, annoying suppliers, and everything to do with running her magazine. The work seemed so trivial and mundane compared to working on a case with Peter. She mostly enjoyed her regular job, but right now she was frustrated and snapping at everyone. A little sleuthing action was just what she needed.

"You know, you worry me. Every time we get a case,

you're like a kid in a candy store," Peter said. She could hear the smile in his voice.

"More, please, sir," she replied in a high-pitch.

"That's what I mean. You worry me."

The doorbell buzzed. Her heart skipped a beat. "Please tell me you're not standing right outside." Larry, the night doorman, would only let one person upstairs this early in the morning. Peter.

"Yes, I am. And I come bearing gifts." He was too smug for his own good sometimes.

"Well, thanks for the heads-up," Diana snapped. She flew out of bed, grabbed a robe, and shrugged into it. She glanced over at Max, her tiny, white Maltese terrier. He was sleeping soundly. He was so used to Peter coming around at all hours of the day and night that he simply didn't react anymore. He had a sixth sense, even in sleep. He always knew when Peter was at the door. Anyone else, he barked his head off. The pizza delivery guy was terrified of him.

Peter hadn't let up on her doorbell. Typical. How old was he? Eight? She hurried to the door and yanked it open, glaring at the six foot two detective who filled up her doorway. His blue eyes twinkled at her, and he flashed her an all-too-pleased grin.

She glared at him. "Stop it," she hissed. "You'll wake the neighbors." She sniffed the air and looked down. He held a cardboard tray with two coffees. "Espresso?" she asked hopefully.

He nodded. "Of course. Am I forgiven?" he asked.

Diana rolled her eyes. "Get inside." She stepped back to let him in. He brushed past her, raising the tray so she could get a better sniff of the coffee. It hadn't taken Peter long to learn that Diana didn't do well in the mornings without coffee. She was not fun before her first cup.

As he passed by her, Diana felt a familiar sense of unease. Peter had gotten to know her very quickly in the time they had been working together. What she allowed him to know, anyway. Ever since her parents' murders, Diana had done her best to keep her relationships as light and as casual as possible. She knew that whomever was responsible for Lydia and John Hunter's deaths was keeping a close eye on her, and she had vowed not to put anyone in danger. Yet she had broken this rule with Peter. He was her friend. Her only friend.

She hadn't told him her backstory. He knew nothing about her parents or the room, just a few yards away, where she kept all their things. They were her secret. She felt guilty. And vulnerable. She would tell him. She owed him that much. And she'd do it soon, she promised herself, before she got so attached to him that her heart would break into a million pieces when he ran the other way.

"So, where's my favorite four-legged buddy?" he asked.

"Asleep, just like I should be," she muttered. "Give." She tried to grab the cup of coffee he was still waving under her nose. He quickly moved it out of her reach.

"You really are a terrible morning person," he said. He took pity on her and handed her the cup.

Diana took it and lifted the lid, inhaling deeply. It would be perfect, she knew. Two sugars and enough milk to give it a caramel color. She took her first sip with a moan of pleasure. "No, I'm not a morning person *at all*. And this isn't morning. It's still the middle of the night."

A sleepy Max crawled into the room and whined pathetically at Peter. "And look who just got up." Peter lowered himself to his haunches and gave Max a good scratch between his ears.

"Traitor," Diana muttered at Max. "You've completely corrupted my dog."

"He's smart. He knows who he can trust." Peter grinned up at her and winked.

Diana hid her smile. Max did trust Peter, and so did she. Up to a point. She trusted him with her life, but not with the truth of her past. Not quite yet.

"I'm going to get dressed." She turned away, her cup of coffee still cradled lovingly in her hands. "Do we have time for breakfast?" she threw over her shoulder.

"Of course," Peter called out. "We have about an hour before they're expecting us." He walked over to the island dominating the center of her kitchen.

Diana froze in her tracks and walked backward until he was in her line of sight again. "You're telling me I could have slept in at least another half an hour?"

"Uh no, definitely not. Remember the last time I dragged you straight from bed to a crime scene without coffee and food? You made one of the uniformed officers puke, you had the rookies practically in tears, and even Doc, the most patient man I know, and Tina, who worships the ground you walk on, wanted to brain you."

"It's not my fault that uniform had a weak stomach," she huffed. "And those rookies were just standing there, gawking, instead of doing their jobs. They were completely incompetent. They couldn't even hold back the crowd."

"For your information, when you explain in detail how bodies liquefy when they decay, and then proceed to provide visual corroboration by poking at the dead body, making it ooze, anyone would throw up," he said.

"You didn't," she pointed out. "And at least I asked Doc's permission before I did it."

"He thought you were trying to determine something

relevant to the case!" Peter threw his hands up in exasperation. "He'd no idea you wanted revenge on that poor constable simply because he found the body, and didn't, as you put it, have the decency to wait until a more civilized time of the day to report it!"

She smiled sheepishly. "At least I waited until the rookies left."

"Well, that's alright then. Thank goodness for small mercies. Now, go get dressed," he ordered.

She snorted. "Why are you in such a rush? It's not like the body's going anywhere." Peter narrowed his eyes and squinted at her. "Alright, alright, I'm going. Might I point out that's precisely where I was heading until you accused me of being a tyrant?"

"Your words, not mine."

Diana glowered, but a small smile appeared when she turned her back. She marched into her bedroom, and slammed the door. "Don't even think of cooking anything," she hollered.

Peter bragged about his famous pancakes all the time. Like a fool, she had once given him carte blanche to put his money where his mouth was. It had been a monumental mistake. The pancakes were incredible, no doubt about it. Her kitchen, though, had been a disaster. Peter was permanently banned from cooking in her apartment. It had taken her three days to clean up!

"Wouldn't dream of it," he answered. He took a seat at the island and sat back. It was hard to beat an early morning tussle with Diana.

# CHAPTER TWO

**P**ETER SIPPED ON his coffee as he waited. He was constantly on Diana's case about how long she took to get ready, but the truth was she was a speed demon. He didn't know any woman, and he'd known a few, who could get ready as fast as she did. No matter how disheveled she was when he found her, she always emerged shortly afterward looking perfectly put together.

Hauling her out of bed at all hours of the night hadn't gotten old, either. And he had a great excuse. She'd asked to be called in on any unusual case. As a senior detective for Vancouver Police Department, most of his cases were unusual.

The first time he had been called out in the middle of the night, he waited until a more reasonable hour to bring her in. She hadn't been pleased. All manner of people had traipsed through the crime scene before she'd gotten there. She had wanted to see it intact, and she made sure everyone knew it. He had learned his lesson well. Now he called her immediately, no matter the time.

When they first met, Diana and Peter had disliked each

other instantly, but as he had gotten to know her, his opinion changed. She thought she was always right, and that she could manage any situation, even if she couldn't. But she was loyal. Intensely so. And she was willing to risk her own life to save someone else, no matter who. Even him. *Especially him?*

More than once he had caught her placing herself between him and a potential threat. She was like a hawk. She noticed the minutest signs of danger and made corresponding tiny movements to deflect them. She would angle herself so she stood between him and whatever it was that had the potential to harm him. He watched her closely and saw that she did it every damn time.

He'd called out her crazy, reckless behavior. He was ex-SpecOps with more than a hundred missions under his belt. He didn't need her to protect him. Diana had exploded. He could shove his sexist, macho views where the sun didn't shine. Apparently, he was imagining things. She hadn't put herself in harm's way to protect him. Why should she? He was a big boy and could take care of himself. Especially when he was often the one antagonizing the suspects in the first place. It had been quite an ear-bashing.

Over time, it had become clear to him that her instinct to protect was subconscious. She had no idea she was doing it. He warmed to her for it, but it also infuriated him. This stupid habit of hers would get her killed one day.

In a short space of time, they had become friends. They still fought like cat and dog, and most of the other cops in the division knew to hide when they started in on each other. It was a lot safer not to get caught in their crossfire. Even Donaldson made himself scarce when they were having one of their arguments. The superintendent had told them they were his best team, but they were as volatile as a nuclear bomb. He loved their results, but he didn't want to get caught in the blast area.

"Diana?" he called.

"Coming," she answered. A few moments later, she appeared, looking more like her usual self. "What is it?"

"How do you eat?" he asked. That sounded a little moronic. Her raised eyebrows and skeptical look confirmed it.

"I put food in my mouth, I chew, then I swallow. You know, like most living creatures." She opened the fridge and grabbed a strawberry. "Like this." She slowly took a bite out of the red, juicy fruit, gazing at him as she chewed.

Peter cleared his throat. "You know I don't mean that," he said. "You spend so much time working for VPD, and I know how little they pay you, so how can you *afford* to eat?"

She shifted her attention back to the contents of her fridge. When she hesitated, he spoke up. "Sorry," he said. "Didn't mean to pry. I know it's none of my business."

She shrugged. "You just caught me off guard. I never worked at the magazine for the paycheck. It was just a nice change of pace from CSIS." Diana had worked for the Canadian Security Intelligence Service after which she became the editor for Crime & Punishment magazine. CSIS conducted covert and overt operations concerning threats to national security both within Canada and abroad. Sometimes these involved local, but serious threats such as drug or people trafficking. Other times, they got involved in counterterrorism. Diana had been a field agent. A good one.

Her sojourn from fighting crime hadn't lasted long. It had taken less than a year for her frustration with her much-too-calm life at the magazine to build up to a boiling point. She had solved the problem by joining VPD as a consultant.

Working on cases with Peter now took up the bulk of her time.

"When I left CSIS, I received a bunch of back pay in a lump sum. I wanted to get the most out of it. So, I did my research, and I learned everything I could about the stock market and currency trading. I took some of the money and put it into long-term investments, while the rest of it I traded on the currency market, multiplying it exponentially."

This was mostly true. The investing part of it, at least. The lump sum from CSIS had been small however, the bulk of the money had come from her parents' estate.

"So, you're a woman of independent means? Rich? he said.

"I wouldn't say rich, exactly. Let's just say that if I never receive another paycheck again, I can still afford to live comfortably and take a nice vacation a few times a year," she said with a small smile.

"You'll have to teach me," he declared. "I'd enjoy having that kind of freedom, able to do whatever I wanted without money being an issue."

"Sure. Why not? It's no big deal. You're already good at spotting patterns, so I don't see why you wouldn't do well."

"I'll hold you to that."

She looked at him.

"I mean it," he said seriously.

"So do I," she replied. There was a pause. "So, do you want something to eat?" she asked.

"I wouldn't say no to a quick sandwich, thanks."

"Ham and cheese, coming right up."

When he bit into his sandwich, Peter moaned in delight. Diana's ham and cheese sandwiches were never as simple as they sounded. Tomatoes, lettuce, pickles, mayo, prosciutto, and Gouda cheese. "I swear, you're even better in the kitchen than you are at interrogating people."

"Why, thank you, detective," she said with a smile. "So, what's this case?"

He shrugged. "Don't know much. Dunway was first on the scene. The victim is male. He's been decapitated." Diana's eyebrows climbed into her scalp. "Thing is that when I last spoke to Dunway, they hadn't found the head. Since he hasn't called me back, I'm assuming it's still missing."

Diana's eyes twinkled. "Sounds like my kind of case."

"You are the weirdest woman I've ever met. You get excited over dead bodies and missing heads and have no problem talking about decapitation over breakfast at 4AM."

She snorted. "Further proof I spend way too much time with you. I know, I know, you're absolutely perfect. You complain that *I'm* a little out of sorts on certain mornings? You put me to shame. You're surly and unpleasant *all* the time," she pointed out.

"No, I'm not. I'm just impatient—"

"And surly. And unpleasant. And bossy. And even obnoxious on occasion." She enumerated a few of his less endearing traits.

"I'm not like that with you," he replied.

She dipped her head and looked at him dubiously from under her eyebrows, long eyelashes splayed wide.

Peter ignored her little dig and polished off his sandwich. He would get her for it later. He always did. He took his plate to the sink, washed it, and put it in the rack to dry. "Come on, madam, let's get going. There's a body waiting for us, and Doc won't hold off forever."

He was right. They couldn't keep everyone waiting. Her phone showed it was half past four. She would make sure she got back in a few hours to take Max out for a walk and feed him.

"Okay, let's go." She shut the door behind them and checked that it was locked. She looked around as she did so, watchful. Nothing was moving.

While they waited for the elevator, she held out her hand. "Keys."

"No," he snapped.

She leveled a glare at him. "I'm driving."

"No, you're not. It's my car."

"You drive like a little old lady."

"Just because I choose to drive safely and make sure we get there in one piece doesn't mean I drive like a little old lady."

She got into the elevator. "When you drive, scooters overtake us."

"And when you drive, they put out a nationwide alert."

"At least I don't watch horses trot by when I'm driving," she muttered. "Hand the keys over."

"You don't know where we're going." He had lost this argument more than once, and if he didn't tie it up now, she would make a run for the car and post herself in front of the driver's door until he gave up the keys.

Diana opened her mouth to deliver a sharp retort but changed her mind. "And you're not going to tell me until you're driving, are you?" she asked after a moment's hesitation.

He shook his head. "Nope."

"Fine. But you still drive like a little old lady," she sniped.

A few minutes later, they were driving through a very quiet Vancouver. "So, where was the body found?" she asked.

Since he was safely behind the wheel, Peter saw no reason to keep it a secret any longer. "Downtown Eastside," he replied, naming one of the worst areas in the city. It was a den for drug dealers, drug addicts, sex workers, and many other people dancing with the darker side of life. No one in their right mind would want to be hanging around Downtown Eastside in the dead of night. Not unless they carried a gun, and even then, it was best to keep one's head down.

"You take me to the nicest places," she said sweetly.

"I know. Thoughtful, aren't I?"

She shook her head. "The best."

## CHAPTER THREE

W HEN THEY GOT there, the crime scene
was already bustling with activity. Spotlights
lit up the corner of the alley where the body
lay, trash and fallen leaves obscuring it from the street.
There wasn't a homeless person, drug addict, or prostitute
in sight.

Diana looked at all the uniformed officers and wrinkled
her brow. "I hope they haven't moved anything." She bit
her lip.

"Don't worry. They know you're coming. They
wouldn't dare," Peter replied.

Diana threw Peter a dirty look. She wasn't that bad. But
some of the constables, especially the rookies, tended to lose
their lunches at gruesome sights, or they were a little
overzealous in their attempt to impress their superiors.
They ended up contaminating the crime scene. Once, after
a rookie had removed a key piece of evidence from a body,
Diana had exploded. While she could be uncommunicative
and come off as snotty – as Peter so quaintly put it – she

rarely let her temper fly. That day though, she'd sent it to Mars. The rookie almost cried.

Since then, everyone in VPD knew if Peter was assigned a case, Diana wouldn't be far behind, and that meant nothing could barely be looked at, let alone touched before she got there.

Diana got out of the car and followed Peter into the alley. "Good morning, Dunway, Gibson," she greeted the two constables guarding the crime scene. "What do you have for us?" she asked.

"Good morning, ma'am, sir," Dunway replied. The constable glanced toward the back of the alley and swallowed. "It's a bit unsettling, Miss," he said. "There's no head to the body."

She waved a hand. "Don't worry about me. I have a strong stomach."

"Well, if you're sure..." Dunway trailed off. When she nodded, he led them to the body. Diana lifted her chin slightly but stared resolutely. Just as Dunway had said, the body was headless.

Peter winced but was far too experienced with the sight of broken bodies to be affected further. He turned to Dunway. "Doc not here yet?" he asked.

Dunway shook his head. "He called a little while ago to say he was twenty minutes out."

Peter pulled two pairs of latex gloves from his pocket and handed one of them to Diana. "Any identification on him?" she asked Dunway.

"No, Miss. I checked his pockets for a wallet but there was nothing."

Diana's lips tightened into a harsh line. Dunway noticed and raised his palms. "I swear, Miss, I only patted his pockets. Nothing else." She nodded, satisfied. Diana stood while Peter lowered himself to study the body. "You see what I'm seeing?" she asked.

"Expensive clothes. Too expensive for this part of town." The man was dressed in a high-end quality suit that Diana would stake her life on was custom made. Just like the shirt and tie.

"Clearly, not a denizen of the area," Diana said. "So, was he in this part of town because he was having a really bad day, or was his body dumped here?" Diana tapped her lip. She walked around the body to take a look at the neck.

"The cut is clean through. This was done with a very sharp implement and by someone very strong."

Peter came around and looked at the wound. Cutting off someone's head wasn't easy.

"What do you think cause of death was?" Diana asked, looking over the rest of the body.

Peter looked at her as if she'd gone insane. "How about removal of one's head from one's body?"

"Ha, ha, aren't you the smart one? How could I have missed that, I wonder? But if your smartass-ness would like to take a closer look, you'll see there is very little evidence of bleeding. Unless of course, your stomach's too weak to take a closer look," she replied sweetly.

Peter frowned. "My stomach is fine, thank you very much." He lowered himself down to the body's level again. "I guess you're right. Something besides the obvious killed him." He looked up. "Dunway, any sign yet of his head?"

"Sorry, Detective, nothing. We have men out searching every nook, cranny, and dumpster on a five-block radius."

"If we don't find it, it will be hard to identify him," Peter said. "I'd like to hope that his fingerprints are in the system, but judging by his clothes, I doubt he's had any run-ins with the law."

"We might get lucky. If he's as rich as his appearance suggests, someone will report him missing, even if it's just to make sure they can get their hands on his money," Diana said.

"You're rather cynical this fine morning?"

"Huh?"

"Well, you know, he might be reported missing because he's somebody's loved one," Peter suggested.

"Maybe, but even if he's loathed by everyone he knows, he'll still be reported missing. Someone will want to get a hold of his money."

"I give up. There's not a single soft, romantic or compassionate bone in that entire body, is there?" Peter gestured at her from head to toe.

"Compassion? You don't even know the meaning of the word. And romance?" Diana snorted again. "I'll let you in on a little secret. Chugging beer while watching hockey in a bar is not romantic."

"She said she loved hockey," he shot back.

Diana looked heavenward.

"They at it again?" a new voice intervened. "Who's winning?"

Peter and Diana looked over. Doc Riddle had arrived.

"I'd say Ms. Hunter is in the lead this time," Dunway chuckled.

Diana looked at Peter and gave him a smug grin. Peter glared at Dunway.

"Leave the poor man alone, Peter. Just because you're a sore loser doesn't mean you should take it out on other people," Diana scolded.

"I didn't even say anything!" he exclaimed.

"Would you two stop bickering long enough to get out of my way?" Doc snapped. They jumped like naughty children. A small, balding man in his fifties and a paper body suit and booties rustled past them into the spotlight.

"Yes, Doc," they chorused and moved out of the way to give the medical examiner room to work.

They kept quiet, well aware Doc didn't like to be disturbed when he examined a body, whether it was during the initial analysis or when he performed the autopsy. After six minutes of complete silence, however, Peter dared, "So, anything interesting?"

Doc didn't look up. "How about a body without a head?" he muttered.

A few minutes later, Doc hummed. "Found something?" Peter tried again. Diana marveled at his courage.

"Maybe," he said, studying the body's left hand closely. He got up and moved around the body to look at the other hand.

"Look at this," Doc motioned them over. "What do you see?" he asked. He showed them the man's hand, palm side up. The finger pads had been eaten away.

"Acid?" Diana asked.

"I think so. It's the only explanation that makes any sense. I'll run some tests when I get the body to the morgue to make sure."

"Pre- or post-mortem?" Peter asked.

"I'm pretty sure this was done after he died. The crime scene is too clean. I would expect to see splash marks on his hands and the ground if he'd been alive when it was done. It looks almost like the acid was painted on. It was done carefully.

"So we can assume our killer wanted to stop the victim from being identified. Or at least delay the process," Peter said. He caught sight of Diana's face. She looked stunned, "What is it?"

"Doc, when you get to the morgue, could you run a full tox screen on him?" she said.

"I was going to anyway, but if you tell me what you're looking for, it'll make things easier."

"Some type of neuromuscular blocking agent," she replied.

"A what?" Peter asked.

"They are a class of drugs that cause paralysis. They're used in surgery, alongside anesthetics, to prevent the muscles from moving," Doc explained quickly.

Peter frowned and raised his eyebrows.

"It's just a hunch," Diana said. She turned to the medical examiner, "Can you look in his pockets?"

Doc slipped two gloved fingers into both of the body's pant pockets, then his jacket's breast pocket. Doc pulled out what looked, at first glance, like a folded blue piece of paper. It was a surgical mask. Peter looked over at Diana, but she was striding away, head down, her hands stuffed in her coat. Something was up.

# CHAPTER FOUR

P ETER DROPPED THE mask into an evidence bag and caught up with Diana. She often opted to keep her early theories to herself until she had a little evidence to back them up. But Peter could see from the worried look in her eyes and stiff posture, there was a lot more going on than just her wanting to keep her ideas private for now.

He pulled her aside, making sure they were out of everyone's earshot. "What's going on?" he whispered.

Diana looked up at him. "We're in a whole heap of trouble."

"You've seen something like this before?"

She nodded. "Kind of."

"Do we have a serial killer?"

Diana shook her head then paused. "Technically, no, but he is a psychopath." She hesitated. "If Doc finds a neuromuscular blocking agent in that guy's body, this was a professional hit."

Peter frowned. "A hit? Come on, Diana. Assassins like to do things clean and quick. A bullet between the eyes usually suffices. They don't normally get down and dirty with their marks. Chopping off heads and burning away fingerprints isn't usually their style. This guy, whoever he was, took his time with our friend over here."

Diana frowned. "If the person who did this is the person I think it is, we've got trouble. He is known as Surgeon on account of the mask he always wears and leaves at the scene," she said. "He's a killer for hire and at the top of his game. He usually does jobs for drug cartels and terrorist organizations. And he only ever goes after high value targets. He travels all over the world fulfilling his contracts."

"How do you know all this?"

"CSIS. We tracked him for a while."

"And you never caught the guy?"

Diana shook her head. "No. He was only loosely connected to certain organizations we were investigating. Nothing concrete. The one time he set foot on Canadian soil, we lost him. Since he was a foreign national and he never returned, the higher-ups in CSIS had no reason to go after him.

"Hmm, well, now they do."

"Yes. Now he's turned up here. I hope I'm wrong. I really do. And it might not be him, cutting off heads isn't his style at all, but the other trademarks fit. And if it is him, then we have another problem."

"Oh?"

Diana shook her head. "CSIS will want in. They might even take the case from us."

Peter frowned. "That will depend, surely? If they want to work with us, I'm fine with that, but this looks like a murder, not a part of a terrorist plot. Technically, they have no jurisdiction."

"We don't know if it's just a simple murder and even if it is—"

"VPD, and me specifically," Peter clarified, "don't take kindly to interlopers. They can't just take the case. They have no authority muscling in."

Diana shrugged. "They won't see it like that."

Peter looked her straight in the eye. Diana was equivocating. That was unlike her. He still didn't know exactly what she had done for CSIS but he understood the workings of the organization enough to know it had to be ruthless when pursuing its objectives. He also understood the power politics that were rife in such an organization and the dangerous work that instilled a loyalty that could seem illogical or out of character to an outsider.

Still, he couldn't help but challenge her. "How do you see it?" He was asking her where her loyalties lay. Would she side with CSIS against VPD? Against him?

She looked right back at him, and without hesitation said, "We'll clean this up. I'll back you up, don't worry. But it won't be easy," she warned. "If this is Surgeon, we're looking at more than one guy's murder. It's likely there's a lot going on, and we might not like what we find."

Peter shrugged. "I'm up for it if you are." Diana looked away.

"Anyhow, it's all moot until Doc does his thing. Let's take a look around and see if we can't figure out who our victim is. Fingers crossed this is just a run-of-the-mill nutcase," she said.

"You know things are bad when you're hoping the perp turns out to be *only* a serial killer," Peter muttered.

"You have no idea," Diana replied.

They spent the next hour combing the crime scene, doing their best to stay out of Tina's way. The head of the crime lab had arrived and had gotten straight to work. They hadn't found much. The scene had been carefully photographed, Tina and her people had done a thorough sweep, and Diana and Peter had done everything they could, including dumpster diving, to find any clue that might uncover the identity of their victim. The head did not turn up.

"Maybe our killer took it with him as a trophy of sorts."

Diana's heart had surged a little at the idea. Her man wasn't known for taking trophies. Perhaps it wasn't him.

"Let's hope so," she replied. "I'd really like to be wrong on this."

"Well, there's nothing more we can do here," Peter said. "Let's get down to the station. Missing persons might have something for us."

Diana took her phone out to check the time. She was feeling depressed and anxious. It was almost seven in the morning. "Can you drop me off at my place? I need to take Max out. I'll meet you later."

"Sure. Anything for my guy, Max," he smiled, "As long as you bring me a coffee when you come in." He saw her hesitate. "Are you okay?"

"Yes, but this case... Oh, it's a long story. And it might not be him," she added, coming to a decision. She swung her arms and gave him a tight smile.

"I'll tell you later. When we know for sure. Let's go."

# CHAPTER FIVE

A N EXUBERANT MAX greeted Diana when she got home. He ran over to her, jumping up her leg, barking his welcome. Then, like an over-stimulated child who couldn't stand all the excitement, he ran away down the hallway to calm himself before hurling himself back again and repeating his performance. Diana knelt down and gave him a scratch between the ears. "Who's mommy's good boy?" she murmured. He yipped happily, rolled on his back, and whined. She scratched his tummy and laughed. He looked hilarious lying on his back with his tongue hanging out and his legs at odd angles.

She sobered quickly. No matter how much joy Max brought her, she couldn't shake the feeling that something very bad was going to happen. She had no way of knowing for sure if this latest killing was the work of Surgeon, but it had all of his hallmarks. She stood up with a sigh and grabbed Max's leash.

Outside, as Max trotted along, stopping every few seconds to sniff, she thought back to her own encounter with the killer. Peter was right. Assassins didn't usually take time liquidating their targets. Typically, they simply murdered their victims as quickly and as cleanly as possible before disappearing into the shadows.

But for Surgeon, killing was something else, an art, something to be savored and perfected. Not for him the sudden, bloody, violence that usually accompanied even a clinically efficient professional hit. Surgeon's preferred method was to administer a blocking agent and watch his victim quietly slip away. A small prick most people wouldn't even feel was all it took to deliver the drug. It took ten minutes at most for the subject to die of suffocation under these circumstances, all without causing a fuss. Or a mess.

As killing methods went, it was surprisingly graceful and effective. Leaving a mask on the body was one of his hallmarks, as was removing the victim's fingerprints. Surgeon liked to play with law enforcement and make their job difficult. That's how he saw killing. Play.

Max whined, bringing her back to the present. "Sorry, boy," she murmured. She walked toward her building.

She felt a prickling sensation on the back of her neck. Someone was watching her. She turned to scan the area but couldn't see anything. Still, she knew someone was there. She was certain of it. Affecting a casualness she was nowhere close to feeling, she shrugged and walked into her building.

She took a deep breath and gave herself a mental shake. Though her gut instinct rarely steered her wrong, she reminded herself that they didn't have any evidence yet that it was Surgeon behind this latest killing. Maybe it was just her imagination playing tricks on her. She was nervous. Surgeon was the only one who had ever gotten close to ending her life, and her experience had led her down a path she hadn't anticipated. He was also the only one who'd got away.

"What's wrong with you, boy? Are you deaf?" Donaldson snapped.

"No, sir," Peter gritted his teeth. "But I don't understand what CSIS wants with this case."

"Hell if I know, either," Donaldson grumbled. "I just got a call twenty minutes ago from the Deputy Commissioner telling me CSIS would be coming in to assist."

"Assist?" It wasn't the first time CSIS had poked their noses into one of Peter's cases, but it was the first time they had offered to "assist."

"Yeah, I know. I found that strange, too. Guess it might have something to do with Diana," Donaldson said. "Maybe they want her help. Or something."

"How did they find out about the case so quickly?" Peter asked. He hadn't had a chance to run a search for their victim or the M.O. or anything, so how had CSIS found out?

Donaldson raised an eyebrow. "You do realize this is CSIS we're talking about – an intelligence agency. Knowing things is their business."

Peter grunted. He didn't buy it. They weren't all-knowing. They had to have found out somehow. From someone. Diana...?

"When will they be here?" Peter asked his boss.

"About half an hour or so," Donaldson said.

Peter turned to leave Donaldson's office. "Hopkinson," his super barked, stopping him in his tracks, "I know this is annoying as hell, but I need you to play nice. If CSIS has gotten involved, there must be much more going on than we know about. Remember, this is about finding the killer and making sure no one else gets hurt, so forget about your ego. Just play nice, you hear?"

Peter nodded with a grunt.

He walked out of Donaldson's office and ran right into Diana. "Whoa!" He grabbed her by the shoulders so she didn't lose her balance.

"Are you *trying* to kill me?" she snapped.

"Diana, we need to talk."

"What is it?" There was fear in her eyes. Diana could be cold, sharp, brittle, but she rarely looked vulnerable. It unsettled him.

"CSIS—"

"Well, well, well, if it isn't the smart ass rookie with a bleeding heart," a male voice tinged with a heavy dose of sarcasm interrupted him. Peter looked over Diana's shoulder to see two men walking up the corridor. One looked in his late thirties, tall, an aquiline nose dominating his features, his hair sharply cut and gelled. The other was younger, clearly the junior of the two judging by his more submissive gait. They both wore dark suits, ties, and had sunglasses in their top pockets. Standard plain clothes investigative uniform.

Diana stiffened. She backed away from Peter a step and turned around. "Why, if it isn't the jerk who doesn't know when to shut up." Diana and the older man glared at each other. Peter tensed.

Suddenly, the guy who'd spoken softened and a wide grin spread across his face. "Di, it's so good to see you!" he exclaimed, holding out his arms. Arms into which Diana ran without a moment's hesitation.

"Kieran, I'm so happy they sent you," she said, her voice

muffled by the fact that her face was buried in the man's suit jacket.

"Who else would they send?" he said as he held her out at arm's length. "As soon as the boss found out you were working on this and who was involved, she told me to get moving." He paused for a moment. "Are you okay?" He looked genuinely worried for her.

Peter took a deep breath and exhaled. He crossed his arms, waiting.

"I'm fine," she said. She hesitated for a moment. "Are you sure it's him?"

Kieran nodded. "No doubt about it. I'm sorry, baby girl. We've been waiting for him to show himself. We got some intel that he was in the country, but we had no idea where. Or why."

*Baby girl?* Who the hell was this guy? It had never even crossed Peter's mind to call Diana anything other than, strangely enough, "Diana." Peter cleared his throat. He felt like a guy in the friend zone at a lover's reunion.

Diana turned, a sheepish smile on her face. "Sorry," she said quickly. "Kieran, this is Detective Peter Hopkinson. He's the lead on this case. Peter, this is Kieran Black. He used to be my partner at CSIS."

*Partner?* Great. "Hi," he replied gruffly, shaking the other man's hand. Kieran's handshake was strong. They were about the same size, but Kieran was a few years older, and he was much too attractive for Peter's liking. Peter squeezed the other guy's hand a little harder.

Kieran's eyes crinkled as he smiled. "You'll do," he said.

"Sorry?" Peter demanded.

"To look after my baby girl here," Kieran replied, inclining his head toward Diana.

"Oh, really?"

"Yup, only the best for my girl. I checked you out. I hear good things, Hopkinson."

Peter bristled.

"Okay, that's enough. We need to brief the Superintendent. We have a killer to catch," Diana intervened.

"Ms. Hunter," another voice interjected. It was the poor sucker who'd accompanied Black and whom they'd completely ignored. "My name's Steven Jones. I'm Kieran's partner. I've heard so much about you. It's a pleasure."

Diana smiled and shook his hand. "Good to meet you too, Mr. Jones."

"Please, call me Steve. And don't worry, he won't get away this time," the young man said. Peter swiveled his head to look at him hard. *This time?*

"Damn right, he won't," Diana replied, her face hardening before switching again, the smile back in full force. "Peter, why don't you go with Kieran and Steve to the conference room? I'll get the superintendent. I need a moment." She had a pleading look in her eyes.

"Sure thing. Follow me, gentlemen," Peter said, starting to walk, his confusion imperceptible to the men around him.

# CHAPTER SIX

D IANA WALKED INTO Donaldson's office. "CSIS are here," she said.

The super looked up. "Will they work with us or will they make our lives harder?"

"They'll cooperate. They want to catch this guy as badly as we do."

Donaldson studied her for a moment. "This is personal for you, isn't it?"

"Yes."

"And that's all you're going to say?"

Diana shrugged. "For now. Until it becomes relevant to the case. *If* it becomes relevant to the case."

Donaldson slapped his hands on his desk and pushed himself out of his chair. "Fine. Let's get this show on the road."

When they walked into the conference room, the air crackled with tension. Diana sighed. The last thing she needed was to be stuck between two alpha males. Kieran and Peter had even sat themselves on opposite sides of the table. This was going to get really old, really fast.

Diana made the introductions and when Donaldson took his place at the end of the table, she sat next to him, making her position clear. She wasn't choosing sides in Peter and Kieran's stupid little war. "So, what do we have?" Donaldson asked.

Diana listened as Peter explained what they had found at the crime scene. For Donaldson's benefit, she explained about Surgeon, his predilection for removing fingerprints and using a neuromuscular agent to disable his victims. "But until we get confirmation from Doc, there's no way of knowing whether it's him," she said, giving Kieran a pointed look.

"That's not entirely accurate. We're pretty certain it's him," he said.

"Why?" Diana demanded.

"Because of who his victim is."

"And how do you know that?" Peter said.

"Because we've been surveilling him," Steve jumped in.

"I thought surveilling Canadians was illegal," Donaldson said, giving him a dirty look.

"It is, unless there is a credible threat to national security. But in any case, our victim wasn't Canadian."

"Well, don't keep us on the edge of our seats. Who was he?" Donaldson snapped.

"He's had many aliases. No one knows his real name, but we knew him as Lucenzo Garibaldi," Kieran said, looking right at Diana.

"You have got to be kidding me," Diana breathed out.

"Hang on, hang on. Who is this Garibaldi guy and what's his connection with Surgeon? And," Peter emphasized without pausing, "if you were following Garibaldi so closely, how exactly did he get himself killed?"

Kieran grimaced, "We heard that he was in the country

to carry out a hit. We lost him a couple of days ago." He turned to Donaldson, "Lucenzo Garibaldi is – was – also an assassin. Word is that Garibaldi trained Surgeon in some of his techniques, although the execution method of paralysis and suffocation appears to be unique to Surgeon, hence the name. Speculation was that something went wrong between the two. They went from being partners to rivals in short order. "

Diana turned to Kieran. "How sure are you it was Garibaldi?"

"As certain as you are that someone's been watching you," Kieran said.

Diana's eyes widened, then narrowed at Kieran. "What?" Peter exclaimed. "Why didn't you tell me anything?"

She turned to Peter, "Because I thought it was just my imagination, that's why. I should have known better." She looked back at Kieran. "Since when have you been watching me?"

Kieran went red. "Just a few days," he mumbled.

"Why?"

"We heard chatter about Surgeon coming to Canada... I wanted to keep an eye on you... you know, make sure..." he trailed off and gave her a helpless look.

"Really, Kieran." She drummed her fingers on the table.

"Beside the fact that I should lock you up for stalking," Peter snapped, "what exactly does Surgeon have to do with you following Diana around?"

"You haven't told them?" Kieran asked, his tone heavy with censure.

Diana shook her head.

"Told us what?" Peter demanded.

She glared at Kieran. "I see you're still very talented at putting your foot in your mouth."

"Don't," Kieran warned her. "You can't expect them to do their jobs properly if you hold information back."

"Okay, stop. What are you talking about?" Peter's voice was strong and commanding, but Diana ignored him. "I'm not a rookie anymore, Kieran. I can handle myself."

"I know you can, but no one can be objective after what he put you through. If you want this to work," he said, waving his hand around to encompass the group, "you need to tell them the truth. All of it."

"So, they suddenly have clearance?" she snapped.

"For this, yes," Kieran said. He placed both of his palms flat on the table in front of him.

"Fine!" Diana turned to look at Peter. "Surgeon kidnapped me. He let me go. The end."

"Stop being childish. Tell them the whole story," Kieran insisted.

They faced off across the table.

Kieran had been impossible to work with for a while after her abduction. She had been a new recruit and he'd been charged with seasoning her. He'd come close to losing a brand new CSIS agent, and he'd taken it personally.

After that, he'd been wildly overprotective and micromanaging to the point that she had taken to avoiding him. When that didn't work, she had gone to his boss to complain. Now though, while Diana didn't appreciate what he was saying to her, she knew he was right. She had to tell the others what had really gone on. She stared defiantly at Kieran then glanced at each of the faces that stared back at her passively, waiting for her to explain. She wasn't getting out of this.

# CHAPTER SEVEN

"I T WAS MY first major mission," Diana said. "A prominent Saudi imam was scheduled to visit Canada, and we obtained reliable intel that an attempt would be made on his life. The death of the imam on Canadian soil would have made us a target for every terrorist group out there, not to mention the strain it would have put on our relations with Saudi Arabia. It was a big deal."

"Come on, Di, get to the point," Kieran admonished. She gave him a dirty look. So what if she was delaying the inevitable? They weren't pleasant memories.

"We learned that Surgeon was the assassin. Kieran managed to locate him. As his rookie, I went along for the ride. We were able to get the imam out and neutralize Surgeon's attempt. He fled. The failure of his mission made him angry. Very angry. It was his first and only miss. He became fixated on me. He was convinced I'd ruined his plans and humiliated him—"

"Well, you were the one who figured out what he was

up to, so you pretty much were the reason he failed," Kieran pointed out.

"We didn't capture him, though. We thought, hoped, that he'd left the country, but we were wrong. One night, he grabbed me. He held me for three days."

Kieran shook his head. "Longest three days of my life," he muttered. "Everyone was convinced she was dead, but I knew if anyone could survive, it was Diana. We kept searching."

"He didn't do much to hurt me physically. It seems he enjoys playing with his victims when he's not on the clock. He drugged me so that I was completely paralyzed and spent three days telling me, in gruesome detail, what exactly he was going to do to me. It was three days of non-stop, extreme, psychological torture. Then he let me go."

"Just like that?" Donaldson asked, his deep voice resonating in the silent room.

"Just like that," Diana agreed.

"Why?" Peter asked. "Why not kill you?"

"We've never been sure. Perhaps to taunt us. The threat of him grabbing Diana again has always been present," Kieran replied.

"He's been slipping through the fingers of the world's intelligence agencies ever since. Once we were sure he was off Canadian soil, our superiors at CSIS reprioritized, and he's been at large ever since."

Peter watched Diana. Her tone was even as she relayed the story, but clearly it still affected her. She was pale, and her pupils were dilated. He looked over to Kieran. Guilt was stamped across his face.

"So you know what he looks like?" Donaldson asked.

Diana shook her head. "No. His eyes but no more. He wore a mask. Never took it off."

Kieran sighed. "That's not the end of the story."

"Every year, on the anniversary of my abduction, he sends flowers and a card to me via CSIS," Diana continued.

Peter's eyebrows rose into his hairline. "Creepy. He's obsessed with you," he muttered.

"Obsessed is putting it mildly," Kieran snorted.

"Do you think he's here for Diana?" Donaldson asked.

Kieran shook his head. "No. Diana's identity was kept secret, so there's no way he knows who she really is."

"How can you be sure?" Peter demanded.

"Because he hasn't tried to grab her again," Kieran said.

"When's the next anniversary?"

Kieran looked at everyone in turn. "Two days' time," he said gravely.

Peter turned to him. "Well, he might change his mind this time. He could find out who she is, it wouldn't be that difficult. If he's in the country, we should be fully alert to that possibility," he said. "And he definitely can't find out she's involved in this case."

Kieran nodded. "I agree."

"She'll have to stay here, under guard. She definitely can't be out and about," Peter said.

"Totally."

"Excuse me! *She* is in the room, and *she* can take care of herself," Diana snapped.

"Diana, don't be your usual mule-headed self for once. You know that if he finds out you're involved, he'll stop at nothing to get at you," Kieran said.

Diana's eyes narrowed. "He's probably long gone by now."

"We don't know that. We can't take that chance." Kieran remonstrated with her.

"Look, you're not thinking strategically. Even if he is

still in the country, we can use his fixation on me to our advantage."

"Absolutely not," Peter retorted. The fool woman was going to get herself killed.

"You don't even know what I was going to say," Diana huffed.

"Yes, we do, and no way in hell are we letting you stick your neck out. It's too dangerous," Kieran replied, siding with Peter.

"Who said you have any say in the matter? The fastest way we can get to him is to use me as bait."

"No, no, and no," Peter said.

"He's right, Diana. It's way too dangerous." Kieran agreed.

Diana folded her arms and looked down at the table.

"So do we know why he killed Garibaldi?" Peter asked, changing the subject.

"Well?" Diana looked up at Kieran angrily.

"Not specifically, no. But we are concerned that he has other business here, beside the Garibaldi hit. We're keeping an eye on a number of events that are taking place next week," he said.

"What's the most high profile?" Peter asked.

"One moment, please," Steve said, surprising everyone. It was the first time he'd spoken since they'd entered the room. He took out a tablet and swiped at the screen a few times.

"We have the Canada Day celebrations on July 1st. The Governor General will attend, along with a number of other dignitaries from various countries, and there's a reception at the Saudi Embassy being held to honor the visiting Crown Prince Nasser bin Hadeel. The Prime Minister will also be attending, along with other Canadian officials."

"Hmmm, they *are* very high profile. That's not really Surgeon's thing. He prefers the covert hits. You don't genuinely think The Prime Minister and these others are at risk from him do you?" Diana asked.

"We have nothing specific, but these events along with his presence in the country are enough for us to be concerned."

Diana cocked her head and Peter looked over at her. "I think we're all forgetting one very important element here," she said.

"What might that be, Diana?" Steve asked.

"Lucenzo Garibaldi. He's a piece of the puzzle. Was his killing part of a personal vendetta between him and Surgeon, or is it linked to a larger operation?"

"None of these targets," Peter waved at the tablet Steve was still holding, "explains why Garibaldi is in the morgue without his head and his fingerprints."

"So that's obviously the first question we need to answer. Why this Surgeon guy went after him," Donaldson, who had been sitting quietly, interjected. "I suggest that's where you start. Presumably you have people looking out for him at the ports."

"Yes, sir," Kieran replied, "although it's something of a fool's errand because we don't know what he looks like."

"Well, let's start with the motive. Hopkinson dig around and follow the Garibaldi/Surgeon angle."

"Yes, sir," Peter replied.

"You, Mr. Black, look out for your high profile targets and let Peter and Diana know whatever else you find out and they will do the same. Diana, desk work only." Diana opened her mouth to object. "No arguments. I don't want you out and about on this case. Update me in twenty-four hours." When no one moved, he added, "So, get to it, people."

## CHAPTER EIGHT

D IANA EYED HER phone nervously. In two days they had barely made any progress on the case. Doc had confirmed the presence of a neuro-muscular drug in the body and certified the cause of death as suffocation, but that only confirmed what they already knew. She was jittery. It was the anniversary of her encounter with Surgeon.

Kieran would call her when the flowers and card were delivered. That had been their practice every year. The first few years that they'd started arriving, he'd kept the information from her. She'd been furious. Ever since, Kieran had faithfully let her know.

She turned back to her laptop, and immediately, her phone rang. She snatched it up.

"Have they arrived?"

"Yup, same as always. Card, flowers. This time, though, he's sent you something else. There was a flash drive with the card. We're having it analyzed now."

"Any trace on where the flowers came from?"

"Nope. Delivery guy was just some delivery guy. But

we're following through with the florist to see how the order was placed and where the memory stick came from. Watch this space. I'll get back to you when I know more."

Diana sighed as she put the phone down. She had been extra vigilant, but she'd refused the offer of extra protection that Donaldson had extended. The anniversary of her abduction was always unsettling, but knowing that Surgeon had been, and possibly still was, in her vicinity had spiked her anxiety.

Her phone rang again. "Yes?"

"We've got something."

"Well, what is it?"

"It's a recording of a call between Surgeon and Bernard Kloch of Blue Panther Security."

"You're not serious," Diana said. Blue Panther Security was a large Canadian corporation. Kloch was their CEO. The company's reputation was less than spotless, and their methods had come into question many times, especially since Kloch had taken over the company from his father seven years ago. Yet they were the good guys. The government contracted with them to support Canadian troops deployed in Afghanistan. Their domestic operation protected some of the most important and influential people in the country. What was Kloch doing talking to Surgeon?

"They're discussing the contract to take out Garibaldi. I'm coming over right now."

Once again the five of them convened in the conference room: Diana, Peter, Donaldson, Kieran, and Steve.

"So what've you got?" Donaldson asked.

"We have a recording of two men arranging the hit on

Garibaldi. We've done a voice comparison on Kloch and confirmed it," Steve hesitated, "Ms. Hunter, we'd like you to listen to the tape and verify that the other individual is Surgeon."

Diana avoided the men's eyes and nodded. "Okay."

Steve pressed a button on his laptop keyboard.

*"It will be my pleasure, sir. Rest assured, Lucenzo will be taken care of in a manner that he unquestionably deserves."*

Diana suppressed a shudder. "Yes, that's him."

"Sounds like a nutter to me," Donaldson growled.

"What do we know about Blue Panther Security? And Kloch?" Peter asked.

"We did some digging into Bernard Kloch and found a few interesting data points in his financials, namely, a payment of five million dollars from one of his personal accounts in the Caymans to an account in the British Virgin Islands," Steve reported. Peter whistled.

"Hmm, that's a lot of money. I wonder who Bernard Kloch is protecting. Undoubtedly Garibaldi was here to assassinate someone. Maybe someone Kloch wanted staying alive. Perhaps he hired Surgeon to kill Garibaldi for that reason. To remove the threat to Kloch's man." Diana said, impressed in spite of herself. Ordering a hit on a hitman to prevent another hit wasn't common even among the world of conspiracy and corruption that she was used to.

"Or he is the middleman. Someone else ordered the hit on Garibaldi and used Kloch as cover," Peter suggested.

"So, the next step is to talk to him," Kieran said.

"I doubt he'll be very forthcoming," Donaldson interjected.

"Do you know him, sir?" Kieran asked.

"I know of him. Wily devil. But as we have a recording of a conversation between him and Surgeon discussing the transaction, if not the details of the hit on Garibaldi, good old Bernard will have a hard time denying his involvement, I should imagine."

"Shall we arrest him?"

"No, don't do that. He has a lot of powerful friends. They might spring to his defense if we go hard on him from the get-go. Let's see if he'll cooperate informally first. Get him in here. Find out what he knows. Then let me know." Donaldson left the room, frowning.

The others stayed behind for a few moments.

"Donaldson seems jumpy about this Kloch guy. Do you know why?" Kieran's glance flicked between Diana and Peter. Diana shrugged.

"Hmm. Not sure. My guess is that we're close to treading on some political toes. He hates that kind of thing," Peter offered. "He's worried this could go very dark and very deep."

"He's demanding his lawyer, but that won't help him," Peter said as he shut the door to the interview room and stepped into the corridor outside.

"He has no idea who he's messing with, does he? You were like the Incredible Hulk in there." Diana was standing outside the interrogation room door.

Peter gave her an amused look. "I do not have a nasty disposition, and I don't turn green."

"I'll agree with the bit about turning green, although you have been known to turn a rather unpleasant shade when presented with a pineapple and jalapeño pizza. We'll have to debate the part about not having a nasty disposition."

Peter laughed. "Sadly I can't jump up multiple stories or punch through walls. Though it would be cool if I could," he grinned.

Diana smiled. "I always wanted to be Supergirl and date Thor."

"You do know they're from different universes, don't you?"

"Yes, but I don't care. The question is, how do you know? Let me guess, you've seen every Marvel movie to date," she said with a grin.

Peter blushed. "Twice. But if you tell anyone, I may have to kill you. Wouldn't do my credibility any good in the bullpen."

"Our secret, I swear," she said crossing her heart. "Soooo...," she said. Peter looked at her expectantly. "Marvel movie marathon at my place after the case is over?" she asked.

He grinned. "You're on. I'll bring beer and popcorn."

"After you two have finished setting up your date, maybe you could get back to work. There's a suspect to interrogate, a killer at large, and other, you know, minor things like that," Kieran said, as he passed them in the corridor.

"It's not a date," they both said at the same time.

"Yeah, right," Kieran muttered. "Can we get on with this?" He nodded toward the interview room.

"Together?" Diana asked Peter.

"Of course," he replied with a grin. "I'll be the Hulk. You can be Supergirl."

"As always," Diana said with a grin of her own.

"Oof. You're cold."

# CHAPTER NINE

P ETER OPENED THE door for Diana. She
walked in with a gentle smile on her face. "Mr.
Kloch?" she asked.

Kloch was a slight man with sparse fair hair and wire-
rimmed glasses. His slim body was draped in a sharp suit, a
Rolex watch wrapped around his thin wrist.

Unprepossessing, thought Diana. Intelligent. She
wasn't going to underestimate him.

"Yes," the man said quietly.

"I'm Diana Hunter. It's a pleasure to meet you."

Kloch was unmoved. "I wish I could say the same."

Diana took a seat opposite him, while Peter leaned
against the wall next to the door. He crossed his arms and
assumed what Diana had dubbed his "brooding killer shark
look." This was a routine they'd perfected over the months
they'd been working together. Peter dominated the suspects
while Diana charmed them into bonding with her in the
face of his intimidating presence. They often told her all she
needed to know, and if not, their unguarded body language
made them easy to interpret.

Sure enough, Kloch kept glancing to the side, monitoring Peter's presence, until Diana drew his attention to her. "Mr. Kloch, have you been informed of the reason for your visit with us?" Diana asked.

The man looked at her and shook his head. "This brute here," he nodded at Peter, "said it was something to do with a professional hit. Although why you should think I had anything to do with it, I have no idea. And holding me like this is against the law." He was haughty, indignant.

"But Mr. Kloch, you aren't under arrest," Diana said, affecting a perplexed look. "We've only asked you to come in because we need your help." She widened her eyes and gave him a beseeching look. She touched his arm.

Kloch, whose gaze had wandered to Peter again, turned back slowly to meet hers. He adjusted his glasses. "Yes, of course. Anything I can do to help VPD." He smiled, "We security forces must stick together, mustn't we?"

Diana saw he was shrewd, calculating. Superficially charming. Deadly if crossed?

A small smile graced Diana's lips. "Thank you, Mr. Kloch. We – I would really appreciate any help you can give us," she replied.

"Of course," he said smoothly.

"Now, Bernard, for our records, could you please confirm that you are the Chief Executive Officer of Blue Panther Security?" Diana asked.

"I am," he said gravely.

"According to our information, your company contracted—" she paused for effect and glanced into the file, "we know him as Surgeon, to perform a service for you. Is that correct?"

"Who?" he said.

"You haven't heard of him? He's a killer for hire."

Kloch's face darkened. "I have no idea about whom you are talking." His tone was clipped.

Diana raised her eyebrows. "Mr. Kloch, I have all your company's financial records right here. You made a payment of five million dollars in installments to a company located in the British Virgin Islands called Elexcor. This company has two major shareholders, also legal entities. One is registered in Jamaica and the other in the Bahamas. These two companies, in turn, are owned by a single entity registered in China. Now, I know China has a non-disclosure policy, but when my colleagues shared their suspicions concerning who owned this entity and indicated that they might leak this information, the company's associates were more than forthcoming. They told us they'd agreed to pay Surgeon the sum of five million dollars. They didn't know why but maybe you do...?"

"I have no idea what you're talking about. We did indeed contract Elexcor to provide additional security for one of our clients, but I have no idea who this Surgeon character is."

Diana cocked her head. She knew he was lying through his teeth, of course. If she hadn't listened to the recording that incriminated him, his micro-expressions would have told her so. He was showing fleeting moments of disgust, annoyance, and fear.

"Mr. Kloch," she stressed his name soothingly, "please don't waste my time. We know you paid Surgeon to assassinate Mr. Lucenzo Garibaldi. What I don't know is why, and that's exactly what I'd like you to tell me."

Kloch appeared unperturbed, but the slight tightening around his eyes and mouth indicated apprehension. He was worried. Good. He had plenty to be worried about.

"How dare you?" Kloch said coolly. "My company

works to protect Canadian soldiers. We don't go around ordering *hits* on people." He jabbed his forefinger at Diana, leaning over the table.

His display was more posture than substance, but Peter stalked over to him. "Sit down, now," he growled into Kloch's ear. His tone was menacing. Kloch calmly planted his behind back in his chair. "You *will* tell us what we want to know," Peter said, ever happy to play the heavy. He resumed his stance against the wall.

"Look, I don't know anything," Kloch stated mildly, his voice steady. He sat back and crossed his legs. It was as though he hadn't a care in the world. But Diana knew better. There was a very slight sheen on his upper lip.

"Mr. Kloch," Diana said with a sigh, "I'd hoped you'd be more forthcoming. But we are wasting time." She took her phone out of her pocket. She swiped, tapped, swiped twice more, and tapped one more time. Seconds later, voices filled the room. She placed the phone on the table between them and watched for Kloch's reaction.

*"Mr. Bernard Kloch?"*

*"Yes."*

*"I've received word that you wish to contract my services. You wish to dispose of a difficult target?"*

*"Yes. Lucenzo Garibaldi. He needs to be eliminated."*

"You can't prove anything with that." Kloch said. Diana watched him carefully. He was cool, still.

"Mr. Kloch, the conversation continues and provides plenty of proof," Diana replied. "You were there. You know what was said."

Kloch shrugged. "Okay, if you insist, yes, I did contract Surgeon's services." He said nothing more. Diana waited, but when he didn't continue, she said, "The question that is begging to be asked, Mr. Kloch, is *why*?"

Kloch tilted his head to one side as he considered the question. "One of our teams in Afghanistan came across information that Senator Riley Greene was being targeted by an extremist Islamic group. They had engaged Garibaldi to eliminate Senator Greene. The Senator was provided with government-sponsored protection on account of his position, but he also contracted our company's services for additional security as a result of this threat to his life."

"Protection doesn't usually cover ordering a hit," Peter pointed out from the side of the room.

The man looked at Peter with the same unfazed look.

"When we discovered who posed the threat to Senator Greene, we felt it was more prudent to fight fire with fire. Why put my men in harm's way when the situation had a much simpler solution? An eye for an eye. A hit for a hit."

Peter spoke up again, "You know as well as anyone that it's as much a crime to order an execution as it is to carry one out."

Kloch shrugged. "It's also illegal to double park, but people do it all the time."

Peter's eyes flickered, and he cut a quick glance at Diana. Kloch thought himself above the law.

"Anyway, it's not as if Garibaldi will be missed," Kloch continued. "He's been responsible for dozens of deaths. You should be thanking me. Agencies around the world have been trying to catch him for years. We were just the first to have the courage to do what was necessary to get him. Thanks to us, he is no longer a danger to anyone."

"You said Senator Greene was the target of this new Islamic terror group, and that he contracted your company to provide him with additional security, correct?" Diana asked.

"Yes, that's right."

"Do you know why he was selected as the target? He's not very high-profile. Why didn't they go after someone like the Prime Minister?"

"Senator Greene is opposed to withdrawing our troops from the Middle East. He's been very vocal about it. He believes we should be increasing our military presence in the region, not decreasing it. His view is that it is the only way to maintain control. As such, Islamic groups consider him an enemy."

"And you agree with him?" Peter said.

Kloch nodded. "Of course. It's the only way to keep the peace. Military might."

"More eye for an eye stuff, right?" Diana said.

"Oh no, Diana," he purred. He looked intently at her through his rimless spectacles. "They take an eye, we take ten eyes, ten tongues, ten noses, and ten hearts. They strike us, we retaliate with a nuke. They hit us, we hit them harder. It's the only way to assert our authority." Kloch smiled. "And, of course, keep the peace."

"Keep the money flowing, you mean," Peter added. "In your direction."

"Okay, but I still don't see how the Senator's stance on our troops in the Middle East makes him a target. He's small fry. He has little power to affect policy changes on his own. Why add him to a kill list and sic a top assassin on him?" Diana asked.

She sat back in her chair and folded her arms.

"Senator Greene will be announcing his candidacy for Prime Minister within the next two months," Kloch said.

Peter pushed himself off the wall and walked over to the table once more. He stood behind Kloch who twisted in his seat, trying to keep both interrogators in his line of sight.

"And how did some extremist group from the other side

of the world find out about that?" Peter raised his eyebrows at Kloch. "And why would they kill him before he makes the official announcement? It would make more sense to wait."

Kloch decided to focus on Diana. He looked squarely at her. "I don't know what to tell you. My job is to take care of the Senator's security. That's all I know." He made the tiniest of shakes with his head, sniffed, then rubbed his nose. Diana perked up.

Kloch hadn't broken eye contact at all. A shake of his head meant he didn't mean what he was saying. Nose rubbing occurred as a result of itchiness associated with an increase in adrenaline. Maintaining eye contact for an extended period of time is an overcompensating action to deflect the idea that the subject is being dishonest.

Bernard Kloch was lying.

# CHAPTER TEN

"**D**O YOU KNOW anything else about the attempt on Senator Greene's life?"

"No, I don't."

"Are you sure?"

"I just said I didn't," he snapped, shaking his head slightly. Lie. She made a tiny movement with her hand. It was a move Kloch wouldn't notice but one that Peter would fathom. Even Kieran hadn't understood her like Peter did. He nodded back.

"So you're saying that you heard that Greene was to be killed because of the possibility that should he become the next P.M., he would have a hawkish stance on Canadian military presence in the Middle East?"

"Yes." Kloch shook his head again. Another lie.

Another slight movement of her hand. Another nod from Peter.

Kloch knew much more about what was going on than he was saying. Peter gestured toward Kloch with his head. It was his signal that she should go on the offensive to get more information out of Kloch.

Diana raised her eyebrows.

Peter paused for a moment. She was asking him to reconsider. Should they tip their hand so early in the game? He nodded slightly. On reflection, he was agreeing with her. They would wait.

"Very well, Mr. Kloch. We will leave things here for now. Someone will be in to keep you company, and we'll come back in a bit." Kloch's pupils widened but he said nothing. "Can we get you a coffee?"

"No, thank you."

"Very well. See you later."

"Maybe," Kloch smiled as he watched them leave the room. Peter was calling for a constable and didn't notice, but Diana saw Kloch's smile didn't quite reach his eyes. She wondered what he was hiding.

They'd found an empty conference room. Peter leaned back in a chair and put his feet on the table, his hands behind his head. His chair teetered on its back legs.

"He knows a lot more than he's saying." he said.

"Doesn't he just? Part of me is afraid to find out what they're up to."

"Someone else is involved. They have to be. It isn't as if you can be party to a terrorist plot, hire someone like Surgeon, attempt to cover your tracks all on your own, *and* keep it a secret."

"What I'd really like to know is whether or not Greene had any idea about Kloch's plan. Did he know that a kill was ordered to protect him?"

Peter snorted. "I wouldn't be surprised. He's a politician. Nothing's more important to him than his hide."

"Yes, but precisely because he is a politician, would he knowingly risk having his name associated with a professional hit? If it got out, it would destroy any chance he had of getting elected."

Peter shook his head. "Oh, I don't know. His popularity could soar just because he didn't wait around to be killed. He might be seen as a man of action rather than a political putz."

Diana quietly tapped the table as Peter warmed to his idea. "As Kloch said, it wasn't as if they arranged for the killing of an innocent civilian. Garibaldi was a killer himself. Many people would agree with the strategy to take him out. Greene might become a hero."

"Politics is *such* a sleazy game," Diana said with a groan.

Peter grinned, "I think it's cool. Watching them have a go at each other is like having a ringside seat at a boxing match, except with less blood."

Diana snorted. "I don't get your fascination with boxing matches."

"I don't get how you're sick at the sight of blood at boxing matches. Seriously, woman? I mean, you must have seen a ton of blood in your time."

Diana sighed. "At times. But a boxing match or any other sport? One drop, and I lose my cookies."

"You're such a girl," Peter said, rolling his eyes.

Diana glanced at Peter. "Really? I hadn't noticed," she said wryly. "Didn't your mother ever tell you not to tip back on a chair like that?"

"Frequently, but it didn't make a blind bit of difference. Used to drive her mad. So, do you think Greene was in on it or not?" Peter asked, turning serious.

"I don't know. We're going to have to talk to him."

Peter sighed and ran a hand through his hair. "I can't wait."

"I know. It'll be tricky."

"If we go in guns blazing, the Deputy Commissioner will have our heads on spikes. Donaldson won't be able to protect us."

Diana sighed. "We can go slower. Anyway, if we start throwing accusations around, Greene will clam up faster than an antelope running from a tiger."

"I'm guessing you'd be the tiger in this analogy?"

She shook her head. "Nope, that'd be you. You're the one who's big and scary with a tendency to snarl at people."

"Wow," he said, rubbing his chin.

Diana laughed. "Well, take it as you will. But I do love tigers." She snarled and clawed the air with her hand.

Peter's gaze flew up to meet hers. Her tone surprised him. In a few fleeting moments of weakness, he'd considered something more with Diana. She was a beautiful woman. He'd have to be blind, dumb, deaf, stupid, and dead not to consider it. But he had drawn a line, and he refused to cross it. She was his partner and nothing more. She could never be anything more. Besides, Diana had always been clear she wasn't interested in a relationship. With anyone. She'd treated him as a friend, a buddy, nothing more.

He expected her to retract her words or pass them off as a joke. Instead, she just smiled at him.

"If I'm the tiger, then what are you? Because I certainly don't see you as the antelope," he said, his voice low.

She hesitated, but then got up and walked toward the door. Peter's heart sank for a moment. He watched her.

"One of us needs to speak to Donaldson so we can get a meeting with Greene. It'll be easier to get to him if the

Deputy Commissioner opens the door for us," Diana threw over her shoulder.

"What makes you think the Deputy Commissioner will help us? He'll want to keep Greene happy more than he'll want to help us."

Diana stopped at the door. "True, but the thought of being accused by the media of aiding a terrorist plot will put a bomb under him. As it were."

Peter's eyebrows climbed into his scalp. "Really? How would you swing that one?"

"You have no idea what CSIS can do," she winked at him.

"I'm guessing you'll be asking Kieran for help with that, then." He sounded irritated, and he knew it. Despite all his logic regarding their strength as a team, why a relationship with Diana wouldn't work, why they should just be partners and friends, Kieran's reappearance in Diana's life annoyed him. In fact, every time he saw the guy, he wanted to rip his face off. Actually, he wanted to rip him limb from limb, then stand over him beating on his chest, showing *his* woman that he was the better, stronger partner.

*Oh God. What the hell?*

"Not Kieran, Peter. CSIS," she replied, tartly.

"It's a good idea," he said gruffly. "Though I'm not sure how threatening the Deputy Commissioner will help us in the long run."

Diana shrugged. "I don't intend to threaten him. In fact, I plan on approaching the D.C. directly and being very diplomatic about it."

"Are you trying to subtly tell me I'm not part of your plan?" he asked.

"Subtlety is hardly my go-to M.O where you're concerned."

"Can't say I'd noticed."

"Very funny. We've got to get it past Donaldson first. And we'll speak to Greene together."

"I'm not very diplomatic."

She smiled. "No, you're not. But you have many other more valuable skills."

Diana left the room and closed the door. Not even a second later, she opened it again and poked her head through. "And I'd be the tigress, watching your back. You catch the antelope, and we rip it apart together," she said with a wink and closed the door as quickly as she had opened it.

Peter found himself staring at the door for a long moment after it had closed, pondering her words. After a while, he shook his head. He was imagining things. Everything was just like it always was. And that's how it would stay.

## CHAPTER ELEVEN

"YOU WANT TO what?" Donaldson exclaimed. Diana and Peter had just finished briefing the superintendent on the information Kloch had provided them and had expressed their desire to have a word with Senator Greene. Their request hadn't gone over well.

"Well, sir," Peter began, "we need to find out exactly what Greene knows and how involved he is in this whole mess."

"And you think that he's going to suddenly find God and decide to tell you the whole truth and nothing but? Don't be ridiculous! Even if he is involved, which I doubt, he won't tell you a thing. And, in the process, you'll have antagonized a Senator *and* the Deputy Commissioner, who thinks, by the way, the sun shines out of Greene's rear end," Donaldson snapped.

"I can read him and at least get an idea of whether he's lying to us or not," Diana said.

Donaldson snorted. "He's a politician. If his mouth is moving, he's lying." He shook his head. "No, no. I do not need this right now. I don't need the Deputy Commissioner breathing down my neck because I let you two squeeze his favorite Senator. And I said desk work, young lady. Not chase down a Canadian Senator and give him the third degree. Find another way."

"Sir, this could all blow up not only into a major political scandal, but also a public terror incident. If we have foreign parties ordering the assassination of a Canadian politician on our soil, it's possible there's a threat to the general public underway too. Garibaldi wasn't a major loss. No one will cry over his death. But what if innocent people are caught in the crossfire next time, and we let it happen because we didn't want to ruffle feathers?"

Diana had to give it to Peter. He was wrong. He could be diplomatic and persuasive when he wanted.

Donaldson gave Peter a dirty look, opened his mouth, and then shut it just as quickly. He glared at Diana. "Fine," he said through gritted teeth. "If, *if*, you get approval from the D.C., I want you leading the interview," he said. Donaldson pointed at Diana. "And you," turning to Peter, "You keep quiet. Not a single word out of you, got it?"

Peter raised an eyebrow. "So what am I supposed to do?"

"Just stand there and look menacing. You're good at that," Donaldson said. "Now go, before I change my mind." He waved them both out of his office, and they left as quickly as they could.

"He said yes," Diana came down the stairs quickly. She'd been up to the Deputy Commissioner's office and pitched the plan about speaking to Greene to him.

Peter grabbed his jacket. "Come on, let's get going," he said. "He might change his mind if he has too much time to think about it."

Diana hesitated for a moment. "Should we call ahead?"

Peter shook his head. "No, let's use the element of surprise."

"You're right. Let's go." They hurried out the building and down to the parking lot.

"You were quite the politician in there with Donaldson earlier," Diana murmured when they were in the car. Peter reversed out of the parking space and quickly turned right into the street, throwing a quick glance over his left shoulder as he did so.

"I'm not just muscle and menace, you know. Even the Hulk has his moments."

"But you let people think that."

"It suits me. Besides, next to you, I'm always going to be the brute. Beast to your Beauty, Shrek to your Princess Fiona."

Diana shifted in her seat and looked at him in surprise.

"I have a niece, Clare. She's seven," he explained, sensing her curiousity.

"And you watch movies with her?"

"Uh-huh. She makes me. I must've seen Frozen one hundred and twenty-two times." He looked over to her. "That's a secret. I definitely will have to kill you if you tell anyone about that."

Diana looked at Peter in wonder. "Can you sing the songs?"

He shook his head. "I can't reach the big notes."

"Bet you know all the words, though."

"Maybe." He smiled at a memory. "She sings into a

microphone, and I play the," he took his hands off the wheel for a second to make air quotes, "camera guy."

"Sounds fun."

"Yeah, she's pretty cute. We have a regular date once a week." He didn't say anymore.

Diana stared at him a moment longer before she turned back to the front. She studiously watched the scenery as it passed by, mulling over what she'd just heard and conjuring up the scene of Peter with his niece watching movies and singing songs together. She felt a stab of jealousy, then longing. Deep, deep longing. She shut her eyes briefly. *Stop this, Diana. Oh, god. Please no.*

Greene's immaculately coiffed and elegantly dressed personal assistant showed Diana and Peter into Greene's office. After they'd showed up unannounced, the assistant had initially refused to allow them to see the Senator, but following an unproductive charm offensive from Diana and some rather more stern rank pulling from Peter, she'd reluctantly informed Greene of their presence.

"Senator Greene, thank you for seeing us. My name is Diana Hunter. This is Detective Peter Hopkinson." Greene looked in his early fifties, with salt and pepper hair and vibrant green eyes. He was attractive, and his confident air made him appear authoritative, ideal for the position of Prime Minister. He'd made them wait half an hour after agreeing to see them. It wasn't clear if that was genuine or a power play, but Diana was wary.

"No, problem at all," Greene said as he shook her hand and then Peter's. He gave Peter a cursory glance, before refocusing all his attention on Diana. "Anything to help the

Vancouver Police Department. Please, sit down," he said, indicating the chairs in front of his desk.

Diana sank into the plush cushions. She realized immediately that the soft chairs were designed to put the sitter at a disadvantage. She quickly took in his office. A large mahogany desk with intricately carved legs dominated the room. Two wine-colored couches faced one another in the middle, and a small, discreet bar took up one corner.

Around the room, dotted on tables and bookcases, were various busts, figurines, and sculptures. Two large pieces of original art hung on the walls. One depicted a red maple on the banks of a river, the white crested rapids forming the backdrop to the tree's scarlet leaves. The other was of an explorer's encampment during an expedition. Diana knew it to be nearly two hundred years old and one of the most expensive Canadian paintings ever.

The decoration in the room was opulent and expensive. Massive, heavy, gold drapes swathed the huge window to the left of the Senator's desk. It was unusual for a Canadian politician to reveal his wealth so unapologetically. Those who represented the Canadian people didn't normally display it quite this openly.

She looked at Peter from the corner of her eye. He was sitting stiffly, his tension so apparent it was almost as if he were a snake just waiting for the right moment to pounce. No wonder Greene kept glancing at him.

She started to speak. "We had a small discussion with Mr. Bernard Kloch of Blue Panther Security earlier. He indicated that an extreme Islamic group had targeted you."

Diana watched Greene carefully. He was affecting an open, inquiring, friendly expression, but she saw his eyes widen almost imperceptibly when she spoke. He swallowed. He clenched his jaw very slightly, probably involuntarily. He was displeased. Why?

"Yes," Greene said, "Mr. Kloch brought this threat to my attention a few weeks ago. I felt it prudent to engage additional security, alongside the protection I am afforded due to my position. I understand the threat has now been dealt with."

"Do you know *how* it was dealt with, sir?" Peter was nothing if not plainspoken.

A minute frown. An imperceptible tightening of his lips. More anger. "I understand the man who was sent to kill me met with an unfortunate accident."

Peter snorted. "If you could call being suffocated and having your head cut off an unfortunate accident."

Now, Greene allowed his anger to show. "Are you accusing me of something, Detective?" he snapped.

"No, no," Peter said, his hands up in supplication. "Just wondering what your role is in all this."

"If this is the approach you want to take, we can continue this discussion some other time, with my lawyer present. And after I've had a chat with the Deputy Commissioner."

Damn it. She was sitting too far away from Peter to give him a good kick in the shin. He was being a bear. "I'm sorry, sir. I can assure you, your welfare is our main priority."

The Senator looked back at her. "I'm glad to hear it, Ms. Hunter, but as I already said, I have Blue Panther Security and my government detail looking out for me."

Diana cocked her head and gave him a smile that she hoped didn't look as pained as it felt. "Senator Greene, I'm sure Blue Panther Security can provide you with protection, but VPD can catch whoever's after you. Right now, although the immediate threat has abated, you are still a target."

Greene gave her a shrewd look. "And pray, how would VPD endeavor to achieve that when the people after me are an Islamic group in Afghanistan? They have suicide bombers, deep pockets, and most likely powerful connections at their disposal. I can't see VPD having much influence on that little lot."

Diana gave him a small, lopsided smile. "That's right. I forgot to mention that CSIS is working with us. They will be able to work with other intelligence agencies around the world to eliminate the larger threat, while we work domestically to ensure that no one has slipped through the cracks and made it onto Canadian soil to specifically target you or other Canadian nationals."

Green's voice wavered. "I don't think that's necessary. Surely it would be a waste of good resources. The threat has been eliminated now. Kloch seems to think so, at least. I'll be just fine. I'm sure VPD and CSIS have much bigger fish to fry than me." He was talking too quickly. Trying too hard.

"Senator Greene," Peter was speaking, "Not only did someone take out a contract on you, but someone else took out a contract on the person who was to kill you. You're in the middle of something. You're in a lot of danger."

"Now, Ms. Hunter, Detective Hopkinson, I'm sure you are blowing this all out of proportion. I'm sure that the people who were after me have rethought their priorities now that – what was his name again?"

"Lucenzo Garibaldi."

"—Now that he has been, um, neutralized."

"I don't suppose you have any idea who ordered the hit on Garibaldi?" Diana asked. There was a very slight drop of Greene's eyebrows and a thinning of his lips. Ah, satisfaction. He thought they didn't know about Kloch ordering Surgeon to do it. So, Greene was in on it.

"I'm sorry, but I really have no idea." Greene got out of his chair. Peter immediately stood, too. Diana followed suit, but more slowly. "Now, if we're finished here, I have work to get back to. Thank you for your visit and your concern, but I feel quite safe with the security measures that are in place," Greene said.

"Very well, Senator," Diana said. "It's your choice. But if you change your mind, you can find us at this number," she said as she handed him a business card. She knew Greene would never actually call, but she wanted to leave the impression that the Senator had succeeded in convincing them of his story.

"Goodbye, Ms. Hunter, Detective. Forgive me if I say I hope we don't meet again."

# CHAPTER TWELVE

NEITHER OF THEM said a word until they were in Peter's car, driving out of the under-ground parking lot beneath Greene's office.

"What a sleaze ball," Peter said.

"No argument there." Diana replied. "And he's up to his eyeballs in this whole mess."

"Yup. I noticed he was really pleased when you indicated we had no idea who hired Surgeon to take out Garibaldi."

"Caught that, did you?"

"Hey, I haven't been spending all this time with you for nothing."

"Well, I'm glad I'm rubbing off on you in a good way."

"So, clearly he is involved somehow. Whether it was his idea or he just went along with it, we don't know. What I don't get is why he wouldn't want us to go after this Islamic group if they present such a threat to him."

"I know. It doesn't make sense. He totally freaked out when I mentioned CSIS. I reckon there's a whole lot more going on than just some terrorists wanting to kill him," she replied.

"The question is what? Politicians don't usually go around hiring hitmen to take out other hitmen who are targeting them. They come crying to the police, to the mounties, to the intelligence agencies, to basically any law enforcement agency for help. They don't hire a private security firm and then have that someone assassinated," Peter said. "It's not a normal response."

"Exactly. And why did this group target Greene in the first place? The guy is a really small fish in a big pond. He isn't important. I hadn't even heard of him before this case."

"Remember Kloch said it's because of his political views and that he'll be running for P.M. They want him removed from the candidate pool.

"I know, but it's way too early to be thinking of killing him. He might not even have made it to the final rounds. They'd have been better off waiting until he was P.M., or at least down to one of two or three candidates."

"Hmm."

"Where do we go from here? I doubt Greene's told any of his staff what's really going on. They'd run for the hills. And Kloch's people aren't likely to help. Who's the weakest link in this whole scenario?"

"Greene. Kloch's seasoned and as hard as nails. No matter how hard we lean on him, he won't talk. We need incontrovertible evidence to implicate him. I don't think Greene, on the other hand, will put up much of a fight."

"But with Greene we have a different problem," she pointed out. "Remember a certain Deputy Commissioner? He'll never let us really lean on Greene."

Peter blew out his cheeks. "We have to approach this from a different angle, then."

"Uh-huh. And I have an idea."

"Are you alright?" Diana was in Donaldson's office. He'd spied her from the window. She'd been sitting on a bench in the courtyard below, lost in thought. He'd called her in.

"I'm not certain what you mean, Superintendent."

The senior police officer sighed. "I know you. You're working on a plan to get Surgeon, aren't you? I can see it all going on behind your eyes." Diana held his gaze. "Look, I don't know how things were done at CSIS, but I care about my people. I will not let you put yourself in this psychopath's sights if you have any misgivings whatsoever. Your safety is more important than making our lives easier. We can still catch this guy without you sticking your neck out, you know."

Diana smiled gently. CSIS wasn't quite as bad as Donaldson made it out to be, but they were undeniably used to putting their lives on the line. Subverting terror plots required it.

His concern for her was a nice change of pace from that, but they were dealing with a man who posed a major risk. Surgeon was only deployed to hit significant targets, often ones that held the balance of political power in their hands. Entire regions of the world had been destabilized by Surgeon's work. The Garibaldi killing appeared an anomaly, a one-off, but she suspected it was of much larger significance. They just didn't know what it was. And they needed to. They simply couldn't afford to let him wander the world, taking out people on kill lists.

"Thank you," she said, "but I don't think we have a choice. We need to find out if he knows anything about the larger reason Garibaldi was here to kill Greene, and what his involvement might be. I am the fastest way to him."

Donaldson sighed but he didn't look convinced. "What if he's finished here?"

"What do you mean?"

"What if Lucenzo Garibaldi was the job? What if that was all he was here for? What if he has no other involvement?"

"Then he'll be waiting for his next hit. Killing is like a drug to him. He needs his supply, his high. He needs to be dealt with."

Donaldson walked over to a filing cabinet and picked up a small imperfectly sculpted figurine. It had been a gift from his daughter when she was in second grade."So, what's the plan?"

"I'm going on TV network news. I'm going to call him out. Flush him out. If he's still here, he'll break cover. I'm sure of it."

"Are you mad?" Donaldson exclaimed. "Are you sure you want to challenge someone like him like that?"

"It's the best way. I've thought it all through. If I can draw him out of hiding, have him come after me, we'll catch him. He'll make a stupid mistake, I know it. And if we throw everything we have at it, we'll get him." It was a risky plan. She knew it. It could backfire so easily. But too much was at stake. This was one chapter of her life she needed to close. She'd had enough of Surgeon being out there, still roaming, never knowing if, or when he was going to come for her.

Her experience with Surgeon had become inextricably linked in her mind with her parent's deaths. Although there was no suggestion that they were connected, her battle with Surgeon coming so soon after she joined CSIS, and her sense that she was being kept under surveillance by her parents' killers had caused her to volunteer for the most dangerous CSIS missions.

Humiliated, terrified, and paranoid by these two threats to her safety, she had trained her way to expert status in close quarters combat, marksmanship, surveillance and reconnaissance. She'd even taken CSIS' advanced Special Operations courses, their toughest. Then, when she'd done that, she volunteered for every course, every mission available to her. She figured it was the best way to stay one step ahead of her parents' killers and beat back the memory of her time with Surgeon.

Driven by her demons and her fear, she had pushed herself to her physical and psychological limits over and over again. Now she was done with Surgeon taunting her. She refused to let this charade continue. She wanted a life without the threat of him looming over her.

"I don't know. I'm still not convinced. You're relying on a lot of 'ifs' here. If he sees you on television, if he reacts to your taunts, if he doesn't go ballistic and decide to shoot you in the head from a distance," Donaldson said, shaking his head.

"Yes, but it's the most effective solution. We need to goad him. It's not like I can send him an invitation. We don't know what he looks like or where he is. I think this is the best shot we have of catching him and finding out precisely what's going on."

"I still think it's a crazy plan." Donaldson shook his head. "I don't like you putting yourself in the line of fire like this."

"It wouldn't be the first time. And I won't be alone," she reminded him.

"You bet you won't be alone. I'm assigning a full security team to you. Where you go, they go," he said.

Diana shook her head. "Just me and Peter. No additional protection. We want to draw him out, not scare him off." Donaldson's phone rang. He took the call. Diana could hear a man barking angrily at the other end.

"Yes, sir. We'll do that. I'll tell her." He put the phone down.

"That was the D.C. We are to let Kloch go and—."

"What? But he contracted a murder!"

Donaldson waved away her objection, "And you specifically are not to go near Senator Riley Greene again. The D.C. mentioned you by name."

Diana looked up at the ceiling in exasperation."The D.C. gave me permission to speak to Greene."

"Well, he's withdrawn it."

"Are we being warned off?"

"Undoubtedly." Donaldson was even more taciturn than usual.

"Ugh, this is so frustrating. What's the D.C.'s game, sir?"

"I'm sure he's been leaned on by someone up above. I thought this might happen."

"But where does that leave us? Leave the investigation?"

Donaldson gave her a shrewd look. "Listen, if you can get Peter to agree to this crazy scheme of yours, we'll do it. Go speak to him. Otherwise, your plan's off, lady."

# CHAPTER THIRTEEN

"**H**AVE YOU LOST your mind?" Peter had known something was up when she asked him to join her for a cup of coffee in the break room.

"It's the best way," Diana said.

Peter took a deep breath. Then another. And another. This was too much. It was almost as if she wanted to die.

"You're right – we don't have time to waste and we need to get Surgeon. But going on TV? Insane. You have no idea how he'll react to being humiliated in public. It will enrage him! His response will be ten times worse. And you know what that means for you."

"Who said I was going to humiliate him?"

"What else can you do to goad him into action? Invite him over for tea?"

"Maybe just seeing me will be enough," Diana said with a shrug. "He doesn't know my name or where I live. He hasn't found me before now. Seeing me on TV should trigger him sufficiently especially if we give him clues as to where to find me.

Peter gave her an incredulous look. "If he'd really

wanted to find you, he would have already. He could have just staked out the CSIS building. He's just been taunting you with the flowers and cards up 'til now. Playing a game."

"And now I'm upping the ante. Giving him the come-on. Taking the fight to him."

"You won't be able to resist throwing a few digs at him. I know you."

"Do you have a better way to get his attention quickly?" Diana asked.

Peter glared at her. He tried to come up with a solution. There had to be a way that didn't involve her challenging an assassin. In public. He considered the possibilities for a few moments, discarding one option after another.

Earlier, he'd spoken to Kieran about the flowers. They had to be paid for somehow and even if it was in cash, maybe they'd find some security footage, or at the very least, a vague description. But CSIS looked into it every year, according to Kieran. No security footage was available because no one stored more than a week's worth. The order was always placed weeks, or months in advance at a different florist each time. Payment was made in cash. The person placing the order was different every year. There were no leads there.

He'd followed up with the florist who'd taken receipt of the flash drive but no one had remembered anything.

He'd considered the possibility of posting a message online but decided that was too random. The chance of Surgeon seeing it was minimal.

He'd chased Tina, head of the crime lab, but she'd had no luck with the crime scene. There was no trace on Garibaldi's body of anything that could lead them to Surgeon.

So, it looked like Diana was right. Again. They didn't

have a way of getting in touch with him directly – if they did, this stunt wouldn't be necessary.

"Fine, you're right. As usual. But that doesn't mean you have to antagonize him," he said.

"Who said anything about antagonizing him?" she asked.

"Don't give me that innocent look. I know you, remember?"

Diana rolled her eyes. "Look, the point of this whole exercise is to knock him off balance. He has never been able to find me and now I'll be inviting him to play. I want him so excited and so angry that he will make a mistake."

Peter raised an eyebrow. "We're talking about a man that CSIS, along with the rest of the alphabet soup of intelligence agencies around the world, haven't been able to catch in over a decade. This guy doesn't make mistakes."

"One of the reasons he's never gotten caught is that he never lets it get personal. But this time, it is personal. He's been goading me all these years. Well, now it's my turn. I'll dangle myself in front of him on TV, and he won't be able to resist. He will make a mistake. And that mistake will be to come for me."

"Fine, but until he's in custody, I'm not leaving your side," he stated.

"Okay," she replied.

Peter gave her an odd look. "Are you feeling alright?" he asked.

"What do you mean?"

"You're not going to object?" he said. He looked as perplexed as he felt. She normally refused to be "babysat," as she put it. He had expected a huge row.

"Of course not. No matter what you think, I don't have a death wish. I want to catch him and not die in the process.

With you by my side, my odds of surviving this little endeavor grow exponentially."

Peter opened his mouth and closed it again. One shock after another. What was this world coming to? Diana and he were in complete agreement. Without an argument.

"Huh. I'll make a note to check the news later – some rare planetary alignment or an eclipse must be happening."

"Yeah, yeah," Diana scooped some coffee into the coffee maker.

"Look, is there something else going on in that complicated head of yours? Something I'm not fully appreciating?" he asked.

"I might be good, but I'm not infallible," she said. She had spoken so quietly, he'd barely heard her.

"Your instincts will take over." He was quieter now, too. He walked over to her and got close. "He got to you more than you let on, didn't he?" he said.

Diana looked up at him. Anxiety was stamped all over her features. "I don't know," she whispered. "I have no idea how I'm going to react. I'm not an idiot. I know I could have an unexpected reaction."

"Then why do this? You don't owe anyone anything."

"I have to," she said, simply. "We need to eliminate him. He's already killed so many people, and he will keep killing on and on. Those deaths will be on my conscience for the rest of my life if I don't try. And, honestly, I can't let him control my life any more. I need to confront him and put him away."

He put his arm around her shoulders. "I'll be with you every step of the way," he said.

"I know. I know I can always rely on you to pull my ass out of the fire." She smiled at him before sobering. "Thank you," she said.

Peter frowned. "You don't need to thank me, Diana. You're my partner, and partners look out for each other." He squeezed her arm and pulled her in, tucking her head under his chin.

"I know but still... thank you." Out of nowhere, tears welled up. She quickly tamped them down, blinking ferociously and swallowing hard, thankful that he couldn't see her face.

"You'd do the same for me."

"Yes, I would."

He dropped his arm and moved away. He pulled out a chair and straddled it as Diana, thankful that the emotional moment was over, focused on pouring her coffee. "So, what's the plan?"

"I may not work in mainstream media, but I have a few connections. Let me make some calls."

Peter frowned. "You're not calling up another mobster, are you?" he grumbled. Diana had a slew of connections, many of them on the wrong side of the law.

"Not this time, I promise," she said with a grin.

Peter was walking down the corridor after a long day of preparing to implement Diana's plan. He was ready to accompany her to the studio where she was about to play her part in the drama. There was a shout behind him.

"Hey!" Kieran stormed up to Peter.

"What are you doing here?"

"I'm here to argue with Ms. I-Can-Do-Anything about this stupid plan of hers!"

Kieran jabbed at Peter's chest with his forefinger. "Which is what you should be doing. Why are you letting her do this? Diana absolutely cannot and must not parade herself in front of that psycho. He will stop at nothing to grab her. He will torture and kill her."

Peter didn't react. He stood motionless and silent as Kieran started to pace in front of him.

"You know what she's like. She comes up with some scheme and goes on and on about it until she wears you down, or carries it out anyway. You should have stopped her. You *should* have shut her down. Why didn't you, you punk? Do you think you're gonna be the one to save her? You with all your medals, and bravery, and crack military experience, huh?"

Peter continued to maintain eye contact with Kieran but still didn't make a sound.

"Well, let me tell you, this guy's clever. We pulled out all the stops, *all* of them, right? And the only reason she's alive now is because he let her go. Next time she won't be so lucky. And you do not want her death at the hands of that monster on your conscience, believe me."

Kieran took a breath and turned to look at Peter, facing off with him. "She cannot die, you got it? She cannot. She's yours now. You have to protect her."

Peter watched Kieran's retreating back as he blew through the double doors at the end of the hallway. The baton had been passed.

# CHAPTER FOURTEEN

"**Y**OU ARE CERTIFIABLE," Peter hissed. "I can't believe you called him a pathetic psychopath with mommy issues." Fifteen minutes after Diana's stint on the nightly news, he'd finally managed to calm down enough to speak.

Just as she'd said she would do, Diana made a few calls and within hours, had been on the seven o'clock news. She'd discussed, under the guise of being a crime journalist, the psychopathy of serial killers. Her connection to VPD was kept under wraps.

She'd shared information about their latest case. Headless corpses always attracted the public's attention. She also slipped in a description of Surgeon in less than flattering terms. A pathetic psychopath with mommy issues was one of the nicer things she'd said about him. Peter had watched aghast but helpless from the studio floor.

They'd spent the previous hours working furiously to prepare for the aftermath of the broadcast. During her interview, Diana had left breadcrumbs for Surgeon to follow, including naming the publication she worked for. Everyone at the magazine had been given a week's vacation. The offices were now staffed by undercover cops.

Diana had also been given a new home address which was, in fact, a VPD safe house. She would be living there for the forseeable future. All of her documents had been changed, showing the new address as her place of residence.

Everything had been set up. Peter had reviewed the plan with her so many times, she'd gotten snappy with him. They were ready. And then in her inimitable way, she had insulted a treacherous professional assassin. That hadn't been the plan at all. The plan had been to put in an appearance so Surgeon could see her. She wasn't supposed to mention him. She certainly wasn't supposed to insult him.

The moment she'd walked off set, Peter's frustration with her once again showed itself. She hadn't said a word until he'd finished. And then she'd shut him up succinctly.

"He's waited almost ten years to come for me already. I had to push him, to force him to act."

"But now you've made the situation much more dangerous."

"It had to be dangerous, Peter. He needs it to be. Danger and risk stimulate him. That's how he gets high. Danger."

Diana sighed. She'd been sitting quietly in the passenger seat as he drove them in silence to the safe house. "We've been over this. He's going to come for me for certain now, which is what we want, right?"

Peter kept quiet. If he said anything, he was liable to get angry again. As the minutes dragged on, the silence became oppressive. "What are we doing in Shaughnessy?" Diana asked out of the blue.

He looked at her with a small frown. "We're going to the safe house."

"In Shaughnessy? Since when does VPD have a safe house in one of the most expensive neighborhoods in Vancouver?"

Peter shrugged. "Since we confiscated the place from a drug dealer a few months ago. Donaldson decided it would be the best option. Didn't you look at the address?" he asked.

She shook her head. "Didn't get a chance," she said with a small shrug. "So, why this place?"

"Quiet neighborhood," he replied.

"Anyone new to the area will be easy to spot," she finished.

Peter turned onto Marguerite Street and then into a driveway. Diana gasped. "Wow, this place is beautiful," she breathed.

He had to agree. On two levels, the house had sloping roofs. There were huge bay windows and stunning, carefully landscaped gardens. He pulled up to the front entrance and turned the engine off. Diana jumped out and looked around. "I can't wait to see this place in daylight."

Despite his mood, Peter smiled at the wonder on her face. She looked enthralled. Cute. A moment of levity amid a steaming pile. He fervently hoped they'd still be smiling in a few days time.

# CHAPTER FIFTEEN

P ETER TOOK OUT the keys, unlocked the front door to the safe house, and swept it open with a flourish.

Diana marveled at the entryway. She turned around, trying to take everything in. The house was decorated elegantly, with ornate yet understated furniture, plush carpets, and neutral colors. A chandelier dripping with crystals hung from the ceiling. Her heels clacked as she made her way across to the sweeping staircase ahead.

She went from room to room, exclaiming over one thing or another. Peter had never seen her like this before. The more feminine, "girlie" side of her. He followed her into the living room. It had brick-red walls, a white ceiling, two tan couches and a mahogany coffee table that gleamed. A huge, stone fireplace dominated the room.

"I can't believe a drug dealer would have such exquisite taste," she said.

Peter grinned. "I'm sure he hired a decorator." He paused for a moment. "So, do you want some dinner?" he asked.

"I wouldn't say no."

"Pizza?"

"Sounds good. I want ham, pineapple, jalapeños and extra cheese on mine, please."

Peter rolled his eyes. "I know," he replied, deadpan. She never ordered anything else. He still didn't understand how what she ordered could be considered pizza, or even food. She'd offered him some once and he'd recoiled as if she'd presented him with a hissing cobra.

"You can have some, if you like," Diana called out.

"No, thank you. I'll order something else."

"You should try it. Expand your palate, your horizons."

"I draw the line at pineapple and jalapeños, thank you very much."

He placed the order, and while they waited, they wandered outside into the private garden. He found a light switch. The garden was bathed in soft light. "This is wonderful," Diana breathed. "Max would love it."

Peter grinned. "Yeah, he would, although it wouldn't be so peaceful with him here. He'd be running around sniffing and digging and yapping."

Diana smiled at the thought, "Yes, he would."

She had hired a sitter for Max. Pet sitting was helping Terri Jenkins pay her way through veterinary school. She was usually fully booked but came running whenever Diana called. Terri loved Max, and Diana paid her double. This might have been a small fortune to Terri, but Diana considered it a bargain. She wouldn't trust Max with anyone else.

They went back inside, and Peter started to check all the entryways and window fixtures.

"Is the house bugged?" Diana asked.

"Yeah, mikes and cameras in every room. All the doors and windows are solid. We can double lock them all and set the alarm."

"Peter,"

"Hmm?"

"Remember why we are here. We need him to breach the place so we can take him down. If we make this place a fortress, all of this will have been for nothing."

"Okay, but we don't have to make it easy for him. And we definitely don't want to be taken by surprise."

The doorbell rang, and they instantly went quiet. Diana drew her gun. Peter peered through the spyhole.

"It's the pizza delivery guy."

"Are you sure?"

"Yup, I order a lot of pizza. That is definitely not an assassin at the top of his game." Peter opened the door, still covered by Diana, and took the two boxes offered to him.

Peter would have settled on eating straight from the box, but Diana insisted on warming the large bone china plates she'd found in the cupboard and using embroidered linen napkins that were lying, ironed and folded neatly, in a drawer.

"You'll be getting out the cutlery, next," Peter teased her as she rustled around looking for what else the kitchen might offer up.

"What? You mean you don't eat pizza with a knife and fork? Really?" Diana smiled. She'd been nervous before her TV stint but now she was euphoric. They sat in the luxury kitchen at the island and eventually settled down to eat.

"How long do you think we'll have to wait?" Peter wondered.

"Not sure. I've worked cases like this before—"

"Why am I not surprised?"

"...And it usually takes up to forty-eight hours for our mark to show himself. The longest I've ever known was fifty-two."

"Hmm, I've worked them where they've never shown up at all."

"Yeah, that too."

"So basically we have no idea how long we're going to be here."

"No."

"Well then, we'd better get used to each other's company. I have to know where you are always, okay?"

"Yes, I know. You told me earlier. At least three times."

"Even when you're in the bathroom, got it?"

"Got it, sir. Yes, sir!" Diana gave him a mock salute, but she was deflecting. Peter was reminding her of her father. A little less overprotective, but the same care and concern was there. The same strong sense of masculinity.

They ate their pizza in silence for a while. Outside they could hear crickets. The neighborhood was truly as quiet as a graveyard.

"You and Kieran. How long were you partners?" Peter blurted out.

"About eight years. He was a few years in when I was recruited, and I was assigned to him once I'd done my basic training."

"You must have been pretty young."

"Yeah, I was. Funnily enough, he was there when I had my first encounter with CSIS back in college."

Peter didn't say anything more. Diana looked at him. A shadow had crossed his face. His lips tightened, and he took a deep breath.

"Peter, what's wrong?" she asked.

"Nothing. Nothing. Why would anything be wrong?" he asked quickly.

"Because this is a funny line of questioning, and you've suddenly clammed up. You're frowning so hard, you'll get a headache. I don't need to be an expert in body language to know something is wrong."

Peter sighed. "Were you and Kieran more than partners?" he finally asked.

"Oh!"

"Sorry, none of my business."

"No, it's not."

There was an awkward silence.

"Well, were you?"

She was tempted to tell him to butt out, but this didn't seem the moment. Peter had never indicated any interest in her romantic life before.

It had been a long time since she'd been in a relationship. She hadn't had one at all since leaving CSIS. Living a normal life was tough after being a spook. Some agents never got used to it and went back, even if it was just to a desk job. Others ended up hiding away from the world, living in remote places or building a life that was as far away from their former one as possible. Civilians had a hard time understanding any of it, especially when those former lives were classified and top secret. There was always an intimacy gap. It was tremendously hard to make a relationship work with someone to whom you could never tell the truth.

That suited her. Max was her companion, and she'd found new projects to occupy her time. Retired spies were like retired athletes. They found some way to stay close to the action.

Donaldson, despite his initial reluctance to have her on board, had developed into a kind of father figure. Their relationship wasn't deep or close, but he was a comforting presence. And Peter was simply awesome. He knew she couldn't always tell him everything, and he didn't pressure her. He made her smile and laugh. He challenged her on an intellectual level. The evenings she and Peter spent chatting about cases, movies, anything in fact, were her favorites. He understood her like no one ever had, except perhaps her friend from college, Teddy. Diana sighed. She missed Teddy. Pctcr would like him.

"No, Kieran and I were never more than partners."

"He would like more," Peter said curtly.

"Maybe," Diana said with a shrug. "But we aren't suited."

"Why do you say that? You don't stay partners for eight years without good teamwork and common values. "

"He's a great friend, very loyal, but we're quite different. It's hard for him to understand the way my mind works. He doesn't trust me enough. At all, really. And I would never date someone I worked with. Don't date, don't get drunk, and never, ever cry. That's always been my motto for getting on in a man's world. Especially this one."

Peter looked at her. "I see." He swallowed the last bite of his pizza. "Do you want another soda?"

"No. I'm good." She watched him start toward the fridge. She was confused by his reaction. He seemed... something. She wasn't sure what, but she decided to let it go. There'd been enough disclosure for one day.

"Okay," she said, slapping her thighs, "I'm going to bed. You know where I am, right?"

"Yup, just across the hallway. Got your weapon?"

"Of course,"

"Okay, see you in the morning."

"'Night, Peter."

Peter walked outside and stood drinking his soda in the dark. He stared out into the illuminated garden, listening acutely to gain a baseline of their surroundings. He watched as a rabbit hopped across the spotlit lawn, pausing every few feet to nibble at the grass. Ever hyper-vigilant, even he had to agree that everything appeared quiet.

# CHAPTER SIXTEEN

"I'M STARTING TO think this is pointless," Peter said as he threw himself down on the couch next to Diana. "It's been three days."

He held out the bowl of popcorn he'd just made, and Diana grabbed a handful. She immediately started tossing pieces in the air, trying to catch them in her mouth. He'd been teaching her. Well, trying to. She was terrible at it. He grinned as he watched. Diana was always so well-mannered and reserved in public, but his being glued to her side these past few days had shown him a completely different side of her. She hadn't argued with him at all. And she was very ticklish.

Boredom during these waiting games was dangerous. Senses got dulled and warning signs were missed. Diana had taught him her best investing strategies and when they'd had enough of that, to keep them both alert, he'd taught her some hand to hand combat moves. She was a quick study and had picked them up very fast. Almost like she'd done them before.

"My gut tells me he's just biding his time, waiting to catch us off guard," Diana responded.

"Maybe he has left the country after all," Peter said with a sigh. If they'd had a photo or even a sketch of the man, they could have run a facial recognition trace against CCTV footage at all the major Canadian airports. "Maybe it's time to take a different approach," he said.

"I think this is our only shot at getting our hands on him. He's evaded CSIS and all the other agencies for years. We don't have a tenth of the resources they do." Diana massaged her eyes with her fingertips.

Peter checked himself. Diana was sounding weary. "We'll find him, Diana. We've got this. We're the 'A Team', remember?" He held up his fist and Diana bumped it with her own. He winked and smiled at her. She smiled back.

"You're right. If anyone can find Surgeon, it's us."

Peter wasn't just paying lip-service or trying to make her feel better. He really did believe in them as a team. They'd had tough cases before. They could do this. They always did.

"I suggest we give it another day or two and then reevaluate," he said.

"Good idea," she said with a smile. "So, what do you want to do now? Watch a movie? Play a game?"

Diana was a total geek. She was the only woman Peter knew who enjoyed playing computer games. She'd laughed when he'd suggested it, but he'd cocked his eyebrow, and she'd given in. She never could pass up a challenge.

"I'll get my laptop," Peter said rubbing his hands together. Diana laughed. "Don't laugh. Get ready for a beatdown."

"Hey, I thought you were supposed to be teaching me," she shot back.

"Gotta take advantage of your inexperience while I can. You catch on fast."

"And you're a good match. Its good to be around someone smart *and* sharp. You don't know how rare that is."

Peter bent over to pick up his laptop that had been left to charge on the floor. His eyes widened, and he was thankful she couldn't see his expression. She sounded sad and wistful. He didn't know what to make of it.

Diana's eyes flew open. Something was wrong. She could feel it. She made no move but opened her eyes and swiveled her eyeballs in their sockets to take in as much as she could. There were cracks of light seeping around the blind at the window on the left side of the room, illuminated by the glowing bulbs outside. The small amount of light cast shadows around the room, but now they were all wrong. Someone was in the room with her.

She slowly slid her hand under her pillow and curled her fingers around her gun. She surged up into a sitting position and trained the barrel to the left of the shadow that was out of place.

"Whoa!" whispered a familiar voice. "It's just me."

"What are you doing? Are you trying to get yourself killed?" she hissed back. She was shocked. That Peter had got that close without waking her meant either that she was slipping, or he was that good.

Peter held up his hand to quieten her. "Someone's in the house."

She threw her covers off. There were footsteps on the stairs. Peter crept over to the door, and hugged the wall, his gun at the ready. Diana sank to her knees, hiding behind the bed, her gun trained on the door.

The doorknob began to turn. Both of them held their breath as the door opened. Diana's heart was racing, and her palms were sweaty. She'd come so far and learned so much since her last encounter with Surgeon, but cold fingers of fear snaked up her spine, causing an involuntary shiver.

A man dressed in black with a ski mask covering his face crept in, pistol raised. He wore a low-voltage headlamp that picked out Diana immediately. As he took one more step into the room, Peter coldcocked him once across the back of the head. He dropped like a stone.

Diana scrambled to her feet and scurried over. "That was easy," Peter said.

"Why did you do that?"

"He had a gun pointed at you, Diana."

"But—"

Diana put her gun down as she knelt by the fallen man. She tore his mask off and looked down. "This can't be him. He's too young."

"What are you talking—"

Diana looked up.

Peter reached his hand over his shoulder. His pupils dilated. He looked her in the eye, "Run!" He started to fall.

"Peter!" she screamed. She tried to catch him but he was heavy. They both went down. A dart stuck out from the back of Peter's shoulder.

Diana scrambled out from under him and dove for her gun. "Now, now, Diana, calm down." The voice was unhurried and composed, one that seemed to have all the time in the world. "Don't do anything stupid. It's time to play." The voice chilled her.

She turned over, the gun firmly in her hand. In front

of her was a face hidden behind a paper surgical mask. She stared into Surgeon's eyes. Blue eyes that she remembered from last time. Like Peter's, but so different. Where Peter's eyes were expressive and changed from chips of ice when he was angry to sky blue warmth when he wasn't, Surgeon's eyes were flat. Lifeless. There was nothing. Just like last time. She froze. It was a mere moment, but it was more than enough to lose any advantage she might have. She felt a pinprick in her thigh. "I really didn't want to do it this way. I hoped we could be more civilized."

Her vision blurred. She clenched her jaw. She would not go down without a fight, but she was no match for the drug now rushing through her veins. She squeezed the trigger and a shot thundered through the room. Everything went black.

Peter rubbed his eyes. Every muscle hurt. He shifted a little. The surface beneath him was much too hard to be a bed. He opened his eyes and scrutinized his surroundings. He was on the floor, in the master bedroom where Diana should be sleeping.

He looked at the bed, but he couldn't see her from his vantage point. He'd have to get up. What the hell had happened?

He turned onto his side and pushed himself up. He had double, no, triple vision, and his head pounded. Beams of sunlight filtered through the blinds, hurting his eyes. He looked toward the bed again. His breath caught in his throat, and his heart began to thump hard. The bed was empty. The covers were a mess. Maybe Diana was downstairs getting coffee. But why was he on the floor? His memories were muddled.

"Diana!" he hollered. No answer. Peter carefully stood up, swaying as he did so. There was a man on the floor by the door. Peter staggered over to him. The man was dead. A syringe lay on the floor next to the body. What the hell? He could see a small hole in the wall, next to the door, about thigh level. He bent down, supporting himself with his hand. He looked closer. It was a bullet hole. The memories came flooding back.

He pulled his phone out of his pants with shaking hands. He tried to dial Donaldson but couldn't get his fingers to work. He took a deep breath. He had to stay in control. He had to find her.

He finally steadied himself enough to punch in the numbers.

"What's happened?" Donaldson barked.

"He's got her."

# CHAPTER SEVENTEEN

D IANA CAME AROUND slowly. She kept her
eyes closed and focused on modulating her
breathing to feign sleep. She knew she was in
danger but she couldn't remember why precisely. Think.
What happened? She remembered playing a computer
game. She'd gone to bed.

It all came rushing back in a flood. An intruder. Peter
decking him. Going down himself. Decoy intruder. That
mask. Those eyes. Reaching for her gun. Freezing. His
advantage. Nothing. She remembered getting a shot off, but
she'd obviously missed her mark because here she was. She
silently cursed the fact that they'd fallen for the decoy.
Where was Peter? Was he even alive?

She could smell salt, metal, diesel fumes, an undercur-
rent of fish.

She tried to move her right hand, but couldn't. She was
strapped down. And she was lying on something hard and
cold. A metal table. How innovative. She tried to move her
legs, but they were strapped down too. Damn it!

"Now, now, Diana, I thought we had an open and

honest relationship. Pretending you're asleep is just so rude." It was a male voice with a cultured English accent. Perhaps a slight hint of something else. Middle Eastern? She couldn't tell exactly, but it was definitely Him. Surgeon. She'd never forget that voice.

She opened her eyes and cringed as the bright lights aggravated the pounding in her head. She closed them just as quickly as she'd opened them.

"I'm sorry for your discomfort, but it was the easiest way to get you here," he said, sounding so courteous and apologetic that Diana might have laughed if she felt better. And had not been in mortal danger.

"Discomfort is the least of my worries when in your company," she said. Her throat was dry and her lips cracked. Her words were rasping and almost unintelligible. She tried opening her eyes again, prepared for the assault on her senses. She blinked a few times and looked around. She couldn't see him. Instead, she saw a table lined with all sorts of tools. They looked like surgical instruments, most of them had sharp edges. Next to them lined up in a perfectly uniform row were a number of syringes and half a dozen small bottles. Injectable drugs.

She tried to look around the room further, but it was difficult. He'd strapped her at the neck. She clenched her jaw and ground her teeth together hard as she lifted her head as far as she could. She cleared the table by barely an inch. She couldn't see any windows. The cement walls were chipped. Mold grew on one side of the room and on the other, there was graffiti. Way, way above her, steel beams crisscrossed the cavernous roof area. Beyond them, higher, two pigeons flew between the crossbeams. An abandoned building. A former warehouse.

Her abductor had made himself at home. The table.

The drugs. The building. The location. This wasn't some hastily set up, opportunistic operation. Maybe she had been on his to-do list all along. Maybe her public insults hadn't been necessary.

"Ah, Diana. Isn't it wonderful to be together again? I've missed you. Would you like something to drink? You must be parched." He sounded like he was inviting her to share a few scones with him over tea. He brought over a cup with a straw and stood behind her as she tilted her head as much as the strap around her neck would allow. She coughed as the water made its way down her throat.

"I must say, you're audacious," he continued in a conversational tone.

"How so?" she rasped.

"Going on TV and talking about me like that. You need some lessons in the tact department, my dear. You were quite rude. You practically issued me an invitation to abduct you."

"I didn't invite you to anything," Diana replied.

"I believe you did. Otherwise why would you even mention me?" His tone hardened, "And why wouldn't your boyfriend leave your side for days on end? He made things *so* much more difficult." He spat *boyfriend* out like it was a disgusting word.

"He's overprotective like that."

"Did he really think he stood a chance against me? So foolish. When I want something, nothing will stop me from getting it. You should know that by now."

"And you wanted me, right?"

"Of course," he said as if it should be obvious.

"But why?"

"For the same reasons you wanted me. You find me

fascinating. And I you," he replied. "We are similar, you and I." He laughed gently.

She was about to tell him that they had absolutely nothing in common, that he was a psychopath, and there was nothing fascinating about him, but she tamped down the urge. She had to keep him talking. Better to keep feeding his delusions. "I doubt we have the same motivations."

"Maybe you're right." He was being charming again. "It's not really that important anyway. I have you here. I won. That loser failed." His voice hardened. "I still can't fathom how you, whom I deem an intelligent woman, could possibly believe that that overgrown ape would protect you. Wasn't that his purpose?"

"Did you kill him?" Diana hardly dare ask the question, and she wasn't sure she could believe the answer, but she needed to hear it. She needed to determine what to do next.

"No, I decided to let him live. For now."

"May I ask why you did that?"

"I thought he was rather beautiful. And he absolutely adores you. He will be going *insane* right about now. He'll be even more upset when he finds your dead body."

He paused, waiting for a reaction from her. Diana held her breath, but couldn't stop her eyes from closing for a second with relief. A tear slipped out from under her eyelid.

"Tears? He's making you sad. Would you like me to take care of him for you?" Diana heard him move again. She remained silent. "No? Well, I'll probably kill him at some point. Eliminate him from the gene pool. Wouldn't want him polluting it. Maybe later, when you're gone."

Diana heard him chuckle. She bit her tongue. He was goading her. She had to play the game. She had to survive.

She had to get him talking. So, she swallowed her relief, her anger, and her fear, and took a few deep breaths.

"I don't think you should waste your talents on him," she said.

"You think I'm talented, do you?" he sucked in a breath. "I don't know why, but I find that quite gratifying. But there's no need to worry on my account. It wouldn't be a waste to kill your friend. It would be quite enjoyable."

"What are those drugs?" she asked.

"A few things to make the experience more pleasant. For me." There was laughter in his voice again. "While I intend to inflict a lot of pain, I prefer to do it using a controlled methodology that will maximize your agony while minimizing the mess. The side-effects of the drug I used to get you here force me to wait a while before using them to make sure the pain you will endure is excruciating. I don't want you to pass out too soon. I assure you though, you will feel absolutely *everything* I do to you," he said.

"That's so kind of you," she snapped.

He laughed. "I see you've changed, Diana. Boyfriend aside, you aren't cowering in fear of me anymore. But you will. And that will make this process all the more delicious."

Long ago, Diana had mastered the assumption of a straight face even under duress, but in truth, she was frightened. Terrified, in fact. She was tied down and completely at his mercy. She had no way of getting free. She had to take that fear and shove it into the deepest, darkest recesses of her mind. He would use her fear against her, playing those mind games he so loved. She couldn't let that happen.

"It's been a while since we were in the same room together," she replied, calmly. "I can't even remember how long." She knew exactly how long it had been.

"Diana, there is no reason for you to lie. You remember our encounter as well as I do."

Diana shook her head and frowned. "How long ago was it?"

"Shut up," he snapped. A chink in his armor. "You remember our encounter in complete and vivid detail."

"I remember some of it," She sensed him relax. "Like how you told me you didn't enjoy conversing with your victims. In fact, I'm pretty sure you said you preferred them to remain silent. What changed?"

"You," he replied, sounding a little more mollified. If only he'd come around the table so she could see him. "You changed everything. You showed me I had become complacent. I thought I was invincible, and you taught me humility. You were frightened, but I couldn't break you. I realized I had to let you go. I had to learn. I would wait. I didn't appreciate the lesson at the time, but I quickly came to see the value in what you had done for me. You made me better at what I do and for that, I thank you. Now I'm back to finish what I started."

"If you're so grateful, why not let me go again? I'd be happy to teach you a little more humility. Free of charge even."

He laughed. "I must say, Diana dear, you are quite delightful. It's almost a shame I have to kill you. You'd make an excellent apprentice."

Diana raised an eyebrow. "That might not work out so well for you. I would kill you, eventually."

"We all have to retire at some point. There would be no greater honor than to be killed by my protégé. If it happened to me, I'd go out in a blaze of glory knowing I fulfilled my destiny."

And Peter said *she* was certifiable?

"Is that what happened with Garibaldi? You, the apprentice, finally outshining your master? What did he feel when he died? Pride? Relief?"

"Probably." Surgeon paused for what seemed an eternity. He sniffed. "It was time for Gari to retire, for certain. The teacher had been usurped by his student. But it was also a contract. I suppose you could say I killed two birds with one needle, so to speak." He guffawed at his own joke. Diana stayed silent.

"So, someone paid you to kill your mentor?" she asked after he'd stopped laughing. "And you accepted?"

"Aren't you the inquisitive one?"

"It's not as if I'm making it out of here alive. I'm curious why you'd kill him, that's all."

"Well, I guess I owe you that much. It's the least I can do for my most special victim. It will do you little good, but it will sate your curiosity."

Diana tried to contain a shiver. "Ah, so there is at least a little unease," her captor observed.

"No, it's just a little chilly in here," she replied.

"Let's make a deal, Diana. I'll be honest with you, if you're honest with me. If you lie to me, you'll never find out who is responsible for the situation you find yourself in."

Diana took a deep breath. "What do you mean? Someone else is responsible for me being here besides you? Who?"

"Nah, ah, ah," he said. "Tit for tat, remember."

"Well, if it's tit for tat, why don't you move over here so I can see you? You have me at a disadvantage. You can see me, but I can't see you."

"You will only see a mask, so it matters little where I stand."

"You're still wearing the mask. Curious..." she breathed out.

"Curious, how?"

"You're hiding your identity from me. If you were sure you'd be killing me shortly, the mask wouldn't be necessary. I'd never be able to identify you. So you're not one hundred percent confident, are you? You think I might get away. Or that you'll not be able to follow through."

# CHAPTER EIGHTEEN

S URGEON DIDN'T SAY anything. Had she pushed him too far? He blew out an irritated breath. "First of all, my plan to kill you will go off without a hitch. Secondly, it pays to be overly cautious in my line of work, and third, I'll show you precisely how confident I am."

Diana heard fumbling behind her, and the scratching of paper rubbing against rough skin, elastic slapping. Footsteps approached her table.

She was surprised. He looked like a regular, suburban guy with olive skin, graying hair, and laugh lines. His blue eyes sparkled now. He was enjoying himself. Around his wrist, like Kloch, he wore a large, elegant Rolex watch, and in his hand was a small tool, a tiny steel hammer. He was wearing surgical scrubs.

"You seem surprised," he chuckled. "Were you expecting the Devil?"

"Yes, I was pretty much expecting to come face to face with Lucifer, horns, red skin, forked tail and all."

He laughed again. "Sorry to disappoint you. Now, I've

bowed to your wishes. It's time you returned the favor. Tell me, Diana, are you afraid of me?"

She looked into his eyes, calculating her answer. "Yes. Not like the first time we met. I'm not so naïve. But yes, of course. This isn't a normal situation," she strained against her straps, "and you've told me you'll kill me. Painfully."

They locked eyes. "Say it. Say you're scared. Show me your terror." She didn't make a sound. He prodded her. "Go on." Still she stayed silent. "Go *on*," he said through gritted teeth.

A bloodcurdling scream ripped through the cavernous warehouse space, the hard, jagged sound cutting the icy air like a scalpel slicing through flesh. Diana was giving it her best shot.

Surgeon clapped his hands gleefully. "I knew it," he crowed. "Our first encounter was quite memorable wasn't it? You did your best to hide your terror, but I could taste it. I could smell it on you. You were such a lovely innocent. A delight!" He was grinning like a lunatic. "You're not quite so pure now, and you're harder to interpret, so it's good to know that you're still perfectly, fatally, human." He sobered instantly. "You are honest, and I appreciate that. Now, it's my turn to share something."

"Please, by all means," she croaked. She didn't want to scream again.

"You know, I've been waiting for you. All these years, waiting for the perfect moment. Oh, please don't think I'd forgotten about you. Far from it. You didn't think I'd do that, did you? I've spent years preparing for our meeting. I scouted out the perfect location. I equipped it with the highest quality tools and I have devised a plan to prolong your suffering as much as possible. I intend to relish every second of the time we spend together."

"I'm flattered," she said.

"You should be," he said, in complete honesty. "Now, it's your turn to answer my question. How exactly did you work out my plan to assassinate that imam all those years ago?"

"You mean, before? When you captured me last time?" Diana stared at him in surprise. He was still stuck on that?

"Yes. Tell me. It's important."

"It wasn't just me. CSIS had an entire team of investigators and analysts. We all worked together, questioning everyone and anyone who had anything to do with you."

"I understand, but it takes a special mind to draw the right conclusions, and I'm certain you were the one who made the final deduction."

Diana's back was beginning to ache from being unable to move. She focused on her breath. In. Out. It helped keep her calm. She inhaled as deeply as she could. The strap around her rib cage restricted her breathing. "I got to know your work intimately. I studied everything we knew about you. I analyzed your clients. I looked at every case that was even remotely suspected of being related to you." She stopped.

"Go on. I'm enjoying this. You *are* fascinated by me."

"You have a certain methodology. I studied it. You like getting in and out of your situations quickly. You move around anonymously, low key. You aren't connected to any ideological group, nor do you have a network that you adhere to. You move around the world, never staying in one place for too long, popping up only when there is a contract to be completed. Then you go to ground again. You truly are a lone ranger. You are feared and revered in many circles. Even intelligence agencies respect you because you've evaded capture for so long."

"You *have* done your homework. Nicely done. What else did you learn about me?" Surgeon was fondling the tiny steel hammer between his fingers, smirking.

"You prefer to terminate your targets in a specific and unusual manner and again, you are low key in the way you do it. No noise, excessive blood, or violence. Not your style. You burn off fingerprints when you can. You've done that in ninety eight percent of your cases, but there was one in São Tomé that was an exception."

"Hmm, I remember that one. Too many people. No time. I try and avoid those."

"All I did was put two and two together from the intel we had. On this occasion, there was some chatter that you were in the country and obviously not for a vacation. We didn't know for sure, of course, no one knew what you looked like, but the imam was here. There had been threats against him. We had to prevent an assassination attempt. So we sat on him, basically from the time he arrived to the time he left.

"I figured that a reception the imam was attending on the last night was the best chance you had of getting near him given that we were guarding him so closely. And that while it wasn't the quiet, peaceful environment you like with time to do your "thing," the one experience you had in Africa proved you would deviate from your plan if necessary to complete a hit.

"The imam's people, and many of my own, were okay with him attending the reception. They said the circumstances didn't suit you and that I must be wrong. But I felt sure that you would isolate him if it were possible, and if not, you would just stick it to him, as you might say, with that death needle of yours. No one would be able to do anything about it until it was too late. While people were standing around helplessly watching him die, you'd be long gone. I got my superiors to agree to pull the imam from the reception at the last minute before you could follow through with your plan. I can't tell you how happy we were to see him fly home safe and sound."

Surgeon nodded. "Hmm, I thought as much. You do realize this means you know me better than anyone else? I find that quite titillating."

"Sounds like you're very lonely," she said softly. Show a little empathy. Attempt to connect. That's what her training had taught her.

Surgeon shrugged. He dropped the hammer back on to the table with the other surgical instruments and rolled a stool over to sit close to her head. He leaned on the edge of the table and propped his chin on his palm. "I like being alone. People can't be trusted. Death is the only certainty in this world, and I have power over it. I *am* the Grim Reaper. I've ended the lives of dozens of people. That power sustains me."

Diana turned her head to look at him and wondered how a man could look so sane, so ordinary, yet spout some of the craziest talk she'd ever heard in her entire life.

"Now, shall I tell you about my beloved Gari?"

"Please, go ahead." Anything to keep him from using those instruments on the table.

"He was like a father to me. Taught me most of what I know, and I did appreciate that. But like a good son, I surpassed him. I became more successful, more skilled at what I do. All parents want that for their children. The good ones, anyway. They want their offspring to be more successful than they are. Gari was a good man, but my kills had become more efficient, cleaner, quieter, than even he showed me, and he knew that. He was proud of me." Diana saw a faraway look in Surgeon's icy blue eyes. He took a moment before he snapped back to the present.

Diana asked, "But what about his head? That wasn't your style."

"Oh, I didn't do that. I didn't dump him either. As you say, not my style at all. So... vulgar. Someone must have come along afterward."

"So why did you kill him?"

"I already told you, silly. Because it was time for him to retire."

"Nothing to do with the five mill you were paid, then?"

"Ooh, so you know about that do you? Yes, this contract has been most gratifying. That it brought you, darling girl, back into my life was a bonus. Did you get the recording I sent you? Do you know who ordered the hit?"

"Yes."

"Were you surprised?"

"Very."

"You were expecting it to be the head of a drug cartel or some other unsavory character?"

"They make up your usual clientele," she said.

"True, but not this time. That's what made this one extra special. Having a bonafide government contractor hire me was pure class! Mr. Kloch personally contacted me to secure my services in order to remove Gari from the equation?"

"Why though? What equation?"

"Now, now, Diana. Don't be in such a rush. We have plenty of time, and it's my turn," he admonished.

Diana blinked and clenched her teeth. The pigeons above her were grunting. She remained stoic and smiled softly at him. "You're right. I'm sorry."

"Why didn't you ever thank me for the flowers? Such ingratitude"

"How could I? There was no contact information."

He surged forward. "What?" he screamed. Diana stiffened. "I gave them a return address so you could contact me!" He seethed. "Obviously, my intermediaries weren't as meticulous as they should have been." His nostrils flared. "They're lucky they're already dead." He dropped the steel hammer and picked up a scalpel.

For once, Diana was in full agreement with him. Considering what he did to Garibaldi for money, she shuddered to think what Surgeon would do to people who failed him.

"Your turn," he said, after a moment. He was much calmer, but he still held the scalpel. He looked at her expectantly.

"Why did Kloch hire you to kill Garibaldi?"

He shrugged. "Why should I care? Gari was here on a contract of his own. I assumed I was hired to take him out before he assassinated someone else."

"Who was Garibaldi's target?" Diana asked.

"Tsk, tsk, Diana darling. You're not playing fair. It's my turn," he said. He pouted theatrically.

"Okay, sorry. Go ahead."

"You left CSIS and disappeared. Where did you go?"

It was Diana's turn to shrug. At least, she tried to. The straps were holding her down tightly. "I stayed right here. I took a job as a magazine editor."

He laughed. "A magazine editor? You? Bit tame. Was it a good cover?" He sniggered at his little joke.

"I work for a crime magazine," she explained. She was finding him hard to read. His emotions, reactions were all over the place. She reminded herself that as a psychopath, he was devoid of empathy and a conscience. "What's so funny about that?" Diana asked.

"Well, you were a CSIS agent." He gave her a shrewd look. "Surely you of all people wouldn't take such a... *banal* job. Not without an ulterior motive."

Diana shrugged. "I thought it might be fun. Easy."

"Humph. Surely not. Not you."

"Why not, me?"

"Because you're Diana Hunter. Woman of mystery. *International* woman of mystery. Working for a magazine is way too mundane for someone like you. Provincial. Like that *boyfriend* of yours."

# CHAPTER NINETEEN

"THE JOB WAS something to pass the time. No ulterior motive, I can assure you. And please don't insult my partner. He's a good guy. Now, it's my turn, I believe."

"By all means," he said, waving his hand.

"If you killed Gari because he was about to kill someone else, who was his target?" she asked again.

"No idea. It wasn't a detail I was interested in. I assume that it was one of Blue Panther's VIP's considering how much they paid. I could have negotiated a lot more, but the privilege of killing Gari made up for it."

"And that's the only reason you came to Canada? Besides me, of course."

He gave her a broad smile that made him look so boyish and innocent, it was hard to fathom that beneath the almost sweet exterior beat the heart of a monster. "Technically, it is my turn, but I'll answer your question – the one you posed and the one you didn't."

Diana tried to nod. The strap at her throat was threatening to choke her. She was finding it difficult to swallow. "Of course."

"To answer your first question, yes, my only reason for being in Canada was to eliminate Garibaldi. You," he winked at her, "are a bonus." Her skin crawled. "And the question you didn't ask but you still want the answer to is that no, I know nothing else. If I ask too many questions, my client pool would shrink exponentially. Satisfied?"

Diana tried to nod her head but the strap around her neck merely caused her to jerk awkwardly. "Yes, thank you," she replied.

He frowned. "Is there anything else you want to tell me?

"No, nothing," she said quickly.

"Hmm." A skeptical look crept into his eyes.

He got up and spent some moments inspecting the surgical instruments, running his fingers over the metal gently, as if he were caressing a lover.

"Don't you have more questions?" she asked, trying to keep the fear out of her voice. The thought of the instruments on the table frightened her, but what scared her more were those small bottles and syringes.

He shrugged. "I'm tired of talking now. It's nearly time to get started. More questions later. Maybe. First, I want to hear that beautiful voice scream one more time."

"I've been told I'm quite irritating when I scream."

He laughed. "I doubt anyone has ever heard you before. You are not a screamer. I bet I am your first in that regard. But I like the fact that you're still fighting, even if it's only with words. It will make this all the more fun," he said as he inspected each of the bottles on the table. He picked one up. "Ah yes, this is my favorite." He walked over so she could see the bottle he held up. "It's a blend of my own design. I've fused various elements into one spectacular compound. The chemistry is very cool, I think. But what will interest you most is what it does."

He leaned down and whispered close to Diana's ear. "It maximizes the pain you feel while flooding your system with adrenaline so you won't pass out. You will feel every agonizing touch. It is quite brilliant," he said with a maniacal giggle.

He picked up a syringe and filled it half-way. Diana's eyes widened, and she swallowed hard as Surgeon made his way over to her. He rubbed her arm with alcohol.

"We need to clean the area first. Don't want any icky germs getting in, do we?"

"Does it matter? I'll be dead soon."

"It matters to me."

"What's your real name? Who should I be cursing while you're having your fun?" she stuttered. It was becoming harder and harder to control her reactions. Her body was starting to shake uncontrollably.

He chuckled. "My name is Montague Ferrier-Hill. My friends call me 'Monty,'" he said.

"You have friends?"

"Oh, yes. We're friends, Diana, aren't we? You can call me Monty, too. Just a little scratch now." He tapped her arm looking for a vein. Diana refused to flinch as he inserted the needle and pushed the plunger all the way down.

But she gasped as ice cold liquid raced through her veins. "Montague?" she asked when she regained her breath. "Not the most intimidating name I've ever heard."

He shrugged. "My mother admired the British aristocracy, so she gave me a name she thought would suit. She coached me in the art of upward social mobility, you know, etiquette, history, the arts. She considered it the first step in her master plan to elevate her own standing." He stood next to her, the needle still in his hand, tapping it against the side of his finger as he reminisced out loud. Suddenly he jammed it into a container, the kind designed to safely dispose of old needles.

*A sharps container. He has a freaking sharps container.*

"But, truthfully, I never fit in. I was too cultured for my working class roots while lacking the connections and the innate breeding to move seamlessly in the circles for which I had been schooled. Her plan failed."

"So what did you do?" Diana asked, her heart and head pounding.

"I turned to killing people. Well, wouldn't you?"

Diana gasped again as he trailed his fingers over her skin. The light contact had her nerve-endings shrieking in pain.

"So, I was right. You are a psychopath with mommy issues."

He laughed. "Your attempt to anger me by referencing my mother was sweet if misguided. My mother only wanted the best for me. She was a wonderful woman."

"Who gave birth to a monster..." Diana said with another pained groan as she shifted slightly.

"No one's perfect. Now, let's get on, shall we?

"Can I have five more minutes? Just to psych myself for what's coming." She tried to keep her tone flippant, but it was becoming more and more difficult.

"Nuh-uh. I have a schedule to keep to," he said, looking regretfully at his watch.

He approached her. He had the scalpel in his hand again. "Now, where shall we begin?"

"How about we don't begin at all?" she suggested, breathing as deeply as she could through her nose.

"You're no fun, Diana darling. But I'll give you another minute. Just so that you can anticipate what is going to happen to you for a little longer."

"How long do you think this will take?"

"It all really depends on how long I can keep you alive. But I've set aside a few hours for this little endeavor. I'm hoping it will be enough, but if it's not, I can always stay longer. Or come back later." His lips curled into a delighted smile. With the scalpel, he lightly stroked her arm where the fine pale hairs stood up at attention, scraping the blade across the goose bumps that rumpled her skin.

"You know, I have always been fascinated by the 'death of a thousand cuts' they practiced in China. They did it until the early 1900s, you know. I was always curious if it was actually possible to keep someone alive for that long. Many people believe that it only involved making cuts on the body, but that's not true. They did other things." He leant down and whispered into Diana's ear.

"Really? How fascinating," Diana ground out through her clenched jaw as he moved away.

"Isn't it?"

"But rather barbaric, don't you think?"

He shrugged. "Oh, I don't know. I think of it as an art form. It's not easy to keep someone alive through all one thousand cuts. I'm curious if I have the ability to do it." He tapped his lip as he looked over his instruments. He put down the scalpel he had in his hand and picked up another. He held it up to the light. "Yes, this will do. It will do just fine." He turned back to her, his eyes shining with anticipation. "Are you ready, my dear?"

As she watched, he lowered the scalpel to her arm. She braced herself.

"Are you *sure* you wouldn't like to scream again? It would help me focus."

Diana knew the moment that scalpel touched her skin, she'd feel pain like never before.

She ripped another chilling scream that caused the air to vibrate. The building shook. The sound echoed off the walls, off the huge, hollow space. The pigeons who'd settled again on the beams high above her head flew out through a broken window, the sound of their flapping wings a calming contrast to the terrifying sight beneath them.

Surgeon leaned over her. "Now, keep still, Diana." She watched the scalpel's blade glint in the sunlight as he lowered it to her arm. She began to pant and look around frantically, the whites of her eyes holding steady as her irises flicked back and forth within them.

"Here we go, Di—"

"BACK *OFF*!"

There was a massive thud followed by a crash as one of the doors to the warehouse smashed open. Peter's furious voice filled her ears. She heard boots running across the floor of the warehouse. It was the sweetest sound she had ever heard. He was here. Just like they'd planned.

# CHAPTER TWENTY

"W HAT'S GOING ON?" Surgeon asked mildly, his hands in the air. He was still holding the scalpel. "How did you find us?" He looked down at her. "You tricked me, Diana dear."

Diana inhaled deeply, one breath after another. The adrenaline was making her heart race. "Another lesson in humility. Except this one's going to cost you. You'll be paying for the rest of your life, at least. I'll make sure of it." Big words. A lot bigger than the way she felt as she lay strapped to the table, shaking and in pain.

Surgeon shook his head. "Well played, Diana, well played," he said.

Peter stormed up to him. "I told you to get away from her!" he bellowed. Surgeon dropped the scalpel and stepped away from the table.

"He moves so much as a hair, shoot him," Peter said. "And I don't care where."

"Yes, sir." Diana could hear at least four other male voices.

Peter was by her side in the next moment. He ripped off

his headset and leaned over her, his wide shoulders thankfully blocking Surgeon from view.

"He admitted to the killing. Did you get it all? He admitted to the killing."

"Shhhh, we got it all. It's fine."

"What happened? What took you so long?"

"Later. Let's get you out of here," he whispered. He smoothed her hair back from her sweaty forehead. He was very gentle, but she still flinched.

"Sorry. I know you're in pain. I heard everything." He went to work on the straps holding her down, being as careful as an angry man of his size could be.

"Can I help you up?" he asked.

She took a deep breath. "Please," she croaked.

He bent over. "Hook your arm around my neck. I'll pull you. Less contact that way."

He levered her into a sitting position and took a step back to give her some room. Another deep breath. She swung her legs around and slipped off the table. "Bad idea," she groaned as she swayed. There was ringing her ears, her vision blurred. Peter was there in an instant. She leaned against him. "Thank you," she whispered.

"Let's get you out of here," he said.

She nodded but paused. "Just a moment." She hobbled over to Surgeon, who was watching her curiously as two members of the Emergency Response Team cuffed him.

"I want you to know that I will forget all about you after I walk out this door. Got it?" she snarled. "Stand back," she said to the ERT. She brought her closed fist into contact with the soft underbelly of Surgeon's rib cage at high speed. She followed up with her knee and hit him hard in the groin. As he folded over, she brought her fist up yet again, this time into his face. A kick to his chest was her final riposte as Surgeon lay bleeding and coughing spittle onto the floor.

"Better?" Peter asked who was standing by.

She looked up at him and smiled through her agony. "Much."

"Now can we get out of here?"

She shook her head. "What's wrong now?" Peter asked.

"I think I'm going to do something very embarrassing," she whispered.

Peter rolled his eyes. "Go ahead. I'm ready for anything."

"I'm never going to live this down..." she trailed off.

Peter waited until Diana started to fall before he swung her up in his arms. He looked down at her. She was mentally stronger than most of VPD put together. But she took crazy risks.

And he was just as much of a nutjob. Listening to her banter with a psychopath had been excruciating. When he heard Diana's scream, shock and terror had thrown him against a wall. He'd been running to his car listening to their conversation through his headset and talking to Ryan, the tech guy who was tracking Diana's movements.

Her being captured had been part of the plan. Him going down had not.

He'd screwed up. He should have given Diana more space. He should not have been in the bedroom when the decoy came in, but he was damned if he'd just let Surgeon take her without a fight. Like Kieran said, she was his now.

And so Surgeon had gained a head start on him during which Diana could have so easily been killed. It had been a lot of terrifying ground to make up, and Peter had found himself praying to a God he didn't believe in that he'd make it to her in time.

"Will she be okay?" Stockton, commander of the ERT asked, looking at Diana's prone body in Peter's arms. Despite her occasional short-tempered ways, Diana had won over most of the people she'd worked with. Her energy, intelligence, and most of all, her loyalty made her popular, if a little intimidating.

"She'll be fine. She's too hard-headed not to be." He paused. "Take care of this piece of trash, Commander," he said, nodding his head at Surgeon, "and be careful. He's not your average criminal."

"I'm delighted you noticed," Surgeon said.

Peter looked at him. "One more word out of you, and I might forget I'm a cop. And I promise you, these guys would look the other way," he growled.

Surgeon blanched and took a step back. He was a predator, but he recognized that Peter was just as dangerous when pushed. And Peter was near breaking point.

"Don't worry, we'll take real good care of him," Stockton said.

Peter walked out into the light, carrying Diana carefully. He blinked to clear his vision and gently deposited her on the back seat of his car.

The plan had been very, very risky, but she'd been right about the principle behind it. If they simply captured Surgeon, they would have gotten nowhere. He would have lawyered up, ducking and weaving around the facts. They would never have gotten to the truth.

When Diana had proposed she get herself alone with Surgeon and use his obsession with her against him, Peter had been worried she wouldn't be able to handle it, but she'd reassured him. It wasn't her usual spiel of "I can handle anything" blather, either. Her considered, thought-out reasoning had convinced him. And the security measures they'd put in place. The conversation, for once, had not been a battle. Well, not much of one.

# CHAPTER TWENTY-ONE

"I DON'T LIKE this," Peter grumbled.

"Letting him grab me is the most elegant solution."

"Elegant? Lady, you seriously need to revise your adjectives. There is nothing elegant about this. Suicidal? Dangerous? Stupid? Yes. Elegant? Not so much. Donaldson will go ape."

"Please don't tell him, Peter. Or Kieran. They won't go for it.

"And for good reason. I'm not sure if I should be insulted that you think me the schmuck you can bamboozle or flattered that you trust me with your wild-ass ideas."

"Of course, I trust you," she said. "You're my partner." He was mollified for a moment, until he came crashing back to Earth in all his fiery glory when he remembered precisely what she was asking of him.

"Look, this is crazy. I won't know where you are. He'll take your phone. How will I find you? And how do you know you'll be able to get him to incriminate himself? How can you be certain?"

"Whoa!" she laughed. "One question at a time. Look,

*finding me will be easy. See this?"* She pointed to a tiny butterfly tattoo on the inside of her wrist.

"Yeah, a tattoo. I've noticed it before. What of it? Are you showing me how to identify your body when he kills you and takes your head as a trophy?"

"Don't be an idiot," she huffed. "I don't intend to die. And this isn't just a tattoo. It hides a tracking device that monitors my position as well as my vital signs at all times. Courtesy of CSIS. You can follow me with this," she said, handing him a smartphone. He looked down and sure enough, he could see her heart rate and her location.

"Well, that's nice. I'll know the precise moment he kills you."

"It's the latest tech. They're being used to track agents to reduce the number of disappearances and kidnapping-related deaths. They're also used by government officials when they travel to high-risk places."

"Hmm, I suppose they're never used to track persons of interest, no matter how illegal it might be," he said, his tone laden with sarcasm. "How did you get your hands on one?"

"Never mind that. If we've got the tech, why not use it?"

"Okay, I can track you. What's next in that big brain of yours?"

"Our guy'll be so pleased that he finally got his hands on me that he won't be able to resist showing me how incredibly intelligent he is. I'll get him to tell me what happened with Garibaldi. We'll be recording it, and voilà, we've got him."

"Of course. Simple. Easy. What could possibly go wrong?"

"Come on, Peter. Where's that 'Who dares wins' attitude? SpecOps, over a hundred missions, decorated war hero persona?"

Peter's face darkened, "That was different. How do I know when to get you out of there? Use my best judgment?"

"Nope."

"Of course not, silly me."

"That's what this is for," she said, pointing in the direction of her cleavage.

Peter refused to take her bait. "Yes?" he said, not taking his eyes off her face.

"There's a tiny, almost undetectable microphone with a five-kilometer range hidden in the wire of my bra. You'll be able to hear everything."

"In your bra."

"Yes, in my bra," she replied. "And, because I know you like to have backup plans to your backup plans, I will turn on my tooth."

"Your what?"

"My tooth. A few years ago, I had a tooth drilled and a tiny device placed inside. When I trigger it, it will send an emergency signal indicating that I need backup. It will also transmit my location. I trigger it by grinding my teeth like this." She bared her teeth and moved her lower jaw from side to side. "As long as I am conscious, it works great." She gave him a big smile.

Peter's face was thunderous. "You're loving this, aren't you?"

"It's my James Bond moment," Diana smiled.

"You do know that that's fiction, right?"

Diana merely grinned back at him.

"I don't know. This CSIS world of yours with all the covert crap, putting yourself in danger. It bothers me. Too much could go wrong."

"You know, you're going to have to tell me a little more about your time in the military one of these days. How is this *any different than that? You were out hunting terrorists in caves!"*

Peter scowled. *"Yeah, but I was armed to the teeth! I had my men – multiple, highly trained, heavily weaponized men – with me. I wasn't handing myself over like a sacrificial lamb."*

She shrugged again. *"Well, unfortunately, collecting intelligence isn't always easy or safe."*

*"You have a knack for understating things, you know. Not easy? Not safe? Handing yourself over to a psychopath who likes to chop heads off and is obsessed with you is just nuts. And I'm crazy for going along with it."*

*"So you will?"*

Peter stared down at the floor first, then gave her a sideways glance. He knew he was nearly worn down.

*"If I didn't know you better, I'd think you had a death wish."*

*"Nope, definitely no death wish here. Just a desire to make the world a little safer. Take the bad guys down."* She leaned over and put her hand on his arm, and looked at him appealingly. *"Just like you."*

*"You know, I really wish your self-preservation instinct was much more developed,"* Peter grumbled. *"Okay, so I'll know where you are and be able to hear everything. What's next?"*

*"Psych. That'll be the safe word. When I say 'psych', it means it's time for you to get on your white horse and get me the hell out of there."*

*"Psych? What kind of safe word is that?"*

*"One that works for me,"* she said and poked her tongue out. She turned serious. *"Look, we have to make this look real. No heroics, alright?"*

Peter took a deep breath. "Will you be alright?" he asked. She looked him in the eye and nodded.

"Yes." She gave him a wink.

"Okay," he tried not to sigh, "I won't charge in before you're ready, but you have to promise me you won't put yourself in more danger than is necessary. If anything feels off, no matter how slight, you say the safe word, even if we don't have the intel. Got it?"

She saluted. "Sir, yes sir," she barked. And then, she whispered, "I promise."

"Good," he said, satisfied with her answer, for once. "One more thing. When you go on that TV show, try not to piss him off royally. He's already insane. We don't need him wound up even more."

"Why would I do that?"

Peter raised an eyebrow. "Have you met you?"

"I'll try to be good."

Peter groaned. He'd known then he wasn't going to like whatever was about to happen.

But all that was in the past now. The plan had worked out. Not exactly as they'd intended but well enough. They had their man, and Diana was okay. He pulled up in front of Vancouver General, picked Diana up as gently as he could, and carried her inside.

"Where are we?" she mumbled.

"The hospital."

"No!"

"Yes," he replied, firmly. It was like dealing with a child. She hit his chest weakly with her hand.

"You're going in to get checked out. Stop arguing. Sheesh."

"VPD! I need some help here!" he hollered into the hospital lobby. A nurse rushed over with a gurney. "She needs checking out. She's been given a cocktail of drugs that's left her in a lot of pain. And psychological trauma," he added quickly as he lay Diana gently on the gurney.

"I'm fine," Diana was slurring.

"And she talks rubbish sometimes, so there's that." Peter turned from the nurse to Diana. "I'll be right here. They'll check you over, then when they say so, we'll go home, okay?" he told her softly. Two more nurses joined them and Peter watched, hands in his pockets, as they rolled Diana away down the corridor.

He turned around, considering what to do next. He was still wired from the rescue but his high had peaked, and he was starting to come down from it. A headache was starting to form, and the "what ifs" were starting to plague him. *What if he hadn't got there in time? What if the tracking devices had been compromised?* He sat down in the waiting area and took out his phone. He needed to do something positive to offset his ruminations. It was time to update Donaldson.

"You better be calling to tell me Diana's fine," Donaldson barked into the phone.

Donaldson had been livid when Peter had told him what had happened. His boss could swear a blue streak but Peter had no idea he could be quite so creative. He'd sensed Donaldson would have thrown out curse word after curse word for five minutes straight if he hadn't understood the gravity of the situation and the need to launch a rescue operation immediately.

"Almost without a hitch. We got the intel we needed.

Our guy confessed. He's in custody. Diana's in the hospital getting checked out by the docs now."

"Is she okay?" Kieran shouted. So he was on speaker-phone. Great.

"She's fine. She fainted, but she sucker punched him first, so I think she'll be okay.

Kieran and Donaldson chuckled with relief. "Stay there. Make sure Diana's alright," Donaldson said.

"I'm thinking that maybe you should consider a deal with Surgeon, sir," Peter said. He hated deals but they were expedient. Surgeon had worked for some of the biggest scum in the world. And the information he could provide would be invaluable.

"I'm surprised at you, Hopkinson," Donaldson replied. "Not your usual style."

"The intel would be gold, sir. Surgeon will sell out anyone if it benefits him. We could take a lot of perps out of circulation with his help. I'm sure Diana will agree," he added.

"He's right about that," Kieran said.

"Okay, Kieran and I will talk," Donaldson responded.

Peter ended the call and settled in to wait. He could barely keep his eyes open now. His adrenaline high had completely dissipated, and exhaustion was blanketing him. His eyes fluttered as his thoughts switched to Diana. Why did she hate hospitals so much? He made a mental note to ask her, but forgot it almost immediately as he slipped into a restless sleep.

## CHAPTER TWENTY-TWO

T HREE DAYS AFTER her ordeal, Diana was back at VPD headquarters, ready to get to work. She'd been forced to stay in the hospital for twenty-four hours, an order she'd found ridiculous. But no matter how insistent she'd been that she was alright, they wouldn't let her go. Of course, Peter had betrayed her. He'd colluded with the doctors and made sure she stayed put. She hadn't been happy. She'd been held against her will. Again!

When she finally made it home, Peter further annoyed her when he didn't let her do anything for another day. He'd stayed with her and done everything, including feeding and walking Max. He'd even gone out and bought her favorite chocolate.

"No, you aren't coming."

Diana opened her mouth to say something. "No," Peter interrupted her before she could get a word out. "It's no, and it's staying no."

She huffed and pouted. "It's been nothing but no for these past few days."

"Hey, you. Remember who put their ass on the line for you," Peter retorted.

"You're so mean," she grumbled, but she smiled at him.

His face turned serious. "Diana, I don't know if I said this earlier, but I'm very glad you're alright."

Diana chuckled. "You have said it. Several times. But *I* should thank *you*. I never had any doubt you would rescue me," she winked at him and Peter blushed. She noticed. Oh, she would remember that. And she'd be reminding him of it in the future.

Diana continued to be crotchety and grumbled incessantly, but Peter hadn't budged, and in the end, she'd relented and relaxed into his care. It felt good. It had been a very long time since she'd last allowed herself to be cared for by anyone.

With Surgeon in custody, she'd put a ghost to rest. She had thought that her past experience with him hadn't had much of an affect on her, but now that he was locked up, she felt calmer, more relaxed. Knowing where he was and that he wasn't about to grab her gave her a sense of security she hadn't realized she missed until the threat was gone.

But now she wanted to get back to work. They could extract a lot of information from Surgeon now they had him. But Peter wanted her to rest some more.

"I think you should stay off work for a while longer," he said. "We've got him behind bars, we're not on a deadline anymore."

She'd objected.

"They could hire someone to replace Garibaldi. Surgeon's not the only assassin in town. If Greene is the target, he still could be hit."

"Another day with you out of action won't matter. The

world doesn't stop turning at VPD, or CSIS for that matter, when you're not around."

Diana threw herself against the back of the sofa. It really was like dealing with a child.

"We have other people, experts even, who are working the case. They can take care of things. You don't have to do it all."

There was more grumbling, but again she relented. She'd met her match.

But now she was back. Her trek up to Major Crimes was something of a victory walk. Just about everyone she passed stopped to ask if she was alright, to tell her what an inspiration she was, and how brave she had been. When she passed through her dad's old department, normally reverently quiet when she went by, the bullpen burst into applause.

She entered the conference room. Donaldson, Kieran and Steve rose when they saw her. They too clapped, and she blushed.

"Thank you, gentlemen. Triumph is sweet, that's for sure. As is putting some of my demons to rest. Peter's not here, but let's not forget what I owe him, the entire team who got me out, and you. But we must move on. There's work to do."

It was a pretty speech, if a little grandiose, but the victory glow only lasted a moment.

"Are you insane?" Kieran shouted.

"Who came up with this lunatic plan? We were going nuts here," Donaldson was just as loud as Kieran. And they kept shouting.

"Seriously, Diana. What were you thinking?"

"Give us one reason why we should trust you in the future!"

She held up a hand, and they quieted. "With you both shouting at the same time, I can't understand a word you're saying. But you're welcome," she said with a grin. Donaldson looked exasperated and Kieran went red as his nostrils flared.

Peter blithely walked in. "Any news?" he asked as he took a seat, oblivious to the atmosphere.

Thankfully, Steve took the reins and order was restored. "We've informed our counterparts, agencies in other countries, that we have Surgeon in custody. There's been congratulations all round. Your profile with the various agencies is substantially elevated, Ms. Hunter."

"Interestingly, the Americans informed us – after a lot of poking and prodding and a few subtle threats – that Surgeon used to be a CIA agent. Apparently, he went rogue over fifteen years ago, and they've never caught him. If Surgeon were to be extradited, there's a good chance he'd be sent to Guantánamo Bay, somewhere he'd obviously prefer to avoid, especially after we might have intimated that we'd get word out among his fellow inmates about his former status. As a result, Surgeon, or Mr. Ferrier-Hill as he has informed us he'd now prefer to be called, has been extremely helpful."

"Quite a few of his former clients are guests in Gitmo," Kieran said, "and I don't think they'd take lightly to hearing about his lack of loyalty."

"He doesn't know the meaning of the word. He is utterly self-serving. Dead inside a week would be my guess," Diana said.

"Luckily for us, Mr. Ferrier-Hill is paranoid and has kept detailed files on all his clients, going so far as to record all his meetings and phone conversations. He generously handed everything over to us," Steve said with a grin.

"Diana, what you did with Surgeon is incredible. Not only did you facilitate his capture, but he's acting like a lamb and given us intel that will save us years of work."

Diana frowned. "I'd be careful with him. He has a way of manipulating people to get what he wants."

"We know what we're doing," Kieran growled.

"Okay, what can we do to clean up the loose ends in this case? We still don't know why Garibaldi was killed. What about Greene and Kloch? Any movement there?" Peter asked.

"Nope. And don't you go messing around, young lady," Donaldson warned when Diana pursed her lips and frowned. "The D.C. has made it clear we are not to touch them."

They all fell silent for a moment. "What about working it from the other end?" Peter asked.

Diana looked at him and her eyes widened. "You're right," she breathed out.

"So far, we've only been looking at it from the target's angle, but how about we start investigating the terror group? I mean, isn't it about time CSIS started doing something?" Peter looked over at Kieran.

Kieran sat up straighter in his chair and looked at all of them in turn. He blinked before replying.

"So, what can I do to help VPD? Seeing as you're looking for some assistance."

Diana snorted. "Kieran, you wanted in on this case, remember?"

He grinned. "You're so good at what you do that I got the impression I'd only be getting in your way."

# CHAPTER TWENTY-THREE

D IANA ROLLED HER eyes, and Peter huffed. She cut a glance at him and tried to hide her smile. He was glaring at Kieran. She checked herself. She was slightly annoyed that she took pleasure from this tussle they were having. She conceded that it made her feel powerful, if slightly appalled at her reaction. Hadn't women in the 21$^{st}$ century refuted this position of relating to themselves in terms of men? She should know better.

"Okay, okay. It might surprise you to know that while you," Kieran looked at Diana, "were playing damsel in distress and you," he looked across at Peter, "were playing knight in shining armor, *we* were following up on some leads at our end. Then, when Surgeon spilled his guts to protect that sorry ass of his, he gave up that he'd heard on the grapevine that his ultimate paymaster for the Garibaldi hit was a group called the Islamic Front, or ILIF for short. We started doing some digging." He opened a folder in front of him and handed out three smaller ones. "This information is sensitive, so understand that all folders must be destroyed after this meeting," Kieran said with a pointed look at everyone.

Diana nodded. It was standard procedure. Never send sensitive information over an unsecured network and always destroy hardcopies, preferably in a very hot fire that wouldn't leave a trace, or more usually, in a robust shredder.

She opened her folder and found precious little. A few photographs and some notes. She looked at Kieran questioningly. "A little thin, isn't it?"

Kieran acknowledged her point. "We haven't been able to find out much about them. They operate mainly out of Afghanistan. We have photos of suspected group members but that's about it. We've got our people on the ground digging into ILIF to see what else they can come up with."

"So, we're talking about a terrorist group that has plenty of money, has a Canadian official on a kill list, is obviously well organized considering they've managed to evade everyone up until now, but we know virtually nothing about them?" Peter asked.

"Yes," Kieran growled.

Donaldson shook his head. "This has the potential to blow up into a catastrophic mess. What if Greene isn't their only target? Maybe he was just a single obstacle standing in their way. What if their ultimate goal is to pull something massive in Canada?" he asked.

Peter objected. "We could come up with all kinds of disastrous scenarios and any or none of them could be true. The fact is they paid for a hit on a member of our government and we don't know why. That's enough for us to be going on with. Speculation about anything more is pure conjecture at this point and not particularly helpful."

Donaldson hesitated for a moment. "Well, what do we do now? We don't even have a starting point. Where do we look? What do we look for? Who are we looking for? I mean, we barely know who this group is. It could just be a few crazies holed up in a cave."

Kieran shook his head. "This group could be two or three nutcases in a cave, but they have money and connections. They could very well be a front for a much larger group. And in our world, it's always best to assume the worst. It's what keeps us all safe."

"First things first. We'll start on the ground. Kieran has his feelers out. We'll see what that reels in," Diana said.

"I'll make some calls and—" Kieran paused and pulled out his phone. It was vibrating. "Give me a second." He got up and left the room.

"I don't like this," Donaldson said. "I don't even want to think about what this might mean."

Kieran walked back into the room. "Diana, a Major Lennox has contacted CSIS. Says he has information for us and wants you in on the meeting. He's an American."

Diana's eyes widened in surprised. "Ethan Lennox?" she asked.

Kieran nodded. "The message was relayed to CSIS through the CIA. Something you forgot to tell me?"

Diana shrugged. "No. Can you organize a secure link?" she asked.

"Sure. I'll have to clear it with the CIA and CSIS command, but it shouldn't be a problem."

"The sooner, the better," Diana said. "If Ethan's calling, something big is happening."

"I'll get right on it. Don't forget to destroy those files," Kieran said on his way out.

"So, who is this Major Lennox?" Donaldson asked.

"I'm sorry, sir, but that's information I am not at liberty to reveal."

"But you clearly know him."

"Yes, the Major and I are well-acquainted."

Donaldson sighed. "I'm liking this less and less. Now the Americans are involved," he grumbled. "Maybe we should just hand everything over to the Mounties. They have their own counter-terrorism unit. Let them deal with it."

"Bring the RCMP in on what?" Peter asked. "We have nothing concrete so far. Just," he flicked the folder in front of him dismissively, " stories and theories."

"Peter's right. The RCMP won't lift a finger until we can provide concrete proof of a terrorist threat. Once we have that proof, we can bring them in. But until we have accurate intelligence, they won't pay any attention to us," Diana said.

Donaldson sighed. "This better not blow up in our faces," he complained, "We'll end up stationed in Alert. And that's way too close to the North Pole for my liking." The tiny village of Alert is one of the most remote places in the world, only five hundred miles from the North Pole.

"Don't worry, sir, we'll figure this out. You'll be a hero," Diana said with a grin.

Donaldson's eyes widened. "I'd rather be stationed in Alert, thank you very much."

Diana and Peter looked at him quizzically.

"If I'm the hero, then the powers that be will force me into a promotion that I don't want," he continued grumble.

"We could give CSIS all the credit, if it bothers you that much," Diana said with a smile.

Donaldson snorted. "You know what? You two solve this and save the world, and then we'll figure out who gets the credit. For now, I don't care what it takes, you two make sure that these lunatics don't succeed, whatever their plans are."

# CHAPTER TWENTY-FOUR

TWO HOURS LATER, Diana and Peter were on their way to CSIS. Lennox had made it clear his message was urgent, and it couldn't wait another day. It was ten o'clock at night. Diana had called Terri and as usual, Max's sitter had jumped at the chance to spend some time with him.

"So, how do you and Lennox know one other? And why does he insist on speaking only to you?" Peter asked out of the blue, startling Diana.

"We may have worked together at one point," she said.

Peter glanced at her quickly, and then looked back at the road. "I know Lennox," he said. "I know what he does."

Diana looked at him in surprise. "You do?"

Peter nodded. "My team was called in to support his task force on an op. He knows what he's doing. He's a good man, if a little unethical at times."

"Huh. I wouldn't say he's unethical, exactly. He does what he has to, to achieve a bigger goal."

"And looks the other way in the process."

"What do you know about his task force?" Diana asked.

Peter's tone sounded even handed but there was a tiny edge to it. He was staring resolutely ahead.

"I know they're called Task Force Indigo. That he heads them up. That they were assembled to counter terrorist threats and that they have a worldwide remit. That they handle everything from intelligence gathering to acting on it."

Diana's eyebrows remained firmly in place but she was astounded. TFI was classified. The fact that Peter knew about them meant something. She just didn't know what.

Ethan Lennox did indeed head up Task Force Indigo. As terrorist threats had grown in number and diversity, TFI was formed as a joint operation between Canada, the United States, and the UK. It was made up of operatives from the three countries' intelligence agencies and Special Forces divisions. It was a secret. A very deep secret.

"What did you do for TFI?" Diana asked carefully.

"I was involved in a raid to take out a cell that was plotting to mount a terrorist attack in North Africa. The operatives were already on the ground, and we worked with the British and US forces in Afghanistan and Morocco to take out the control and field units. TFI coordinated the mission."

Diana frowned, her mind working furiously. "Ethan is a good man. He cares about results." she said.

"Did you work for TFI?" he asked. He spun the wheel smoothly to take a corner. Peter knew the Vancouver streets like the back of his hand and loved driving the streets at night when they were clear of traffic.

Diana nodded. "For a while."

"Clearly, Kieran has no idea," he said.

She sighed. "Kieran thinks I left CSIS two years ago."

"But you didn't?"

"Technically, I did. I was reassigned to TFI but the level of classified work meant that no one could know, not even the people I worked with at CSIS."

"And you only worked with them for a year or so?"

Diana hesitated. "Technically."

Peter looked over to her. "Technically?"

"I still do."

"What?" Peter exclaimed. He pulled the car over sharply and killed the engine. "What are you saying? How do you still work for TFI? I thought you were a magazine editor!"

Diana rubbed the bridge of her nose. "I am a magazine editor... most of the time. I just sort of do work..." She trailed off. She was reaching. "For TFI... now and again... like VPD. When they need me, they call and I go."

Peter was staring straight ahead.

"I haven't worked full time for them for over a year, Peter. And I haven't heard from them at all in the time I've been working with you." She finished in a rush. She felt like a kid who'd been caught stealing candy. Ashamed, but desperately trying to justify her actions.

Peter tipped his head back against his headrest and closed his eyes. "You've been lying to me all this time." He looked away out of the window, his elbow on the ledge. He banged his curled fist against his mouth.

Her face hardened. "Don't. Don't you dare! You know exactly what it's like. I'm bound by so many rules and regulations that I could end up in jail just for telling you. Do you think I like hiding these things?"

He sighed and turned to look at her again. "I don't know Diana. Do you? You seem to find it awfully easy to lie to everyone."

Diana's heart constricted in pain. Of all people, she

expected Peter to understand. The loneliness she constantly braced herself against threatened to overwhelm her.

"Forget it," she said. "Let's get to CSIS. Ethan's waiting."

"So it's Ethan is it? You two sound awfully close," he snarled, putting the car in gear. He tore away from the curb.

"We are close," she snapped back. "We've been in some tough situations together. And watch your driving, I'd like to get there in one piece."

"Not driving like a little old lady now, am I?"

"Now *you're* being childish."

Peter ignored her. She was right, but he couldn't help himself. "I assume Ethan doesn't have a problem with you lying to everyone. Oh, but you don't have to lie to him, do you? He knows exactly who you are and what you do. The rest of us have to guess."

"You know what? I never lied to you. I never said that I'm only a magazine editor or that I don't work for TFI?"

"A lie by omission is still a lie," he ground out.

"Really, Peter? So, when you worked for SpecOps, did you tell all your friends on the outside exactly what you did?"

Peter didn't reply. Not another word was spoken until they arrived at the unmarked CSIS building in center of Vancouver.

# CHAPTER TWENTY-FIVE

PETER SWOOPED INTO a parking space under the CSIS building way too fast. He wasn't angry with Diana for keeping TFI classified. He well understood why she couldn't tell him, it was standard protocol for all agents employed on covert ops. He was angry that she had this whole other life that involved TFI and Lennox and she'd kept him out of it.

And maybe he was a little jealous, too. Several years ago, Peter had been offered a position with the task force but had declined it. Bad timing. His brother had just been murdered and the drive to investigate his death had over-whelmed his other ambitions. Working with VPD was the best option open to someone with his skills and experience while still allowing him to work on what he called his "side project," but it had been a big step down for him. He cheer-lessly wondered if he'd have met Diana earlier if things had broken another way.

He remembered Ethan Lennox well. A decade older than Peter, Lennox was a great guy, a true American hero.

He was a natural leader, the type who'd throw himself on a grenade to protect his men. He was one of the most decorated serving officers in the US military and charming to a fault. He oozed charisma, in fact. Diana was obviously close to him and had kept all their secrets. It made him irrationally angry with her.

He knew he should apologize for being an ass, but he couldn't. Not yet. An emotion he refused to acknowledge was choking him. Why was everything such a roller coaster with her? He pressed his lips together in a thin line and kept his mouth shut. He knew if he opened it, he'd end up hurling even more unpleasant accusations around, and he didn't want to ruin his relationship with Diana completely.

He took a deep breath. He needed to get control of himself. Anger aside, this news made sense. The idea that she'd gone into the private sector after CSIS and no longer used her skills had seemed out of character to him all along. Her desire to right wrongs seemed deeply embedded in her psyche.

"I'm sorry," he said with a sigh.

"Doesn't matter," Diana said softly. She looked out the window. He'd hurt her. He could hear it in her voice. But what could he say? *I'm sorry. I'm not angry with you. I'm angry with me for being an idiot and not being able to respond differently.*

"It does matter," he said. "I had no right to get angry. You're right, I do know what it's like, and I understand why you couldn't tell me. I'm sorry," he continued.

"It's okay," she said. She hesitated for a moment. "I was going to tell you," she continued softly.

He flicked a look at her.

She sighed. "I applied for you to be vetted by CSIS and by all the other agencies involved in TFI so that I could, you know, tell you. It's been a long and arduous process, because there are so many agencies involved. I submitted your file four months ago, and I received approval last week, but I just hadn't had time to tell you..." she trailed off.

*Shoot.* He felt like a complete jerk. He knew all about the vetting process. The agencies would have run multiple background checks to determine whether he were a threat or not. And when they checked, they checked everything, including what brand of diapers he'd worn as a baby and the books he'd read in middle school. They would have undoubtedly known about his brother's death. None of this would have been shared with Diana.

"I'm sorry, I'm an idiot. I just, oh, I don't know, I appreciate you putting me through the vetting process. Thank you," he said. He smiled apologetically.

"It's okay. I get it. I'd probably be angry too if you had a secret life I didn't know about."

He glanced at her quickly. "What you see is what you get with me. I promise." *Liar,* a voice whispered inside his head. He cringed. As soon as this case was over he'd tell her about his brother. He'd tell her everything.

Diana and Peter sat in a conference room. It looked pretty much the same as the one at VPD.

Getting from the lobby had taken time. Despite it being late at night, once they'd arrived and gone through five different levels of security checks, those staffers working late or on the night shift kept stopping Diana to speak to her as they traversed the hallways. Some of them obviously knew her, but others appeared to simply want to meet her.

"You've become kind of famous around here in your

absence," Kieran had said with a grin when they'd finally reached the fourth floor. He turned to Peter, "Some of Diana's ops have been used as case studies in training exercises for CSIS operatives. They're all eager to meet the woman who has become something of a legend."

Diana rolled her eyes. "I have no idea why. It's not like I did anything they couldn't do."

Kieran snorted. "Sometimes, your modesty is irritating. You were damned good – one of the best – and you know it."

Diana shrugged. "Perhaps I was," she said with a small smile.

"Here we are." Kieran showed them into the conference room. "You need to wait for a moment. Amanda and Clive are coming too," he explained as he made his way to the door.

"You're not staying?" Diana asked.

"Don't have clearance. See you later," he replied, ruefully. He glanced at Peter.

Diana wondered once again about Peter's background.

"Amanda Stone is the Deputy Director of Operations, and Clive Inglewood is the Assistant Director of Intelligence," Diana explained to Peter.

"I see," Peter replied. "I'll be careful what I say."

Peter knew well enough that the politics within an organization like CSIS were always rife. When multiple agencies were involved, the political interference could multiply exponentially. Unchecked, it could impede the progress and success of individual missions and endanger operatives on the ground.

The door to the conference room opened.

"CSIS has learned the hard way to never discount

Diana Hunter," a woman said as she walked into the room. She smiled warmly at Diana. Amanda Stone. The man Peter assumed to be Clive Inglewood brought up the rear, closing the door behind him.

Ms. Stone was in her mid forties, a homely woman with a stocky build and a bowl-shaped haircut. She wore a boxy teal suit like a uniform and paired it with unadorned brown shoes that Peter suspected she wore with everything. While her look was rather plain, she was composed, confident, and authoritative. There was no doubting that she was in charge.

In contrast, the man next to her seemed an insignificant presence. The difference in their relative positions was obvious. Inglewood was a small man and not at all polished. His suit was too big. It made him look even smaller. His thinning, fair hair needed a brush, and he walked quickly and nervously to keep up with his striding, assertive superior as though by being in close proximity, he could absorb some of her gravitas. Peter wondered how such a person could have ascended to the position of ADI.

"How are you, Diana?" Amanda asked, giving her a hug. "It's good to see you, my dear."

"You too, Amanda."

Diana made the introductions, and they settled down to talk.

"We've spoken to the CIA, and this connection will go through them. MI6 will also be on the call. Lennox insisted," Amanda Stone said glancing at Diana and Peter in turn.

Inglewood typed something into the table. Peter realized it was a smart desk, with an inbuilt computer. So not so much like VPD after all.

The screen on the back wall lit up, and Ethan Lennox appeared. Up in the corner, two smaller screens came to life. Two men sat in one and a man and woman in the other. CIA and MI6, presumably.

"Good morning, everyone," Amanda started. While it was late at night in Canada, for everyone else it was the next day. "So, Major Lennox, we are all here – Prentice and Michaelson in Washington, Norris and Hirst in London. Here in Vancouver, I'm joined by Diana Hunter as you requested, along with Hopkinson from VPD and Inglewood and myself from CSIS."

"Thanks everyone for coming. Hey, Diana," the Major said with a smile.

"Hi, Ethan. It's good to see you," Diana replied warmly.

"Sorry to drag you all away from your important work, but I have something that can't wait," Lennox said. "We need to get straight to business."

"Okay, fire away" Amanda directed.

"Our agents in the Middle East have recovered some documents, and I don't like what I'm seeing. It looks like a new group calling themselves the Islamic Front has formed. Anyone heard of them?"

The faces in the two screens at the end of the room indicated they hadn't.

"We've run across them just recently." Amanda said.

"What do you know about them?" Lennox asked.

"We think they were behind a planned assassination attempt on one of our senators. The hit was eliminated before it was carried out but our intel is that this group is out there, active, and bankrolled by someone with significant funds.

"That lines up with what we've uncovered. They appear to have the perfect trifecta: backers, brains and, well, balls. We are concerned they are planning some kind of attack."

"There's always some extremist group planning to attack us," one of the men in Washington interjected.

"Yes, I know that," Lennox retorted sharply. While TFI was made up of people from CSIS, MI6, and the CIA, it wasn't subordinate to any of them. It had a large amount of autonomy and reported directly to the Chiefs of State, the British Prime Minister, the Canadian Prime Minister, and the US President. As head of the agency, Ethan Lennox was extremely powerful.

"The amount of money this group has at their disposal concerns me. It is highly unusual and elevates the risk substantially," he continued.

"Do you have any idea who is funding them?" the woman from MI6 asked.

"We have our suspicions, but I don't want to say anymore. That's why I wanted Diana here."

"While this is indeed a worrying situation, I'm not certain I understand why Diana Hunter is so essential to you," Inglewood said curtly. Peter gave Diana a questioning look.

*Later,* she mouthed. He turned his attention back to Lennox.

"We have a mark, someone close to the group who we think is vulnerable. Diana, I need you to come out here. We're running an op, and I need your help on the ground for this one." Lennox responded.

"Diana no longer works with CSIS. We have active agents that can assist on the ground," Inglewood said quickly.

Lennox' expression hardened. "Diana, everything's organized. A plane will pick you up from Canadian

Forces Base Comox at 1400 hours the day after tomorrow."

"Okay. I'll be bringing someone with me," Diana said, looking over at Peter and raising her eyebrows. He dipped his head.

"We're expecting you, Hopkinson. It'll be good to work with you again."

# CHAPTER TWENTY-SIX

A LL EYES TURNED to Peter, appraising him.
Diana looked at him shrewdly.
"Likewise, Lennox."

Clive Inglewood looked staggered. His mouth opened and closed, not a sound coming out.

"This is highly irregular," he finally choked out. "Two civilians cannot be involved in such an operation."

"Clive," Amanda snapped warningly. "You're over-stepping."

"Mr. Inglewood," Lennox said, his tone frigid, "this is not a CSIS operation. This is a mission for Task Force Indigo. CSIS has absolutely no business telling me how to allocate my resources."

"What? *Your* resources?" Inglewood asked, his face pinched and pale.

"Clive, shut up or leave," Amanda ground out through gritted teeth. She turned to Lennox, "That's fine by us, Major Lennox. As Clive said, Diana is not employed by CSIS any longer. We don't," she looked hard at Inglewood, "need to give our permission."

"It's okay, Amanda. Mr. Inglewood, I should probably tell you that Diana works for TFI. This is something you wouldn't have known had it been up to me, but the urgency of the situation forces my hand."

Amanda and Inglewood glanced at Diana. A small smile glanced off Amanda's lips. "Very well," Inglewood snapped. "But this is highly irregular. The Director of Intelligence will hear about it."

"Thank Richard for referring Diana to me in the first place, would you?" he said. Clive blanched. Peter stifled a grin. Lennox always had had a talent for putting people in their place. Like Diana, he didn't suffer fools.

"Now that we've sorted out the particulars, can we get back to that part about powerful people helping this group?" Peter asked. "What exactly did you mean?"

Lennox shook his head. "I'd rather we discuss that in person," he said with a pointed look at Diana. She nodded.

"Where exactly are we going?" Diana asked.

"Kandahar. All the arrangements have been made. We'll talk more when you arrive. Does anyone have any questions?"

"Will you be sharing intelligence as you receive it?" one of the men in Washington asked.

"Most likely. But we will evaluate it first and classify it accordingly before sharing via the normal channels."

"So you aren't guaranteeing that you will share the intel with our government?"

"No, Michaelson, I am not. I never do. As you well know."

"Well, I'd like to represent most forcefully the view of our government—"

"Sorry, Michaelson, that's how it is. Always has been.

Now, that's all for today, people. Fly safe, Diana, Hopkinson. I will see you in a couple of days."

"See you there, Ethan," Diana responded.

Lennox cut the connection. The faces in London and Washington disappeared from their screens.

Amanda Stone got to her feet, cueing the others in the room to do the same. "I want to be kept apprised of everything as it happens. Diana, that means directly from you, okay?" Amanda said.

"Yes, ma'am," Diana snapped, but she was smiling.

Diana and Amanda had always gotten along. The older woman had helped Diana assimilate into CSIS. She'd recognized her talent and had invariably supported her throughout her time with the agency, despite Diana's relative youth. Amanda had recommended Diana for promotion and supported her when things got tricky as they invariably did thanks to Diana's habit for bending the rules. Between them, there was a sense of sisterhood and solidarity as they traveled the murky world of government secrets and clandestine activities, a world dominated by men.

"Clive, you and I need to have a talk," Amanda said.

Inglewood didn't move. "*Now*, Clive. Good luck, Diana, Hopkinson. We'll speak soon," Amanda said. The woman strode out of the room with a snapped, "Come, Clive." The man scurried after her.

Diana and Peter followed, although much more slowly. Kieran was waiting for them outside.

"I see Clive hasn't changed," Diana said.

Kieran snorted. "You expected him to?"

She shrugged. "I guess I hoped that after three years, he'd have softened a bit. At least in his view of me."

Kieran rolled his eyes. "Diana, you know he's always

had it in for you. Didn't help that he only got that promotion because you turned it down. Or that you were offered it at an age when you were fifteen years younger than he is now."

"And there was that incident in Bali," Diana said thoughtfully.

Kieran snorted again. "Bali, Mumbai, Islamabad, Cairo, and on."

"Not my fault he wouldn't listen to me," Diana said.

Kieran shrugged. "Clive will always be Clive. He's a bull-headed analyst and will never be more than that. He just won't accept it." Kieran paused for a moment, "So," he drew himself up tall. "What's going on?"

"You know I can't tell you that, Kieran. I'm sorry," Diana said gently. Peter glanced between the two of them.

Kieran looked up to the ceiling and sighed. "Well, I guess we'll speak soon then," he said sadly. Peter felt for him. It was never easy when your girl moved on. And up.

Diana approached Kieran and leaned up to whisper something in his ear. He softened, drawing her into his arms and giving her a big hug.

"You look after yourself out there." Kieran looked straight at Peter. "Whatever it is you're doing, bring her back in one piece, you hear. You might have to tie her up and lock her away to do it. And then you'll need to find a very remote place to hide."

Peter grinned. "I hear there are job openings in Alert."

Kieran laughed. "Might just be far enough away."

"I so love it when you two talk about me as if I'm not here," Diana said.

Kieran and Peter shook hands but said nothing. "Well, I guess we should get going. It's really late," she said.

It was almost midnight. They left CSIS headquarters and twenty minutes later, pulled into VPD's parking lot.

"If only traffic were always like this in Vancouver," Diana said with a sigh.

"Wouldn't that be something? Too bad we can't work nights all the time," Peter replied. "Donaldson's waiting for us. I'm going to have to make a few calls before we talk to him or it might be too late."

"Too late for what?" Diana asked.

"I need to get put back on active duty. I don't know how long it will take to renew my security clearance. I doubt it will be in time for our trip, but it can't hurt to try. I want the request to be on the right desk first thing tomorrow morning."

"You go ahead, and I'll make a few calls too, to speed up the process."

Peter looked at her in surprise. "You have no idea how quickly people move when the request comes from TFI," she said with a grin.

"Thanks," he said.

"No, thank you," she said.

"What for?" he asked in surprise.

"For coming with me. And for not being angry that I put you on the spot like that."

"Did you really think I'd let you go off on your own? You're my partner, and I've got your back, no matter what."

Diana smiled. "Thanks."

"Anytime," he said with a wink. "By the way, you're going to have to tell me about you and Clive Inglewood."

"Yeah, I will. It's a long story, though."

"It's a long flight to Kandahar," he reminded her.

She nodded. "True.

"Okay, come on. Let's make those calls and give

Donaldson the bad news."

"He's going to have kittens, isn't he?" Diana said.

"Probably not. As long as VPD doesn't have to pay for our little jaunt, he'll be fine."

At two in the morning, Diana finally walked into the lobby of her apartment building. "Hi, Larry," she greeted the doorman.

"Hi, Ms. Hunter, working late again?" the man inquired with a smile.

"What can I say? The criminal element doesn't seem to need as much sleep as us mere mortals."

Larry laughed. "I highly doubt you're a mere mortal, ma'am."

"Thanks, Larry. You have a nice night now," Diana said with a grin as she got onto the elevator.

"You too, ma'am."

She leaned against the wall and closed her eyes for a moment. She would have to get used to sleeping when and where she could again.

Peter had been right about Donaldson. He'd actually been pleased they were going. Vancouver was his city, and he had a proprietary interest in what went down here, criminally speaking. If something really nasty was going on, he wanted to be in on it. Peter and Diana were his "in." Donaldson had been smart enough not to ask too many questions about why they had been called away, he was just satisfied they were staying on the job and that VPD wasn't paying for it. In the meantime, he'd promised to continue digging into Greene and keep an eye on Kloch.

She took a deep breath. She'd have to get her gear out of

storage tomorrow.

When the elevator doors opened, she stepped into the corridor. The area around her apartment was dark. She made a note to speak to the building manager about getting the light fixed. And she'd have to speak to Terri about taking care of Max for the next few days.

When Diana opened the door to her apartment, she was met by a whirlwind of white fur. Max leapt as high as he could, trying to get into her arms. He seemed very glad to see her.

She bent over and picked him up. "Who's mommy's good boy?" she murmured to him as he licked her face excitedly. She scratched him between his ears as she made her way into the living room. She dropped her purse on the table and sank into the couch. Max jumped on her lap. She knew that when he was certain she wasn't going anywhere, he would relax and settle himself down for a nap.

A moment later, however, her phone started ringing. She groaned. "Sorry, boy," she said as she deposited Max on the floor. He let out a disgruntled yip but followed her over to the table. Suddenly, he started barking furiously. Diana looked down and shushed him. "Max, quiet," she said as she pulled her phone out of her bag.

"Peter?" she asked. "Is everything alright?" She switched on the lights.

"There's a problem," he said, his tone urgent. "Surgeon's escaped. We have no idea where he is. They're scanning the ports looking for him, but he could be anywhere."

"I don't think so," she said quietly.

"Why do you say that?" Peter asked.

"Because he's standing in my kitchen with a knife to my dog sitter's neck," she said.

*"Hello, Diana. Did you miss me?"*

# CHAPTER TWENTY-SEVEN

"**D**IANA!" PETER STARTED to run. "Diana!" he yelled, again. There was no reply. He'd heard Surgeon on the other end of the line. A chill ran down his spine. Surgeon had killed two guards during his escape and instead of fleeing, he'd gone after Diana. Her dog sitter would die just as soon as Surgeon no longer needed her. Would he kill Diana before or after?

Peter yanked his car door open and jumped in. Within moments, he was tearing out of the parking garage with a squeal of tires. He kept his phone glued to his ear. The line was still open, but the words on the other end were muffled.

On the way, he raised Donaldson on his police radio.

"He's got her again!"

"What?"

"Surgeon. Diana's apartment. We need armed backup stat!"

Outside Diana's building, Peter threw his car on to the sidewalk and ran through the doors. Diana's apartment was at the back of the building, on the third floor.

"Hey, you can't park there!" Larry shouted, coming out

of his office. He was rubbing his eyes, his hair standing up askew. Peter skidded to a stop and sprinted back to the front desk.

"I need a key to Diana's apartment?"

"Sir, I couldn't possibly—"

"Diana and another woman are being held hostage."

Larry blanched and dashed into the small room behind the front desk. He ran back out with the key. "I'll go with you," the doorman volunteered, squaring his shoulders.

Peter shook his head and started toward the elevator. "No, stay here. Direct the armed unit to the apartment when they arrive." He changed direction. The stairs would be faster.

"Yes, sir, right away."

Peter sprinted up the steps, taking them two and three at a time. In a few moments, he was outside Diana's apartment with his ear glued to the door. He could hear voices, but he still couldn't make out what they were saying. Damn it!

There was a scratching sound and a low whine through the door. Peter put his phone to his ear again to listen in on what was being said in the apartment. A few moments later, Diana's voice sounded loud and clear.

*"You look a little tired. Why don't you sit down? The sofa's right behind you."*

Surgeon wouldn't be able to see the front door from there. *Good girl.* Peter slipped the key into the lock and turned it as gently as he could.

*"Just let Terri go, Monty. You don't want her. You want me. And I'm here."*

*"Ah, but while I have the girl, you are much more amenable."*

The lock quickly clicked open, and Peter eased the door

open gently. Max shot through the opening and latched onto Peter's pant leg with his little teeth. The terrier tried to pull him into the apartment. Peter got down on his haunches and scratched Max's head to calm him down.

"I'm here to help her," he whispered. Max looked up at him and let go of his pants. Peter could have sworn the dog nodded at him. Max then trotted back into the apartment and sat in the hallway, looking at him, waiting for him to make his move. That was one smart dog. Peter slipped inside and closed the door.

He looked around, taking stock of the situation. Ahead of him, he could see Diana. She was in her living room, standing sideways to him.

"I promise I'm not going anywhere. Let Terri go, it's me you want," she said. To Surgeon, she'd seem calm and collected, but Peter could see the tension in her jaw and posture. She was angry. She was blinking a shade rapidly so she was scared too.

"I'd rather not. It's more fun this way, don't you think? I can see you better, Diana dear." Peter couldn't see Surgeon from his viewpoint, but there was a noise and a gasp from the girl he was holding.

"I don't think it's a lot of fun for Terri," Diana said.

Diana made a tiny movement to the right with her head. Peter glanced down and noticed she was making a gesture with her hand. She was using sign language.

"It's not supposed to be fun for her or you," Surgeon said smugly. "It's supposed to be fun for *me*."

Diana gave her thigh a small pat as though she were calling Max over. Was that "dog?" in sign language? Then she closed her hand into a fist, with her thumb on the outside. Peter was pretty sure that stood for the letter "A." But then she gave another sign that he didn't understand followed by another "A," maybe a "C," and one more he didn't know. What was she trying to say?

"But really, Monty, I thought you wanted to be alone with me," Diana purred, her voice low and sultry.

He heard Surgeon inhale sharply. He also heard Terri gasp and then gurgle. He must still have the knife to her neck.

"That's true," Surgeon said. "Maybe you're right. Maybe I should let her go." He grunted and there was a small cry from Terri. "To her death. Then you and I truly would be alone," he ended viciously.

Diana shifted on one foot slightly so she could see Peter in her peripheral vision. He shrugged apologetically. She quickly refocused her attention on Surgeon.

"But wouldn't it be better to have an audience? I could switch places with her. Terri could watch. See how brilliant you are at what you do."

Peter glanced down at Diana's hand again. She pointed at Max. "ATTACK." She'd switched to military hand signals. His eyes widened as he looked down at Max. She had to be kidding.

"I don't know," Surgeon sounded both eager and hesitant at the same time. "She is such a sweet morsel. She could be the appetizer. Or perhaps dessert. *You* are the entrée, my dear."

Peter saw Diana's jaw clench. She was gritting her teeth in irritation. She glanced at him and he circled his finger at his temple. *You are crazy, babe.*

She thinned her lips and gave a look he knew all too well. *Just do it.*

Okay, she knew her dog better than he did. He waited until she spoke again. "Max," he whispered under the cover of Diana's voice. The tiny, delicate, white, soft, fuzzy furball looked up at him expectantly. Trust shone out of his big black button eyes. One of his floppy ears twitched. "Attack," Peter whispered and pointed toward the living room.

To his astonishment, Max quietly got up and sneaked in a low crouch along the wall and into the living room. Peter moved to the edge of the hallway, flattened against the wall, gun ready.

"Sweet she may be, but she isn't a challenge, is she? And I know you like a challenge," Diana kept talking. "Am I not the one you're really looking for?"

The seconds ticked by. Peter tensed, his muscles coiled, ready to spring into action. He listened for every sound. He heard a low growl and then a snarl. He spun around into the living room as Max launched himself at Surgeon, his tiny teeth like needles piercing Surgeon's skin and sinking into the muscle around his ankle bone as he took a firm hold.

"Arrggh!"

Diana reached out and tore the knife from Surgeon's grasp. She yanked Terri to safety. Peter saw his chance and let off a round just as Surgeon reflexively tried to shake Max off. The bullet caught Surgeon in the shoulder and a high-pitched scream rent the air as he was blasted back against the wall, Max still clinging to his ankle. Peter winced. He felt sure that Max's neck would break if he didn't let go, but no. The tableau was surreal.

## CHAPTER TWENTY-EIGHT

"**D**ON'T MOVE!" PETER shouted. Surgeon was trying to shake Max off but he stilled as soon as Peter stood above him, pointing his gun at Surgeon's face.

Max remained firmly clamped to the killer's leg, the tips of his teeth buried out of sight in Surgeon's flesh. He growled continuously.

"I've got him covered. Armed response are on their way. Do you want to call Max off?" Peter said to Diana, breathlessly.

Diana walked over and stood next to him looking coolly at Surgeon's prone body, his face contorted in pain. "No, but let's give his jaws a rest. Ready?" Diana asked Peter.

"Yup."

"Max, leave it!" she barked. Max immediately opened his jaws and detached himself from Surgeons's ankle. "Guard!"

Puffing himself up, Max began to growl again. He stalked round to Surgeon's face and bared his teeth. Surgeon painfully tried to push himself up and away from

Max until a jerk from Peter's gun stopped him. They could hear sirens in the distance.

"Reinforcements. This time, I'll go with him." Peter said. "At least until they transfer him to Kent."

Diana directed her words at Surgeon. "You'll be going to Kent Institution, our local maximum security prison." She nudged his injured shoulder with her foot. Surgeon yelped.

"And after this stunt, as soon as we can arrange it, you'll be going to Gitmo as our long-term guest." Peter said, "He killed two cops to get here."

"Seriously?" Diana nudged Surgeon's shoulder again, a little harder this time. "Maybe we should do the world a favor and just shoot him here and now," she said, her voice cold.

Peter looked at her in surprise. She meant it.

"He broke into my home and held someone I care about hostage. He would have happily murdered both of us, all of us. And now you tell me he's destroyed two families?" She crouched down and got her face close to Surgeon's. Max growled a little harder. "But it's all in a day's work for you, isn't it? All a bit of fun, Sunshine. You make me sick." She stood again. "Shooting him wouldn't be a problem. I'd see it as saving the multiple lives he would undoubtedly take if he ever got away again.

"Diana, come on, you're no cold-blooded killer. That's not you," Peter said, still not taking his eyes, or his gun, off Surgeon. He'd never seen her like this before.

She looked at him then, her face hard and cold. "You have no idea how far I would go for the people I care about," she said. "He should consider himself extremely fortunate he went after me instead of you."

Diana took a deep breath. "Give me your gun. Call Donaldson with the news."

"Sure you won't shoot him?"

"Yes, yes," she said impatiently.

Donaldson answered immediately. "Yes!"

"Surgeon is down," Peter said, with a sigh. "We're all okay."

"Good. ERT there yet?"

"Not quite. Thanks for sending in the big guns."

"Of course," Donaldson said, seemingly surprised that Peter would even consider he'd take any other course of action. "Twice in one week is some kind of record, though. Don't get used to it. They're expensive. Let me call them and apprise them of the situation so they don't storm the whole building or something."

Peter looked at Diana, "ERT will be here soon. They'll transport him," he said.

Diana looked up. "Good. Here, take over." She gave the gun back to Peter and walked over to Terri. "Are you okay?" she asked.

The girl nodded. "Yeah, I'll be fine. Just a bit terrified." She smiled weakly. Diana put her arm around the girl's shoulder and gave it a squeeze. "Max is pretty special. I had no idea," Terri said.

Diana grinned. "He's pretty awesome, isn't he?"

A loud knock sounded. Diana walked over to the door and opened it, coming face to face with a squad of men in dark fatigues, all armed with automatic assault rifles.

"Ms. Hunter?" one of the men asked.

"Yes, that's me. Thanks for coming."

"No problem. We understand the suspect has been subdued."

Diana nodded. "But you're going to have to come in and see to believe it," she said.

She invited them in with a sweeping gesture and they swarmed into her hall. It seemed tiny now that it was filled with six very big, heavily armed men. "That way," she pointed to the living room.

They filed in while she shut the door and locked it. "Good to see you again, Hopkinson," one of the men said.

"You too, Stockton." Peter put away his gun. He wouldn't be needing it now that there were several assault weapons in the room all attached to fierce looking men who knew how to use them.

"You've got to be kidding me," Diana heard one of the other men say.

She walked into the living room with a smile on her face. Max was still in the guard position next to Surgeon, his tiny stature offset by his teeth-baring growl and his proximity to Surgeon's face. He snapped his jaws a few times, just for good measure.

"This is really Surgeon? The notorious assassin? Scared of a tiny piece of fluff?" one of the men asked, eyeing Max carefully.

"Yes, that's him. I know it seems unexpected, but trust me when I say that 'tiny piece of fluff' is a highly trained guard dog. And I'm grateful for that, because otherwise this might have been much more complicated and unpleasant."

"That's for sure, ma'am." Stockton shook his head in wonder. "But how did he let him in?"

"Clearly, we have some more training to do. He probably didn't even wake up. He's used to Peter coming over in the early hours."

Stockton looked over at Peter who put his hands up.

"Ah, purely business."

"Well, let's get the big guy out of your hair," Stockton said, laughing.

"Max, heel," she said. The white fluffball obediently turned around and trotted to her side. Diana sat on her haunches and scooped him up into her arms. "Who's my clever boy?" she cooed, burying her face in his fur. "Who's the smartest dog in the whole world?"

Terri, whose minor neck wound was being attended to by one of the first responders, reached out to give Max a good scratch. Peter might have joined them, but he didn't feel comfortable being quite that soft in front of ERT, two of whom were barking orders at Surgeon while they applied first aid to his shoulder wound and cuffed him. The other three stood staring, incredulous.

"Coming with us?" Stockton asked Peter as he pushed Surgeon along in front of him.

"Right behind you," Peter said. He wasn't taking any chances. There might be six of them, all armed with MP5/10 submachine guns, but they had no idea exactly how wily Surgeon could be. When not faced with a tiny dog, of course. He eyed Max critically.

Peter looked up and opened his mouth but before he could get a word out, Diana cut him off. "Don't even think it. He's done enough for tonight. I'm sure you and the big, strapping ERT boys can contain Monty here until he's behind bars again."

"It was just a thought," Peter mumbled. "Are you going with Terri to the hospital? She should get checked out," he asked.

"Of course. If she's not kept in, I'll have her spend the night here," she said.

"Thanks, I could use the company," the girl's voice was

still shaky, and she was as white as a sheet. She had been wrapped in a silver emergency blanket.

Peter snuck a quick scratch between Max's ears, and they all headed out.

As Diana climbed into the back of the ambulance with Terri, Peter said, "I'll call you tomorrow. Try to get some sleep. It'll be your last good chance for a while."

"Call me when he's locked up," she said. "I don't care what time it is. I want to know that he's fully secure, and you are on your way home, okay? I want you, and only you, to confirm that."

"You'll be asleep by then."

Diana glared at him. "Just call me. I want to make absolutely sure."

Peter nodded. "Will do. Good night, ladies," he said, stepping back so the paramedic could close the doors.

As the ambulance rolled away, Diana looked out at the scene outside her apartment building. The area was lit up in a revolving pattern that mimicked the lights of the police vehicles parked around. A few bystanders had gathered. They showed no signs of moving on even though it was early morning and the air was chilly.

Diana observed the retreating backs of the ERT as they clambered into their armored vehicle. She saw Peter put Surgeon in the metal cage at the back of the police van and strap him in. Two ERT members hopped in beside Surgeon to accompany him on his journey.

*If you lie to me, you'll never find out who is responsible for the situation you find yourself in.* What had Surgeon meant when he said that to her? She thought for a second or two before putting it out of her mind as she watched Peter join the driver of the police van up front.

She wondered when exactly she had decided to put her

faith in Peter. And why. Was it because he kept saving her life? Or because he was nice to her dog? Or was it because he didn't put up with her nonsense? She didn't rightly know. But she knew she cared about Peter getting home again safely. Really cared. *And he absolutely adores you.*

Diana sighed and let the tension in her body seep away. She looked out of the window until she couldn't see Peter any longer. She closed her eyes. This feeling was unfamiliar, but good. And she simply couldn't fight it any longer. She had a partner. Support. Her life was a-changing. It felt good not to be so alone.

To get two free books, updates about new releases, exclusive promotions, and other insider information, sign up for Alison's mailing list at:

https://www.alisongolden.com/diana

DIANA HUNTER WILL RETURN...

THINGS START TO unravel for Diana and Peter in the next book in the series. What more will we learn about them? Find out in the subsequent book in the Diana Hunter mystery series, *Exposed*. You'll find an excerpt on the following pages.

# EXPOSED

## PROLOGUE

SALAH SAT SILENTLY in the back seat. Abdel and Jawad were talking urgently in the front. Hip-hop was coming out of the speaker by Salah's head, the staccato beat of the words at odds with the bass note of the track. Salah leaned over.

"Here."

"What, bro?" Abdel was driving. He glanced up into his rear view mirror to look at the boy in the back seat, black fuzz peppering his upper lip, his chin.

"Drop me here. I'll walk the rest of the way," Salah said softly.

"You sure?" Abdel pulled the car over.

"Yeah, I'm sure."

With a languid stretch, Salah opened the door and loped out, dragging his backpack behind him. He hefted it onto his shoulder in one drawn-out move.

Jawad wound down the passenger door window. "See you in a few, okay?"

"Yeah, see ya."

The black BMW flicked its lights on and pulled away,

and Salah, his head down as he took the weight of the pack on his shoulder, turned toward home.

He walked past the shops and businesses that lined the main road: a loan shark, a barber shop, an auto repair. They were all closed now. A takeout advertised "Authentic Salvadorian Food." Often, Salah would stop to pick something up, but today he didn't feel hungry. He kept on, his tall, sloping gait telegraphing his mood better than any words. It started to drizzle.

Salah thought back to the events of his day. Things had begun as a bit of a laugh, then morphed into a mixture of excitement and danger, a personal calling, and finally, a noble cause. Now though, he wasn't so sure.

He put the key in the lock and opened the front door of the wooden-slatted bungalow he called home. It was badly in need of repair, almost a shack. The black door was smeared with white paint where someone had attempted to clean off graffiti and given up halfway through. Rusted, broken guttering hung uselessly from a gable. Two of the three front windows were boarded up.

His family's detritus littered the front yard, sodden cardboard and plastic cartons, mainly. No one had cleared it in months. His mother was too busy working her three jobs, his father was unable as he struggled to manage the cancer the doctors had taken too long to diagnose. Salah and his brothers didn't care for yard work.

He shut the front door with a bang and walked to the bedroom he shared with his two siblings. It was empty. He flung his backpack onto his bed and sat down heavily. With his elbows on his knees, he put his head in his hands, his fingers splaying around his eyes as he stared at the faded, filthy carpet.

Salah sat immobile, deep in thought, before he heard his

father's voice, weak and tremulous, calling out his name. Salah stood wearily.

"Coming."

He propped himself against the wall of the bedroom. His brown eyes, framed with lashes so long that girls at school had teased him, blinked as he took a moment to look out of the window. White emulsion, inexpertly applied, was now cracking and peeling away from the metal window frame. Salah, who'd loved the escape from daily life that English Literature had provided when he was in school, ruefully considered the metaphor. He missed the rhythm of language, the way it transported him, introduced him to new worlds and ways of thinking. He missed his friends, his teachers, their collaboration. He missed the feeling of hope the most.

Salah heard his name again and returned to the present. He regarded the dreary view from his window a moment longer before he pushed himself off and went to his father.

To get your copy of *Exposed* visit the link below:
*https://www.alisongolden.com/exposed*

# BOOKS BY ALISON GOLDEN

## FEATURING REVEREND ANNABELLE DIXON

*Death at the Café* (Prequel)

*Murder at the Mansion*

*Body in the Woods*

*Grave in the Garage*

*Horror in the Highlands*

*Killer at the Cult*

## FEATURING INSPECTOR DAVID GRAHAM

*The Case of the Screaming Beauty* (Prequel)

*The Case of the Hidden Flame*

*The Case of the Fallen Hero*

*The Case of the Broken Doll*

*The Case of the Missing Letter*

*The Case of the Pretty Lady*

# ABOUT THE AUTHOR

Alison Golden is the *USA Today* bestselling author of the Inspector David Graham mysteries and Reverend Annabelle Dixon cozy mysteries. As A.J. Golden, she writes the Diana Hunter thriller series.

Alison was raised in Bedfordshire, England. Her aim is to write stories that are designed to entertain, amuse, and calm. Her approach is to combine creative ideas with excellent writing and edit, edit, edit.

Alison is based in the San Francisco Bay Area with her husband and twin sons. She splits her time between London and San Francisco.

For up-to-date promotions and release dates of upcoming books, sign up for the latest news here: https://www.alisongolden.com/diana.

*For more information:*
www.alisongolden.com
alison@alisongolden.com

facebook.com/alisongolden.books

twitter.com/alisonjgolden

instagram.com/alisonjgolden

## THANK YOU

Thank you for taking the time to read this box set. If you enjoyed it, please consider telling your friends or posting a short review. Word of mouth is an author's best friend and very much appreciated.

Thank you,

54701368R00338

Made in the USA
Middletown, DE
14 July 2019